PENGUIN BOOKS

THE DEATH OF AMY PARRIS

T. R. Bowen spent much of his childhood in India and Egypt. He was briefly at Winchester Art School. At Cambridge most of his time was occupied by acting and he became president of the Marlowe Society. For a number of years he has written screenplays for TV and has continued to act. This is his first crime novel.

T. R. BOWEN

The Death of Amy Parris

PENGUIN BOOKS

PENGUIN BOOKS

Published by the Penguin Group
Penguin Books Ltd, 27 Wrights Lane, London W8 5TZ, England
Penguin Putnam Inc., 375 Hudson Street, New York, New York 10014, USA
Penguin Books Australia Ltd, Ringwood, Victoria, Australia
Penguin Books Canada Ltd, 10 Alcorn Avenue, Toronto, Ontario, Canada M4V 3B2
Penguin Books (NZ) Ltd, Private Bag 102902, NSMC, Auckland, New Zealand

Penguin Books Ltd, Registered Offices: Harmondsworth, Middlesex, England

First published in Penguin Books 1998
1 3 5 7 9 10 8 6 4 2

Filmset in 11/14 pt Monotype Bembo
Printed in England by Clays Ltd, St Ives plc

September 1991

Three miles offshore a yacht thumped through the waves. The wind, westerly and soon to veer northerly, pressed it over as it cut and lurched its way into the darkness that was coming down over The Wash. The boat's engine grumbled on low revs to keep it pushing on where, under sail alone, it might have been stopped short by the steep seas that develop quickly off this coast.

Snugged into his bunk, riding with the boat's motion, the owner knew he should unhook the lee-cloth supporting him, pull on his sweater, struggle aft, open the hatch and check that all was well. Something had woken him.

'Ah, sod it. She knows what she's doing.'

A heavy man, uneasy about his own condition, he rolled on to his back. In the dim red light he stared at the deckhead a few feet above his face. His head was thick from the wine he'd shared with his young crew. He reached out for the plastic water bottle he'd remembered to leave on the saloon shelf. He swigged it laddishly, then swilled it between the gap in his front teeth. He wondered if this trip might make some sort of article for one of the yachting mags. He wasn't exactly fond of the yachtie mag culture, preferring the newsroom where he thrashed out a living. It wasn't even paid properly; but it was bunce, fun scribbling, something different.

He glanced across at his wife who had retired to her bunk as soon as the sea began to pick up. She was seasick.

'As usual . . .'

He was glad, mind, that Ellie'd buggered off. Or she'd have been on to him for chatting up the lass. Harmless diversion but he'd not have heard the end of it for days. Little punishments . . . he knew them all. Boring. Not that he'd got anywhere with the girl. Pleasant enough, but some sort of maths boffin. Patronizing or what? She'd said she'd interface the Decca navigation system to the autopilot, something he'd never even tried. Well, there you go, she'd done it, the snooty bint. As he turned over in his warm sleeping bag, he touched the wart on his forehead as if it were a charm; an old friend. He could hear from the cockpit, above the force-five wind, the ratcheting of the toothed rubber belt as it spun the wheel, balancing the boat on its electronically determined course.

'Clever little cow,' he murmured to himself. He listened briefly to the steady beat of the engine and went back to sleep, satisfied that all was well with his boat. All was indeed well with his boat. The Decca receiver was picking up undisturbed signals from the chain of transmitting stations that ring the North Sea. Assessing them against the waypoints plotted into its computer, it transmitted instructions in turn to the autopilot. The autopilot's fluxgate compass sensed the boat's heading. Its electric motor spun the toothed belt, turning the wheel.

The boat was set fair to continue its uncomfortable journey as far as Spurn Head without further human attention. In fact, until the owner woke later and came on deck, the boat would receive none. The cockpit was empty.

Amy, the clever little cow, was dying, miles astern in the cold sea. In about ten minutes she would be dead. She was beginning to drift into the merciful warm dream which precedes hypothermal unconsciousness. In the distance the indifferent eye of Haweshead light rhythmically spread and disappeared, soon to be replaced by the greater light which signals the dying human brain.

I

September 1992

On the tidal island of Scales Howe, the beach glistened. The sea, beyond the Haweshead light, was calm.

For the past month – Scales Howe being inaccessible in rough weather – Mrs Boland had walked nearby beaches. The surf had thundered. She had felt in her face the sting of the sand blown from the dunes. Now the division of wet beach and sea was hardly visible: both stretched flat, mirroring the sky. The air was as still as it ever is at the coast. The family's three dogs, two labradors and a whippet, were loving it.

Not far away, another woman was lying in the dry sand of the dunes above the beach. She muttered to herself as she watched the dogs chase and stop, and chase again.

'Bloody dogs; bloody, sodding dogs. God forgive me. Thy will be done. What's that? What're they doing?'

Two streams of snot ran down from Grace Carver's nose as they often did. Displaying a violet jumble of blood vessels on its underside, her tongue, long and pointed, curled up over her top lip and licked at the amiable saltiness. On she grumbled to herself in her posh voice.

Grace was the daughter of one of the grandest Norfolk families. She was a graduate of the Slade School of Art and Fulbourn Hospital, where her schizophrenia had been investigated and controlled.

Now, in her fiftieth year, self-preservation prompted her to take her medication at the prescribed intervals. If she did not, she reminded herself daily, with ritualistic dread, the black insectoid beings would come scuttling across the dunes and join voices with the choruses of the sea inviting her to drown herself. Or was it the postman she should drown? Which would be naughty and unproductive. Both bad. And her hands made of cloth. Keep taking the tablets.

The dogs had found something, no doubt about it. Mrs Boland called them. You never knew what you might find on a beach. Even here on Scales Howe, which after all belonged to the Norfolk Nature Conservation Trust, syringes had been found last summer.

Her dogs, usually obedient, ignored her. Could dogs get AIDS? Mrs Boland hurried towards them, calling as she went.

The object of the dogs' attention only became clear to Mrs Boland when she was a few feet away and had them under some sort of control. Most prominent was the fabric: the sleeve of a waterproof coat. Protruding from the coat sleeve and lacking a finger (courtesy of Aida, the whippet) was a slender human arm and hand, quite black except for a threadlike golden ring which was hardly discoloured.

Was it really a body? At first it reminded Mrs Boland of something she'd left too long in the oven. Then she remembered a visit to the British Museum she'd made many years before and the mummies she'd seen there. She was convinced. She was looking at a dead body.

After initial shock and bemused disgust, Mrs Boland found herself in tears: it was the ring, she said later recounting to friends, it was the ring that made her so sad.

Grace Carver, the iodine perfume of the sand in her nostrils, watched from above and crossed herself as Mrs Boland began to cry.

Mrs Boland sensibly waited by the sad relic until other dog walkers came along, as she knew they would. She sent them for help and stayed to guard the body.

While she waited for the police, she heard a distant singing from the direction of the tiny ruined chapel behind her in the shifting maze of the dunes.

'Eternal Father strong to save . . .'

The voice was high, girlish. It frightened Mrs Boland more than anything she'd seen that morning. On it wavered, slipping on and off the notes. It was the childish mocking tone which so disturbed her.

'Who bidd'st the mighty ocean deep
Its own appointed limits keep . . .'

She knew it would be the bag woman Grace Carver

who was reputed to live on Scales Howe, although Mrs Boland personally couldn't see how it was possible, especially in winter.

Mrs Boland had seen the woman often enough, in the library. She knew the staff didn't like Grace Carver going in because she smelled. She also muttered to herself and had a violent temper when provoked.

'Oh hear us when we cry to thee
For those in peril on the sea . . .'

The singing stopped suddenly. Mrs Boland looked south to where the valley through the dunes emerged on to the beach, about a quarter of a mile away. A small group of people, two police amongst them, was hurrying towards her.

The day that Amy Parris's body was found by Mrs Boland's dogs, an animal-rights activists' bomb exploded in a Cambridge University laboratory car park, severely wounding two lab. technicians, so the discovery of the body was hardly front-page news.

It was news of sorts. A dead body, even one which went missing in unsuspicious circumstances, is likely to be news and it meant a minor mystery had been solved. Nevertheless, in those newspapers which thought of it as copy, it was clear there was a struggle to make anything of the event. Most was made of the body's remarkable state of preservation, which was correctly attributed to the dryness of the dunes in which it lay. Many days of gale-force northerly winds blowing along the wide and empty Norfolk shore had uncovered it, just as in similar circumstances a year and more before it had been covered.

The authorities rapidly established to their satisfaction that the causes of death were exposure and drowning. This was consistent, they found, with Amy's loss overboard from the yacht *Seahorse* on which she had been crewing. Preserved inside her foul-weather gear was Amy's personal organizer containing all that it should, even a brief log of *Seahorse*'s passage from Aldeburgh until the evening watch when she was lost overboard in darkness, never to be seen again until now. All was consistent, all was in order.

A few days later, Amy Parris's remains were on their way to the Suffolk churchyard in the shadow of whose flint tower they would shortly be buried. Saddened and sickened at first, her family found themselves relieved: there is little worse than uncertainty in such matters.

So it was that a coincidence of interests hurried Amy Parris to her grave, not exactly out of carelessness but because people thought that was where she ought to be.

There was, however, an inconsistency in the business which her family, her friends, the police and the press were genuinely blind to. It was simple enough, and there were two people who, when they read the newspaper reports of the discovery, knew immediately what it was.

One of them would soon be dead.

2

The taxi pushed on through Bangkok's nightmare traffic, thinning now in the suburbs. Rain fell on it like a waterfall; dynamic, cleansing, deafening. Then, as suddenly as it had begun, it stopped.

The taxi drove on along a road out of the city that was beginning to steam.

In the back of the taxi sat a large Englishman watching the sky lighten to a diffused brilliance. The roadside cane grasses had the battered look of roadside vegetation the world over, but the fields beyond were restored to glittering viridian; tropical green. John Bewick watched these startling transformations with apparent indifference.

He was a big-framed man with a square face and a hard, powerful body: an immediate impression of muscular strength; a man who wouldn't disgrace the pack of an international fifteen. This impression was accurate, but only one part of the truth. Few, however, got beyond it.

He was slumped in the back corner of the old Mercedes. The driver of the taxi was a member of the Thai BPP, the Border Patrol Police, which is the most respected of the Thai domestic security forces.

They had been driving now for seven hours with frequent doublings back over their own trail; even, once, driving straight past the airport, towards which they were now once again headed.

The decision to move Bewick out came within hours of the death of Bewick's friend, Samai Churan, gunned down in the streets of Chiengmai – thus meeting the nemesis he had more or less recklessly courted for three years.

Bewick hadn't protested at his own removal from the country. His purpose in remaining would have been to liaise with Samai, and now that Sam was dead there was no point in being there, whether or not he was in danger himself, as General Kwon had claimed he was.

His contract to give seminars, the subject being the training of instructors at the Criminal Investigation Bureau Academy, had been genuine after all. In fact the contract had preceded the request to help Sam. Every move he had made since entering the country could be rationalized in terms of that assignment: which he had completed to universal approval. Nevertheless, for form's sake, an open fax had been sent from CICS requesting his return to England.

Otherwise he had handed himself over to General Kwon; human baggage.

The deputy head of station, who had briefly prepared Bewick for his journey south, had been surprised by the indifference to his fate displayed by the big man, which had bordered on rudeness. Bewick didn't even seem to care that the business was unfinished; that it had ended in failure.

Sally Vernon watched the man making his steady way up the aircraft towards her. She had one of the two seats by the wing emergency exit. They were the best seats outside club class: the broad aisle to the exit gave room to stretch out. She was hoping that for one stage of the journey at least, the one next to her would remain empty.

The engines of the gigantic machine wound up to a roar. She glanced at her watch. The man approaching her had cut it finc. She found herself resenting the fact. He was standing a few feet from her now. She saw quite how large he was.

He stared at his boarding pass as if it confused him, as if the simple information on it was too much for him. Then she found herself caught in the attention of a pair of grey eyes and heard the rumble of a meaningless pleasantry as Bewick stepped forward to claim the window seat beside her.

She watched him unobtrusively as he sorted out his flight bag and papers. As she observed the steadiness of his movement and took in the scale on which he was constructed, she was amused for some reason.

Bewick had arranged things to his satisfaction and he sat down. He seemed sensitive to his size and didn't crowd her in any way. Sally was surprised. She flicked a glance at him and found herself caught again in the cool grey eyes. Bewick turned away, then settled his head on the small pillow he'd taken from his bag and went to sleep.

As she read her way through the long flight to Delhi, she found it impossible to rid herself of an awareness of the man sleeping beside her: despite the fact that he slept so quietly. She took a deep breath and tried to concentrate on the book she was reading – and was enjoying, she reminded herself. She couldn't do it.

She settled herself to sleep, which was worse. The life she was returning to was enviable in the eyes of the world, privileged by any standard. Behind her closed eyelids it appeared to her as a dark knot of complications.

She sat up and stared out at the endless blue beyond the silver tip of the wing.

Sally Vernon was thirty-four. She was a career scientist. She ran a laboratory, which was a sub-department at St Giles' University College in Norwich. It mostly did forensic analysis for the police, when the Home Office labs were unavailable. There were other users, but the police were its main clients. She also ran her own research project into lab sample contamination.

Sally was engaged; within six weeks she would be married. Here the misgivings began. She was unsure of him. It was as simple as that. She had taken this long journey to cousins in Australia to try to clear her mind. It hadn't worked.

James was charming and he was undoubtedly bright. In fact she loved his company; as companion, as lover; but . . .

So what was wrong? Nothing. Well, small things, tiny things. The odd cruel remark immediately retrieved by a warm smile. The occasional black deafness of his mood – so momentary, so quickly controlled that few would even have seen it. The greed sometimes with which he reached for the whisky when he'd come home, and the evident relief it gave him.

All this, she objected again, was normal, human, negotiable. Perhaps it was the fact that they had never seriously argued; anger had never been traded. She didn't know what his anger was like. All she knew was that when she was away from him the seed of doubt grew and flourished. When she was with him, it was all forgotten.

Then there was the business of the wedding . . . which looked fit to dwarf a durbar.

The plane began its long descent to Delhi airport. The alteration in the plane's angle of flight woke Bewick. All that Sally noticed was that his breathing changed. The next moment the seat was empty and he was on his way to one of the toilets.

A few minutes later Bewick returned to find Sally kneeling on his seat craning to see out of the window. He stood watching her, waiting. He was so still that for some time she didn't notice him. When she did, she jumped. 'I'm so sorry, I didn't realize.'

She returned to her own seat. As he stepped forward, Sally realized that he'd been looking at her for some time and was going to talk to her.

' . . . And now I'm researching the contamination of blood samples,' Sally explained.

The land beneath the plane was visible in clear detail now as they closed with the runway.

'The greatest advantage of DNA, you see, is also its greatest drawback. Because it's replicable through PCR, you only need have the tiniest amount of material to work on. Once you've got it, you can make more of it. So quite comprehensive tests can be carried out on micrograms of blood or tissue.'

'And the drawback?'

'If only tiny amounts of a sample are needed – and theoretically you can work on a few molecules – then some of the material you work on could be an airborne contaminent of the sample. Dust, for example, could contain dried blood which had been floating around for days and be nothing to do with the event under investigation.'

'But surely . . .'

'It sounds like an extreme example, doesn't it? But most people are killed or assaulted or raped by someone they know. Someone may be under suspicion who could well have been at the scene of the murder in a quite innocent capacity at another time.'

'Yes. I see that. But surely common sense . . .'

'Ah yes. Common sense . . . but scientists are the new magi. We're believed. We're supposed to be ruthlessly objective. Juries don't understand how we got up the mountain and back, they just want the tablets of stone. Men have been sent to their deaths on the say-so of pathologists whose carelessness we'd think was outrageous nowadays. Judges believe pathologists because they're educated and speak a specialized language, like lawyers do. Lawyers respect them, as they expect to be respected themselves. Sometimes it's a big con.'

'Sure. So where's your lab?'

'Norwich St Giles's.' Something about the way Bewick had asked the question made her suspicious: 'And you: what do you do?'

'Oh. I'm an ex-copper. I'm a sort of consultant now. We used to use your lab.' Sally blushed hot. 'Christ. You might have told me. Christ, how embarrassing.'

'Not at all. I wasn't aware of the problem. I know about establishing the chain of evidence, of course, it's standard. But I didn't know there were those problems with DNA. It ought to be better known. I'm very glad you told me.'

They were interrupted by the plane landing and the intercom seatbelt and smoking announcement.

The possibility of this man being police hadn't entered Sally's head. She met police often in the course of her work. He didn't fit. She glanced at him surreptitiously. No; he didn't fit.

She realized she was full of irritation at herself for her mistake. 'DNA profiling is still going to revolutionize individual identification,' she said defensively, 'but it's got to be understood what you're getting.'

What did this self-anger mean? She thought of James; or tried to. She couldn't, didn't want to.

But if this man was an ex-policeman, what sort of consultant would he be? He seemed more like a . . . but she couldn't categorize him. 'Where is your consultancy then?' She knew he was reluctant to answer. 'I'm being nosy. But you're a very unexpected man.'

'I'm part of CICS.'

'I see.'

She smiled at him. He returned the smile, but not without reserve. She had seen him earlier noticing her engagement ring. There was a dazed quality to him. She wondered what he had been doing in Thailand.

At Delhi airport refreshments were very expensive cokes dispensed with supreme lassitude by a tiny man with a murmur of a voice.

Outside the air shook, quivering and coiling, distorting all beyond it as it rose from the oven-hot concrete. Sally stood by herself at the plate window watching the shifting patterns.

So he was part of CICS.

CICS had been seen, in informed circles at least, as one of the more outrageous Thatcherite sell-offs.

Three years before the foundation, in 1959, of

Cambridge University's Institute of Criminology, the ancestor of CICS had started life partly funded by the Home Office, under the wing of its own Research Unit. It was then called the Nashe Criminological Research Foundation after its principal benefactor. With the advent of the University's Institute, moves were made to close it down. It had however been launched by private donation. In order not to discourage future philanthropy it was decided to keep it running as an advisory service and consultancy.

It served whoever considered it useful: domestic police forces, foreign governments, large companies. It was a success. The direct government funding which was available to it was in fact never required: it was one of the very few Home Office institutions which was consistently profitable.

Now privatized, it was the Cambridge International Criminology Service. It had brochures.

She finished her drink and made her way back to the plane.

'We have brochures,' Bewick said, somewhere above the Arabian Gulf. 'Glossy. You can see to tie your tie in them.'

She smiled.

'I'm the token copper,' he added.

Bewick had been the youngest superintendent in Britain when he was head-hunted for CICS to become one of its consultants.

Apart from its work on the sociological aspects of

crime, CICS's claim to commercial attention was that it assessed the latest investigative methods thrown up by technology and science: computer modelling and mapping of multiple crime, for example, the software for which was coming through; DNA-matching methods; offender profiling.

Essentially its staff of consultants were educators; academics who were also trained communicators. Following a visit to the FBI Academy at Quantico, however, the Director of CICS had insisted on the inclusion of someone who had actually investigated crime; hence Bewick.

Between Delhi and Tel Aviv, Sally Vernon discovered the bones of this more easily than she'd expected. Bewick seemed content to talk about the work he did. Remembering his earlier reticence, she wondered why. Eventually she asked him. He didn't answer at first.

'I'm being nosy again,' she said.

'Not at all. Talking about work is pleasant: as if the world conforms to solid values, that sort of thing.'

'Which it clearly doesn't?'

'How about a nightmare, dreamt up by an acid-dropping astrologer, roaming the jungle with a Kalashnikov.'

Sally laughed. 'What were you doing in Thailand?'

This time she didn't get an answer at all. Bewick looked out of the window for a moment and then he said, 'And you're engaged?'

'Yes. Yes, I am.'

'Is that going to get in the way of your work?'

'Not for a few years. I think I can put off babies for a bit longer.'

'That's good.'

'Why?'

'I'd like to know more about your work. Perhaps you could give us a seminar at CICS?'

Sally wondered if he meant this or whether he was sparing her earlier blushes. His general tactfulness was another surprise; like a tiger with a conscience. 'Do you mean that?'

He looked at her. 'Yes. It relates to our work at the service.'

'Then I'd like to. Very much.'

At Gatwick Airport, which was crowded, their parting was awkward. It was full of regrets, so it was formal, disguising.

They stood looking at each other in the middle of the shiny concourse floor, under the towering windows. Around and past them streamed a tide of fellow passengers.

'So I can call about a seminar, can I?'

'You can call me anyway.'

'Do you come to Cambridge much?' Bewick asked.

'Every so often. Shall I ring you?'

'Yes please.'

'Good. Then I shall.'

They shook hands. Holding his hand, Sally, who

considered herself tall, found herself going on tiptoe to kiss his cheek.

The fresh smell of his skin gave her a pleasant nudge of surprise. She tucked her shoulder bag under her arm and went. Almost immediately, she turned. 'Are you married?'

'No. Was.'

He watched her go, until she'd almost disappeared. Suddenly she turned again. Seeing him still looking at her, she smiled before waving briefly.

He raised his arm to return the gesture, but at that moment a child pushing a baggage trolley ran it into him. Meeting the immovable Bewick the child was thrown forward on to the bar. He hurt his face and began crying. The mother gave Bewick a filthy look, implying, 'Why don't you look where you're standing?'

Her husband and two other children straggled up, sunburnt and overweight, wearing pink and lime-green cotton hats. The husband looked at Bewick, as if measuring him for his strength, then turned idly to the crying child and clouted him.

An immediate row began. Sally had disappeared. Bewick moved off.

At Victoria, Bewick telephoned his home number in Cambridge to pick up anything on the answer machine that might be usefully addressed while he was in London. There were several messages from George and Kit Enwright, followed by two messages left by Alec Dundas. He tried George and Kit with no result, then rang Dundas.

'Alec?'

'Yes.' It was Dundas, unmistakably. The voice was backstreet Scots, overlaid with years of law practice at the highest level, adapted to an establishment tradition where lawyers tried to sound judicious. Nothing could disguise the energy, however.

Alec Dundas leant back in his chair and smiled. He was glad to hear Bewick. The scars of youthful bad skin and an awkward angular face were overcome in Alec Dundas by the brightness of his eye, his intelligence and his unnerving energy. Everything he did seemed decisive. His gestures were bold. He had a laugh like a donkey.

'John Bewick! . . . Where the hell have you been?'

'Thailand, matter of fact.'

'Some pointless consultancy, I suppose?'

'You're so well informed. What can I do for you?'

'Ah. Yes . . .' Dundas hardly hesitated, but Bewick read it. 'Something which might be of interest to you.'

Since Dundas only came to Bewick with problems, his putting it like this meant it would be a stinker.

Bewick's reply was loaded with caution. 'Yes?'

'Do you have anything on?'

There was a silence.

Dundas waited only briefly. 'Do you?'

Dundas knew that Bewick always considered anything he proposed to him. Eventually Bewick replied, 'As long as it doesn't mean travelling, Alec.'

'No, no. On your doorstep.'

'What do you mean, my doorstep?'

Dundas could still hear the reluctance. 'Cambridge. A killing. DCI Jones handled it.'

'I see. Gio Jones. OK. All right.'

'What about tea-time tomorrow, here?'

'What about today? I'm in town now.'

'Four-thirty, then.'

Bewick put the phone down. He stood quite still, his hand on the replaced receiver. After nearly a minute, a man waiting outside tapped on the glass. Bewick turned, as if for a brief moment not understanding why the man, who looked now questioningly at him, had done it.

Soon after Bewick's call, Dundas's secretary Mrs Clyro made an excuse to come into his office. She wanted to know Bewick's response. She knew that Dundas was keen to see Bewick on board.

'He's coming in to discuss it, which is a good sign.'

Mrs Clyro nodded. Dundas had never seen Mrs Clyro smile. When he first employed her several years before, he had wondered if she ever would; and she never had.

'When is he coming?'

'At tea-time. He seemed reluctant but, as I said, he knows this man Jones who's in charge of the case. They were colleagues when Bewick was a cop; quite close, I understand.'

3

Two weeks earlier, Detective Chief Inspector Giovanni Hywel Owen Jones had been in his small pigsty of an office at the City West Station in Cambridge. He had been complaining in his energetic way to a colleague about the move of the West Anglia Police HQ from Huntingdon to the edge of Cambridge only ten minutes away.

'God man, you could spend half a day getting over to Huntingdon to get your paws on a piece of paper. Now they've moved the bloody toybox over here, you're expected to be back within the hour. If that's progress I'm a Tory minister.'

To the north of Cambridge the A45, as it was then known, curved in an arc round the city which spread out to meet it, and amongst the high-tech palaces on the western edge of the science park stood the regional HQ of the West Anglia Police Force, so resented by Gio Jones. Built of brick and flirtatiously painted steel, it housed the most advanced technical equipment enjoyed by any police force in England.

The HQ's control room was the clearing house

for 999 calls in the region: air-conditioned home to twelve computer terminals, telephones and other communications hardware.

That morning a broad, round-shouldered man, Inspector Laffan, was in charge of the dozen officers that were usually present in the control room. Suddenly he found himself focusing. A WPC across the room from him was listening with abnormal concentration. As he turned, her eyes flicked up at him. Laffan picked up an earphone. The WPC, he noticed, had gone red in the face. In the earphone Laffan heard a country voice, slow and authoritative: 'You better get someone over here . . . You better send someone down.'

Laffan glanced down at the WPC's pad.

Parbold Cottage
Washpit Lane
Chalcote.
Julia Kelleher, resident owner.

A few minutes later, a line of cars, heading west along the A45, braked to within the speed limit. In their mirrors, the swivelling blue light of the police car.

Chalcote stands on one of the low chalk spurs overlooking the shallow valley of the Cam as it heads north into what was once the inland sea of the fens.

Parbold Cottage bridges the angle of two lanes, backed by a small orchard.

Percy Snaith, a retired college gardener, was there to meet the two policemen. He led them to the front door and pointed to the letterbox. The DI went down on his haunches and glanced through it. He straightened up and turned to Percy Snaith. 'If you could wait in the car until my chief gets here, Sir?'

He addressed the young constable. 'We're sealing it. I'll get on the radio. There's only one gate. You stay on that. No one . . . no one comes in.'

Gio Jones put the phone down. He looked around his room and then up at the tall figure slouching in the doorway. 'You're in charge of the office until further notice, Frank. Come on.'

Inspector Frank Dalmeny unwound his lanky body off the door frame to let his chief past then loped after him down the corridor to Scenes of Crime.

Gio Jones had been born in the dock area of Swansea. Apart from his bright eye, he was a short, plump, nondescript figure. Few people who met him, however, forgot his energy or his pungent realism.

He marched into the office known as Scenes of Crime. 'Baynes, Inglis, you're with me. A body at Chalcote.' He turned to Dalmeny: 'Frank, if HQ haven't come through in the next twenty minutes, tell them what I'm doing.'

Frank Dalmeny hummed some sort of acknowledgement of this and went back to his computer.

'All right, you two.' Baynes and Inglis followed Gio Jones out of the office. Frank Dalmeny watched them go. Computers were the love of his life. If the others went boy scouting after criminals, it left him more time to refine the office's use of these wonderful machines. He leaned back, his hands clasped behind his neck, smiling at the screen in front of him.

Giovanni Jones sat in the back of the police car alone, the two younger men in front. He looked out of the car at the autumn fenland as they moved quickly out of the city westwards. Suddenly they were braking hard.

'You do that again, Kevin Inglis,' said Jones, 'and I'll disembowel you, very, very slowly.'

'Silly sod pulled out, Sir, saw us and bashed his brakes.'

'Just get us there, will you? I'm too beautiful to die young.'

'Sir.'

Kevin Inglis easily found Parbold Cottage lying snug between Washpit Lane and the Haslingham Road. The other police car was parked in a kind of lay-by, cut by successive car tyres into the verge opposite the gable end of the cottage. In front of it was a six-year-old Renault 5, battered blue.

The body was a woman in her mid-thirties. She lay on her side, propped up against the staircase opposite the front door. Her clothes were torn and the lower half of her body was naked. There was a lot of blood; on carpet, walls and banisters. Baynes was unrolling a metre-wide strip of heavy polythene across from the front door to where she lay. Jones made his way over to the body. It was cold and stiff.

'Who's been called?'

'Dr Garrod. He's on his way.'

'OK.'

There was no doubting she was dead. Giovanni Jones could see bruising on the neck and there were terrible wounds to the back of the head.

He looked around him. The door to his right was open, revealing part of the sitting-room. There was an abstract painting on the wall, a chair upholstered in yellow, a glass table, the glossy fronds of a large potted plant.

Not a house with children, he thought, remembering the battlefield chaos of his own home.

Minutes later the police surgeon, Dr Garrod, arrived. He looked exhausted as usual. Garrod stared at the body for a few moments then went to work.

'Yes, it's murder. Ring forensic and try to get Sandy on to it, will you?' Giovanni Jones was on the phone to Frank back at Scenes of Crime. Sandy was Professor Sir Arnold Sandham.

Professor of Morbid Anatomy and Histology and Fellow of St Margaret's College, Sandham displayed a lip-smacking enthusiasm for dead bodies which many found distasteful. Jones found him useful. He trusted his judgement but kept out of his way.

Frank Dalmeny promised to do what he could in his jokiest manner, which suggested the opposite.

Jones restrained himself. Dalmeny was irritating but he was also sensitive and liable to fits of non-cooperation if handled roughly.

'I look after her garden for her. She's a busy woman.'

Jones looked around him at the island bed of flowers, old orchard trees, the lawn. 'Nice job you do.'

'Easy garden. No vegetables. She's not interested in the fruit.'

Percy Snaith said this as if he had been raised in a harder school where vegetables and fruit were the test of a man.

'I'm retired now,' he added unnecessarily: he was as wrinkled as a walnut, with snow-white hair under a greasy flat cap.

'Yes?' Giovanni Jones was polite.

'So I spend a bit of time in her garden. We were friends. She were a friendly woman. Three pound an hour. Only pocket money. But what do I need at my age? Work for an hour, drink for an hour. Good beer at the Horseshoes. Free House. Tolly's. Adnams. Greene King.'

'Friendly, was she?'

'Arrr,' said Percy Snaith, 'she were a nice woman. Some thought she were pushy. I like 'em a bit cheeky.'

'She was cheeky?'

'She were . . .' The old man searched for a definition and failed. 'She were all right.'

'How did you find her just now?'

He explained how he'd found her. Looking through

the letterbox, because it was the second time he'd got no reply. He'd seen her – 'like that'.

Memory silenced him.

With encouragement, other details emerged. Julia Kelleher had been married. Her parents lived locally. She'd been employed by Sirius Software. Her ex-husband lived 'out Bury way'.

Jones spent some time with the old man. He liked his stiffness, his old-fashioned prejudices. His apparent inability to tell anything but the truth was useful.

At two o'clock a not very new Toyota rumbled to a halt outside Parbold Cottage and was abandoned by its driver.

'He's not going to leave it there,' said Kevin Inglis who was sorting the video equipment. 'Not like that.'

'He has left it there,' said Baynes, 'just like that. You've got to admire him.'

'Have you?' asked Inglis. 'You move it then.'

A figure in a khaki tweed suit hurried from the Toyota to the cottage. Professor Sandham had arrived.

'Ah, aha!' Sandham shouted from a few feet away. 'What do you have for me today?'

Sandham was excited; he was all eyebrows and challenge.

Jones, irritated, remained calm. It was an effort. 'I'll show you,' he said.

'Parbold Cottage!' bawled Sandham. 'Mentioned Parbold Cottage to Dunkeley as I was leaving. There an orchard, is there?'

'Yes. Out at the back.'

'You'll find it's pears, I dare say,' triumphed Sandham. 'Dunkeley on Parbold: comes in some Norfolk rents book of about 1200. "A house where pears grow." That's what it means – Parbold. So they'll be pears, I dare say.'

Sandham entered the cottage. Julia Kelleher's body lay where it had been found.

'Yes. I see. I see. I see.'

By lunchtime a small crowd of the curious had assembled near the cottage.

Watching, Jones stood at the window of the woman's bedroom.

'Reckon we've nearly finished with the videoing.' Inglis spoke from the doorway.

Jones nodded and turned back to look out of the window. Mostly women and old men, the crowd spilled over the corner of the recreation ground and on to the road. In the distance he could hear the hue and cry of the school playground.

'Vultures gathering, then?' said Inglis, subdued. The care and order of the house contrasted grossly with the beaten dead body downstairs.

'How many teams, do you reckon?' asked Inglis.

'Be applying for three at first.'

'Right.'

Inglis seldom sustained a conversation with him voluntarily. Jones realized that Inglis didn't want to point the camera again at the mess of death downstairs.

'We're keeping the Incident Room at City West,'

said Jones as he thought about this. 'They've started on that.'

'Right.'

In the road below, Baynes was re-parking Sandham's car.

'Has Baynes ever used that video? Don't think he has, has he? If Sandy wants to cover anything else then let Baynes have a go, if it's not treading on your toes.'

'No. Shouldn't think so. Right. I'll get him on to it.'

Inglis went, disguising any relief he felt.

After looking round it once more, Jones closed the door on the clean room.

On the landing outside, Sandham was examining the surfaces. In the hallway at the foot of the stairs, Baynes was videoing the carpet quagmired with blood. Sandham glanced up as Jones emerged from the bedroom.

'A lot of blood spraying about,' he explained. 'I want to see how far. Don't think any of it got up here. It was a hammer, almost certainly, by the way. Got one perfect indentation the size of a two-bob bit.'

'Well done,' said Jones and made his way downstairs.

Jones spent most of the afternoon by the phone. The incident-room technicians asked him questions they knew he couldn't yet answer. They always did, part of their modus. He was granted the three extra teams he requested, including the personnel of his choice. His increased budget request fell on less fertile ground, but he was allocated 80 per cent of what he wanted. This was what he'd expected, almost exactly. He was an experienced officer.

'What a nutter!' Ian Aston laughed.

The first team was back reporting from their initial house-to-house in Chalcote. In one of the council houses they had come across Keith Dawes. Keith Dawes was a bike freak.

'Could tell you the kind of spark plug the bloody thing has, just from a sight of the left-hand bit of the bloody thing's mudguard! I tell you, a right malco boffin!'

Mixed with his intense interest in what he had just been told, Jones felt something like regret. He knew that he already had a breakthrough. His intuition told him that this would lead to an arrest. He nodded, half a smile.

'Get checking then.'

'Sir.'

The younger men left the room with enthusiasm.

Left alone, Jones's smile faded. He rapidly developed doubts, or at least felt less sure. Worse still, he didn't really know what he felt.

This sensation of confusion, this blurring of his best intuition, had been with him some time. He knew its cause, having worked it out some months before. There was no one in the station now that he could spark off. Since John Bewick had left, there was no one to whom he could entrust his more bizarre theories, no equal to argue with. Bewick was an outsider like himself. Jones missed him profoundly.

'Old bastard,' he grumbled, then thought about what Aston's team had discovered.

Keith Dawes had heard a bike the previous evening. He'd heard it start up near Parbold Cottage. He would swear on his mother's steak and kidney, Aston said, that he knew what the bike was. It was a Ducatti 888. Such bikes were uncommon, expensive. Any local purchase of such a machine could be traced within hours.

Later that afternoon, Jones went to report to Superintendent Hutchings, his immediate superior. He was told that Hutchings was out shooting.

'Oh. I could wear a tramp through the woods, mind. Nice day for it.'

'Not pheasants, Gio – targets. Rifle club stuff, you know? The Royal Cambridge.'

Jones knew. The Royal Cambridge Rifle Club wasn't just about poking holes in cardboard with high-velocity metal. It was a coterie of men who valued the social contacts made there far more highly than the sport itself. The clubroom cases were full of trophies, but few were current. The ambience of the Royal Cambridge was self-advancing, exclusive and masonic; few of its members had more than a nodding acquaintance with firearms.

Gio Jones found Hutchings on the club's six-hole golf

course. He was playing a round with a shy-looking, silver-haired man whom Jones recognized.

Muir Hammond was the director and founder of Sirius Software, the firm where the victim Julia Kelleher had worked. With them was an elegant Asian man whose aristocratic air was somehow masked by the more immediate effect of his perfect golden skin and thick black hair, which was greying so exactly at the temples that it looked as if a make-up artist had been at work.

Hutchings spotted the inelegant figure of Jones wandering over the grass catwalk of the links. He excused himself from Hammond and his friend. He met Jones some distance away. He wasn't pleased.

'What is it, Gio?'

'A killing. Woman in her own home.'

'Yes?'

'Thought you should know. And quite frankly I fancied the fresh air. She had her head pulped.'

'You've got the teams you asked for?'

'I got what I need, Fred.'

'There you are. We all have to live in the real world, Gio.'

Jones nodded but said nothing more and made no move to go.

'Anything else, Gio?'

'Not really, just that . . .' Jones flicked a glance in the direction of Hammond, '. . . she was one of his employees.'

'Hammond's?'

'Yeah.'

'He has hundreds of employees.'

'Sure.'

'Quite difficult to avoid being one of his employees.'

'Sure. "Nerd instinct: the Gates crasher".' Jones quoted the headline of an article about Hammond which had appeared in the *Guardian* a few days before.

'One of the entrepreneurial spirits of the age,' Hutchings countered. 'OK. I'll tell him. It can hardly put him off his game. He's already playing like a cow on crutches. That Asian friend of his is eating him for breakfast. You'll want to speak to his people, I suppose.'

'Wouldn't hurt. Specially if she worked at the HQ.'

'All right. Leave it with me. OK. Thanks Gio.'

Jones wandered back to his car across the stylized greenery of the course.

Yes, everything was falling to hand. He had a definite sense of anti-climax. Oddly, that pleased him. If he was disappointed, it meant at least that his interest in his work, excitement even, hadn't deserted him.

It had taken ten officers six hundred man hours to establish that Keith Dawes must have misidentified the motorbike. In that respect the first week had been a write-off.

Jones summoned Ian Aston, the detective who'd brought Keith Dawes to his attention. 'This bike nutter Keith Dawes . . .'

Aston was embarrassed. 'Yeah. I thought he was the type, you know. Knows the size of your bolt on your mudguard flange. One of those. Thought he was genuine.'

'What d'you think now?'

'Got him wrong, didn't I?'

'How confident did he seem?'

'Well, that was it. That was the thing. He seemed so sure.'

'What did he actually say to you?'

Aston had known what the interview was to be about. He opened his notebook, although he knew it by heart. 'He said, "What you're looking for is a Ducatti triple eight." He was definite; dead definite.'

'He didn't tell you where he was when he heard it?'

'No, Sir. I told him about that Eastern Electrics bloke passing a bike at speed in Washpit Lane which he couldn't identify. And Keith Dawes said, "You're looking for a Ducatti triple eight." End of story. Expert witness.'

'Sure.'

Jones walked to the window of his muddle of an office and stared out at white clouds drifting eastwards.

'Thing is,' he said after a bit, 'I feel it in my old Welsh water . . . we got to find the bike.'

'Yes, Sir.'

'Get this Dawes lad in, will you? I'd like a word with him myself.'

Apart from the fruitless search for the motorbike owner, the database on the Kelleher murder was expanding rapidly. The woman's parents lived locally. Jones had spoken to them himself and done his best to protect them from the obscene ritual of media attention.

He hadn't taken to the father at all and in other circumstances would have had little sympathy for the man; Julia Kelleher's mother was so shy she seemed barely sane.

Julia's ex-husband David Toner had been questioned early on. He was cooperative and had no objection to being blood tested, despite the fact that his alibi for the evening in question was as solid as corroboration by his girlfriend could make it.

Julia Kelleher's employers, Sirius Software, had given the police all the help they could, thanks presumably to Hutchings's influence. It was quite a famous company; nevertheless, the MD, Muir Hammond, and the Personnel Manager had found the time to talk to Jones for over two hours.

Jones had been interested to meet Hammond properly after glimpsing him on the green acres of The Royal Cambridge. He was, after all, one of the stars of the continuing so-called Cambridge Phenomenon: those small, specialist, science or technology based companies which captured national headlines with the cleverness of their inventions, with their multi-million-pound contracts. Many of the entrepreneurial heads of these enterprises had gone public. From being paper millionaires, they overnight became the real thing. Hammond had resisted this choice and still owned his company. Some said that he had missed the boat, that bigger companies were ripping off the principles of his software, manipulating the grey area of unprovable copyright infringement to their advantage. Why otherwise was the company needing to expand its less creative Systems Installation Division?

Hammond was very welcoming to Jones and to the young woman detective who accompanied him to Sirius House.

Hammond was taller than Jones had remembered, wearing a silver-grey suit. Socially he was awkward, protecting himself with a slight, fixed smile. His handshake was slack for such a lean, angular man. When talking, his natural habit was to consider the upper corner of the room, as he followed his own thoughts. He had taught himself however to pull his eyes back, from time to time, to the person he was talking to. When this happened, it was accompanied by a small widening of the smile. Jones reckoned he was a natural for a Nutty Boffin of the Year trophy. Mind you, there was so much competition in Cambridge.

Hammond talked freely about the murdered woman, praising her astuteness and willingness to learn. Jones had an instinct about places where he would learn something to help an investigation. He would learn little here. On the wall, he noticed, were photographs of gleamingly restored vintage cars, some empty, some with Muir Hammond at the wheel smiling. One, taken at an event, showed him driving; possibly even racing.

As expected, little was learnt. The day Julia had been killed was like any other. She had no enemies in the workplace; was generally well liked.

As he left the spruce, well-ordered environment of Sirius House, Jones remembered that all was supposed not to be well with Sirius Software. Well, there were no cracks showing here. The efficiency of the place was a standing reproach to him.

It was all rumour, Jones decided. He had long ago taught himself to discount rumour, except for what it told you about its source. He knew that there is very often smoke without fire – the smoke usually being downwind of a malicious rival or a frightened neurotic, indulging in fearful imaginings of what might be: dreamt monsters.

Few rumours surfaced from the questioning of Julia Kelleher's neighbours. As predicted, they had seen and heard little. Julia Kelleher wasn't well known in the village but had made a friendly impression. She'd only owned Parbold Cottage for two or three years and most of her time was spent away from it.

Gossip came up with visitors to the cottage, of both sexes, but nothing that aspired to the status of a 'relationship'. Julia Kelleher's desk yielded no financial complications. The only letters she'd kept dated from over a year before and were from another woman describing a trip through the French canals.

Jones wanted to find the motorbike.

*

Next morning, the scruffy and amiable Keith Dawes found himself the target of Giovanni Jones's threatening charm.

Jones looked at the bluff, ploughboy's face gazing across the desk at him with its permanent half-smile of appeasement. He could see why Aston had trusted the lad. He was the type, all right. Kicked around, sent up and patronized by his mates, written off by his teachers, Keith had needed that smile of appeasement; until, one day, his solitary passion became useful.

Keith Dawes lived for motorbikes: he went to sleep thinking about them and woke up in the morning to remember his dreams about them. When his friends began buying bikes, Keith came into his own. His knowledge became currency.

Keith was now cool. Despite the fact that he still lived with his parents, in his own world nineteen-year-old Keith Dawes was a man of substance. Jones had the sense to realize most of this.

'Keith, we're most grateful for the help you've given us,' Jones said, man to man, 'but we're a bit baffled still.'

'Oh yeah?'

'That bike you recognized for us . . .'

'Triple eight, yeah?'

'Tell me how you saw it, and where it was and so on, will you?'

'No, no, I didn't see it. Who told you that? No, no – I heard it. Ducatti triple eight. Big bang engine. I heard it.'

'You heard it?'

Jones had tried to keep the scepticism out of his voice but clearly hadn't succeeded. Keith Dawes was looking defensive. He explained to Jones as if to an eight-year-old: 'That's what it was. Here, listen . . .'

Keith Dawes held up a blunt imperious hand, ingrained with engine oil, for silence. They listened. Jones heard a medley of traffic noises from the Newmarket Road outside.

'Hear that bike idling at the lights out there?'

Jones heard traffic noise, a blur of noise, nothing else.

'You go and look,' commanded Keith Dawes. 'It's a Kawasaki. Probably red.'

Jones peered down out of his window. A red bike stood at the lights, an insignia gleaming on its tank. A patrol car was just easing itself off the premises into the road behind the bike. Jones squinted at the bike and then went to the phone. 'Charlie Maddock is just setting off up the road behind a K reg. red bike. Ask him to get alongside it and see what sort of bike it is, will you? Thanks. Tell him it's an experiment. I'm investigating the audio-recognition of bike engines . . .' Jones smiled, pleased with himself. Then he glowered. 'Of course it's bloody important . . .'

He put the phone down and turned again to Keith Dawes. 'It's all right. I'm as sure as I can be that you're spot on . . .'

'Red, wasn't it? Like I said. There are a few black ones round here, not many.'

'Sure. You see, Keith, if you're right about all this – which I'm sure you are – I've got a problem.'

'Oh yeah?'

'So what I'm asking you, Keith, is this: could it – I mean is there even a possibility of that Ducatti being anything else?'

'Nah.'

Keith was undented, sunny, confident. What a witness he'd make, thought Jones: unshakeable he'd be, even by the slithiest QC.

He told Keith how two of his teams, five officers each, had checked on every Ducatti 888 sold in the area from Boston to Chelmsford, from Norwich to Bedford; and then, after that, in the whole of the UK. How each sale had been followed up; the policework, the whole damn thing; the good old shoe leather and telephonic earache of it all. He didn't even hint at wasted time.

The phone rang. The details of the red bike were read back to him and it was just as Keith Dawes had predicted. Jones put the phone down. He considered the lumpen figure of Keith Dawes, as innocent in his way as some batty professor, and as deeply entrenched in extraordinary, specialized detail.

'So you heard the Ducatti about when?'

'I was working on a mate's bike out the front and Sharon Whittaker was being a real mong, so I told her why don't she bugger off home and play with Mr Blobby and I was thinking I might watch *Neighbours* but I didn't want to put my tools away when I heard it: that started up over Washpit Lane way . . . and then I really told Sharon Whittaker to put something in it.'

'So it was faint?'

'No, no. That wasn't it. I just wanted to hear it.'

For Keith Dawes it was divine harmony he was talking about and he looked as if he was remembering it now.

'You heard it start up Washpit Lane way, so it must have come here earlier – wouldn't you have heard it then?'

'I thought about that, but then I was out road testing my mate's bike earlier, wasn't I?'

'How much earlier?'

''Bout half an hour.'

'I see. So what did the bike do?'

'Sat there for half a minute and then it went.'

Keith Dawes grinned.

'It sat there for half a minute, you reckon?'

'Bit less, maybe – bloke wanted to hear it without his helmet on, something like that.'

'A Ducatti 888?'

'Yeah.'

'It was unmistakable, was it?'

'Couldn't've been nothing else.'

'I see.'

Jones pondered a moment.

'We can only rely on you, Keith. You're the man with the knowledge . . . The only other bit of information we got, see, is a bloke driving into the village about that time who has a bike go past him like a lunatic which he couldn't identify, though he reckoned it might've been a Honda.'

'Wasn't no Honda I heard.'

'Sure. You're the expert. Then let me put this to you, Keith. Is there anything, anything else on the planet – a one-off, a ten-off, anything – which you might not expect to hear . . .'

Jones stopped.

Keith's eyes, with their thick sandy eyelashes, had half-closed in thought. He was frowning.

Jones waited. For something to do meanwhile, he tried to read Keith's jeans which were painstakingly graffitied in biro with bike badges, the names of favourite groups and the odd joke copied from *Viz*. Through carefully crafted rips protruded a pair of hairy knees.

'Bleeding heck,' murmured Keith. He looked up. 'An RC45. Could've been. A 66 per cent engine. Pair firing. That'd throb all right, that would. Yeah!' There was the light of passion in Keith's eyes. 'That's a Honda, an RC45. A race bike. You pay 18K for that on the road then anything you want on top of that to tune it. I never heard one before.'

Keith Dawes turned to Jones, a smile of pure joy on his face. 'That'd murder a Ferrari, that would.'

The next day a suspect had been fingerprinted, blood tested and genetically profiled. Soon after that he had been arrested and charged.

4

Bewick walked through Lincoln's Inn Fields, the gardens fenced against the intrusions of the homeless. He turned the corner into Lincoln's Inn itself. There, suddenly, was Georgian London, the only evident modernizations being Victorian gas lamps. The thunder of the traffic was reduced to a murmur here. Shoes clicked on cobbles. Calm terraces faced each other across a lawn of collegiate smoothness. The legal profession feathered its nest with unfailing confidence.

Dundas came down to find Bewick in reception talking to one of the two women who worked on the front desk. The receptionist was surprised by this mark of respect. Dundas noticed immediately. 'We were schoolchums, Shelagh,' he said. 'St Matthew's. Mr Bewick used to defend me from your unprincipled southern bullies. I was a shy, retiring boy with all the delicate sensibility you'd associate with a product of the Glasgow docks.'

Dundas laughed, a loud joyous yelp which echoed up the unadorned stone staircase. He and Bewick set off up it.

'How's your old man?' Bewick asked.

'Oh! Still on the McEwans. Still toothless. Still in Govan. I tried to buy him a tasteful little villa so he could get away from being burgled every two minutes. He wasn't having any of that. "They're my burglars, thank yih!" So there he is, still partying, in defiance of all medical prediction. Eighty plus, poor old bugger.'

Once it was realized that Alec's father's alcoholism was intractable, Alec Dundas's general care and education had been taken in hand by his uncle, his father's elder brother. He had taken Alec with him to London, hence St Matthew's.

St Matthew's had been in the vanguard of a new concept in English public-school education – the Direct Grant system. This was a Trojan horse of egalitarianism, whereby a quota of selected pupils were accepted into public schools and paid for by the state, on so-called state scholarships.

The Direct Grant idea, which could have led to state control of the entire public-school ethos and could have modernized the British class system within a generation, was abandoned by Wilson's Labour government.

Dundas led the way into his room on the first floor. It was high, panelled, full of light, and uncomfortable in a superior way.

Ushered to a wing chair which looked as if it was contemporary with the building, Bewick lowered his seventeen stone into it carefully.

'Tea?'

'Only reason I came, tea.'

Dundas picked up a small silver bell which stood on the top of a computer. It produced no immediate result, but Dundas clearly expected it to have been heard. He looked at Bewick quizzically. 'You look different. Are you in love or something?'

'No.'

'Are you ill?'

'Not as far as I know.'

'You have a problem.'

It was a statement, a diagnosis.

Bewick said nothing and managed with a smile to indicate that questioning him would be fruitless.

'You're a close bastard, pal,' said Alec Dundas, with some admiration.

'It's been a curious couple of days. Long flight. That's probably it.'

'Oh aye? Shall I tell you why you're here?'

'Please.'

'The facts are these,' said Dundas, and proceeded to give them as if reading them off a page.

Bewick had expressed admiration of this talent of Dundas, even though he was in possession of similar skills himself.

'One. The murdered woman was sexually assaulted, although there was no sign of penetration. She had apparently defended herself, as traces of skin and blood – not her own – were found under her fingernails and traces of sperm were found on her thigh. The genetic profile of both samples was found to be identical.

'Two. An expensive motorbike was heard near her cottage on the evening she was killed.

'Three. The owner of the bike was eventually identified. He was known to be an acquaintance of the victim. He was blood tested. His genetic profile matches that of the material found on the victim. He also has marks consistent with healed scratching on his back.'

There was silence briefly in the elegant room. Bewick smiled bleakly. 'You've got a problem, Alec, if the biker is your brief.'

'His family are retaining me, yes.'

'And . . .?'

'I want to know what happened.'

'You've just told me what happened.'

'No I haven't and you know it,' said Dundas. There was a delicate knock at the door and a tray of tea was brought in by Mrs Clyro.

'What I mean,' said Dundas when she had gone, 'is that there's no discernible motive.'

Bewick looked at him, awaiting an explanation.

'I know the family. They're a thoroughly decent lot.'

'Doesn't mean a thing,' Bewick said.

'Oh yes it does. I've met the lad as well. He's not unpleasant. Bit spoilt. Little short on manners like most of his age group. He's not a rapist or a murderer.'

'None of them are until they do it. That was what my old Super used to say.'

'How very existential of him.'

'There are always surprises, Alec. This may be one of them.'

'I don't think the boy did it,' said Dundas. He put the flat statement in a way which suggested it was the result of some thought.

'Has he denied it?'

'Not exactly. He hasn't admitted it either, and they've been at him for days.'

'Alibi?'

'Claims he was doped out: doesn't know where, for how long, anything.'

'The lad's going to have to do better than that.'

'That's why you're here.'

'What was he hitting?'

'Hash, some acid . . .'

Bewick voiced a sceptical grumble deep inside his chest while Dundas sorted out the tea. Bewick took his cup and added, as if it were part of the grumble, 'And Gio Jones is in charge of the case.'

'You know him well?'

'Very.'

'What do you know about DNA profiling, John?'

Bewick smiled: 'As it happens, I had an impromptu lecture on it on the plane. It's not infallible – like fingerprinting isn't infallible, I guess. But most things being equal, everyone accepts it now.'

'Is there any possibility of a mistake in this sort of case?'

'I doubt it. Gio Jones is very good. He would have

double checked. On the other hand, procedures can go wrong, as you know. I'll look into it.'

'If you would.'

'How do you come to know the family?'

'They were libelled by some local rag. A friend of mine is their GP and he put them on to me.'

'I didn't know you handled libel.'

'I don't. Geoffrey does all that. Never came to it in the end. The opposition settled. But I used it as an excuse to go to a College feast I'd been invited to. So I met them and heard the libel. You know them too.'

'I do?'

'George and Kit Enwright.'

Bewick froze. This was the ace Dundas had held back.

'Christ . . . Hang on, this doesn't make sense. Bill is what? Must be thirty-five by now. Last I heard . . .'

'It's not Bill. He's in the States. It's their nephew. George's brother's boy.'

'Thank God for that.'

'You know the boy's father is dead? George's brother, Phil.'

Bewick nodded: 'They didn't get on. George didn't approve of Phil. I met him once; very fly. Very pleased with himself. Misplaced self-confidence.'

Bewick lapsed into a thoughtful silence. 'Christ . . .' he said at last, then he focused on Dundas. 'I'll help in any way I can of course.'

The taxi took Bewick from Cambridge station to the

garage in Trumpington where he had left his car while he was abroad. He threw his bags in the boot and drove straight to George and Kit's house, which was a large modern bungalow on the outskirts of the fen village of Beach.

The garden was professionally landscaped and the house, on its couple of acres of rising ground, was invisible from the road. Halfway along the drive, an electronically operated gate swung open obligingly to let Bewick's old Volvo through.

George was on the forecourt to greet him; he looked exhausted. He and Bewick hugged each other.

'Hello John mate. Told Kit you'd be here soon as . . . you know.'

Over George's shoulder Bewick saw Kit, the tears starting as soon as she saw him. She sobbed in Bewick's arms while George held her hand.

'It's been bloody awful John. You find out who your friends are, I tell you. We were going mad. Ringing and ringing you. Then George rang the Institute and found out you were abroad. Then the buggers wouldn't tell us where.'

'I came as soon as I heard.'

'I knew you would really. When I heard you was coming, I felt so guilty for doubting you.'

Kit led the way in.

In describing his friendship with George and Kit – some people thought it surprising – Bewick would say that a perfect couple never existed, but George and Kit ran it very close. They were cousins of Bewick's ex-wife Nina, of whom George and Kit were surprisingly tolerant, considering how Nina was the golden girl of her family and knew it – the first of her kind to go to university, with a starry career in the civil service to follow. Nina quickly learnt that Kit wouldn't take any sort of condescension from her, but was always there to be dumped on in the early years of Nina's children: hers were grown up.

When Nina walked out on Graham, her first husband, and soon after teamed up with Bewick, Kit began to take her seriously. Kit was impressed by Bewick, immediately noticing his hidden quickness of mind. She revelled in his politeness towards her, the unlikely sensitivity of such a powerful man. Virtuously, she included him in her circle of people to love.

George was wiry and short, a lean monkey face with a ready grin. Kit was tawny haired and tall, with big breasts and elegant hands. Kit laughed a lot and was an instinctive, efficient book-keeper. Kit's Dad had owned a garage and George had married the boss's daughter.

When Dad retired, Kit and George's reputation for honesty, their charm and their capacity for work expanded the business to a group of four garages. When they sold out at the end of the eighties they had two million in the bank.

And now this.

George was talking about Phil, his dead brother, father of the accused boy.

'All that sex stuff Phil used to get into, it used to put me off. He was like one of those doorstep Christians, what d'you call them, Jehovah's Witnesses, except with him it was sex. Yeah, if you hadn't done it hanging upside down from a tree, dressed up as a bishop or something, you hadn't lived.'

Kit grinned at him: a flicker of startling intimacy. 'I know what he was up to with all that talk,' she said. 'He wanted a bit of wife swapping, that's what he wanted. He was the good-looking one; he thought he could have anything.'

'Mum was a bit fond of him.'

'Bit fond? She was obsessed, George, that's what she was and it never did him no good. No good at all.'

'Anyway he made a pass at Kit one day . . .'

'Wasn't even pissed, the rotten sod,' Kit interrupted, angry. 'His brother's wife!'

' . . . So we only saw him at family do's after that. What I'm saying is, I don't know what was going on but . . . it wasn't the sort of house I'd want my kids growing up in. Like that.'

'Yeah,' Kit added, 'when we made our wills it wasn't Phil we put down to look after the kids, I can tell you. Go on George, you be mother.'

George poured three glasses of champagne. They drank.

'Cheers,' said George. 'Don't know what to drink to, mind. I tell you, John mate, this thing stops you looking forward to anything. What're you going to be able to do?'

'The best move you made was instructing Alec Dundas. He'll do the best defence job you can get; if it comes to it.'

'If it comes to it?' George frowned.

'It'll come to a trial all right,' Kit asserted. 'It's got to do that. They've got everything. They've done it by the book and they've got everything!'

'Except a confession from Joe.'

'Well I shouldn't think most people who do anything as horrible as he's supposed to go and confess, do they?'

'But it makes a difference that he hasn't. Until I know why he hasn't, I won't be able to tell you what sort of future there is for the boy.'

'No, no. No, I see.'

Kit and George looked at each other as if the idea of Joe having any sort of future hadn't occurred to them. Neither would be unwise enough to start hoping, however.

'What happened when his father died?' Bewick asked. 'How did Joe react? When did Phil die, by the way?'

'Just over a year ago now,' said George.

'In his car, wasn't it?'

'Yeah. On his way back from Ely. Came off that bend – near the Twenty Pence Inn. Nobody saw the car till the next day; it was under water. Coroner said drowned . . . Joe? I don't know. He seemed to take it in his stride somehow.'

'Everyone said how well Joe seemed to be taking

it,' said Kit. 'You know what I think? I think he was really excited.'

'Didn't he like Phil?'

George seemed reluctant to answer, as if mention of his brother's death had brought home to him the extent to which he was criticizing him.

'He was scared of him. Wasn't he, George?' said Kit. She sounded guarded too. 'Don't you reckon Joe was scared of Phil?'

'He was always very quiet when Phil was around.'

'Phil used to flatter him in public. Joe used to hate it. I could see he hated it. It made you think this wasn't how things really were, you know? I don't think Joe liked his father at all. Then suddenly he was gone. For a bit Joe thought his life belonged to him. That's why he bought the bike.'

'Oh Gawd . . . the bike . . .' groaned George.

'He bought his first bike – that was his first bike. Phil had never allowed him one. It was a bit of a celebration. It wasn't a very nice thing to do but Phil hadn't made his life very nice.'

'Should see his bike . . .' George muttered.

'What about his mother? What did she think of the bike?'

'Lesley didn't . . . think, not really,' George replied. 'I'm not sure she took it in. You know how ill she is? She's very ill. That's why the lad came to stay with us.'

'Not that we've seen much of him.'

'He's been using Lesley's new house some of the

time. She hasn't even unpacked properly. He leaves it reasonable. We didn't say nothing. It was his.'

'Sure.'

'Lesley was being treated for years before Phil got killed. She's very bad now, in and out of Addenbrooke's all the time. Don't think she thinks about anything much.'

'Yeah, she comes here, Lesley does, when they let her out. Her house isn't unpacked, like George says. She's asked us to get rid of it. She knows she won't go back there now,' said Kit looking away.

'I go over and sort the mail for her every week. I agreed with Joe and her . . . before all this, you know . . . to put it on the market, but nothing's selling.' George sounded apologetic.

Bewick smiled and Kit noticed.

''S not your bleeding fault, George,' she said.

'She's dying. She'd like it settled. I feel bad about it.'

'He's told Lesley,' complained Kit, with pride, 'he's told her he'll look after all her affairs for her. What more can he do?'

George got to his feet. 'What time's dinner?' he grumbled.

'When you like.' Kit turned to Bewick. 'You will stay?'

'Kit, this is the first time I've ever said no to you, but I've been on the go for nearly two days. May I come back tomorrow?'

It isn't the first time, Kit thought. 'I'll let you off this time,' she said.

'I was going to show you my pool table,' George said. 'Still, tomorrow'll do.'

Bewick was sitting in his car before he remembered.

'Do me a favour, George – I forgot to ring Mrs Woods. Alec Dundas's message put it out of my head. She'll want to know I'm coming back.'

'Leave it with us.'

As he drove out of Beach, a row of willows obscured the view for a moment, then it opened up. A dramatic expansion: the black flats of the fens stretching to a horizon lost in mist; ten, twenty miles away, the shrunken bed of an inland sea.

Home for Bewick was a modest mid-terrace in the village-like suburb of Homerton, which lies on the banks of the Cam, separated from the city proper by playing fields, some municipal parkland and a willow-studded fen belonging to Homerton College, still grazed by cattle.

As his car turned into Water Street, Bewick noted that a promised traffic-slowing scheme had been introduced since he'd been away. He passed the Co-op, the post office, the butcher, the greengrocer on the corner, the chemist and the hairdresser's: they were all still there at least. He drove into his street.

His part of the village was a triangle of three streets. The terraced houses had been built in 1902 behind some Victorian artisan cottages which fronted the main road. At the back, the gardens of the houses ran together: each street's line of gardens was divided from the others by a footpath. The three footpaths met roughly in the centre of the triangle to form a Y shape.

Coral Woods was waiting on the doorstep. 'Hi, how are you? You're looking well. Was it hot?'

Coral Woods showed Bewick how she'd left things, what expenses she'd incurred from the plumber, what cleaning materials she'd bought at Sainsbury's, what she'd left for him in the fridge. Bewick wrote her a cheque. Then she left.

Bewick had put the kettle on as he entered the house. A mug of tea now stood on the bedside table. Bewick climbed naked into bed. He took a sip of tea but then decided against it. He settled himself down to sleep: seconds later he was unconscious. The tea steamed, untouched, and went cold.

5

Bewick woke nine hours later at six a.m. He got up and took a shower.

Bewick contacted CICS early enough to be reasonably sure that the head of the service, Sean Halliday, would not be at his desk. In the name of teamwork, Halliday was an exploiter of his personnel.

Bewick left the message at CICS that he would be taking the two weeks contractually granted after any overseas assignment.

He thanked Mrs Kay, Halliday's assistant, for the fax requested from CICS. Mrs Kay, who was organized and probably underemployed, reassured him that everything he had said would be handed on to Mr Halliday. No, there was no need to confirm anything.

Bewick parked his car in front of the elegant new West Anglia Police HQ. He paused as he got out. Standing a few feet away with his back to him was a teacher telling a group of art students something about the bronze sculpture which occupied the centre of the forecourt.

Like a cracked-open, empty eggshell, the giant head

had flat, incomplete discs, like damaged slices of its own brain, suspended within it.

'If you look at it from here,' the teacher was saying, 'it looks like the horizon. You see? Then drop your eye down and the world seems to be tipping. So; what do you think it means?'

'Well, it makes a nice roundabout; different definitely,' murmured a cynical Welsh voice, quietly enough for the teacher not to have heard.

The short, scruffy figure of Gio Jones hadn't changed.

'Shut up,' Bewick murmured back, 'and give the man a chance.'

'Of course on one level,' the teacher went on, 'it's saying: look inside the object. The surface of living objects is always deceiving: too charming, too off-putting. So; look within. But then I think it's also saying: if you do look inside, what you find is never comfortable – you'll find a world which is sliding around, impossible to see whole or straight . . .'

'Think my brain slides around too much to grasp what he's on about.' Jones eyed Bewick for a moment. 'God knows what you're playing at, Mr Bewick.'

'Why're we meeting here, Gio?'

'We got the Home Office lab round the back now.'

'Neat.'

'Oh yes. Anyway I was picking up some stuff. Thought you'd like to see this place. Horrible, isn't it?'

Bewick looked at the pleasant building.

'Let's get my bag, Monsieur Bewick, and bugger off to the Old Muscovy.'

The two men entered the reception area, where a hedge of potted palms divided a glittering floor. Jones waved a contemptuous hand.

'Course you'd know all about this, wouldn't you? Image and all that.'

'Sure.'

'Glad I don't work here. Like operating inside a bleeding toybox. Hello Big Ears! Sod off Noddy . . . give me the grown-up boring version any day.'

Bewick glanced round the space: light, airy and a tribute to the architect's skill.

Jones collected his bulging briefcase from reception and led the way out of the building again. 'Least the Old Muscovy's still here. Just about.'

The Old Muscovy pub stood at the head of a cut which led to the river. Once isolated in the wastes of Quy South Fen, it had been a watermen's pub in the days when Fen Ditton down the river had been a thriving inland port. Now it did a better trade serving the science park whose high-tech palaces glittered on its doorstep.

Bewick brought two pints, Adnams and Greene King, across the uncarpeted floor of the pub to where Jones sat by the fire.

'Cheers.'

The two men lifted their glasses and drank, Jones still glowering.

'How is it then? Your international consultancy?'

Jones emphasized 'international' with full nasal contempt; very Welsh.

Bewick shrugged. 'It's good.'

'Don't believe you. You should come back into the force, John Bewick, that's what you should do. And if you think that's flattery you're mistaken.'

'Well, let's say I feel very mistaken then, Gio.'

'What're you messing around with this Kelleher case for? It's open and shut.'

'Sure.'

'We've got everything. Motive, opportunity, witnesses, fingerprints, fibres and matching DNA.'

'Sure.'

Jones looked at the big man dwarfing the pub table in front of him. Bewick seemed patient, interested. He smiled. Jones was irritated. 'What're you pissing about at then?'

'I've been asked to make sure that everything's being done that can be done. That means a look at the evidence, obviously.'

'Kid doesn't even deny it, you know.'

'Does he admit it?'

'No. The little darling was out of his skull on hash and acid. Or was it bangers and mash? Couldn't even remember the substances, never mind the circumstances. Can't admit what he can't remember, can he?'

'How long have you had him?'

'Nearly a week.'

'So you've sewn it up in what? Ten days?'

'Fortnight, thereabouts.'

'Well done. Sounds classic to me, classic. I said as much to – '

'Don't give me that diplomatic bloody garbage,' interrupted Jones. 'Who d'you think you're talking to? Little Bo Peep?'

Bewick laughed: 'Was it easy?'

'Easy? It was like falling off a motorbike.'

Anyone seeing Bewick and Jones together at that moment would have understood that they were friends. Few would have guessed their profession.

Jones drank deeply and looked distrustfully at Bewick. 'Who's the kid's brief then?'

'Alec Dundas.'

'Posh, is he?'

'Depends what you mean. His background is Glasgow back streets. He's out of the top drawer now. QC. He's clever. Natural actor.'

'There's lovely. Have to be a posh shite of a lawyer, wouldn't there?'

'Why should you care? You've got a cast-iron case.'

'Lawyers make me envious.'

'Doesn't it worry you, Gio, that the lad hasn't admitted it?'

'What? What's this? Don't you start. Leave that to the bloody brief, mate. No, it doesn't worry me. What worries me is you. You worry me. You ought to have better things to do at your age.'

'Sure.'

After they'd eaten some lunch, Bewick drove Jones back to City West Station.

'Hallo John, Guv. You're looking well; very well. Where've you been?'

Frank Dalmeny was as tall as Bewick, but a bean-pole compared.

'He's been sorting out the entire drug problem of South East Asia, Frank, that's what. The fact that he hasn't come back a millionaire is just an indication of how wet behind the ears he is. Lovely tan for the time of year, though, I agree.' Jones grumpily elbowed his way past the two men and down the corridor ahead.

Frank Dalmeny had been the fifth person to greet Bewick on the brief journey from the front door to Jones's office.

In the office the untidiness was rampant; defiant.

'So you've spoken to the victim's ex-husband,' Bewick said, 'to her friends and her parents, the pub, the vicar, the gardener . . .'

'Yeah, Percy Snaith. He found her; he was helpful.'

'And her employer . . .'

Jones didn't seem to be concentrating. He looked at Bewick suspiciously. 'Anything wrong with you?' he asked.

'Wrong?'

'There's something up with you. You look different.' There was a knock at the door and a woman entered with her arms full of files.

'You two know each other I suppose? DI Quinney – John Bewick. Karen's the one nobody makes sexist remarks about. Local regulation. Police choir's only got so many places for castrati.'

Karen Quinney was fair with dark brown eyes. 'Yes, we know each other,' she said coolly and pleasantly.

Gio Jones was alert immediately, but made no comment.

'Hallo Karen,' said Bewick. 'We were just about to mention the victim's employer.'

'Bloke who runs Sirius Software – Hammond,' added Jones.

'I know. Skinny git in a shiny suit,' said Karen Quinney. 'Silver specs. Looked like a bit of his own office equipment.'

'One of the entrepreneurial spirits of the age, Detective Inspector Quinney. He's survived into the nineties, what's more. And a good citizen too. After the Hungerford do, he handed in a couple of guns under the amnesty.'

'Yeah, so how many did he have? Millionaire gun clubber? Royal Cambridge? You know? Why didn't he give them to the club? Look at me, good citizen! Creepy or what?'

'Creepy,' said Bewick.

'Anyway, he was helpful,' said Jones.

'Yeah, he gave us a decent amount of time. And they do a good coffee at Sirius Software.'

Karen Quinney dumped the files on the desk. 'The Kelleher case, Sir.'

'Ah yes. We'd better find Mr Bewick a spare office. Dare say you can brief him on the files?'

'I'll take them down to Green Four, shall I?'

'Thank you.'

Karen Quinney picked up her files again, and left. As the door closed on her, Jones turned to Bewick. 'Well?'

'Well what?'

'What's going on?'

'Going on?'

'Karen Quinney – perhaps that's another reason you should come back into the force.'

'Karen Quinney?'

'She'd give you a welcome you might not forget in a hurry. You're very slow today.'

'What're you talking about?'

'I was watching her. How well do you know her?'

'Hardly at all. I administered a course she was once on, that's all.'

'Uh huh. Uhuh. I see. I see.'

Bewick smiled but didn't respond.

'Better get on with it then,' groaned Jones.

In the spare office, Green Four, Karen Quinney had laid out the material on the Kelleher case.

'We had several teams on it. Gio Jones got the usual lot together. He's good at that . . .'

'Sure . . .'

'Anyway, you'll see who did what. Once they'd got a fairly positive ID on the bike . . .'

'Yes; Gio told me about that. What was the bike in the end?'

'A Honda RS something. Want to know how much they cost?'

'Yes.'

'Twenty-five grand.'

Bewick was silenced for a moment. 'I didn't realize it was that much. That was the money he got from his father, you know, when his father died. That means he blew the lot on the bike. Every penny.'

'Is that stupid or is that stupid?' Karen Quinney said, shaking her head in disbelief.

Bewick stared at the wall. 'Perhaps . . .' he said eventually. 'Thanks Karen,' he added and gestured to the files. 'I just . . .'

'Yeah, right.'

'How are you, by the way? Been promoted I see.'

'Yeah. I'm fine thanks. Fine.'

There was an awkwardness about her.

'Give me an hour or two, will you? Are you in the building for the rest of the afternoon?'

'Yeah. I'll be around. See you later.'

Bewick's capacity for absorbing information seemed somehow unlikely to those who knew about it. His physical power, his relaxed manner and his athleticism suggested someone used to taking practical, active decisions. He looked like a man who should be out of doors. Sitting at a desk he seemed out of place. He spent much of his life looking out of place.

Jones peered in through the glass door panel at Bewick where he sat like a statue in front of the files. It was the second time he'd passed the office. Nearly two hours Bewick had sat there. Jones felt irritable.

What was Bewick doing? What on earth was there in the case to interest him?

Julia Kelleher had lived for just over thirty years and nobody, not even her killer, according to the papers Bewick was reading, knew why she died.

Julia was a local woman. Her parents lived in Chesterton. Her father, Brian Kelleher, ran a small local travel agency, Home and Away Travel. Her mother had a history of minor mental illness which had left her pathologically shy.

At twenty-two Julia had married David Toner who was twelve years older. They had run a wholefood shop together for a few years. They were, it seemed, motivated by principle rather than money. Nevertheless they were able to sell the shop as a going concern when the marriage began to falter. Toner, using training he'd received in the army, set himself up as an electronic engineer, self-employed. By the time Julia was twenty-seven they had separated.

Julia found herself a job at Sirius Software as an assistant manager in marketing. There had been no boyfriend after the marriage as far as anyone knew. Two friends were mentioned: Amy Parris who had worked with her and a man, Julian Rae, whom she'd gone to the theatre with and had brought to company functions twice.

The name Julian Rae sparked a sense of recognition in Bewick. Unable to place it, he moved on.

Julia Kelleher's personality survived the blunt CID

interview notes: a lively, not entirely conventional person emerged from them, someone who was remaking her life with independence and spirit, someone whose early death prompted a feeling of absurdity, a chilly tremor of meaninglessness.

Bewick closed the post-mortem file, where the violations of a murderous death had been multiplied by the surgical procedures of the post-mortem itself.

Karen Quinney found him still sitting at the desk an hour later. The late-afternoon sun was blazing full in his face. He sat with his eyes lowered from the sun but it was clear he wasn't looking at the document in front of him.

'All right?'

Bewick turned slowly, as if out of sleep. She could see that the sun had left his face flushed. Almost immediately he reverted to his usual sociable self. 'Hello Karen.'

Karen was dressed to go home.

'Is it that late?'

'Yes. Gio Jones had to go off to some burglary on the Henderson. Thought I'd see if you wanted anything.'

'You want to go home.'

'I don't.'

'Good. OK, let's get some tea.'

On the Henderson Estate, Jones stood outside a ground-floor flat where a break-in had left a broken glass panel in a side door. It had been the eighth in as many days, all within three or four streets of one another.

Jones had decided on a heavy presence and extensive questioning of neighbours; a demonstration of police concern, of solidarity with the community. And, you never knew, it might actually turn something up, probably local, probably juvenile.

He stood looking up at the bleak block, a sixties edifice hardly distinguishable from the factory units half a field away. Then he began searching the grass between the building and the road. He quartered the small piece of lawn methodically, the wind off the fens tugging at his coat. As his last sweep reached the pavement again he became aware of a man shivering a few feet away.

Jones glanced up. The man gave a weak apologetic grin. His arms were crossed to keep himself warm and he was hopping from foot to foot.

'Police,' he said and chuckled.

'No, we're the East Anglian Mountain Rescue Club, matter of fact,' said Jones.

''S me motor,' explained the man.

Jones took in the tattoos on the forearm, the ancient Iron Maiden T-shirt faded to a slaty grey, the dirty hair; the noticing, helpless eyes.

'Come to the car, we'll freeze to death out here.'

''S me mother,' the man apologized, once they were in the Vauxhall with the heater going full.

'Thought you said it was your motor.'

'Yeah, 'S me motor. Only me mother said to see you 'bout me motor. Stupid – I got it back, didn't I? But she said.'

'What's your name?'

'Jim Spilby.'

Jones had seen something in the man's eyes, a sense of humour, an inventiveness, he wasn't sure, but something that made him want to hear Spilby out. Not for the first time he was disappointed. Like the good cop he was, however, he took brief notes and dated them. Five minutes later he prompted himself with them, as he checked the information back to Spilby.

'So. Your motor is a B-reg. Escort, red, on its second re-spray but still scruffy and who would want to nick it?'

'Yeah . . .' Spilby laughed.

'And on the night of the sixteenth it gets nicked from outside The Hero pub. You see this theft as a let off from driving, an excuse to get blittered, well and truly, and a mate drives you home. Lunch time next day a different mate rings you and, with what is left of your brain, you take in the fact that he's seen your motor abandoned in the lay-by just before the A45 on the Histon road. You walk over and pick it up. Yes?'

'Yeah. That's it. Not a scratch on it; not except those what was there already.'

'Does my heart good. Thanks Mr Spilby . . .'

Spilby was already laughing his apologies.

'Apart from getting me back in here to warm up for a few minutes . . .' said Gio Jones, pausing for a moment to watch Spilby's eyebrows which suddenly shot up of their own accord, for no reason, unless amazed at their owner, ' . . . I think you get my prize for the most boring reported crime of 1992.'

'Yeah. Interesting, innit?'

They sat in a café-brasserie which, although it was buried deep inside a shopping precinct, was pretending to be a corner of rural Italy.

Neither Karen Quinney nor Bewick even noticed this daft fantasy.

'You're an athlete, aren't you, Karen?' Bewick asked.

'I do a bit of running.'

'I saw you once running in the half-marathon. You looked very cool, very fast.'

'You watch the half-marathon?' She was surprised.

'My car was held up by it.'

'Right.'

'You looked very good. What was your time?'

'One forty-ish. Nothing to write home about. I'm not a club runner or anything. I just like being faster than the lads at the station.'

Bewick chuckled.

'You swim, don't you? I've seen you at Parkside,' Karen said.

'Yes, I do.'

'You looked all right an' all.'

She remembered her surprise. She had noticed a smooth, high-elbowed front crawl, of club-competition standard. The man had been tall like many good swimmers. When she'd seen him standing in the shallow end, she'd appreciated how strongly built he was; then to her amazement she'd realized he was a senior officer at the station.

'Well,' said Bewick, 'this Enwright business . . . I'm just covering the ground really, but I've read it all and . . .'

'And what?' Karen asked. 'Are you on to something?'

'Not really . . . No. Nothing. It's the lad, Joe Enwright, I can't . . . I just don't see why he did it. Simple as that. All very well to talk about him being out of his skull on hash and acid . . . Do we know anything about that, by the way?'

'How do you mean?'

'Is either drug a memory wiper? Are they in combination? Has anybody asked?'

'No. We've got his DNA.' She smiled. 'The teams kind of relaxed after that.'

'I see that, sure. I suppose it's just that I don't see how he got himself into a position where . . . well, where killing Julia Kelleher was the only option.'

'Unless he was a natural for the job, a power and violence merchant.'

'Has he been profiled? There are no notes . . .'

'As I say, we got his DNA. There's a dodgy old

childhood too, isn't there? Truancy . . . he attacked a teacher once, didn't he?'

'Yes . . . Yes. I'm interested in that. Murder still doesn't look quite right though, even with everything you've mentioned.'

'But does it ever? You know . . .'

'Sure, sure.'

All investigators are tripped up sooner or later by the calm ingenuity of sociopathic individuals, in their need to disguise where they were, what they had done; even from themselves. Bewick had been taught this and acknowledged it now, but went on to discuss remembered profiles of murderers and how none of them seemed to fit Joe Enwright. It was an astonishing display of memory. Karen knew he wasn't out to impress her – if only he had been.

'What about the bike?' Bewick asked. 'Any ideas on that?'

'Nobody's been able to work that one out. Twenty-five grand. On a bike. You tell me.'

'Have you interviewed him, Karen?'

She shook her head. 'I was there for about ten minutes of one of the interviews.'

'What did you think?'

'Spoilt brat. Quite a dish, mind, definitely. Doomy gloomy good looks. Sexy. Could've. He hasn't denied it.'

Bewick mumbled something about having heard that, then looked away, frowning at a fake pitchfork hanging on the wall.

When he looked back, it was into a pair of clear brown eyes which stayed on him longer than was ordinarily acceptable, in a kind of resentment.

'Where's he being held?' Bewick asked.

'City West.'

'Can you organize it for me, Karen? Would that be a drag?'

'Course not. Defence are entitled. And Gio Jones has said you're to have full cooperation.'

'Get off.'

'He said we're obliged to help you,' she said smiling.

'That's more like it.'

'Have I got your home number? I'll give you a bell.'

Bewick gave her one of his CICS business cards which also had his Homerton address on it.

She smiled. 'Consultant Director.'

'That's me. I thought it'd be a tosser's charter joining CICS. Then you meet people who run forces which haven't been trained properly. You realize it might not be so stupid after all.'

'Gio Jones thinks you've gone mad. He says, how's the force going to do what it has to, if people like you leave.'

'I'm not a good team person.'

She put the business card in her bag. She stood. 'Excuse me . . .'

Bewick paid for the coffees. When Karen came back to the table, she smelt of Cristalle.

The smell was still in Bewick's car when he drew up outside his house in Homerton after driving her home. He sat in the car for a few moments. It would have been clear to anybody that Karen had wanted the evening to continue.

He stared down the lines of parked cars crowding the street.

He went into his house and rang the Norfolk phone number which Sally Vernon had given him.

'Two four seven two.' The woman's voice was county set, upper class, acute. Bewick didn't reply for a moment. It wasn't what he had expected.

'Two four seven two – Hello?'

Bewick asked for Sally Vernon.

'Yes, she's here somewhere. I'll get her for you. Hang on.'

Bewick waited.

Mrs Vernon had heard a plainness of accent in the man's voice on the phone: enough to tell her that he was not of her daughter's class. Mind you, few were. She was curious. Now that Sally was engaged, it was unusual for her to be phoned by a man unknown to her.

Mrs Vernon entered the sitting-room, a wry smirk on her face. 'It's a man – for Sally,' she announced, throwaway.

Sally shot her a glance. What game was she playing? She hated her mother's capacity to suggest that she possessed knowledge which somehow put you in the wrong.

'Get on with it girl, I want my supper,' grumbled her father from the depths of a copy of *The Field*.

Sally got to her feet very deliberately and left the room.

'Yes, hello? Sally Vernon.'

'John Bewick. We met on the plane. You rashly said you'd explain DNA fingerprinting to me . . .'

'Hello John Bewick. Of course. I'd be very happy to. I've got to come to Cambridge anyway: Scientific Periodicals Library. Yes . . . Let's make a date for next week.'

'Good. How's it all going?'

'All right. I think I've got a firm offer for my house. It'd better be firm: I've just moved all my stuff.'

'Where are you now then?'

'At my mother's.' Sally heard herself being called. 'I'd better go. We're supposed to be eating. I'm really looking forward to seeing you.'

They settled on a train. Bewick agreed to meet it.

Bewick put the phone down and crossed to the kitchen table where he poured himself a glass of Australian red. From next door, very faint, came the sound of a piano and someone singing.

An hour later there was a call from Karen Quinney. The day after tomorrow he was to meet the young murderer.

'If that's what he is, a murderer I mean,' Bewick said.

'Like I said – don't you start. Leave that to the bloody brief, mate!' Jones shouted down the phone at him, above the mêlée of noise around him.

Jones was crouched in the corner of the hallway of his house, a refugee from the maelstrom of family life which swirled around him, a finger in one ear, the phone at the other.

'What did you say?'

'I said I've been dreaming of the sun. The first night it was coming up over the sea. Last night it was coming up over the horn of Africa, Upper Egypt. I checked the time when I woke up. It would have been.'

'I tell you what it is. It's your brain following your body home. Tell me when it catches you up, will you? You might start making some sense.'

'I'll see you at City West tomorrow then?'

'If I haven't got anything better to do.'

6

As he was shaving next morning, Bewick emerged from the bathroom frowning. Over breakfast he scowled at the empty bottle of 13 per cent Australian Shiraz-Cabernet.

Bewick unearthed his bicycle from the cellar. He reached the pool just as it opened at seven-thirty. He swam a kilometre and a half.

Showered and dressed, his head clearer, he biked home. A big man, hurtling through the traffic on the stripped-down bike with its narrow racing wheels, he attracted attention, but seemed oblivious to the figure he cut. As he turned on to the asphalted path which crossed Sidgwick Fen, he began planning his day.

The first call was to Sirius Computers where Julia Kelleher had been working at the time of her death. Shamelessly parading titles – Chief Superintendent, Senior Consultant at CICS – he persuaded Muir Hammond's assistant that he was not only harmless but important.

Repeated phone calls to Julia Kelleher's parents' home bore no fruit.

He opened a database on his PC.

Sirius Computers rang back at ten-fifteen to ask him to come at around twelve-thirty when Muir Hammond would be able to see him briefly. Another call to the Kellehers was unanswered. Bewick rang City West to check the address and the number with Karen.

'Who're you?'

Bewick turned.

A smallish man, neat with a tidy moustache, specs and a bow tie, approached his own front door. He carried a full plastic shopping bag on which was reproduced a gigantic postage stamp.

Number four Erasmus Close was an undistinguished house in a small development on the outskirts of Chesterton. Thin conifers stood beside a paved drive in which stood a small grey Rover. The curtains of the large window on the ground floor were drawn.

Bewick's wait on the front doorstep had lasted a couple of minutes: long after he'd heard someone approach the door from inside the house.

'Because if you're the press,' said the man with the moustache, 'I'm not talking to you. Neither is Mrs Kelleher; and I give you to the count of ten before I set the dog on you.'

'I'm not the press, Mr Kelleher. I've come over

from the police station.' Bewick lied for simplicity's sake.

'They assured me! They said we'd be left alone now.'

Bewick explained his position.

Despite himself, Kelleher found himself trusting the candour of the big man on his doorstep. He'd suffered too much however in the past two weeks and was determined. 'No. Won't do. I can do without this. Why should I? Answer me that.'

'It's what they might say about your daughter in court. I'd like to move the defence away from the need to raise the issue of your daughter's character: if they mention the subject at all it can only be valuable to them to question it, you see.'

There was fear briefly in Kelleher's eyes. For form's sake he grumbled a little more then invited Bewick into the house.

The three cups rattled in their saucers despite Mrs Kelleher's attempts to move slowly and to keep calm.

Patricia Kelleher was a woman who wanted to be somewhere else. She was pale, with pale eyes, diffident, yielding; as if she were continually trying to evaporate. The effort required to serve tea to her husband and Bewick was titanic: the self-control she exercised in the course of it would lay her out with a nervous headache for the rest of the day.

Bewick watched her as she put the tray down on the table. It was the climax of a heroic journey.

'It's a very nice room, this . . .' he said.

It was a mistake. Patricia Kelleher reacted as if she'd been punched. The milk, which she was transferring from tray to table, began to judder and slop within its jug. She put it down quickly. A painful smile flickered and disappeared. 'Biscuits,' she said and fled.

Kelleher's reaction to his wife's social terror was to ignore it, whatever its consequences and however long its effects took to subside.

He had perfected the trick of rendering his wife invisible. He only referred to her when she was absent.

'Odd thing: Julia's death has made Patricia quite a lot calmer. Given her something to think about, I suppose.'

Bewick stared. 'Ah,' he said.

'Yes. The headaches have got less too. She was even able to talk to one of the journalists on the phone.'

'Ah.'

Patricia Kelleher re-entered the room, hair drifting, a ghost. Kelleher ignored her. His cheek was plump, pink and well shaven, his moustache perfectly clipped.

'So, what do you want to know, Mr Bewick?'

'Julia'd been married, I understand?'

'That's right. David Toner.'

'They're divorced?'

'That's right. Three years ago. Julia reverted to her maiden name, you see.'

'Has there been a regular partner since?'

'No, nothing like that.'

There'd been a flicker of hesitation before Kelleher

had replied. Patricia Kelleher fiddled with her clothes.

'Do you know why they divorced?'

'No idea. He'd just started to make money. We liked David.'

'So she lived alone?'

'Yes. Generally. Yes.' Again there'd been the hesitation. 'Friends would stay, of course. That's what we'd understand, yes. Tea?'

Tea was handed round. The room was done out in maroon and magnolia, as neat as a catalogue. Its surfaces were dotted with trinkets, mostly glass and china animals with expressions of sickly sweetness; it was a room full of fear and rejection.

Patricia Kelleher kept her eyes averted as her husband answered Bewick's questions. Every so often her left hand strayed to the collar of her blouse to make sure it was folded as she wanted. Always the left hand, always to the same point.

'Did Julia begin working full time before or after her divorce?'

'Before. We don't think David wanted her to work. They'd got a good price for the shop. He was working all the hours God gave. He was earning quite enough. More than enough. He was successful. Last thing he needed was a wife who was out all day. We think that might have had something to do with them divorcing.'

Bewick nodded, ponderous and charming. His square, bony face was creased into a look of slight puzzlement. It was a face that people wanted to explain to; a presence to confide in.

'Did he get angry with her?'

'I dare say he did. I would've done. I've been angry enough with her in my time. Can be an awkward cuss, stubborn as a mule and half as friendly, when she wants. We'd very little to do with her, you know, recently. We wondered sometimes how she could be our daughter. I mean, who did she take after?'

Patricia Kelleher was as still as ice – as if she'd stopped breathing, or was willing herself to disappear.

'She took after no one in my family, that I can tell you. She was always in debt.'

'Where did she work?'

'Sirius Software. You know, that chap Muir Hammond's computer company. Don't mistake me. She earned enough. No sense of economy, that's what, or discipline, of any kind. She upset us a great deal more than I can say . . . Oh yes. I'll say.'

Under the neat thatching of the moustache, the mouth became set. Then, without warning, Kelleher smiled. 'Of course you know there are something like three hundred computer companies in and around Cambridge; in and around. Over twelve thousand people employed, maybe more . . .'

Bewick interrupted as soon as he could: 'Are you able to tell me how long it was before she died that you last saw your daughter?'

'Oh, about a week.'

Out of the corner of his eyes Bewick saw the tremor of Patricia Kelleher's neck as she stopped herself shaking her head in denial of this.

Bewick remembered that Kelleher ran a small travel agency in Cambridge. He asked Kelleher about his work, what commitments he had, when he'd be returning full time to his office.

Bewick emerged from the house fifteen minutes later, leaving behind a man who thought of him as a friend. He took two deep breaths as he walked back to his car. In his pocket were the keys to Julia Kelleher's cottage.

From the file on the seat beside him, once he'd regained the privacy of his car, he took a photograph of the murdered woman.

It had been difficult, he would later tell Gio Jones, to connect the Julia Kelleher in the photo with the house he'd just left. He returned it to the folder. Then, in his steady handwriting, he began making notes on what he'd seen and heard in Number Four Erasmus Close.

'Kelleher? Her father? You serious?'

Jones was horrified. He shoved a stubby, splayed hand through his thinning hair. 'You're serious, aren't you? Here we are with a perfect case . . . this case is the sodding Parthenon of investigations. Perfection of form we're talking here. And you're asking me what Kelleher was doing on the night of the sixteenth?'

'Calm down, Gio. All I'm saying is that Kelleher is a man who has no imagination and who hates the memory of his own child.'

'It wasn't his semen we found on her body.'

'I'm only ringing to check that Karen's arrangement stands – that you're happy with it.'

'Yeah, you can see the lad. Course you can. Defence is entitled, you know that, for God's sake . . . Look here, man . . . Tell me what you think. Tell me why he did it, why don't you?'

Jones put the phone down. He realized he was sweating. He propped his stomach against the window-sill and stared unseeing out at the street, hazily sunlit.

Suppose Bewick were on to something? He quickly ran the major evidence in his head. It was rock solid. CPS were happy. What more could he do? Nevertheless, as he turned from the window it took an effort of will to address his next task of the day. He looked up at the ceiling, his voice loaded with twenty-four-carat South Welsh sarcasm, and swore: a long, inventive string of filthy expletives.

Sirius Software had two sites: a state-of-the-art factory in the Trinity Science Park and an extended Georgian house overlooking Parker's Piece, which was where the company's extraordinary acorn-to-oak history had begun.

Bewick arrived a little before his appointed time and was asked to wait in reception.

When he appeared, Bewick recognized Muir Hammond immediately from Karen Quinney's description of him. Apart from the pink in his cheeks,

Hammond was monochromatic – shades of grey and silver from top to toe.

Hammond, on the other hand, didn't know what to expect at all. He took in the big, square-jawed heavyweight and instinctively made towards the other man who was waiting.

Bewick stood. 'Mr Hammond?'

'Ah. Yes . . .'

'John Bewick.'

'Yes, of course. Come up to my office.'

Muir Hammond walked quickly through the building that was his little kingdom.

'It's very good of you to spare me the time, Mr Hammond,' Bewick said, when they were seated in a minimalist white office with a view clear across Parker's Piece.

'Not at all. Now as I understand it, you're acting for the family of the accused man.'

'That's right: Joe Enwright. His mother is very ill, terminally ill. His uncle and aunt are paying my fees. They have no convictions either way. They just want to be sure justice is done. I said I'd run a ruler over the police evidence. I've no reason to believe it isn't sound.'

'How can I help?'

'I read the notes of the interview you gave Inspector Jones about Julia Kelleher's time in your company. They were very useful.'

'Good . . .'

Muir Hammond looked at the big man opposite

whose muscular face was creased into a conciliatory frown, who seemed to be at a loss for words. Hammond was unaware of being observed: Bewick looked so preoccupied.

'I'd prefer to tread carefully . . .' Bewick began. 'I'm acting for the defence . . . but, after reading the files . . . I don't want the defence to start a character assassination of Julia Kelleher; even by implication. I don't think it would be right.'

'Yes, I'm sure you're correct in that; she was a splendid person.'

'I mean to be present when the defence lawyers prepare their strategy . . .'

'Why employ you otherwise?' suggested Hammond.

'Quite. I'd like to be able to give the defence team a full and clear picture of Miss Kelleher.'

'Sure.'

'I was wondering if there was anybody in your company whom I could talk to, who knew Miss Kelleher well.'

For a moment it looked as if something out on Parker's Piece had taken Hammond's attention as he stared rigidly ahead of him. 'Unfortunately,' Hammond said, bowing his head as if pushed from behind, then lifting it to meet Bewick's eyes, 'unfortunately, the person she seemed to know best, although she was definitely younger, you know . . . well, she met with a tragic accident over a year ago now: lost at sea . . . She worked here. She was very clever, very.

A mathematician out of the top drawer. She and Julia were great friends. I don't know that there's anyone else who could tell you much that was specific. Julia was generally popular – everybody would be able to tell you that – but I can't think of anyone who might be able to tell you much more.'

'No, I see.' Bewick's disappointment was evident.

Hammond touched a button and said, 'Tessa, I wonder if I might have a word?'

An alert woman in her thirties entered; she was smartly dressed and had a short-back-and-sides haircut. She carried a dictation pad. Hammond first explained who Bewick was, then said, 'Tessa, Mr Bewick is very properly looking for evidence of Julia's character. He wants to persuade the defence lawyers that it would be inappropriate to raise the issue of her character as part of a defence strategy. I think Miss Parris was her only really close friend, but I can't be sure, of course. If you'd be good enough to ask around, identify who knew her best? Perhaps you could communicate with Mr Bewick directly?'

Bewick obliged with his card.

Five minutes later he was walking across Parker's Piece towards the multi-storey where he'd left his car.

The fine weather had tempted out hundreds of lunch-time picnickers, most of them young. The warmth of summer had not yet left the weather system. It looked as if it would be a classically calm and misty autumn.

★

Gio Jones had felt fidgety all day after Bewick's phone call. He had snapped at three or four colleagues, including Frank Dalmeny: had told him to sod off and play with his sodding software. Bad move, with Frank as sensitive as he was. It'd take days to put that one right. Hearing about it, Karen had suggested he send Frank some flowers, so he bit her head off too.

Later that afternoon found him knocking at Bewick's door in Homerton. He was nervous. He needn't have been. He had forgotten how Bewick's secrecy was ordinarily so camouflaged by his manner. Bewick didn't look at all surprised to see him.

'Come in. Come in. Tea? Drink? Soft drink? I'm off out soon, I'm afraid.'

'Soft drink, ta.'

They went into the living-room where Bewick's computer hummed on a glass table. When Bewick disappeared to the kitchen Jones wandered over to read the computer screen where Bewick was typing in notes on his interview with Hammond. He'd hardly had time to identify what the screen contained before Bewick returned. He didn't disguise what he was doing. He knew that if Bewick had wanted the screen not to be read, he would have switched it off before he answered the front door.

'What did you think of him, then?' Jones asked.

'Hammond?'

'Yes.'

'Very defensive.'

'In what way?'

'Felt to me as if he was manning the battlements . . . I don't know in what way. He saw to it that I didn't know.'

'There are rumblings about his company.'

Bewick nodded. 'Could be that. I didn't like him.'

'No?'

'Too used to giving orders and no talent for it. All that courtesy coming at you and no friendliness. "I'm being polite. Respond or get out of the way." Courtesy as a juggernaut.'

'Bit like you, really . . .'

'Drink your fucking elderflower cordial and fuck off.'

Jones grinned. This was more like it.

'And talk about tight-arsed. That office . . .' Bewick continued.

'Oh yes,' Jones responded. 'And the convent-bred secretary with the schoolboy haircut. They suit each other. Arses as tight as melons in a box.'

They laughed.

'You don't mean it about Julia Kelleher's father, do you?'

Bewick stretched, clasping his hands behind his head. 'Matter of fact, now you ask,' he said, smiling, 'I do.'

Bewick stood under the clipped arch of hawthorn, taking in the topography of Parbold Cottage, its garden, its orchard, the roads nearby and the surrounding fields. Once satisfied, he walked to the rear of the cottage.

At the bottom of the garden he stood on the grassed-over tump of an old compost heap. The main St Neots road was visible from there. Flickering behind the crown of the old orchard, its traffic moved past a belt of trees which formed the horizon. With the breeze in the south as it was now, the traffic was silent at this distance: about half a mile.

The land between was flat, treeless, hedgeless, dissected by deep ditches and uncultivated, now that farmers were being paid to grow nothing.

Bewick turned back to the small garden to see a wrinkled brown face watching him from over the garden gate.

Bewick explained who he was. Percy Snaith introduced himself. Bewick told him why he had come. The two men were soon mooching around the yellowing garden, enjoying each other's company.

'Young bloke who took over from me at the college,' said Percy Snaith in wonderment, 'he had a degree: "Landscape Gardening". Good gardener, mind – Irish. A degree!' He shook his head in disbelief and laughed.

They were sitting on an old bench at the back of the cottage now, the sunlight still just clearing the nearby trees to warm them. Bewick brought the subject round to Julia Kelleher.

'This last year or so, she weren't herself, not at all.

I never asked her why direct but I got it out of her by an accident, you could say.'

The old man took off his tweed cap and scratched the top of his head. 'It embarrassed me, I can tell you that. She's standing over there,' he waved to the small lawn, 'and I wa' telling her it wa' too late for wallflowers this year – we wa' into January by then. "No one'll be selling them no more," I said. "I'll sow you some April time," I said. "If you want to buy the plants, you have to tell me September–October time, you know that. Well," I says to her, "you didn't tell me to buy 'em, did you? On account you was never here, on account of that friend of yours goin' missing, I suppose . . .' Well I knew I'd said the wrong thing. She go pale and went indoors.

'What happened was, she'd lost a young friend of hers, drownded she was. I didn't know what it meant to her.'

This must be the same friend mentioned by Muir Hammond.

The old man rumbled on. 'Well, she'd no spirit for ordering of flowers. She wa' haunted by that girl. Anything could start it up, even an old bugger going on about deaths at sea. Talking of ghosts, I can see 'em now, I can . . .'

Snaith was very matter-of-fact. Bewick looked up, as if to see if spectral figures were in fact approaching through the leaf-filtered light. Snaith said, 'I can see 'em now. Used to walk around the garden arm in arm, laughing together.'

'Who was the friend?'

'Aah . . . I don't know her proper name – I called her Spex. She worked at the same place as did Julia. Clever, Julia said. Genius-level wa' what she said. Computers.'

Like a true East Anglian, Snaith pronounced it c'mpooters.

'What was she like?'

'Like? Like a student, I should say. Studious. She wa' pretty when she laughed – she sparkled. She wa' pretty enough anyway, but she never bothered. Nice hair too, but not done, you know. Made her look plain as day till you really looked at her. Then you realized she wa' a bit lovely.'

'Was her name Miss Parris?'

The old man thought, then shook his head. 'Might've been. I called her Spex. On account she wore them.'

It was nearly dark by the time Percy Snaith left. The front door to the cottage was set off to one side. Bewick unlocked it, reached in and switched on a light.

To the left of the entrance was a kitchen occupying most of the ground floor; to the right a smaller sitting-room; ahead was the staircase, on which the body of Julia Kelleher had been found.

The kitchen was bright with painted furniture, some of it in need of repair. It was colourful and comfortable. Olive and sunflower oils stood near the stove, well-thumbed cook books next to them. A Victorian pink lustre bowl full of shallots and garlic occupied the centre of the table. The window bay overlooking the back garden was furnished with an upholstered bench strewn with cushions. It was the room of an imaginative person who had come to some sort of accommodation with herself.

Bewick took his time before leaving the kitchen: what had taken place in the hallway now had to be imagined.

Julia Kelleher had probably been within a foot or two of where she had been found when she was first struck. According to Sandham's notes the first hammer blow was violent enough to have killed her. The other half dozen blows would have been unleashed after she had collapsed against the staircase.

The police case was that Joe Enwright visited Julia on the late afternoon, early evening, of the murder. He had known Julia some months. After he left (his departure by bike being logged so memorably by Keith Dawes) Julia had drunk some wine and cooked herself some pasta. She'd then watched TV: this had been noted by a neighbour out walking a dog. As she had passed back down Washpit Lane towards the village, the neighbour, Mrs Childerley, had heard the News at Ten jingle and the sound of washing up, although she hadn't actually seen Julia.

Enwright's version was that he had *cycled* over much earlier to Julia's house. He had stayed some time and then had returned later, in the early evening, to find her out. Under pressure, he admitted that although she didn't answer the bell, her car was still outside the cottage. The second time he came, he said, was to show her his new bike.

The police placed the second visit much later than Enwright's statement – after ten o'clock. And it was then that he killed her. She had realized what was going to happen and tried to defend herself. Joe Enwright was at this point naked, at least to the waist. She had scratched him down his back. Minute quantities of his skin were still lodged under her fingernails. He had then stripped the bottom half of her body and masturbated – a small quantity of his sperm was found dried on her legs. No penetration had taken place.

The evidence was grim and sound. Bewick faced an unavoidable wall of it.

'Evidence is evidence,' he muttered to himself.

Bewick went upstairs and into the main bedroom.

He stood in the pale bedroom for a few minutes. Because the investigation of her murder had been so copy-book and been brought to such a quick conclusion, most of Julia Kelleher's belongings had been left undisturbed by the police.

The room was soft and neutral: light blue carpet, white Indian cotton bedspread. On the cream painted chest of drawers stood a small cluster of gold, white and green perfume bottles: Dior, Chanel and Ricci.

There were two splashes of colour only – a Mondrian grid and a vivid abstract by Olive Mayo.

Bewick opened the wardrobe. Lined up inside were the suits for work together with variations on a navy cardigan/white shirt theme. Beyond them jazzy tops, tiny skirts – magenta, violet, lavender, jungle green, electric blue. As a language, fashion was Chinese to Bewick, the wardrobe a territory for which he had no vocabulary and no grammar. What, for example, to make of the morning suit – trousers and tails – with the wafflefronted dress shirt and white tie hanging inside it? Bewick compared the jacket with others in the wardrobe. It was the same size. In the small ticket pocket he found a single tampon still in its cellophane; relic of forethought one evening not long ago.

Shoes broadly repeated the story of the clothes, again unintelligible to him in its details. There were dark-coloured and black shoes and boots – everyday wear, he assumed, which made up the bulk. Then there were evening sandals aiming to expose: tiny glittering straps, little cones of lipstick-red leather into which toes were supposed to go. Bewick pulled from the shoe rack something he did understand – two pairs of trainers, one Asics and one Nike. He looked at the condition of the uppers and at the deep-cut, evenly worn tread, grubby but unclogged. Good running shoes, but they hadn't been used to run in.

Outside it grew fully dark. The dry evening gave way to a blustery wet night.

Bewick's inquisitiveness about Julia Kelleher's life

was as intense as a lover's. He ransacked her house. For hours he went through photographs, keepsakes, old diaries, recipes, bank statements, tax returns, insurance policies, credit-card statements, her books, her music.

The phone rang in George and Kit's luxurious bungalow at nine. George and Kit had been arguing about whether Bewick would ring to say when he would come to see them again. George had told Kit not to set such store by Bewick's ringing. 'He's a busy man. And if he's looking into this girl's murder he'll be even busier.'

George was in his dressing-gown watching a Jeanette MacDonald movie on video. Seeing his wife's set mouth, he paused the tape with the remote. 'Here, love, it's all right.' George put out his arm. Kit came to him on the sofa. George turned off the TV and VTR.

'I know I shouldn't expect nothing. I know really, but then . . .' Kit controlled herself. George claimed not to mind her crying, but she knew he didn't like it.

The phone rang. It was Bewick.

'Where are you, John?' asked Kit.

'In the phone box in Chalcote. I've been looking at the cottage where Julia Kelleher lived. I got very absorbed, sorry; forgot the time. I won't make it tonight, I'm afraid.'

'It's all right; we realized that.'

‘I’ll ring tomorrow.’

‘We’ll look forward to that. That’s fine.’

Bewick heard the need for reassurance in her voice. ‘This business isn’t over by a long way, Kit.’

‘All I want is the truth.’

Bewick stood in the phone box for a moment after he’d replaced the receiver. Then he walked back to the cottage, lifting his face to the rain.

Bewick sat at the table in Julia Kelleher’s silent kitchen, a small pile of credit-card receipts in front of him.

His concentration had been revived by the discovery of a sequence of petrol receipts from a filling station at Scalder Staithe on the north Norfolk coast.

They began a year before, and there were three in the month leading up to Julia Kelleher’s death. There was no accompanying evidence of overnight stays in hotels or B & Bs, so the visits Julia made were either to a friend’s house or she had driven there and back in a day: not impossible at all, but unwelcome. The visits were probably not connected with work, as most were during the weekend.

Bewick knew that the first receipt fell at about the time when, according to the gardener, Julia’s young friend had been lost at sea. Had these journeys been in the way of visits to a watery graveyard?

Bewick stretched and rubbed his face. He continued making notes.

By the evidence, Julia Kelleher had been a level-headed woman. She had taken from her divorce what was due to her in terms of property; no more, no less. There were no children and she earned more than her ex-husband, David Toner, so there was no question of maintenance. Her fiscal affairs were ordered.

Amongst all the photos of her, none was sombre, most were sober.

Her taste in reading and music was middlebrow. Her charities were RSPB, Amnesty International, Friends of the Earth, WWF.

With her instinct for order and for an organized life, how had she allowed someone so out of control to come close enough? How had she missed sensing the chaos of such a man?

Sociopaths were born deceivers and then self-perfected deceivers, that was how. In fact the most dangerous were the over controlled, fitting their niche in society: quiet, utterly disguised.

Also, living this tidy, self-sufficient life of hers, she may have grown insensitive to life's dangers: the skin of her existence had possibly hardened a little. She had forgotten, perhaps, how to sense disaster. How otherwise could such a woman have come to be the target of a murderous psychopath fifteen years her junior?

Bewick returned to the photographs, a drawerful of which he had found in the desk in the living-room. One stood out. 'Julia at nine years old' was pencilled on the back of it. Hands on skinny hips, unsmiling, a defiant jaunt to the pose, a dark bell of hair framing a face which looked older than the unformed swimming-costumed body. It was the face of a child who knew she had to stand up for herself.

There was nothing he could recognize amongst the photographs which hinted at why it had all ended so disastrously.

Bewick decided to call it a day. He tidied up and let himself out. A soft wind now: the air was warm and very humid. He turned from locking the door and checked.

Just inside the gate, in the dark shadow of the clipped hawthorn arch, a tall figure stood watching.

'Yes?' Bewick challenged.

The figure shifted.

Bewick relaxed himself, easing his weight forward on to the balls of his feet. 'I'm John Bewick. Who're you?'

The figure emerged from the shadows. He stood a few feet away: a tall man in a long raincoat. 'Christ, you scared me.'

'You're Julian Rae.'

Bewick had recognized the actor's voice. Rae had made a popular name for himself playing amiable idiots in TV comedies over the past decade or so.

Rae was also one of two men who had refused to take the police blood test.

'Yes, I'm Julian Rae. Christ, you scared me,' he repeated. 'You've got the keys . . . Are you official or something?'

Bewick told him how official he was, then asked Rae why he was there.

'Same reason as you: trying to work out how the hell this could have happened. And . . .'

There was a silence.

'And?'

'It's my house. It will be. Julia left it to me. The solicitor wrote to me. So . . . but, well, I want to know what happened too. The police've got medical evidence, according to the papers. But I don't know. It seems . . .'

Rae gestured: a dancer's movement conveying disbelief, protest.

'So what were you going to do?' asked Bewick.

'Sorry?'

'Do you have means of entry?'

'Oh. Well, yes. I've come here from time to time.'

'I understood the police had changed the locks. The keys Mrs Kelleher's given me are new.'

'Yes. Everything except the little scullery door – which was the only key I had anyway. I used to check up on things for her when she was away.'

Bewick nodded. 'Why don't we go in? I'd like a word.'

'Well . . .' Rae's panicky reluctance was unmistakable.

'I promise to be civilized. They've arrested the murderer, you know.'

'Yeah, but have they?'

Bewick didn't respond, but led the way inside.

*

'We weren't an item, if that's what you mean. We had fun going around together. We were outrageous, Julia and Julian. We used to cross dress in a kind of low-key send-up way.'

'Really?'

'You got a problem with that?'

Bewick smiled, spreading his arms wide and shaking his head. 'No, no, not at all. I've been trying to get a line on her. It interests me. She wore a morning suit, yes?'

Rae looked surprised. 'Yeah . . . What I'm saying is we could play all sorts of games which would embarrass a real couple. I loved her.'

A determined stare was holding back Rae's tears. Bewick waited.

The actor's beautiful, bony face, which was drawn tight in lines of pain, relaxed and softened. 'I'm gay and Julia was – well, on the edge of the sisterhood, you might say. She'd had a bad time with a couple of blokes and her father's a nightmare, never mind her husband.'

'Her father?'

'Have you met him?'

'Yes.'

'Well?' Rae was challenging Bewick to say what he thought.

'I didn't like him,' said Bewick.

'Nightmare. He wouldn't get away with it today. One hopes. Luckily for Julia he was quite unwell when she was in her early teens. He'd been in the

RAF and picked up something nasty in Asia – story of our lives, dear – anyway he was in a military hospital for nearly two years, then invalided out.

'He came home properly when Julia was fifteen. She'd been doing pretty much as she wanted for two years. Imagine. She's virtually running the house, never mind her own life, when nice Mr Hitler moves in.

'Her mother gives up. Can't take it. Decides to star in the mouse-of-the-year competition. She's left to battle it out with her father. The stupid shit'd hit her. It wasn't just a casual slap, you know, but what he called "punishment".

'She put a stop to it by standing on the front lawn and screaming that he was a fucking bully so that all the neighbours could hear.

'He only hit her once more after that, she said. He locked the doors that time and went for her. The front door was glazed, though. Julia threw her mother's sewing machine through it, then cut herself dreadfully getting out. She stood in the street covered in blood and screaming until the police got there . . .'

Bewick frowned. 'I had an image of her as someone who was very together,' he said.

'Yeah, she was. But she wasn't boring. She made her own way. She'd had to and with the start she'd had, it took her a while. She had her crummy marriage to get through too, but she got there all right. She was lovely, outrageous. She'd been very poor in her life and had been OK. It gave her courage.'

Rae's hand was quivering as he ran it through his hair. For a moment the vitality seemed to drain out of his face, leaving it gaunt and distressed.

'Do you know the lad they've arrested?' asked Bewick.

'Joe Enwright? No . . . I've heard about him from Julia, but I think she wanted to keep us apart, matter of fact.'

'Why was that?'

'Joe is supposed to be drop-dead gorgeous. Well, he is, if his pics are anything to go by. She wanted to keep him to herself.'

'Were they lovers?'

Rae smiled, cool and dry. 'It was more like she was his favourite aunt. Joe's mother is dying and his aunt and uncle are as old as God. Julia was his mother, his friend, older sister, you name it. Although he's not at all stupid, Joe I gather is quite tongue-tied, whereas Julia was very articulate. When they were out together she could wrap him up in a shawl of words and he'd be safe.'

'You don't think he killed her, I gather?'

Rae shook his head. 'Why would he?'

'You sure they weren't lovers?'

'I think it was something they wouldn't want to do in case it didn't turn out well. They had a secret bond all right but it wasn't that.'

'What was the bond?' Bewick asked.

'They both knew what it was like to have a vile father.'

'You'd know about that too, wouldn't you?'

'Oh yes. I'd know about that.'

'Weren't you itching to meet Joe?'

'I was trying to be grown up about it for Julia's sake.'

'I suppose you could have bumped into him without knowing it?'

'I suppose. Though I knew him from photos. Like I said.'

'If you had met him, where would you expect it to have been?'

'In a club, probably.'

'He likes clubbing, certainly.'

'Yes?' Rae looked uncomfortable.

'Were you out clubbing the night Julia was killed?'

'Yes.'

'You sure you didn't see him? I'm not asking you to swear to it. It wouldn't be evidence. I'm still trying to get a line on things.'

Rae sounded irritated. 'No. Anyway, if he'd been where I was . . . the pound in his pocket would have to have been pink.'

'I see.'

'Mind you, I don't remember much from that evening, quite frankly . . .' Rae smiled, dazzling charm. ' . . . I was drowning sorrows, I'm afraid.'

'You don't remember when you got home?'

'Not really. Working backwards from my hangover level, I think I reckoned about two o'clock.'

'How did you get home?'

'Cab. I live in Grantchester.'

Rae only now seemed to recognize the turn their conversation had taken. His face closed; pain in his eyes. He pushed his hand through his hair again. 'Why don't you ask me', he said bitterly, 'why I refused the blood test?'

'Presumably because you have some fear of being HIV positive.'

Rae looked aside. The slightest nod and he stood. 'I'm going now.'

'I wanted to talk to you about Julia's husband. Quite a chequered career . . .'

Rae shook his head, not looking at Bewick. 'You talk to Toner yourself.'

'OK. Drive carefully now.'

Rae heard the friendly warmth in Bewick's voice. He turned sharply as if warmth were something he no longer trusted.

'If you remember anything about the boy, ring me, will you?' Bewick asked. 'I'm in the book: John Bewick. Baccata Lane, Homerton.'

'OK.'

'It looks very bad for him,' said Bewick. 'Anything might help.'

'OK. And I'll tell you something about Toner. He's a bastard. Julia married him as a poke in the eye for her father. In the end the two bastards ganged up on her.'

'Right. Thanks. What sorrow were you drowning?'

Rae stared impassive for a moment, then there was

a mocking smile before he said drily, 'Usual thing, you know. The death of a friend. Usual thing.'

He turned and went. The front door of the cottage slammed. Rae's footsteps disappeared.

After Rae had gone, Bewick paced up and down the bright kitchen. It had begun raining again, light and persistent: the glass of the windows was freckled and streaked. Somewhere a rainpipe dripped.

He had passed the dresser half a dozen times before the object registered. Tucked behind a jug on the crowded shelves was a small photo-frame, lying face-down. The frame was old rubbed gilt tin; a hint of art deco, polished up. It surrounded the quiet, watchful features of a woman in her twenties.

Carefully Bewick dismantled it. The photo of the young woman was recent. It was written on, neat and very small: 'With love, Amy.'

Bewick took the photograph to the table and sat down. He contemplated the young woman's face: was she the Miss Parris mentioned by Muir Hammond? And was that the same woman described by the gardener? Certainly she fitted Snaith's description. There was nothing distinguished about the features, but the face was alive with an intelligence of the sort which does not expect itself to be understood.

Gio Jones didn't want to be in his car at this hour. As he turned off the St Neots road towards Chalcote, he swore at Bewick, knowing as he did so that he was angry with himself. He'd been to Bewick's house.

Finding it empty, Jones remembered Bewick saying he'd be having a look at Julia Kelleher's cottage that afternoon. Knowing him, he'd probably still be there.

The itch to know what Bewick was up to wouldn't leave him alone.

At their evening meal, his wife had been trying to make a decision with him about their daughter's GCSE course. She didn't succeed. After *Newsnight*, Eilean discovered what was getting to him and told him to go and sort it out; not to come home till he had.

Bewick woke, his head bowed on his arms which were folded on the table. A car was being parked outside the cottage. A minute later, Jones was at the front door. He looked suspicious. Bewick smiled at him. 'You woke me up.'

'Don't tell me. You were dreaming.'

'I was as a matter of fact.'

'What was it this time? Sun coming up over Sardinia, was it?'

'No, it was gilded temples this time, behind big white walls. Grey trees, orange-robed monks, that sort of thing.'

'Thailand?'

'Yeah.'

They were back in the kitchen now. Bewick was at the table where he sat blinking for a few moments as he considered Jones's question. Then with extraordinary speed he was on his feet and reaching for the light switch.

Standing in the sudden darkness, Jones thought he saw a movement at the edge of the garden. Or was it only imagination? A trick of a teased retina?

'Someone out there?'

Sliding through the house and out of the door took Bewick time to accomplish silently. Jones tried to follow, his skin burning with consciousness of objects around him. By the time he was outside the house, Bewick had gone. Jones couldn't think how he'd done it. His own eyes had only then adjusted to the lack of light.

Then, in the deeper dark of the outgrown, overhanging hedge, he spotted Bewick moving. It gave him the courage to move out into the darkness after him. When Bewick was a metre or two from where Jones thought he had seen something move, he stopped.

Jones tried to listen, but the rain on nearby leaves seemed deafening. There may have been a squeak from the far end of the orchard, but the road two fields away was audible and it may have come from there; it may have come from a nearby clash of waterdrops striking a twig.

Jones made his way over to where Bewick was standing on the grassed tump of the old compost heap. He looked out: the bleak, ditch-intersected fields were just visible.

Nothing moved.

'Anything?' Jones whispered.

Bewick shook his head.

'What did you see when you were in the house?'

Bewick shrugged. 'Something moved, I think.'

'I thought so too.'

Both men were uncertain. Then, as if in confirmation, far in the distance, at the edge of audio-discrimination, they heard a car start up: the laboured, wheezy starter motor of a cheap old banger. In the darkness out by the road, over to their left somewhere, gears were crashed and the car moved away.

Over a glass of red in the kitchen of Bewick's house, they argued.

'What's all this about Julia Kelleher's father? What're you up to? You know the case is solid.'

Bewick said nothing at first, then, 'Suppose Joe Enwright was one of Julia Kelleher's lovers.'

'Who told you that?'

'Nobody. Nobody told me. In fact I've been told it's not likely. It's not impossible though, is it?'

'OK. But he wasn't. He's denied it. You know that, do you? He's denied being sexually involved with her.'

'Yes. I know that. It's in the notes. But he would, wouldn't he? Unless he knew it was his only possible defence.'

'What? Well you better ask him then, hadn't you? Like I said. You're talking to him soon, aren't you?'

'Yes.'

'Well, you ask him then. You explain to the little

bugger that he could still get away with it if he plays his cards right.'

'This isn't a contest, Gio.'

'Oh yes it is. Our lovely old legal tradition sees to that, doesn't it? It's winners and losers in our system. Winners and losers.'

'Suppose for the sake of argument—'

'OK,' said Jones, tired. 'Just explain, please, what the hell you mean about it being his only possible defence.'

'All right. Joe Enwright visits her the afternoon of the night she was killed. Yes?'

'That what he says. Our version is different – early evening.'

'I thought you had corroboration from Keith Dawes?'

'Yes, but it was later, early evening. Enwright says it was the second time he went there – to show her his bike, he says. We say it was the first.'

'Perhaps he was telling the truth. Perhaps she didn't answer the bell because she was already dead.'

'Jesus . . .'

'Just listen, eh? Suppose on the earlier visit they'd begun to make love. She's playful aggressive. She scratches him. At some point he ejaculates prematurely. Some of his semen ends up on her thighs. Something, a phone call perhaps, interrupts the sex. She's obliged to give the call her full attention. It takes time. He gets fed up with waiting and leaves.'

'Then what? She cooks herself something, don't

forget. And washes it up. Hands in and out of water.'

'I know. But look at the amount Sandham got out from under her nails – it was a minute amount, miniscule. You can do the DNA test on micrograms of material. That sort of amount wouldn't necessarily get dislodged washing your hands. There were rubber gloves by her sink, anyway – she may have used them.'

'So what happens then?'

'Then, later, someone else comes to her cottage. Or perhaps the second time Enwright turns up, as I said, she may already have been dead.'

'Then who the hell was doing the washing up at ten o'clock?'

'The murderer. There was a lot of blood.'

Jones glowered. He looked at his watch. It was one o'clock. 'You got anything to eat?'

'Porridge.'

'That all?'

'Porridge is one of the basic essentials. It has a molecular weight, I shouldn't be surprised.'

'What the fuck are you on about?'

'Do you want some porridge?'

'Yes. But you don't cook.'

'I can cook porridge. Sophie taught me.'

'OK.'

Jones remembered the warm-skinned girl with her mother's dark watchful eyes, a cartoon scatter of freckles around her nose. He knew that of his three step-children Sophie was the one Bewick missed the most. Jones had maintained an interest in her story as she was to go to university in Swansea. When he thought of Sophie, he thought of home – of Gower, archetype coast, of the past. He waxed sentimental Welsh for a moment, then pulled himself together. 'Sophie beat me at Boggle when I was waiting for you once. Beat me hollow. She's got a lovely laugh, I remember – really grubby, you know. A gurgly drain of a laugh . . . What the hell are you doing?'

Bewick was pouring oats into a cup. Water stood by in a measuring jug. 'I've tried improvising but it always goes wrong. I have to do it just as she told me.'

As Bewick put the saucepan on to the stove both of them heard a car start up a street or two away. It seemed to have the same loose-ringed, coked-up quality of the car they'd heard out at the cottage. They strained to confirm it, but it was travelling away from them into the distance. Gio Jones looked at Bewick, who shrugged non-committally and went on with his cooking.

Jones said he was going for a piss and left the room.

He was straightening up from lifting the lavatory seat when he heard it again. Some trick of sound as it passed a gap between buildings, the night silence, something, brought the engine's sound to him again, faint and clear.

This time he knew. It was the car they had heard at the cottage.

Jones came down to find Bewick wooden-spooning the cooked porridge into bowls.

'Heard it again. It was the same one.'

Bewick said nothing but took the saucepan to the sink and ran cold water into it. He looked troubled. Or did he? Nothing about Bewick had altered, but Jones sensed something was troubling him nevertheless.

'What's up?' he asked.

'Eat your porridge.'

7

Bewick's answering machine held four messages from CICS: requests from the Director that, if he was in Cambridge, would he please make contact. Bewick ignored them.

Today was the day he was to meet the young prisoner, Joe Enwright. Shortly before ten Bewick set off on his bike for City West to keep his appointment with him.

Bewick passed the Granta pub. A car drew level with him. The nearside electric window sank into its door. 'John!' a voice called from inside. 'Can you pull over? I'd like a word.'

It was the Director of CICS, Sean Halliday.

'Shit,' Bewick said to himself.

Bewick sat in Halliday's office. 'Those weren't the terms of my contract,' he said quietly.

'But I need you to do it,' said Sean Halliday, for the fourth time.

'I made it clear', Bewick said, 'that I was going to take the time on my return. I faxed you. I rang Mrs Kay.'

'I thought you needed the time for semi-medical reasons, not for doing an investigation of your own.'

'What I do with the time owed to me is my business.'

'Is it?' Halliday asked.

Sean Halliday was small and always well dressed. His incisive manner was something he had developed to demonstrate he had no fear of being disliked. It was also used to wind up flagging committee meetings, the management of which he was famous for. It was he who had drawn lessons from his visit to Quantico, and insisted on employing investigators of crime. It was he who had had Bewick headhunted and had tempted him away from the police.

Halliday now needed Bewick to go to Glasgow University. At a three-day conference there, he was to sell the virtues of the independent criminological service to sceptical academics.

'Sean, look at my contract,' Bewick said. 'I commit to CICS thirty-six weeks of the year. At the end of any identifiable overseas assignment I am entitled to two clear weeks, and a third if CICS require a report. The Thai police force job was as identifiable as you get.'

Halliday knew he was getting nowhere. 'It's also in your contract that you do nothing that might reflect badly on CICS,' he said.

Bewick smiled, spreading his hands wide. 'Sean . . . I can see this means a lot to you. Or you wouldn't have said anything so – '

'So what?'

'So crass, I was going to say. But don't forget you forced it out of me.'

'I don't see that it's crass. You're nailing your colours to a lost cause.'

'Perhaps, but there's nothing dishonourable in that. Besides I'm hardly going to attract attention if the defence fails.'

'If?'

'Well, there you are. Giovanni Jones will get the credit. No one will even know I've been involved. You know that line of attack is nonsense, Sean. I'm not going to Glasgow, whatever you say.'

'You've never let me down before.'

'I'm not "letting you down" now. You presumed too much, that's all.'

'You're letting me down: severely letting me down.'

'I don't see it.'

'Clearly not. What's the matter with you? You're not normally disloyal.'

'My contract – ' Bewick began.

'Fuck your contract!' Halliday shouted, eyes glaring. 'If everybody stuck to the letter of their fucking contracts, we'd still be living in fucking caves. I didn't recruit you to this consultancy for you to give me a lecture in commercial law every time I ask you to do something that isn't in your contract. What's the matter with you?'

Bewick sat frozen. He seemed to be at a loss. Sean Halliday watched his normally accommodating expression turn to stone.

Bewick stood up, towering over him. He looked as if he didn't know what to do next. Then he picked up the chair he'd been sitting on as if to return it to where it had stood against the wall.

Sean Halliday wouldn't have been able to describe what happened in the next few seconds, although he witnessed it. Bewick's eyes were on his briefly. Then his arm moved violently quickly. There was the crack of splintered wood. Then the room was empty.

Halliday heard the door at the end of the corridor open and shut. He looked across. The heavy solid-beech chair leant at an angle to the wall, its legs broken, the plaster above it gouged by the impact.

Bewick walked out of the building. An astonished Mrs Kay watched. She had heard raised voices, the edge of violence.

As soon as Bewick left the building, she hurried through to the Director's office. Halliday, somewhat to her disappointment, was uninjured. He had regrettably had a disagreement with Mr Bewick, he said. The chair's condition was a result of Mr Bewick's surprising clumsiness.

Bewick emerged from CICS. 'Fuck him,' he said, jamming his arms through the straps of the small rucksack he carried when cycling. He flung the bike forward and straddled it on the move. 'Fuck him!'

Skidding at the junction with Grange Road, his bike shot up Garrett Hostel Lane. It was a beautiful morning, sunlit, still.

Across the lawns of Trinity, the golden stone of

Wren's Library caught the sun, appearing and disappearing between avenue trees.

He accelerated towards the bridge.

'Fuck him!' he said, scattering tourists as he shot down the other side.

The walls of Trinity and Trinity Hall narrowed the stone-crumbling, medieval lane. Bewick's alarming journey continued through the ancient centre, up Jesus Lane and out along Maid's Causeway. He parked his bike outside City West. He was hot from the speed of his ride. He went to the station toilets and spent time splashing his face with cold water.

The man who emerged ten minutes later was indistinguishable from the steady, mostly amiable colleague the officers at City West remembered.

'Has anybody explained to you why I'm here?'

Joe Enwright didn't respond for a moment and then shook his head. 'Norreally.'

Bewick recognized a type: it had glowered down at him from the confectionery of pop posters on his step-daughters' bedroom walls: various versions of male don't-give-a-shit nineties cool.

They were the sort of kids whose heads he'd banged together of a Saturday night when he was a young cop, but in the posters raised up as icons, gilded by brilliant photography which fingered their ephemeral smoothness, trying for both prettiness and danger.

'I didn't hear that,' said Bewick.

'Not really.' He said it over-precisely, deliberately prissy.

The boy was lean and bony with dark brown hair which flopped over his eyes at the front and was shaved up the back of his neck. He looked at Bewick now with what looked like resentment.

Was he trying to be one of those poster icons? How to be cool when charged with murder: the ultimate challenge.

'Your uncle and aunt want an independent investigation of your case,' Bewick said. 'I'm doing the investigating.'

'Yeah?'

Bewick waited a few moments.

'My . . . case . . .' The boy tested the words as if he had never thought of himself as a 'case'. He slid a token glance towards Bewick before hiding again behind his flopped hair and his mumble. 'OK.'

'I'm on your side, in other words. Nothing you say to me will be passed on to the police unless you want it to be. Understood?'

Joe Enwright nodded, barely perceptibly.

'So – is there anything you'd like to tell me?'

'Norreally.'

'OK. That's fine, except it'll be you who does your twenty years amongst some extremely dodgy male felons if we get this wrong.'

Grey-blue eyes looked at Bewick through the hair. In its way the face was beautiful – although there was something about the eyes, a suggestion of intense pain, a vigilance, a suspicion, that would make those who came close pay dearly for the privilege.

'I've persuaded them to return your bike, by the way. They'll use photographs at the trial, if it comes to that.'

'If . . .?'

At last a response, if only one of nervous despair. Bewick ignored it. 'They're taking the bike to your aunt and uncle's. OK?'

Joe Enwright nodded again. It was a different nod from the previous one, and progress of sorts. He raised his head but his eyes avoided Bewick's.

'Interesting machine.'

A glance this time, nothing else. Bewick moved on.

He established that Enwright stuck firmly to his story of having first cycled to Julia's and later returned to show her his gleaming new superbike toy. For twenty minutes Bewick probed and withdrew, neither condescending nor ingratiating himself, before he returned to what was vital. 'Why did you say it was nothing to do with you?'

'I don't remember anything.'

'Nothing?'

'I went clubbin'. Don't know if I remember that or not. Could've been other times what I remember. Don't remember nothing else.'

'Not Julia Kelleher's cottage?'

'No.'

The reply was indifferent, uninterested. 'I don't remember,' he added.

'What do you know about your own memory?'

'Eh?'

'Do you think there are things you might remember – under hypnosis, for example?'

'I'm not doing that.'

'What I'm asking you is whether you think your memory stopped functioning because of the condition you were in? Or . . . are you now unable to retrieve something which is in fact there, somewhere in your memory?'

The shutters came down. 'I don't fucking remember, right?'

To have elicited any sort of response, even this, was an achievement. Bewick sat opposite the boy in silence.

Joe Enwright, in spite of himself, couldn't avoid the impact of the big man, the continuing benign attention. The impulse to distrust was too strong, however. He continued to say nothing.

'If you talk to me, I may be able to help you. If not . . .' Bewick smiled and shrugged. He folded his big hands on the plastic-topped table.

Joe continued to hide behind his hair.

'What's in it for me?' Bewick asked rhetorically. 'Well, I love George and Kit, you see. I suppose that's it, really. Also, I've taken on a job looking after your interests. So I'm committed all ways round.'

In the next silence that followed, Bewick listened to the hum of the building, its voices, the blur of machine noises and human presences.

Finally he tried again. 'Can you remember what you took that evening – at least at the beginning?'

'Norreally.'

'I'm not expecting you to remember everything, just something.'

Bewick managed to convey that this was Joe Enwright's last chance.

There was a pause, then the boy responded. 'Was a mix'n'match sesh, yeah?' There was a faltering in the voice. As if, without some sort of aggression to ride, he couldn't control the tone of it. He swallowed and stretched his neck.

'All right,' Bewick said. 'Tell me something you were taking. One of them.'

Silence and the boy frowned to himself.

Bewick looked out of the window at the car park. Gio Jones was listening to a young PC and he was frowning. It looked as if Gio had heard something he didn't like.

'Blow and blotters, wasn't it?'

Bewick looked back. Joe Enwright was hidden again behind his hair. Bewick tried to put himself in his favourite stepdaughter's shoes. He had the unwelcome intuition that Sophie would find this boy very cool, very appealing.

'Being hash and acid?' he asked.

'Yeah.'

'Did you take anything at the club; E or anything?'

'No, earlier. Bit of whizz. Think. Not sure. Maybe whizz. Maybe. Yeah. Then a jelly I reckon, later.'

'Do you remember getting on your bike when you left the club?'

A shake of the head, a mumble, was all Bewick got. He took a deep breath, knowing that his opportunities to question the boy were going to be limited. 'I didn't hear that,' Bewick said patiently. He was met by another mumble which he interpreted as, 'Just rode it, didn't I?'

'Yes, you seem to have done. And there wasn't a scratch on it. Impressive really.'

Again Bewick allowed the silence to stretch beyond discomfort into a kind of amiability.

'One of the things you were asked by the men in blue was if you were having any kind of affair with Julia Kelleher. You said no, you weren't.'

'I wasn't. We was friends.'

'OK. If I told you it might be important, for your own benefit, for you to admit that you had had an affair with her – would that . . .'

'What?' The boy had interrupted him. This was progress.

'It might be helpful to your case . . .'

'What? Well I didn't, did I?'

'Nothing sexual?'

'Don't you know nothing about her?'

'You mean that Julia came to prefer women?'

A mumble, then, 'Only Amy. She loved Amy.'

'Amy Parris?'

'Yeah.'

'You ever meet Amy?'

A nod and an aversion of the eyes.

'I've been trying to imagine her. What was she like?'

'She was all right.'

'People say she was super clever.'

'Maybe. Wouldn't know . . .'

Then it was as if clouds parted for a moment. Joe Enwright smiled broadly, showing perfect teeth. Even his eyes lost their congested look. 'Gave Amy a go on a mate's bike once. She liked that. Thought she'd be scared, but she wasn't. Wanted me to go quicker.'

'Did Julia want to go too?'

'No. She said she could think of better ways to get herself killed.'

The clouds rolled in again. Invisible barriers slammed.

Bewick waited, then he said gently, 'You had quite a lot in common with Julia, didn't you? Well, I say "a lot" – what I mean is one very important thing: you each experienced great difficulty in your relationship with your father . . .' Bewick was looking away from the boy. When he turned back to face him, he found himself confronted by a glare of frank hatred; of hurt malevolence.

It was only momentary. Joe Enwright was soon hidden again behind his curtain of hair. It had not been Bewick's imagination, however – the emotion was still there in the tension of the way the boy held himself.

'Fuck off. I didn't touch her.' Joe Enwright stood

up. As far as he was concerned the interview was over.

He was returned to his cell.

Gio Jones came in. 'How d'you get on, then? Do we give the little scumbag a balloon and a party hat and let him go, or what?'

'He says he didn't have a sexual relationship with Julia Kelleher.'

'That old chestnut! You believe him now, do you?'

'I think I do.'

'There's lovely.'

'I also believe he doesn't remember anything. I didn't realize he was taking jellies.'

'Temazepam? He didn't tell us that.'

'That's what he says. I don't know where chemically induced amnesia stands as far as a legal defence goes. Do you?'

'No, I bloody don't.'

'Anyway, your version stands. I'm going to have to think of something else.'

'Let's have some lunch.'

'Amy Parris?'

Munching a sandwich, Gio Jones was slumped in the chaos of his office as if in defiance of the clear, bright day beyond the window.

'Yes. Amy Parris,' said Bewick.

'She was a friend of the victim. She's dead. Drowned; yachting accident, about a year ago. But they didn't find her body till the other day. We've got a file somewhere. Want to see it?'

'Where did they find her body?'

'Norfolk. A beach near Scales Howe. On it, perhaps.'

'Really?' Bewick's interest was unmistakable.

''Ello. What does that mean?'

'Julia Kelleher went to that area about ten times in the last year. According to what your suspect's just told me, Julia Kelleher was in love with Amy Parris. She had no grave to visit, so I guess she did the next best thing.'

'Nice to know you haven't changed. You like the human story angle, don't you? Ever thought of tabloid reporting?'

'Don't give me that. If we're talking soft evidence, who's the man who clings to intuitions like a drowning rat?'

'Me? Bollocks. You know what you said to me once? "People do things for a reason," and you didn't even smile.'

'Relationships are data. There's another for you.'

'Oh, ta . . .'

'So tell me about this yachting accident.'

'Only oddity, I reckon, is what she was doing on the boat in the first place.'

'How do you mean?'

'Not the type, I'd have thought.'

'You met her?'

'Yeah. Sirius set up the computer network in the

new regional HQ; in the toy box. Sod off Noddy. She was in charge. Very, very clever.'

'Why did you say "not the type"?'

'On a yacht? I wouldn't have said she was the outdoor type, that's all. She was more the type we drag out of the river just before the university exams week. All maths and skin and bones. Anyway, she was on the yacht one night and then she wasn't. Perhaps she decided the river wasn't big enough for her.'

'Has anyone talked about suicide?'

'No, no. Nobody. That's just me. Welsh bonhomie. No, she was an experienced sailor, according to the report. You'd never have guessed it . . . Wouldn't think I give talks to raw recruits on the danger of stereotyping, would you? There was something about her, mind. Fragile, suppose you could say. Oh God, you decide. I'll get Karen to get you the file.'

Jones looked round to check the door of his office was shut. 'How about Karen, then? All right there, are you?'

Bewick gave him a cool glance. 'I suppose you're going to say it anyway,' he said.

'I am. She wants her fingernails in your bum, man. What are you? A lucky bastard.'

'So you say.'

Jones dialled an internal number and asked Karen to take the Amy Parris file to Green Four.

'What've you been up to since your Nina buggered off then?'

'Let's talk about your alleged murderer.'

'"The man refused to reply to the question." Fair enough, I suppose, but you don't have Karen walking in and out of your office every half hour.'

'Are you in love with her, Giovanni?'

'Try not to be a dickhead. I'm a realist. Let's talk about my favourite murderer. How did you get on with him? Communicative little toerag, isn't he? What d'you reckon?'

'As I say, I think he's telling the truth when he says he can't remember what he was doing.'

'Where does that get us?' asked Jones.

'I don't know,' Bewick said. 'But you'd think, wouldn't you, that smashing somebody over the head and killing them . . . on some bizarre sexual power-trip . . . well, you'd think it would be likely to lodge itself in your brain – however many neurones were misfiring. Lots were.'

'Oh yeah?'

'The amnesia could've been genuine,' he repeated to himself. 'I mean chemically.'

'Explain please.'

Bewick explained how, as the amphetamines wore off and the time-bending effects of hash kicked in and the hallucinogenic effects of acid washed over all, the boy could well have been moving in a timeless dream without walls. And that was without the known amnesiac effects of temazepam, under the influence of which people had been known to have been involved in serious fights and remember nothing. 'So the cocktail he took could actually have wrecked his ability to remember anything ordinary,' Bewick summarized.

'I think he doesn't want to remember so badly that he doesn't remember.'

'Has the psychiatrist come up with hysterical amnesia since? It wasn't in his report.'

'The psychiatrist needed treatment himself after his last session with young motor-mouth. He was getting about four grunts an hour.'

'I did well, then . . .'

'You did. No, he hasn't talked about hysterical amnesia. So; you think he's telling the truth, do you? Where does that get us?'

'Well,' said Bewick, smiling, 'either it's totally unhelpful and means nothing. Or . . .'

'Or?'

'Or it's totally helpful and means everything.'

'Thanks.'

'Either way your case stands; as I said.'

'So why don't you leave it alone? Why are you bothering?'

'Well, it's the other suspects, I suppose.'

'What!?' Jones shouted. He looked apoplectic.

'There are three suspects – so far,' Bewick replied. 'One of them you've got locked up. Then there's Julia's father and there's Julian Rae. Both are unstable and had a strong emotional connection to her.'

'What the smoking Moses are you on about?'

'I'm trying to explain why I'm still motivated. I know you don't like what I'm doing.'

'I hate it. I bloody hate it. I think you've sold out, tell you the truth,' Jones said, without a flicker of amusement.

Bewick looked at him stonily.

'I do,' said Jones, 'and that's a fact.'

Bewick said nothing.

It was the first time, Jones realized, that he had displayed such hostility towards Bewick. Why did he feel this way? Sod it, he just did.

'What is it?' Bewick asked. 'What's up?'

Jones shrugged. He knew, but wouldn't tell. He resented Bewick's having left the force, not on principle as he pretended, but for where it left him. Since Bewick's departure he felt isolated, exiled within the force. No one else could make him think like Bewick did. The world without him was greyer and sometimes he hated Bewick for it.

'What's all this about?' Bewick insisted.

Eventually Jones replied. 'Got a problem on the Henderson: theft, vandalism; the usual. We arrest the little buggers and the magistrates have to let them go because they're juveniles. The stipendiary magistrate is OK, Jim Dolben – he'd like to see them sorted. He can't do a blind thing. I'm not a control freak, but feeling impotent pisses me off.'

Karen put her head round the door to say that the file was now in Green Four.

Karen entered Green Four ahead of Bewick and pointed to the file on the desk.

'What's the matter with Gio?' Bewick asked. 'It's not just the bother on the Henderson, is it?'

'It's you, probably, Sir,' Karen said. 'I think he's realizing how much he misses you.' She smiled at him bleakly and closed the door behind her.

The Amy Parris file consisted partly of photocopies of the Norfolk Constabulary findings; the rest had been generated by City West, Cambridge.

The story began forty-eight hours before she joined Mr and Mrs Caird on their yacht *Seahorse* on the Friday.

Amy had worked late at Sirius on Wednesday evening, at the Science Park site. According to Security, she left at about nine p.m. This was common enough. Sirius management were a tight-knit dedicated work-force. She had left on her own, by bike. Muir Hammond, the director, was always willing to offer late workers a lift home but he was away that day.

A neighbour, a retired civil servant, Mrs Brett, heard her return home: she thought there were 'more phone calls than usual' for Amy, 'especially as it was late'. If the TV and radio weren't on, Mrs Brett could hear Amy's phone ring.

She didn't hear Amy go out, but she heard someone go up the stairs to her flat. Then she heard Amy's front doorbell being rung twice. Then one person came back down the stairs. No it didn't, according to Mrs Brett, sound like Amy. It sounded like someone much heavier. The assumption therefore was that Amy had refused to answer the door. Mrs Brett heard her moving about later that night, about two a.m., 'which was most unusual'.

The next day, Amy failed to turn up for work. Nor did she ring in to explain. This had never happened before in Sirius's experience of Amy Parris: she was a model of consideration when it came to organizing or re-organizing tasks within her department.

Indeed, it was so out of character that someone from the company turned up that afternoon to ask Mrs Brett, who held a spare key to Amy's flat, if she would mind checking that Amy wasn't hurt or worse. The flat turned out to be empty; the bed made. Her laptop was still there but her handbag and filofax weren't. Sirius Software didn't hear from Amy again. Where she spent Thursday night was never established.

The next report of her, Friday lunch-time, was seventy-odd miles away at Aldeburgh Yacht Club, Slaughden Quay. She was asking if anyone knew of a cruising yacht that might be for hire. She had sailed since she was a child and knew the East Coast rivers well.

She found nothing local that could be hired and seemed reluctant to try a charter company. When she discovered that Mr and Mrs Caird were heading north to lay up for the winter and would be glad of a crew, she asked to join them. She spent Friday night on board *Seahorse*, which left Aldeburgh on Saturday.

Nightfall found *Seahorse* off Cromer. Amy volunteered to stand the first night-watch alone. As she had interfaced the Decca positioning system to the autopilot, it would be a piece of cake. Only insisting that she wear her harness and safety line at all times, Mr Caird agreed and turned in. His wife was already below, as she was sea-sick. When Amy was discovered missing, Caird turned back and radioed for help. Air sea-rescue and the RNLI searched all the next day, but found nothing.

Lost at sea.

Amy Parris's flat was burgled four days after she was lost. Her electronic equipment was all taken: the laptop, a sound system, a TV, a state-of-the-art PC.

Then at the bottom of the last page in the file, a stick-on note: 'Body found 16th Sept '92. Scales Howe. ID, PM, returned to family.'

Bewick read the post-mortem report which was attached. Death by hypothermia.

What had Amy Parris been doing?

Had she, after all, been the depressive Gio Jones took her for?

Was this wild departure from normality meant to be a complex suicide as he suggested?

Or what?

8

Sally Vernon shut the door on the house in which she had lived more or less happily for six years. She piled the cleaning equipment into the back of the car outside.

Standing under the SOLD notice by the front gate she looked back at the house for a moment. It had been hers entirely: bought with her own money and without help. Ownership had given her great pleasure, profound content.

It was a Victorian terraced house on what had once been the fringe of the city, built in the 1890s. Ordinary enough, but she had loved it in the way she might love a person. Now it was clean, bare, fresh from her ownership, awaiting its next occupant.

She turned her back. She realized for the first time just how much it was going to hurt her to leave it.

James came up the steep street carrying bottles of wine. 'Are you sad, darling?'

She nodded. He kissed her, open mouthed, as if knowing she wouldn't feel at all self-conscious at that moment.

James was handsome, with a commanding beak of

a nose above a mouth which readily showed amusement. It was a soldier's face. 'I'll make it up to you,' he said, smiling.

'When?'

'Now.'

'How? You're back in the office in ten minutes.'

'The office can take a hike.'

So they drove to his house near the cathedral and made love.

James was what she expected of a lover: mostly gentle. She loved the moment when the hard definitions of his body, rigid with orgasm, began to soften into smooth inertia; pliable, lazy, dreamy.

James flung himself off the bed. 'I'll go straight to the site meeting,' he announced. 'When did you say you were going to Cambridge – tomorrow, was it?'

'Thursday. Scientific Periodicals Library.'

'And who're you meeting? You're meeting someone, aren't you?'

'A policeman. He needs to know about DNA.'

'Will the poor plod understand a word you say?'

'I think so. He's quite bright.'

James shot a glance at her where she lay on her back, cosy and sexy in the white bed.

'Yes,' she smiled, 'I think you should be suitably jealous.'

'I vill make you pay for ziss!' he hissed. 'I vill fuck you to vizzin a centimetre of your life!'

'Yes please,' she said as he hurried away.

When she had been alone for a few minutes, tears

ran out of the corners of both eyes and fell on the pillow.

A door it seemed was closing quietly behind her and she was powerless to stop it. Her body glowed, she was spread with the warm smell of him . . . and still she was unsure.

The two officers looked at each other in desperation. Joe Enwright glanced at them in turn, then shrugged. It was as if his being under arrest and his forthcoming trial were their problem, not his.

Gio Jones took out a handkerchief and wiped his face with it. 'Open the window, will you?'

Baynes got up immediately and did so. The atmosphere in the interview room was heavy with controlled anger. The open window brought a cool breeze and the rumble of traffic passing in Maid's Causeway.

Jones looked at the meagre notes on the pad in front of him. Made nervous by Bewick's continuing interest in the Julia Kelleher case, he had decided to check and re-check the chain of evidence.

Joe Enwright's movements on the evening of the killing were obviously crucial. After leaving Julia Kelleher's cottage on his bike he'd gone for a burn up along the A45 nearly to Newmarket, returning to Cambridge via the A11-M11: a round trip of about thirty miles. 'And on that machine,' thought Jones, 'it'd take him about a quarter of an hour.' Nothing amongst the notes was new.

What time had he got to his mother's house? Joe

didn't know. He watched some telly before he went out. What telly? He couldn't remember, could he? He'd changed, got some drugs from his cache, then gone round to George and Kit's and told them not to wait up for him as he'd probably go clubbing.

He went first to The Anchor on Silver Street Bridge. Then he'd gone to a club called The House. From there on, it was a blur; finally a blank. He was woken up on a Midsummer Common bench by a hedgehog making a racket in rubbish which had spilt from a bin.

He thought he'd lost his bike, but eventually found it leaning against a tree not far away. He splashed his face in the river, he said, then drove around Cambridge in the dawn in low gear: full volume.

'Why?'

'To wake up them snotty, fucking uni types, that's why,' said Joe as if he didn't mean it.

That was all. They had corroborative witnesses who had seen him at The Anchor and The House about midnight, but between those times and after one in the morning, nothing.

The small plane circled the green acres of the airfield, waiting for the even smaller RAF trainers, cheerful scarlet, to land.

Bewick stood in front of the airport building. Conceived in the heyday of the great ocean liners, curved, white and steel-windowed, it was a remarkable survival: financed presumably by the service hangars on the far perimeter, from which the gigantic tail fins of Tri Star jets protruded.

The little red training aircraft were bumping across the turf now, away from the runway where Dundas's long-nosed plane was just touching down. As it turned towards him, Bewick set off across the grass towards it.

A minute or so later he was standing in the shadow of the Cessna. 'Time for a coffee? We can be in Fen Ditton in five minutes.'

'That would be good.'

Bewick led the way through the low white buildings.

In Fen Ditton, Dundas changed his mind about the coffee, saying he'd rather stretch his legs, so he and Bewick walked down the High Street to the river.

Dundas had explained on the phone that he was flying to York and would like to land at Cambridge when conditions were good, as he was piloting himself there the following week.

'I'm only a weekend flyer and you never know.'

'Why are you coming to Cambridge?'

'There's a dinner at St Margaret's I've been invited to. Managed to get the guest room on the river; bloody nice . . .'

'Perhaps we could meet up?' Bewick suggested. 'Bring your hangover to breakfast. I can't cook my way out of a string bag, but I can sort a breakfast.'

'Porridge?'

'Porridge and codeine: it always works.'

'Good. Thanks.'

Bewick summed up the case for Dundas. It was a quiet performance, unexcited, done in a slightly pedantic tone: Bewick's version of the policeman being official. Dundas realized it was masterly, though and told Bewick so and thanked him.

'If Enwright went on trial tomorrow,' Dundas speculated, 'how do you think it would go?'

'Badly for Enwright. Three–one to the Crown, I'd say.'

'Yes,' said Dundas. 'The only thing they haven't got is a confession. And, what's worse, we have no alternative version of events ourselves: just four hours of amnesia. Self-induced too – in a manner hardly calculated to appeal to any jury I've ever met.'

'You'd have to focus on those four hours though, wouldn't you?'

Dundas grumbled an acknowledgement of this. Then he shook his head. 'Och, we could muddy the waters with this actor fellow inheriting her house, I suppose. And we could set up her papa as a violent shite, but . . . What d'you think? Do you think it's worth going on with it?'

'I haven't finished yet,' Bewick said.

Dundas marvelled at the rock-like confidence that seemed to underlie this statement. Earlier, just after he'd landed, still exhilarated by the flight, he'd been surprised by Bewick's being untypically subdued. Dundas wondered if it had anything to do with a curious, unexplained meeting he'd had a couple of days before.

'I bumped into Musselwhite just now,' he said, watching Bewick for a reaction.

Musselwhite had been at school with them both at St Matthew's. Dry witted and very clever, he had gone into the Foreign Office. When Musselwhite had been recruited into SIS, or even if he had been, neither of them knew. It was an acknowledged assumption between them, however, that he had.

'How is he?' Bewick asked.

'Greying at the temples and drier than ever. He . . . quite odd, really. He asked me how *you* were.'

'But I haven't seen him.' Bewick snapped off the remark.

Dundas wondered what Musselwhite might know about Bewick's affairs that he didn't. In his hierarchy of friendships from university days, Dundas placed himself closer than Musselwhite to Bewick. 'He actually sounded concerned about you, John.'

Bewick smiled and made light of it. 'I should hope so. Perhaps getting some grey hairs has humanized the bastard. No wonder his wife went off with another woman.'

'You're not ill, are you?'

'Good God, no. And if I were, you'd hear about it before that skinny Whitehall git, let me tell you.'

Dundas realized he was being told that Bewick understood that this was what he wanted to hear.

Bewick was also telling him to mind his own business. 'OK. Good.' Useless to speculate.

'Do you think you'll find anything before you do finish?' Dundas asked, returning to the case of R *v.* Enwright.

'Don't know. I wouldn't go on with it if I didn't think there was something to be found . . .' Bewick shrugged. 'Don't know.'

Dundas was comforted and it surprised him that he was. Then he was suddenly possessed by a certainty that things would go better than he'd hoped hitherto. What a strange being Bewick was, Dundas thought – so hidden, so self-protecting, and yet capable of provoking such powerful feeling.

Ten minutes later the wheels of Dundas's plane rumbled across the turf towards the concrete runway. Bewick watched the long nose of the Cessna lift and climb and turn north-east. Its flicking lights blurred into the brightness of the sky, until the plane was no more than a small noise melting into the sounds of the A45 a mile away.

He had phoned CICS before leaving for the airport. He needn't have bothered to check.

'Mr Halliday's in Glasgow; didn't you know?'

Bewick parked in Clarkson Road and made his way past the Newton Mathematical Institute site to the buildings which housed CICS.

Mrs Kay had always been on Bewick's side.

She understood the point immediately. 'I realized you'd had an argument, so I would have been alert to anything he'd initiated since. He's done nothing; promise. I think he wants to forget the whole thing.'

'I suppose I should be grateful to be still employed, then,' said Bewick.

'But somehow you find yourself curiously indifferent?'

Bewick laughed.

'I suspect he'll exercise the letter of your contract with regard to your two-week break,' said Mrs Kay apologetically.

'Tell me,' said Bewick.

Bewick drew into a lay-by on the main St Neots road. To his right, on the far side of the road, was a windbreak of trees. To his left, open uncultivated fields stretched towards Chalcote, and just visible beyond its small orchard was Julia Kelleher's cottage.

There was a snack wagon at the far end of the lay-by. An old Rottweiler was lumbering up and down the edge of the ditch barking at something in it; a rat, perhaps.

As Bewick watched, a barrel of a woman appeared at the back door of the wagon and shouted at the dog, which eventually obeyed her. Bewick smiled. 'Hello Bella.'

Little brown eyes, currants in the big pudding of her face, squinted then opened in delight. A blunt paw swung and thumped Bewick on the shoulder. 'John Bewick. Well, well. Here I am, still.'

'Yeah,' said the other customer at Bewick's elbow, 'you can't keep a good woman down.'

Bella had been closed down more times than anyone could remember. Hygiene was cited, but most thought it was officious tidy-mindedness which was at the bottom of it. Bella's wagon was a scruffy outfit.

'The buggers haven't finished me yet.'

'Good,' said Bewick.

'You've left the force, haven't you? Gio Jones told me.'

'When did you see him last?'

'When that woman was killed . . .' Bella jerked a greasy thumb over her shoulder, ' . . . over there. Chalcote way. Wanted to know if I was here that night.'

'Were you?'

'Oh, so you're still a copper then?'

Bewick explained himself, and asked her again if she'd been in that lay-by on the night of the killing.

'No – I have to keep moving nowadays. The buggers haven't closed me down but they've got me on the run. No . . .' Bella laughed; high, youthful. 'No . . . I was down at the Cottage that night.'

The Cottage was a lay-by on the A11, big enough to warrant a public lavatory, which was a gay pick-up joint; hence Cottage.

'There were some tinkers up here then. Only a couple of vehicles – just one family, I should think.'

It had been in the notes. The travellers had seen nothing, heard nothing. They'd been watching TV. After being questioned they'd moved on.

'When did you get set up here, Bella?'

'Yesterday.'

'What time do you pack up usually?'

'This time of year I'm usually gone by about seven, 'cept Saturdays. Saturdays I go on as long as there's custom.' She laughed again. 'Sounds as if you've got your work cut out with this business. What can I get you to keep your strength up, eh?'

Bewick asked for a sausage sandwich and tea.

The tea came in a pint mug: 'Bella's Mega Mug – 60p.' A couple of lorries hauled in. Bewick took his tea and his greasy sandwich and wandered the length of the lay-by in the overcast drizzle.

He scanned the terrain between the lay-by and Parbold Cottage. There was no cover except the ditches. He walked over to the nearest, which was only a few yards away. It was deep: well over five feet. Certainly it would be cover for a man moving carefully. To make out the run of ditches from where he stood was impossible. He returned to the snack wagon.

He was greeted by a man in his sixties, lean and lined, his grey hair back in a pony tail. 'Mr Bewick, how the devil are yer?' The accent was town Suffolk, wry, shrewd.

'Muldoon! Is that your rig out there?'

'Yeah, I'm the Eddie Stobart of Stowmarket now. Don't even break the speed limits these days.'

Bewick raised an eyebrow. As a criminal, Muldoon had been clever, always able to improvise, incorrigible and living for today. Bewick looked at Bella, who winked, as if to confirm his doubts.

'I'm impressed,' Bewick said. 'Can you do me a favour?'

'He'd better,' Bella chipped in.

'Depends. What is it?'

'Let me climb on top of your rig for a few minutes.'

Muldoon gave a brief mirthless chuckle which implied that Bewick was losing it. He shrugged. 'Sure.'

Muldoon showed Bewick how to climb on to the top of the big trailer and then went back to Bella's Snax.

The view from fifteen feet up showed Bewick what he wanted to see: the pattern of the ditches from near the garden of Parbold Cottage to the road. Someone could move across the area quite unseen – indeed they could reach the Long Toft Road as well, half a mile to the west. He could also see a light on in the cottage.

'You didn't find the drugs in me trailer, then?' said Muldoon without taking the cigarette out of his mouth.

'No, it was all those boxes marked swag got in my way.'

Outside Parbold Cottage was parked a grey Rover. The light was on in the kitchen. He knocked very gently and then stood well back so he could be seen from inside the cottage. He waited.

Eventually he was rewarded by an almost imperceptible movement of the door. It opened barely an inch and a voice whispered, 'What do you want?'

'Hello Mrs Kelleher. You wanted to tell me one or two things, I know. You saw me notice that you did, when I was talking to your husband. I haven't forgotten that you want to tell me these things about your daughter and I'd feel very privileged if you felt you were able to tell me now.'

Again Bewick waited. From behind the door came the sound of a sigh, then silence, then another. The door opened a few inches more, then nearly closed again. Finally it opened about halfway. Bewick stepped forward. Mrs Kelleher had disappeared. He found her in the kitchen, biting her nails by the window.

Bewick said nothing. He went to the table and sat down to wait again. Mrs Kelleher turned suddenly from the window. 'He didn't tell you everything.' The spirit of a monstrous accusation lurked behind this simple outburst. 'He didn't at all! And some of it . . .' Mrs Kelleher said, as if outraged beyond belief, ' . . . some of it wasn't true!' She subsided, spent. Bewick nodded, a model of understanding. He waited.

Mrs Kelleher came to the table and sat down. With intense malice, she began, 'He hated her. He hated everything about her: always did. He's even accused me of having another man's daughter. Julia had the measure of him, you see. She saw him for what he is and she didn't mind saying it. She was wonderful. I don't know how, but wonderful. She wasn't able at first, after he came back from being ill, but after a bit she stood up to him. Then she just grew and grew. She gave me her books to read. I knew Brian wouldn't have liked them. So I hid them. It was a secret between us. I've got all those sort of her books.'

'What sort would those be?' Bewick asked.

'Feminist,' she whispered as if to admitting to a perversion. 'I've got them all now. I took them. I keep them in a secret place.'

Mrs Kelleher glanced shyly at Bewick, bright eyed and excited for a moment as she talked about her heroine, her murdered daughter. 'I don't think she should have married that man, Toner. He wasn't good enough. But he was older. He'd been in the army, one of those tough regiments, you know. He'd been through the mill. He was her new daddy. And they were what you'd call idealists – with their shop. Well, she was. She was a real Green. She campaigned for the natural life . . . Brian didn't like Toner at first, but when Toner went back to his drinking, well, Brian was more on his side then, because Toner started being horrid about Julia. They'd gang up on her. It only made Julia stronger. She was running everything – the shop accounts, everything. Then one day, when he'd been drinking, he hit her. Julia walked out. She never spoke to him without a solicitor being there ever again, not once; not ever. I so admire her for that . . . not ever.'

Mrs Kelleher flicked her hand in front of her face, little darting movements, as if to bat away an appalled self-consciousness at this outpouring. 'And it wasn't true what Brian said about there not being someone in Julia's life after Toner, and not knowing why she divorced! Untrue! Julia walked out because Toner was a drunken bully. When they said she'd been killed I thought it was him. I did!'

Mrs Kelleher was startlingly defiant. She seemed to expand as confidence in her own defiance grew. Bewick's receptiveness, his unobtruding presence drew her boiling emotions to the surface. 'And I don't mind telling you she was in love again after she left him, and not with a man either. And I don't blame her! She deserved some love.'

Bewick nodded; half a smile. Mrs Kelleher was shaking. 'The poor girl was lost at sea. They only found her body the other day. Buried in the sand . . .'

There was a silence. Mrs Kelleher was breathing fast and shallow. She took control of herself and breathed deeply.

Bewick risked a question: 'Did Julia go to the funeral?'

'Of course. Of course she did. She went to Suffolk for it. She went to Norfolk first, she told me, to see the place where Amy was found. She met a mad-woman there, she said, who talked like the queen.'

'How long was this before she was killed?'

Mrs Kelleher stared at Bewick as if this was one question too many. 'A few days. Four days.'

Bewick nodded.

'At least', Mrs Kelleher went on, 'Julia was able to say goodbye to Amy. I loved Amy too – she was such a special person. I think everybody would have loved her if she'd allowed them to.'

'In what way did she prevent people loving her, do you think?'

Mrs Kelleher stared and thought. Then she shook her head. 'She made no effort to . . . I mean she didn't seem to need people much. Even with Julia, she . . . She didn't try and charm people. You know? Julia was a charmer. Amy was much cooler, but so kind. She was very kind to me. And when you thanked her, she just smiled. She smiled like as if it was the first time anyone had ever thanked her for anything, you know, as if it was a new thing to be thanked!'

'What about before she met Julia?'

Mrs Kelleher looked confused. 'I didn't know her before she met Julia.'

'No, that's right. Did she talk about her life before, though?'

'She didn't talk much at all.'

'Was she ever married, do you know?'

'Not as far as . . . why are you asking me about Amy?'

'I want to know as much as I can about Julia's life and Amy obviously meant a lot to her, as you've told me. Also, I've been wondering why Amy went off for no apparent reason to join that sailing yacht. Did Julia ever talk about that? About her being on the run or anything?'

Mrs Kelleher shook her head, not just in denial but as if to fend off any more questions. She seemed to subside, to shrink. Her left hand strayed to the collar of her shirt as if to check how it was folded. She looked as if she were on the threshold of tears. Bewick stopped asking her questions.

He put one of his address cards on the table in front of her. 'If you ever need help, Mrs Kelleher, I don't mind being contacted at any time.'

She didn't pick up the card but looked at it for some time. Then she whispered, 'Thank you for talking to me.'

Bewick smiled. He tried one more time. 'Have you any idea why Amy Parris might have been on the run? Or who from?'

Mrs Kelleher looked ashamed at her inability to help. 'No idea,' she murmured.

Bewick took his leave. He was about to set off up the path when Mrs Kelleher cleared her throat, so unobtrusively that few would have bothered to respond. Bewick turned.

'That David Toner. He's going to get the life insurance. They took it out together and Julia never cancelled it.'

'How much for?'

'Two-hundred thousand.'

Bewick nodded. 'Thank you,' he said.

The fire in the grate at The Old Muscovy burned low,

but nobody bothered with it; it was a mild autumn and the bar was crowded.

Jones squeezed his way through the assembled suits of Science Park employees and found Bewick's seventeen stone perched on a stool by an open window. He handed Bewick his pint. 'Adnams. Here's death to your investigation,' he said, drinking.

Bewick didn't reply.

'I had another go at Enwright – see if he'd managed to remember anything.'

'Let's see. A bike ride. Telly. George and Kit's. The pub. The club. Waking up by the river. Any advance on that?'

'No. Nice to know some things don't change, isn't it? So . . .' Jones looked beadily at Bewick, 'You, what've you come up with?'

'Tell you later.'

'Oh, it's keeping me in suspense now is it?'

'I want to ask you something. Your advice.'

'All right, what is it?'

'When we've drunk these.' Bewick lowered his voice and gestured to the crush around them.

'OK.'

Bewick and Jones sauntered along the bank of the lode, just wide enough for a barge, not much more than a ditch. Choked now with reeds, it connected the staithe at The Old Muscovy with the river.

'I know you don't want me to go on with the case,

but I'm going to, so you might as well accept it. I've got ten days . . .'

Jones, who knew Bewick's doggedness, snorted. 'Oh yes? And then you'll go away and leave us all alone, will you?'

'It'll be a spare-time thing. If I still have a job.'

'What's that mean?'

Bewick told Jones about his confrontation with Halliday. 'That's what I wanted your advice about.'

'Your job? Jack the bugger in, mate. I've told you often enough: you're a fish out of water with those varsity arseholes. You're going to argue with them. And don't think it'll get easier. You're a first-class copper when you put your mind to it. Get back in there. You could do it. The chief wants you back. That's my advice.'

'It wasn't advice about the job exactly . . .'

'Bloody hell. Yes? What then?'

'I told you about that to show how things stood.' Bewick mumbled something inarticulate.

'What's getting to you?'

'What I want your advice on.'

Whatever it is, it's serious, thought Jones.

Jones knew that Bewick long ago had narrowly escaped an assault charge against someone he'd been arresting, and another against a fellow officer.

The lode stretched ahead, its surface yellow with the litter of willow leaves, man-dug, straight as a ruler between its high banks.

Jones glanced at the big man beside him. Like

himself, Bewick was self-made: poor childhood, state-paid education and advancement in a profession. There, similarity ended. Jones had retained his natural ebullience: he was open, said what he thought and often gave offence. Bewick was hidden, partly behind his sober charm; self-made in more senses than one. Jones knew that Bewick's congenial, attentive presence was not just a front. It was what Bewick tried to be.

They were at the junction of the lode with the winding river. There were a few more trees here, and among their roots the tunnels of water voles. The meadow beyond was being grazed by wild geese. Earthy, rivery smells came off the water. Constant drone of traffic.

They retraced their steps towards the pub. 'So,' said Jones, 'what's getting to you?'

'No, it's all right.'

'What? What d'you mean, you great Anglo-Saxon monolith? Advice on what?'

'Nothing. I shouldn't have mentioned it.'

'Come on, man, what?'

'Forget it.'

'Come on!'

More strides in silence; then:

'That car we heard out at the cottage – '

'Yes?'

'Are you sure you heard the same one when we were back at my place?'

'Why?'

'Are you?'

'Why?'

'Answer the question.'

'No, not sure. How many old bangers are there in a city full of students, for God's sake? And it was nearly two in the morning and I'd had a jar or so. With my hand on the Bible I'd only be able to say they were similar.'

'I thought you might say that. I don't know if it makes it better or worse.'

'What?'

'The feeling I get . . .'

'You think someone's staking you out?'

'Sometimes . . . sometimes I do, yes.'

So that was it. Bewick, he knew, would want him to be practical. 'Well, you're experienced enough . . . perhaps someone is . . . You be careful. No routines. Do you want us to do anything?'

'Not yet.'

'Keep me posted.'

'Sure.'

'You scared?'

There was a long silence. 'Whatever that means. It's . . . a feeling I don't like. Like a kind of background hiss.'

'White noise?'

'Yeah . . . nearly. Yellow noise. Funky. The sound of funk.'

They both laughed uncomfortably as if they had been joking about terminal illness.

They were nearly back at the pub.

'Anyway, you were going to tell me what you've come up with.'

'It was just that I wasn't sure you knew that Julia Kelleher's ex-husband, Toner, had a policy on her life for two hundred K?'

Jones's head reeled. No, he didn't know it! Mentally he scrambled through the David Toner file to try to recover a hint he could have missed: nothing.

'Where d'you get this?' he asked savagely.

'I wasn't sure how well your teams checked his alibi. I got it from Mrs Kelleher.'

'We checked. Anyway, so what, even if we find his alibi creaks a bit? There's the small matter of two sources of the same DNA, both belonging to the little vomit-bag we've got banged up. Not David Toner.'

'Ah, but how did they get there?'

'Get lost. You can't buy the stuff in Tesco's, you know.'

'Joe Enwright may have been Julia Kelleher's lover, whatever you say.'

'It's what he says, mate. He denies it. He even denied it to you.'

'I know he did. But there may be a reason for that.'

'What d'you mean – may be? There is a reason. He denies being her lover because he wasn't her lover. That's the reason. You're like a tart being shagged in an alley, John Bewick. You're banging your head against a brick wall. I know it in my old Welsh water – the boy is a killer.'

'OK. I've always respected your instincts, Gio.'

Jones looked at him sharply: no hint of irony, not a squeak. 'My instincts are data, are they? That it?'

'Why be sarcastic? Yes, they are. As far as I'm concerned they are.'

Jones realized he should have really liked to hear this. Why did he hate it? Same story. He shrugged.

'Amy Parris,' Bewick was saying. 'That's an interesting problem, don't you think?'

'What?'

'I dreamt about her last night.'

'You ought to take a good look at Karen Quinney, that's what you ought to do. You've been without a woman for far too long. Have you actually clocked what Karen looks like? Can't you imagine it, man?'

Bewick lengthened his stride, forcing Jones to walk unnaturally quickly to keep up.

'John . . .'

'You're being a boring arsehole, Gio,' Bewick said quietly as they walked into the pub car-park.

'Yeah, well, I got a degree in it, en't I? You want me to deny my roots?'

Bewick unlocked his car and got into it.

'All right, all right. Come on. I want to know what you think of Amy Parris. Really I do. All right?'

'Sure. Sometime.'

Bewick started the car. Jones had to stand aside when it moved off.

'Sod you then.'

Jones watched the car disappear and he wondered if Bewick regretted his confession. Angry with himself and angry with Bewick, he headed back into the fug of the bar and ordered more bitter. Again he'd bumped up against Bewick's unpredictability. Bewick could be faultless in his logic, hungry for data, open. Or he could be superstitious, touchy, listening to his own dreams, silent, deaf to ideas.

Jones had thought this time, wrongly, that what Bewick really wanted to talk about was fear . . . how he was dealing with it. He knew how such an imagined threat would ruin his own life, every waking hour, never mind the nightmares. When they had worked together as young officers, Jones had made a rule for himself never to judge Bewick by his own standards. Yet here he was, all these years later, doing exactly that. He also wished he could work out why he kept trying to shove Karen under Bewick's nose. He did it without thinking and always regretted it. Was it to prove to himself her total unavailability as soon as possible?

Gio Jones stood at Bewick's front door half an hour later, feeling foolish. The door opened. Bewick didn't even look surprised to see him.

'Hi. Just came to lick your boots and analyse your dreams about Amy Parris.'

'Too late, unless you want to come to Norfolk with me.'

Jones found himself writing off his planned afternoon at City West. 'OK,' he said.

'It'll be the rest of the day. And you'll need wellies.'

'Sure. You lend me some.'

'OK.'

'I'll drive you if you like . . . What am I doing?' Jones shrieked in an undertone.

'It's what they call creative irresponsibility,' said Bewick.

'Yeah. Good. Yeah – that's what it is. Brill. Thanks.'

They were heading up the A11 towards Thetford Forest before the subject was raised again.

Jones asked Bewick about his dream. Bewick obliged. 'It was like being at the theatre, except I was in the play as well as watching it. There was a character, me, running through a dark wood. It was some sort of fairy tale. The trees were plywood cut-outs. But as he/I tried to run, he realized I was running through brambles; and they were real enough.'

'Just stick to one pronoun, will you? I've got the idea.'

'I was being chased by dogs. I could see the torch beams of their handlers behind the trees. At some point I acquired a companion. I was running hand in hand with her. I thought at first it was my step-daughter Sophie but I came to realize it was Amy Parris.

'I don't remember much else of it . . . there were some knights in armour . . . anyway I found myself on a beach. Amy left me and ran away into the sea. She turned into some sort of sea creature, a dolphin-cum-seal creature and disappeared.

'Then I woke myself up by speaking aloud. What I said was, "On the run." The dream was so clear still that I took notes to remember it.'

'Sure you didn't say "On the rum"?'

'Fuck off.'

'Amazingly enough, it occurred even to this mentally challenged copper that Miss Parris might have been running away from something. In fact it's difficult to see what the hell else she might be doing. Refusing to answer her doorbell. Turning up at a yacht club asking to be taken somewhere, anywhere.'

'Running away from something is different from being on the run. "On the run" in my book means being under external threat. She could have been "running away" from a relationship . . . from embarrassment . . . from her family's nosiness . . . from being outed as a gay . . . from herself. What I meant is that she felt in danger.'

Jones was parking on the quay at Wells-next-the-Sea. Bewick had gone to see if the café was open.

Jones squinted down the long channel, a silvery sheet of light leading out to the sea. Three fishing boats were coming in against the young ebb, clouded with gulls. Yards from him, other crews were unloading their catch, tidying away their gear – the clunk and ring of steel on steel.

He found Bewick in the café being served by an old man in a red apron. Bewick had bought a large-scale map of Scalder Staithe and a guide book.

The coastline east and west of Wells was low-lying, strewn with sand bars. Channels wound inland to shallow drying harbours and the surrounding muddy creeks of marshes and saltings – to Scalder, to Burnham, to Brancaster. Of these harbours, Scalder Staithe was notorious for its two sand bars. One, guarding the entrance channel, was forever on the move and was re-buoyed after each bout of rough weather. The second lay well inside the entrance and caught out many a visiting yacht, although only the shallowest draught boats ever attempted an entrance. The effect of this second bar was to cause the incoming tide to pile up against it, creating back eddies which ran out towards the sea. This continued for the first couple of hours of the flood until the volume of water entering the harbour overwhelmed the back eddies. Then for some time a fierce rip poured through the channel. A similar phenomenon occurred on the ebb. This interval of tidal power, moving sometimes at six knots, was known locally as the Scaller Falls. Even a top international swimmer can manage little more than three knots in the flat water of a swimming pool. The Falls had been responsible for many fatalities. Where the waters of the haven at Scalder Staithe finally ran out into the sea stood Scales Howe, a small rough island of sand dunes.

'Get a load of this,' said Jones, delighted. 'This is the sort of thing that makes you think Britain isn't finished.' He waved the guide book at Bewick.

'Let's hear it then.'

' "Scales Howe has long defied the geography of the East Anglian coast. According to the rules, it should have been washed away generations ago; at the very least by the end of the seventeenth century. As at Dunwich and elsewhere, successive nights of storm-force winds driving spring tides down the funnel of the North Sea should eventually have overwhelmed Scales Howe and reduced it to legend. It would then have been rapidly eroded to become a merely fatal bar further complicating the entrance to Scalder Haven.

' "The tidal anomalies which preserve Scales Howe have long been debated by hydrographers, to no agreed conclusion. Its forty acres of steep dunes, its ruined chapel half buried in the sand and its derelict lighthouse stand in awkward defiance of thc best that scientific ingenuity and natural violence, that Cambridge and the North Sea can throw at it." There's lovely now, isn't it? "Scales Howe and Scalder Staithe, Romance and Legend, Flora and Fauna. By W. A. Lund, MA."'

'When was it written?'

Jones looked inside the front cover. '1965.'

The coffee and tea arrived. Bewick asked to see a local telephone directory. There were two Lunds in the book. One at Scalder Thorpe and a W. A. Lund at The Mount, Scalder Staithe.

'Who is that?'

A distinctive figure emerged from the village shop.

Grace Carver, who was having a bad day, stood for

a moment, mouthing her curses at the small world of Scalder Staithe. Her weathered face stared out from under an ancient waxed-cloth sou'wester, topped off with a plastic carrier bag, its handles tied under the chin with orange baling twine. The chin was thrust forward as if in constant challenge to anything that the world of the sane and reasonable might throw at it. She was holding two tins of steak in gravy, to which she and the hedgehogs whose company she cultivated were partial. An added advantage to her of the brand in question was that it came in ring-pull cans.

Aware of the fact that she was being watched, which she disliked, Grace stuck her tongue out, although not directly at the car where Gio Jones and Bewick sat. She made a few faces in variation on the theme, then walked off.

'Hands off the gear stick, you! What're you doing in there? Big man! Craggy. Craig-y-nos!' A snort of laughter. 'All the elements of light, eh?'

From the observation room built at the end of his house, a man watched this encounter with some of the old amusement he used to feel when watching Grace Carver's antics. Before, that is, she got as bad as she had recently. He could date the onset of her increased paranoia, but he had little idea what might have caused it.

Lund watched the two men getting out of the car. He didn't like the look of them. They looked soiled by the world; engaged with problematic events. They had that air, which was to be seen everywhere now, of weary aggression; of men who had no time, men too tired and impatient for courtesy. They were of the present, bound up in it; whereas Walter Lund lived for the past, in the past, surrounded by beautiful things.

Lund frowned. They were coming to his house, to his front door. He wondered if he should call the police, but called his wife instead.

Jones looked at the flint and brick house on its patch of rising ground which gave it an uninterrupted view of the salt marshes. It was very charming, with the two tones of off-white paint on its windows recently done. Even the boot scraper had just been painted. He rang the bell.

The end of the house was built into a squat tower. On this was constructed a glass and timber room, from which you could probably see clear over the dunes of Scalder Staithe to the sea itself.

The man Jones had noticed up there earlier didn't move when he rang the bell. A woman came round the side of the house. She was wearing herringbone tweed trousers tucked into rubber boots and was carrying a hedging hook. Margaret Lund gave the two men a brief glance, silently agreed with her husband's description of them as 'unsavoury' and said, without welcome, 'Yes?'

Jones smiled sweetly and held up the small guide-book. 'We came to consult your husband. We like his prose style.'

Margaret Lund thought for a moment. She didn't

think prose style was an issue in most criminal lives, nor in most salesmen's.

'I see. Who shall I say?'

'Detective Chief Inspector Jones and Superintendent Bewick,' replied Jones, giving the titles a bit of a flourish.

'Wait here, please.' Margaret Lund went into the house.

'Celtic gigolo,' said Bewick.

Lund came down to talk to them largely because of the seniority of Bewick's rank.

The drawing room was lined with books, a whole case of them dedicated to oriental ceramics, examples of which were on display.

Walter Lund was a soft-featured man who cultivated a benign absent-mindedness. He was bald, apart from two fluffy clouds of white hair above his ears. He wasn't any more welcoming than his wife. 'Please sit down gentlemen. Why are you here?'

Outside, Margaret Lund was raking the first of the autumn leaves from the lawn.

'We're inquiring into the death of a young lass,' Gio Jones replied, 'whose body was found near here the other day.'

'I thought all that had been resolved.'

'Mostly, yes. We read your guide . . . Your local knowledge . . . We thought . . .'

'Yes? There was nothing suspicious about the girl's

death, was there? The inquest seemed very straightforward.'

'You went to the inquest?'

'Oh yes. As a local historian, you know. A local tragedy weaves its way into local myth. It's something I should know about. That's why I went. Nothing else has come up, has it?'

'Not directly, no. One of the things we're interested in is people who may have come down immediately after she disappeared.'

'Well, quite a few – immediately after. But it was tremendously filthy weather. People braved it for a while, especially the family, of course, but they soon gave up.'

'These were people looking for thc body, were they?'

'Yes. They searched all the beaches east of here. That's where they expected her body to come ashore.'

'Which it didn't?'

'Which it didn't.'

'Then why were they searching there?'

'Someone had told them to expect it.'

'Who was that?'

Lund hesitated then he smiled. He clasped his hands together and rested them on his knee. His smile was arch, malicious. 'There is a colleague of yours in the local force who is, not to put too fine a point on it, a self-satisfied fool. Let's call him Smith. He has what one might call an executive manner. Anything that appeals to him he executes immediately.'

'So what did "Smith" do?' asked Jones. He knew who Lund must be talking about.

'Someone suggested he ask one of the Scalder fishermen where the tides might take a body which had fallen into the sea eight miles north-east of here. Good idea! thinks Smith and immediately asks the one man most likely to mislead him.'

'Wasn't he a fisherman?'

'Oh yes – he was the oldest fisherman that Smith could find, one Oswald Sutton. Trouble with Ozzie is that the old charlatan hasn't been out in a boat for twenty years. Also, he's very vain – far too vain to suggest to the executive-type Smith that he might ask the people who really know – the lads who are out fishing in it every day.

'No, Ozzie delivered his opinion and from then on that was the official line: if it comes ashore at all, the body will be found somewhere to the east – perhaps as far as Holkham.'

'And the unofficial line?'

'In the bar of the Lord Nelson they were talking, quite rightly, about west of here. The tidal eddies would hold it back. They doubted if it could even get as far as Scales Howe, never mind beyond it.'

'Which is where it was found?'

'Yes. What the lads in the bar hadn't properly allowed for was the wind strength. They knew it was strong – that's why they weren't at sea after all – but they didn't know how strong. In fact it blew at force nine for over six hours on one day, gusting much more.'

'How do you know that?'

'I have an anenometer on the roof of my study, my observation room.'

'Would anybody have looked for the body on the island?'

'Good God no. The splash was a torrent. No one in their right minds would have crossed to the island in those conditions. It was a proper storm, visibility was about zero.'

Lund was enjoying himself under Jones's mild interrogation. When Bewick spoke for the first time, his enjoyment evaporated. He had almost forgotten Bewick's presence.

'Why didn't you advise the girl's family?' Bewick asked. 'You have the knowledge. You're articulate. They would have listened to you.'

'Personally, I hoped they wouldn't find her. A body which has been in a North Sea storm of that magnitude would be a very distressing sight.'

'I'm sure it would,' said Bewick, 'but they were expecting it. As it was, they had a year of uncertainty and a sand-mummified corpse to deal with. Still, I'm sure you acted for the best. I suppose the fishermen, having not been consulted, volunteered nothing?'

'That's right.'

Jones could see that Bewick had somehow not offended Lund, whom he reckoned was a very touchy man. How did the bastard do it?

'If we were looking for anyone else,' Bewick was saying, 'apart from her family who came down immediately after Amy Parris was lost from the yacht, do you know who we should ask?'

Jones watched Lund's suspicion and vanity fighting with his desire to help Bewick, simply because of the man Bewick was. Suspicion won.

'No, I don't really.'

'Of course not, why should you? Thanks for your help.'

Bewick nodded to an exquisite sculpture of a Buddha, smooth and minimalist in dark stone, which stood carefully lit on the far side of the room.

'That's Thai-Cambodian, isn't it?'

Lund shot him a very sharp glance then confirmed that it was.

'I've been out that way recently,' Bewick said.

By the time they were leaving the house ten minutes later, they had a recommendation to talk to the postmistress Mrs Cahn, 'an observant woman', and had been given a sketch map of Scales Howe with instructions of where and when to cross to it.

On the doorstep, Lund volunteered more. 'There was one person I noticed, come to think of it. A young woman. She was part of one of the search parties, but then, later, she used to come down at weekends. She used to mooch about by herself.'

'Do you remember what she looked like?'

'I'm sorry. The young all look alike to me.'

Bewick smiled. 'Sure,' he said. 'Did you get to know Amy Parris's family at all?'

'No, I kept my distance. I find myself upset by others' suffering.'

Bewick took out his wallet. From it he took a couple of photographs of Julia Kelleher. 'This is the young woman you probably remember. Ring any bells?'

The fellow is eating out of Bewick's paw, thought Jones, in irritated admiration.

Lund nodded and admitted it was, but said that he'd never spoken to her.

' "That's Thai-Cambodian, isn't it?"' quoted Gio Jones, outraged. Bewick laughed.

'I just happened to see some. One of the diplomats was a collector. They're very distinctive once you've taken a good look at them.'

'Oh yes?'

Mrs Cahn in her post-office shop was a disappointment. She recognized the photos of Julia Kelleher, who had come in a number of times over the past year, but she hadn't said much to her.

'She seemed private, you know, kept her counsel.'

She'd seen her with a man once, 'When they all come looking for that girl's body, but only that once.' Her description of the man only amounted to a waxed jacket and glasses. Gio Jones reckoned this was probably Muir Hammond, her boss at Sirius, who said that he had come down to join the search for Amy's body and had gone afterwards to the family's home near Wickham Market.

'Aren't we doing this the wrong way round?' Jones complained, as he stomped along the gravelly sand in a spare pair of Bewick's wellies which were four sizes too large for him.

'Are we?'

'We should be talking to Amy's family, shouldn't we? Or maybe the good yachtie folk at Aldeburgh – not tramping around her last-but-one resting place. I mean, how is any of this going to tell us that she was on the run? If she ever was.'

'I thought we should see it, that's all. What about this evening? Think you can get permission from Eilean to stay out late?'

'Don't come the smug bachelor with me, mate.'

'If you can, we'll do that. We'll go to see Amy's family in Wickham Market.' Bewick walked in silence for some time. 'I wanted to see Scales Howe,' he said, 'because before her body was found, Amy's lover came here to mourn . . . came often. Then, once Amy's body had been found, Amy's lover, her mourner, was killed.'

'It's the most boring thing in the world to my wife, a map. She has the sense of direction of a lobotomized mole. Maps don't make it into three dimensions in her head, you see. She hardly even knows that up is generally north. Me, I love maps. Spatially I'm brilliant.'

Jones and Bewick were looking at the sketch map given them by Walter Lund.

'It'll be there,' Bewick said, looking at the water. 'The smooth patch there.' He pointed.

'Oh yes?'

'That disturbance to seaward will be where the water falls off the edge of the bar. The bar is the smooth bit.'

'Well, well.' Jones folded up the map and put it in his pocket.

They set off across the gravel shallows, the water about a foot deep. Their boots were flattened against their ankles by the pressure of the ebbing tide. The sun went in. The wind off the sea was now more noticeable.

Looking to landward, banks were beginning to dry, boats were canting over, some were already stranded near their mooring buoys. There was still a huge volume of water yet to leave. The sense of its power was beginning to impress itself on Jones. They were about a third of the way across.

'This is right, isn't it?' he asked Bewick. 'You don't think we should leave it another half hour?'

Bewick didn't deign to reply.

'It's all very well for you, junior champion freestyler and all, you'd probably survive. We who boast 48 per cent saturated flab, on the other hand . . .'

'Shut up,' said Bewick.

A couple of minutes later they were across, standing near the emergency beacon.

The cloud which had earlier covered the sun was the outrider of a thick shelf, darkening to the horizon. Over the island, the heaped dunes with their mops of grass were brighter than the sky now. Billions of grains of pale sand caught and seemed to hold the light. The grass hissed in the wind.

They read the notice by the beacon showing how the black barrel should be hoisted into the gallow trees either to indicate a stranding or an emergency. Nearby stood a hut, the survival shelter, its back to the sea. Nailed there was another notice, this time pleading with the reader not to vandalize the hut.

A boardwalk led inland along a valley between the dunes. According to Lund's map, it traversed the entire island. He had told them it was built to transport mussels brought ashore from the hard on the far side of the Howe. The valley had for some reason been fancifully named Vallombrosa.

The oak boards hadn't been maintained for years. Many of them were under the drifting sand and were broken, but the structure just about served. Bewick and Jones set off along it.

Bewick stopped. He was listening.

'What is it?'

They stood in the mid-section of the valley. A bend behind them deadened any noise off the land. A bend ahead blanketed the noise of the sea. Bewick stood still in the unusual silence. What was he up to?

Then Jones heard it himself. Someone was singing; not very well. The notes slipped, the rhythm slipped. The intonation was childish; the voice mature. The effect was a bit crazy.

'Eternal Father strong to save,
Whose arm hath bound the restless wave . . .'

Then another voice interrupted, high above them. Canada geese, a tidy V of them, flew overhead to unknown feeding grounds. The leading bird regularly repeated its haunting call. And then:

'Oh hear us when we cry to thee . . .'

The singing stopped. Jones heard the next line in his head.

'For those in peril on the sea.'

Bewick remained still for a moment longer. The silence was deep, a presence. He moved off.

Some minutes later they emerged on to the north-westerly shore of the island. The sands stretched flat for a quarter of a mile to a line of breakers sparkling white under looming cloud.

Ahead was the hard – a masonry ramp, later refaced in concrete, which ran out across the sand for about two hundred feet.

To their left, the ruined Victorian lighthouse stood on its islet. To their right its modern replacement, the Haweshead light, stood on its steel lattice base above another shoal just off the end of Scales Howe itself. Automatic, it shone its double flash every thirty seconds relentlessly, day or night; too bright to look at comfortably even in full daylight.

They heard the melancholy honk-honk of the geese again and looked upwards. The sky was empty. From behind them they heard a high childish laugh. For a moment they caught a glimpse of a delighted Grace Carver jumping up and down, mouth open. Then she ducked and disappeared. They heard her goose call again, muffled now by the dunes.

'Is that the woman mentioned in the Amy Parris file, do you think?' Bewick asked.

''Course! Yes. That'll be her. Should've realized when she came out the village shop just now. Yeah. Grace Carver. Sculptress and bag-lady.'

'That's right. Sculptress . . .'

'Sculptress, vocal impressionist, schizophrenic and recluse. The witch of Scales Howe. Not so much your care in the community, more your no-care on the desert island.'

'I'd like to meet her,' said Bewick.

They walked along the northern shoreline towards the lighthouse. Tiny amber red pebbles, washed into ridges, lay across their path like miniature groins.

It was clear that Grace was keeping pace with them, out of sight behind the cliffs of sand and grass. Snatches of hymns Ancient and Modern came to them on the wind. Once they heard the high night-barking of a dog fox perfectly imitated. Later it was the sharp knocking sound of a pheasant alarmed.

Bewick stopped and looked around. 'I reckon it would have been about here.'

'Yes?'

'Where the body was found.'

In the quietness which followed the stilled crunching of their boots, they heard a new sound. At first Jones thought it was the wind blowing across the tops of the dunes or a fog warning offshore. Despite thickening cloud, however, visibility was clear over the sea. The wind was light.

It was a moan, a non-human sound, rising and falling like the natural music made by a gale blowing across the chimneys and cracks of an old house; but there was neither house nor gale.

Realizing it was Grace, the two men looked at each other. From the fade and rise of the sound, she would be walking about not far from them, behind the sands.

Bewick walked down the beach towards the sea, then turned back to look at the rising ground which was now visible to him in the interior of the island. The moaning sound stopped.

'Big man,' Grace murmured to herself. She was wary of this pair. Wary of her attraction, wary of her wariness.

Most people in Grace's world divided into two lots: Dere-Deres and Yahoo Scum.

Dere-Deres were patronizers. Mad with neatness.

Very grown up. Pat-pat patronize. Pat chaos on the head and call it a good dog. There there. As if you could pat the ocean. Never tried to paddle in it, never mind navigate. Never been out on it. Knew nothing.

Yahoo Scum were foul and stupid. They were the ones with pus brains, with built-in malice-beforethought. They had locked doors in their heads, doors they couldn't open. They went running up and down dim passages of closed doors. Sniffing and shitting. Maddened, they went in search of other people's to crash through.

Yahoo Scum she feared. Luckily they were stupid enough to think her stupid, so she had always outwitted them so far.

This pair though. . . . They were like the other one who had come; who wouldn't tell her what he wanted. He had known she wouldn't give it to him if he named it. So he wouldn't name it. Yet he wanted to desperately.

This pair were seekers too . . . Big as a truck, look at him. Lorry and Hardy. Seen it all.

Oh look, bowing . . . Sir Walter Bicycle . . .

Jones saw Bewick bow courteously from the waist. He'd seen her.

Grace shivered. She began her moaning lament again. Yes, they were different . . . The big one had been there; the place where no one wants to go. He'd been there. He knew what it was like. He hadn't forgotten. Lord Foden, Sir Walter Scania.

She turned away, singing, knowing he'd follow, wondering if he'd see.

It looked like the chapel it had once been, even though most of the stones had fallen long enough ago to be buried. It had been a ruin since the middle of the previous century, appearing on Victorian maps as such. In the late 1940s it had briefly been the responsibility of the local council, who had ordered the stabilization of what was left.

Walk past, glance briefly and it was a ruin, nothing else. Even the knowledgeable who came here regularly, who could tell you that the original chapel pre-dated Henry VIII's destruction of old Catholic England, or that the stone dressings of the flint and rubble walls were very similar to the stone of Norwich cathedral and probably came from northern France – even they could stand and look and not see it.

It required a receptive mood, observation and a moment of innocence perhaps, to see what it had been transformed into; transformations intended to be invisible at first and even second glance; transformations, code.

The two men climbed the sand scarps up to it. Jones was left well behind and when he finally caught up, Bewick was standing in the arch at the west end. He was looking around the ruin full of interest.

'It's going to rain,' said Jones as he came panting up.

'There's something . . .' Bewick gestured to the four ruined walls.

'What?'

'I don't know. It feels odd.'

Jones looked around the walls, bare but for scrappy vegetation. All he could see was a crude hand shape, partly following the shape of the lid of the tinned ham from which it had been cut. It was rusty, jammed into a crevice on the northern wall. 'It's going to rain.'

'Yeah.' Bewick nodded and looked up at the clouds.

A hiss of wind through the surrounding grasses heralded the arrival of the rain. It came in a cold torrent as the dark squall-line of cloud passed overhead.

Jones and Bewick sheltered in the lee of the chapel's western wall. As they stood there they saw they were almost on the highest point of the island, only the hollows beyond the taller dunes were hidden from them.

When the rain eased, they hurried directly across the island towards the Splash.

She was bitterly disappointed in him. How could he run off without seeing it? She nearly called out to him, to tell him what a suck-faced vermiculate bastard . . .! She would! But when she tried, all that came out was a hoot of laughter, a wild cackle.

Neither Jones nor Bewick heard Grace's laughter as they followed the sand valleys. They were quickly lost in a natural maze with dead-ends and doublings-back of deceptive familiarity. Eventually Bewick decided that by following the passage of the squall-line above them they could give themselves a direction.

They climbed and descended for several minutes, Bewick waiting at the top of each dune for the panting Gio Jones. At the top of one of them he pointed down and to the left. In a narrow cleft between two dunes which were in the process of joining was a small shelter made of driftwood and weathered plastic sheeting. Above it, planted high up in the slope of sand, like a witch's cloutie-tree, was an old carousel clothes dryer, turning in the wind. It was hung with beach-combed objects: manes of seaweed, tins, plastic bottles, shreds of polythene, bits of bleached tree root, pale abraded wood, sand-ground glass jars – all objects evidently touched by the sea.

The squeak of the turning clothes dryer followed them as they pressed on. As it faded they briefly heard singing again; this time discordant, angry.

'So now we have to ask the difficult ones: like what the hell were we doing here?'

'And was it worth the effort?'

'Exactly.'

'It was worth the effort.'

'Convince me.'

They were sitting in the car on the quay at Wells.

The car windows were open to stop it steaming up from their damp clothes. They'd found the café closed but had come across a fish and chip van and were each eating a portion of fries. Polystyrene cups of tea steamed under the windcreen.

'We now know that the body was washed ashore at a point invisible from the mainland.'

'We knew that anyway.'

'No we didn't. We also know that local people don't like going to the island, won't go there, in fact, in rough weather. Also there's a sensible explanation for them looking for the body in the wrong place.'

'That makes it worth it?'

'We know too that Julia Kelleher came here.'

'To mourn. I mourn therefore I'm killed? Come on.'

'Or she might have been coming here to look for the body. She might have been trying to investigate what she thought was a murder.'

It was dark before they parked outside the terrace in Wickham Market. Richard Parris's voice on the telephone had been quick, authoritative. Jones had been expecting a larger house from the voice, which had confidence, authority. Richard and Emily Parris were teachers and Catholics. The house was bursting with their children.

Richard was giving a 'cello lesson elsewhere by the time they arrived. Emily Parris showed them into a small room littered with sheet music and books. On a torn sofa a cat slept in an open violin case. She cleared a chair and one end of the sofa. She sat at her desk in the corner.

The pressures she was under were obvious. The condolences and courtesies were quickly out of the way.

'In danger? Felt herself to be in danger? Would that be it? You're not suggesting . . .?'

'No,' said Bewick. 'We're confident at present that her death was an accident . . .'

'An accident?' Mrs Parris sounded surprised and looked at Bewick curiously.

As Bewick looked back, she saw the flare of immediate understanding and something else; an illusionless sympathy, which she valued greatly.

'Amy had . . . My daughter had a history of mental upset. She admitted herself to Fulbourn twice when she was an undergraduate. All I can tell you is that it's unlikely Amy would have been in the cockpit of a boat at night without being clipped on, unless . . . unless she intended harm to herself.'

'I see . . .' Bewick's voice rumbled. It was a long-drawn-out sigh.

'Clipped on?' Jones asked. 'You mean a safety line of some sort?'

'Yes. They were set up on the boat in question. I asked the skipper – that rather unprepossessing journalist. They weren't Gibb locking clips, mind you. They were the old-fashioned sort and they can come open far too easily. So I suppose there's some room for doubt.'

'It makes a difference to the way I think about the case, nevertheless. That possibility hasn't been mentioned before,' Bewick said gently.

'Nobody seemed interested.' Emily Parris smiled. 'It's not the sort of information one is likely to offer to the uninterested.'

'Did you know Julia Kelleher, Mrs Parris?'

'Julia was obsessed with my daughter: it really was like a crush.' Emily Parris blinked and coloured slightly as if ashamed of her own suspicions. 'I think it was a reaction to her marriage. Amy told me that David Toner was a frightful man. He said he hated the army but behaved as if that was the only place he really wanted to be. He'd been in one of those outfits that prides itself on its toughness, but doesn't have the discipline of the elite regiments. Amy called him a self-deceiver, stupid and brutal.'

She stopped for a moment, a brusque turn of the head as if to rid herself of thoughts of her daughter in front of these strangers.

'Do you know if Amy had a man in her life, Mrs Parris?'

'She had men after her, which was quite surprising really as she made very little effort to attract them. She'd had affairs . . . well, we discussed contraception more than once. I honestly don't know what was happening in her private life at the time she was lost.'

'Would you say that Amy would be the sort of

person who would come to you if things became critical in her life?'

'Yes I do. Anything to do with her work she seemed to deal with easily. Her emotional life . . .' Emily Parris stopped. She looked at Bewick candidly. 'I realize I haven't thought about it much,' she said. 'As a matter of fact I don't think she would have come to me by the end. I think she would have dealt with her own crises in the end. Well, she did, didn't she?'

'Do you think she may have joined that yacht with the intention – '

'I don't know,' interrupted Mrs Parris. 'How is that important?'

'She should have been at work. It was very uncharacteristic of her, I understand, not to turn up for work without making arrangements.'

'What?'

Bewick described Amy's movements, as far as they'd been able to interpret them, before her joining the yacht.

Emily Parris frowned. 'I didn't know any of this.'

'I expect Mr Hammond didn't want to trouble you when he came to see you.'

'Possibly not. Although he didn't seem particularly sensitive to me.'

'I have a theory that she was on the run. Someone was hounding her. That this oppressed her enough to do what she did.'

Emily Parris was silent for some time. 'Yes,' she

said, 'that would make sense. But I have no idea what it might have been, I'm afraid.'

They drove back to Cambridge. As if they had exhausted their capacity to speculate about the case, they began talking desultorily about the Swindon road killings, which had been in the papers that week. The driver had killed five young people doing eighty in a forty speed-limit zone. He'd got five years.

'A year per life. The families must be pissed off as hell.'

Bewick remembered that he had promised to ring George and Kit that evening to give them a progress report.

Gio Jones saw a phone box in a lay-by near RAF Lakenheath. Bewick retrieved his address book from his bag and made his call.

Jones watched a pair of fighter bombers come in to land. He had once been told that one of these machines was capable of devastating an area the size of Birmingham. He smiled as he remembered this. It was meaningless. Like death itself, it was beyond thought.

Bewick got back in the car. Jones asked him about the Criminal Justice Act 1991, which had just come into effect. He knew he should know about it and hadn't had the energy to read the bumph. He knew Bewick would have it at his fingertips, despite having been abroad for months. The meat of the legislation was the fact that a range of fines were now means-tested. He was right. Bewick knew. Bloody Bewick always bloody knew.

9

The woman's face jerked sideways. She made no effort to defend herself: as if she was offering her passivity as a form of defiance.

Drunk, the man sensed the defiance, but it was her passivity which frustrated him. He hit her again. A sob of anger came from him as each blow drove home until the woman was collapsed across the darkened hallway of the small house.

The front doorbell rang. The man, stooped over her, froze. The woman's breathing bubbled through the blood in her nose and the back of her throat.

The bell rang again. The man lurched towards the lit room at the back of the house. Slowly, painfully, in the darkness, the woman climbed to her feet.

Bewick stood at the front door of David Toner's house. The small house was one of a row fronting the brook which ran the length of the village street. Each house had a bridge from its garden across the brook on to the street. Each bridge embodied a different idea of what a bridge should be. Across the road stretched a long range of thatched barns, punctuated by a red phone box. Dallington was undoubtedly picturesque.

The door opened. The woman stood staring at Bewick stupefied, snoring through her own blood. In the orange lamplight, the blood looked brown.

Without a word, Bewick took her hand and with an arm around her shoulder helped her quickly over the threshold and down the path away from the house. When she was sitting in the passenger seat of his car, a rug round her, he asked her, 'What's your name?'

'Mary Crofton.'

'Do you live with David Toner?'

A nod greeted this.

'Did he do this to you?'

Another nod.

'Is he still in there?'

'Yes. Listen, he's drunk, be careful.'

Bewick ignored this. 'What do you want to do?'

'Do?'

'Do you want to bring charges?'

The woman turned away. In the streetlight Bewick could see that the side of her face was beginning to swell; the skin stretching, shiny.

Bewick waited for her to speak. A tractor, a warning light swivelling, came noisily down the village street, preventing Bewick from hearing the movement behind him. The woman turned back. Her eyes widened. 'Look out!'

Bewick, who was on his haunches at the open passenger door, moved too late. The door thumped him; the breath hissed out of him. He bounced the door outwards. Then he flung himself flat and rolled. The man's kick caught him but was neutralized by the roll.

Bewick fell and slid through nettles and hit the chill of water. He was on his hands and knees. He floundered a short way, his feet in soft mud. As he straightened up, a boot swung at him but missed. Bewick moved into range. Toner kicked out. Bewick lunged and grabbed. He had Toner around the waist, his head pressed into Toner's chest. Toner's fists flailed but only hit Bewick's back. Bewick released Toner enough to head-butt him.

As the hard bone crunched into his face, Toner grunted. Bewick pushed him away. Blind with pain, Toner lashed out, stumbling forward. Bewick rammed his right knee into Toner's balls. Toner stretched forward, his mouth gasped open. Bewick hit him on the back of the neck, lifting his knee again as he did so.

Toner turned away and began to crawl up the steep bank of the ditch. He was whimpering. Bewick hauled himself out of the water. He stood over Toner. He stamped very hard on one of Toner's ankles. Then he kicked out savagely at the back of the thigh of the same leg. Toner roared with pain, then collapsed moaning. Bewick returned to the car.

'What did you do that for?'

Mary Crofton could see that Bewick was shaking. He looked pale and disturbed. Suddenly his head reared up and panted air into his body, straightening and arching his back. 'Always kick a man when he's down. It's a rule,' Bewick said. 'Or he might get up again.'

He reached across his body to touch his left shoulder, the one which had been hit by the edge of the car door. He didn't complete the movement. He froze, and the breath whistled out of his body as the pain hit him.

Bewick walked the few yards to the phone box. He was soon speaking to City West.

It took the two police vehicles twenty minutes to arrive. During that time, Toner tried twice to move off, but the pain from his crushed ankle dissuaded him. Only one person walked past. He stood for a moment on the opposite pavement trying to work out what was going on. Eventually he asked, 'OK?'

'Thanks. I'm CID,' lied Bewick. 'I'm waiting for my colleagues.'

'Uh-huh. Right.'

A mist began to form above the brook. A Ford Orion came slowly round the bend, its headlights reflecting off the mist. It stopped and reversed. The driver's window lowered and a woman surveyed the scene. 'Did you hit him?'

'Yes,' said Bewick.

'With your car?'

'Not with my car.'

'Pity. Bastard shite, that one. Hit him with your car next time, why don't you?'

Mary Crofton sat in the car slumped with her eyes

shut. Occasionally she voiced a protest at the pain which was taking her over, otherwise she was silent. Bewick checked twice to make sure she was warm enough, otherwise he ignored her, keeping his eye on Toner.

Toner, the inheritor of two hundred thousand pounds, beat up women. His alibi depended on the corroboration of the woman now sitting in Bewick's car: someone he could intimidate.

Gio Jones, when he arrived, grasped this point immediately. He took Bewick aside. 'You don't need to say it. History of violence. Two hundred K. Fuck you and I've got the picture. What happened to him? He's going to sue every copper south of the Wash, he says.'

Bewick pulled open his jacket and shirt to show Jones the crush wound spreading across his back.

'Self-defence? Fair enough. Will she witness for you?'

'More to the point: will she stick to her alibi corroboration?'

'DI Quinney is taking her to a women's refuge. She can ask her. But you know the form. What the girlfriend says tonight and what she says tomorrow may be chalk and cheese. Still, worth a go. She a drinker too? He stinks.'

'I don't think so.'

'That's something. There are doormats and there are drunken doormats. So there's hope. Right . . .' He turned to go, then turned back. 'That injury – take it to a medic. You've got to have something in writing in case the stupid bastard has a stupid bastard lawyer in tow. Meanwhile, we'll charge him with assault.'

'OK.'

'Off you go then. You all right to drive with that shoulder?'

At the City Hospital it took Bewick nearly two hours to be seen by the appropriate medic. He had changed his sodden filthy clothes and showered before he went.

'Yes, yes, I see. The diagonal welt and associated bruising would be where the edge of the door caught you.' Dr Carvalho made notes. 'And this other bruise is where you were struck by the boot. Very good.' Carvalho glanced again at Bewick's torso, which was a manuscript of faded scars. He wondered what had caused them. He was sure that few of them were contemporary with one another.

The door opened. A nurse had brought X-rays. Carvalho clipped them up on a light-box. The nurse left.

'Nothing broken, as you can see,' he said. 'Good. Are you all right to dress yourself?'

'I'll help him.' Karen Quinney stood in the open doorway.

'A colleague,' Bewick explained.

Carvalho smiled as if Bewick had said something fatuous. 'I'll leave you in her capable hands. You will be receiving a letter from me. Please allow five days. Excuse me now.'

Karen Quinney helped him into his vest and shirt. She stood very close to him doing up the buttons, her head bowed. She was wearing Cristalle. There were blonde hairs on her wrists, paling the brown skin.

Karen didn't look at him until she had finished buttoning his shirt and moved away.

'What did you do with Mary Crofton?' Bewick asked.

Karen looked at him. She saw that he had been holding himself back. She was relieved. Where there was lust there was hope. She was hot. It took her time to answer. 'We took her to a refuge. One of those streets off Mill Road . . . you know, what's her name? Sister Patience! That's it. Sister Patience – the fourteen-stone bride of Christ. It was either a road gang or the veil for her. I don't know many blokes who'd take her on, with or without gloves. So Crofton'll be safe enough there.'

'And Toner's alibi?'

'Grey area, I reckon. She was prepared to talk about it being crap. But I don't think she'd go to a signed statement. She's a very confused woman.'

'What do you think?'

'I don't think she was in a state to remember much.'

He was looking at her steadily, without speaking. She found it intimidating and looked away.

'Why did you come here?' he asked.

'To see you were OK.'

They were only a few feet apart. It would be so simple, she thought, to take that step towards him. Even as she thought it, she knew she wouldn't.

'That was good of you,' Bewick said.

What did that mean? 'Thank you, I fancy you, but keep your distance'?

Karen shrugged and smiled, making light of it. 'I only live a few minutes away. Didn't know if you'd be driving, with that shoulder.'

They walked through the never-sleeping hospital.

'You really sorted out that Toner bloke.'

'He's stupid.'

'Why did you go to talk to him?'

'I could spin you a theory, but . . .'

'No, go on.'

'Gio Jones wouldn't approve.'

'I need his approval?'

'Something like this then. Toner realizes that Joe Enwright is having an affair with his ex-wife. He's furious. He's pissed. He wants to kill. He also realizes that if he does kill, he pockets two hundred K. He goes to Julia's house.

'He's hidden in the garden. He sees Enwright getting dressed. They've been screwing. Julia's on the phone and doesn't get off it. Enwright leaves on his bike, fed up with her phoning.

'Toner goes in. There's a row. He kills her. All he thinks is, if Enwright's been having sex with her then the evidence will be there. Nowadays, he knows, that can be traced. He thinks he's got both of them; and two hundred K.'

Karen Quinney walked in silence for a few yards. Then they both stood aside to let a trolley past. 'I don't see what's wrong with that, except . . .'

'Except for two things. Firstly, Gio Jones has spent much longer with the boy than I have, and he has him down as a killer. I spent years profiting from Gio Jones's judgement. Why should that suddenly change? Secondly, the boy denies any involvement with Julia Kelleher. It's been made clear to him that things may go better if he admits to having an affair with her. He won't admit it.'

Outside, the car park was deserted. Karen insisted on seeing Bewick at the wheel of his car and being satisfied that he was able to change gear before she left him.

He took her hand through the open window. He looked into her eyes for a moment as if he was going to say something important. Then he looked down. 'Thanks,' he said and withdrew his hand.

Karen drove like a teenage drunk to get to her house, five minutes away.

In the spartan modern bedroom, with the teddy bear on the chest of drawers and the weights in the corner, she lay naked on her back, tears flowing, her fist thumping the mattress.

'All I want is for him to fuck me,' she said to the empty room. 'Is that too much to ask?' But she knew it wasn't all she wanted; and she knew it was too much to ask.

George glanced at Kit. She met his eyes for a moment and then looked away. 'I don't know,' she said.

'What is it?' asked Bewick.

Kit nodded to George. 'He's telling me to keep my mouth shut. That's what it is.'

'Tell him,' said George, resigned.

They were sitting, in sunshine, on the terrace of George and Kit's house with its view of the vast stretch of the fens. They were out of the wind, which was bending a line of poplars below them into goose quills.

'Well, there was something wrong,' said Kit. 'But there'd never been the publicity, not then – even if it has been a bit hysterical – it wasn't something as crossed your mind in them days . . . I mean people using young children for sex. Do you see it? I can't see it. What do they get out of it?'

Bewick looked at George, who sat staring at his hands for a moment before he looked up and explained. 'We talked about it when all that stuff came up in the papers. We thought, you know, that maybe there'd been something going on like that with Phil's children . . . As I say, we couldn't prove nothing. Anyway, after a bit we reckoned it wasn't going on no more, if it ever had been. Joe was the youngest and he was changing girlfriends like racing tyres by then.'

There was a silence.

Then Bewick said, 'The plea would have to be guilty to be able to use it.'

''Course. Sure.'

'And then Phil got himself killed. End of story. I just felt, you know, that you should hear about it.'

'What made you think it in the first place?'

'Oh lots of things – little things, you know,' Kit replied. 'Things weren't right. You couldn't put your finger on it, but . . . like that pool business.'

'Yeah, we'd just had the pool built,' George chimed in, 'and we had a party. We were still talking to Phil in them days.'

He nodded to Kit, who said, 'There was a bit of horseplay going on in the shallow end with some of the youngsters. Phil was showing off up the deep end. Then he swam down to the shallow end. He puts his arm around Joe's shoulder, friendly you know. Joe froze; just froze. Phil took his arm away. Joe didn't look right or left. He walked straight out of the pool and kept going. And it wasn't an ordinary moody from a fifteen-year-old. It didn't seem, well, real, if you know what I mean. It was as if he knew people might be watching and he wanted to tell them something very important. It was things like that.'

Bewick nodded and pondered. 'It could have been a reaction to straightforward bullying of some sort or another,' he said.

'Sure,' said George.

'Which could have been nearly as harmful in the

end,' Bewick went on. 'Shame, powerlessness – it all makes for self-damage.'

'Sure. You tried to talk to him about it, didn't you?' George said to Kit.

'Dare say I wasn't too clever about it,' Kit replied.

'Anyway, he wouldn't tell us about it. If there was anything to tell.'

Bewick smiled. 'He's not one of life's great communicators, is he? Did he ever have a regular girlfriend?'

'No.' George took a deep breath; he was uncomfortable. 'I reckon, you see, John, that the girlfriends were . . . well, quite honestly, John, I think he's just as interested in men.'

'That might make sense.'

'When he come to live with us,' Kit said, 'I tried to read books about it; but I'm too stupid. That's another thing I won't understand, I reckon.'

'Did you talk to his mother about any of this?'

'Lesley's been very ill.'

Again, Kit and George exchanged a glance.

'We don't know much about Lesley, where she come from,' Kit went on. 'Phil more or less said: "This is my wife – take her or leave her." Nobody knew about her. She had no family.'

'But you heard rumours?'

'There'll always be rumours to fill in, won't there?' said Kit.

'Some said she was a tinker. A gippo from Soham Fen was how they put it. She was dark haired and highly coloured when she was younger. Maybe that was the start of that one.'

'And lovely teeth. She was a beautiful young woman when Phil found her. She put on a bit of weight later.'

'There was another idea,' said George, ' – that Phil had picked her up in Soho and never let her go back. Well, what did that make her? A stripper was the kindest thing they said.'

'It was her looks,' said Kit. 'Exotic, a bit, you know. A touch of the Ava Gardners. And she wouldn't never go into church. She just wouldn't. You can imagine what people thought up to cover that one.'

'I like her, mind,' said George. 'Can't say as I really knows her. But what I seen, I like.'

'How bad is she now?'

'No so good. I'm not sure she takes much in. They keep her so full of drugs now, it's difficult to talk to her.'

In the annexe stood George's full-size snooker table. The walls were decorated with pre-war metal advertising signs. Outside the glass doors, the bubble-wrap-covered swimming pool was still full.

George gestured to it. 'Did you know we get the same rainfall here as Tel Aviv?' He squinted along the line of his cue. 'I was swimming last weekend. It's very sheltered.' He was quiet for a moment as he played his shot. He was giving Bewick a pasting.

'Did you go to Phil's inquest, George?'

‘’Course I did. Misadventure, they said. In other words he was pissed.’

‘Do you miss him?’

George straightened up from the table. ‘No I don’t. I didn’t like to think he was my brother. I didn’t wish him dead, but I wished he wasn’t part of my life. I had this idea he might go and live in Australia. He mentioned it once and I thought it would be great if he did. But – ’ George shrugged.

‘The house you’re trying to sell – Lesley’s house – is that the house Phil and Lesley always lived in?’

‘No. Lesley sold up after he died. She took this place quick for cash.’

‘Would it be all right for me to have a look round?’

‘Sure. I’ll get you the key.’

‘Why did you come by cab?’ George asked as he opened up the garage.

‘The car . . .’ Bewick said and gestured vaguely. ‘Think I’m going to have to hire one.’

‘I could’ve come and fetched you.’

Bewick didn’t tell him how he had left his house under the cover of a delivery van serving the shops nearby. A brisk few steps past some lock-up garages, then a short narrow footpath and he was in Milburn Avenue, which leads to the Barton Road. The taxi had been waiting in Milburn Avenue. No vehicle in his street would have had a chance of following.

George drove him to Newmarket Road, where Bewick hired himself a car.

★

It was an anonymous house on an anonymous estate. From the outside the house looked just completed. There was no garden to speak of, just a couple of squares of grass which George kept in order.

Bewick opened the door. There was still a smell of newness in the air: glue, varnish, paint, the factory smell of the new carpet. Net curtains dissuaded the curious from looking in. Not that there was much to see. In one room stood a sofa with a sleeping bag slung over it, facing a TV on the floor in the corner. Apart from this the ground floor was empty.

Upstairs it was different. One room was crammed with furniture and there were tea chests and cardboard boxes everywhere. Objects had been taken out to be used and those disturbed by this had been left as they lay. Some had been tidied – George's conscience probably – but none returned to its box.

Bewick wandered around the litter of Mrs Enwright's and her son's interrupted lives for about twenty minutes. Then he left, leaving the place exactly as he had found it.

The nurse's shoes squeaked on the shiny floor. 'Mr Enwright, her brother-in-law, comes nearly every day,' she said. 'I'm very impressed with that man. He said you might come.'

Bewick stood in the doorway of the side ward. Lesley Enwright was dying, there was no mistaking it. Whatever blood was being pumped around her thin body wasn't reaching the surface. Her skin was grey and chalky. Hair and small blemishes stood out unnaturally on it; the writing on the wall.

She gave him a brave smile of greeting. 'You're the fellow who's going to help Joe, aren't you?'

'That's right.'

As Bewick and she talked, despite the fact that she seemed to drift in and out of the reality of the present, it was clear that she was capable of taking in more than George had suggested.

Bewick told her how he was trying to discover an alternative explanation for the evidence the police had found. He didn't tell her, nor did she give any indication of knowing, what that was. He asked her if Joe had any particular friends. She told him she wouldn't know them even if he had. There was no girlfriend.

Bewick watched the woman sucking air in and out of her wrecked body. He turned away and looked out of the window at the flat extended fields which stretched away to the Gog Magog Hills. When he looked back, it was to meet a pair of dark eyes fixed on him in a kind of query. They clouded and then, without prompting, Lesley began speaking: a painful effort.

'Joe was supposed to go in the car with Phil that night, you know, the night of Phil's accident. He wouldn't go. He had a bad relationship with his father at that time. And he knew his father would be drinking. He hated that. Joe serviced the car for Phil mind, he'd always do that. Joe loved anything mechanical. I used to say to him, a girl'd have to grow wheels before you could love her. Nothing would make him go that night. He'll be drinking, he said, and that was that. Nothing'd make him go. Perhaps . . . he felt something.'

Her face troubled, she panted rapidly and closed her eyes. Soon her breathing regularized into a shallow wheeze. She was asleep. Bewick took Lesley Enwright's hand briefly: he would never see her again.

The onset of sleep had been so rapid, Bewick went to find a nurse.

Bewick stood watching the parking bay outside Radiography where he had left the hire car. He waited just inside the door, with it held ajar so that he was invisible from outside. He watched for about three minutes. Then he ran to the car. He drove quickly round the main complex, past the Frank Lee Centre to the Long Road exit. He turned left. The traffic was normal. He kept pace with it, checking his mirrors to watch for signs of abnormal driving behind him. There were none.

10

Sally realized as she walked up the platform that she felt nervous; a faint chill in the stomach, a drying of the mouth. Her pace slowed. A man behind nearly walked into her. She was oblivious.

She had, she knew, been behaving oddly that morning. As if to demonstrate to herself a carelessness about her meeting with Bewick, she had put on old clothes, dead nonchalant. The clothes might have been old but they suited her: the top with just enough stretch to emphasize her breasts, the skirt revealing exactly what it should. The part of her which understood this had been stifled; until now. Of course she cared what she looked like! Now cross with herself, as well as nervous, for this crass attempt at self-deception, she was hoping John Bewick would be late and not waiting to meet her as promised.

She saw him as soon as she turned into the station foyer, his size emphasized by his stillness. She had an impression for a moment of his being a rock, around which the people near seemed to flow like water. Then the observing grey eyes were on her, the sombre face was lighting up with recognition and she found herself a moment later being kissed on the cheek.

'It's a hire car.'

They had turned left at the Catholic church and were now driving along Lensfield Road past the Scott Polar Institute.

Sally had said nothing to prompt this: just glanced around the very clean, impersonal interior surreptitiously as she leant over to the back seat to retrieve a tissue from her bag. The sureness of his observation could have irritated her, but she found herself delighted by it.

'I suppose the first thing to know is that about 70 per cent of our DNA is junk,' said Sally, ten minutes later.

'Junk?'

'It doesn't code for anything. It's the other 30 per cent which codes for everything, from the shape of your nose to the chemistry of your liver.'

'I didn't know that.'

'DNA which codes for something is quite similar between individuals. So it wasn't until the junk was known to be junk that DNA profiling for individuals became possible. By their junk shall ye know them.'

'How?'

'Imagine a number of children. Each child is given a jumble of letters. First of all, from the pile of letters each child is asked to spell out certain words – the same words for every child. These recognizable words are then laid out in a line with gaps in between.

'Now each child is asked to arrange other letters, any letters, to fill these gaps, quite randomly. When they've completed the task, the spelt-out words will be roughly common to all the children. What'll be unique to each child are the random bits in between. You see what I'm driving at?'

'You're saying that the "words" represent genetic material which codes for something – the shape of your nose, say – and which is roughly common to all human beings. The random stuff on either side of it will be unique to the individual.'

'You've got it. That's it, very crudely speaking.'

They were standing in the Cavendish Laboratory's small private museum. In front of them was one of the great icons of science: a model, about a yard high, of the double helical deoxyribonucleic acid molecule – DNA. Made in monochrome metal with the four nucleotide bases boldly marked and one of the helixes omitted for simplicity, it was a half-sized version of the model built for Crick and Watson in the fifties. Near it were references to Bragg's pioneering work in X-ray crystallography which made the discovery possible. Sally liked the model, its low-key functionalism.

'So there it is,' said Sally. 'Crick's monument. The technicolour version is in the MRC lab at the New Addenbrooke's . . . The Cavendish was in Free School Lane in those days, you know. Although they did the double helix work in the old bicycle shed at the back, on the museums' site. Does The Eagle still do lunches?'

'Yes. I think so.'

'The Eagle is where Crick used to hold court in the fifties when it all happened. If you're going to have your ear bent about DNA, it really should be in The Eagle.'

They drove from the New Cavendish in its spare, landscaped setting to the west of the city, along the Madingley Road to park in Queens' Road.

There was a gateman on duty at the Backs entrance to King's. Sally explained that she was a senior member and they were allowed in. They walked along the avenue towards the bridge, the meadow to their left grazed by cattle.

They paused on the bridge and looked across the expanse of lawn: one of the most famous views in the world, and at its centre King's College chapel.

'I never get tired of it, even though it's such a cliché. When I'm dying there are two places I'll remember: Scales Howe and King's chapel.'

'Scales Howe?'

'Do you know it?'

'There was a body found there a couple of weeks ago.' Bewick looked as if he might say more, but left it.

'Oh yes. I remember. Are you involved in that?'

'In a way.'

'Scales Howe is ordinary enough, I suppose. It's

probably only special to me,' said Sally. 'It's somewhere I went as a child. I'm quite careful with it: I don't go there often enough to blunt the magic.'

They walked on, past the Gothic buildings on the south side of the court.

'There's a set of rooms in there,' Sally said, pointing upwards to a square-bayed window, 'where the doors and panelling were decorated by Dora Carrington.'

Bewick, who didn't know who Dora Carrington was, had it explained to him that she was the suicidal lover of Lytton Strachey who was the friend and lover of the great economist Maynard Keynes who was for a while the bursar of King's and who was married to a Russian ballerina, who . . . 'Do you have a favourite place in Cambridge?' asked Sally, conscious that she was talking more than she liked.

'I'll show it to you after lunch if you like.'

They entered Bene't Street. Opposite the small church with its Saxon tower was the gateway to The Eagle's courtyard. Sally turned and pointed to an alleyway running under the high wall of Corpus Christi, beyond the churchyard railings opposite.

'Up there,' she said, 'up Free School Lane, that's where the old Cavendish is. And in there,' she said, pointing to the dark medieval court behind the thousand-year-old tower of St Bene't's, 'in there, Faustus made his bargain with the devil.'

Bewick looked at her sharply. She laughed. 'It was where Christopher Marlowe had his rooms as an undergraduate.'

Bewick thought for a moment. 'Marlowe wrote plays, didn't he?'

She was surprised that he wasn't familiar with Marlowe. But then, she asked herself, how many policemen would even know that Marlowe was not just a village on the Thames, if that? 'Born the same year as Shakespeare,' she replied. 'You know *Dr Faustus*?'

'Remind me.'

'In his play, Faustus bargains with the devil. The devil can have his soul for eternity if Faustus can have anything he wants while he lives.'

'I remember. We read some of it at school. I only believed in living hells then, like double German. Seemed like a classy deal for Faustus.'

The Eagle was an ancient survival, with a galleried first floor overlooking its paved and cobbled yard, this feature making it a forerunner of the first theatres. In its time it had rung to the sound of verse drama, as well as to theories of how nucleotides manage to pair off inside a double helix of coiling atoms.

On the brown ceiling of the bar, written in candle-smoke and varnished over for posterity, were the names of the pilots and bomber squadrons who flew against Germany from the airfields around Cambridge fifty years before. Ten years after that, in the peace which the airmen had helped to win, two men had probed, played with and finally resolved the enigmatic structure of the vital molecule which informs all life on earth: DNA.

Sally explained how the four nucleotides which make up our DNA are like invisible chains of frightening durability, which bind us to a past more ancient than our own humanity; more ancient than our history as apes, than our status as vertebrates.

A fire crackled in the grate.

Bewick listened with complete attention.

'You're doing well,' Sally said.

'You explain it well. And it's a great story. It makes me wish I weren't so ignorant.'

Sally laughed. 'Do you know', she said, 'that there are students today, reading medicine at leading universities, who still believe in the biblical version of creation? Who won't accept Darwinian evolutionary theory?'

They had lunched early. The bar was beginning to fill up. Bewick made his way to the bar to replenish the glasses.

Sally watched him walk through the crowd of younger people. He moved carefully, aware of his size. Moving through a narrow gap he lifted one of his arms. She saw he was in pain as he did so. How had he hurt himself? She really wanted to know. She laughed at herself. Her level of interest in him was much higher than it should be. She didn't care.

'Have you hurt yourself?' she asked when he returned with the drinks.

'Who told you?'

'I noticed.'

'I was in a fight.' Bewick seemed to regret admitting this.

'A fight?' Sally hadn't managed to keep the surprise out of her voice.

'Yes,' he said. 'DNA profiling: where were we?'

'What makes you uncomfortable about being in a fight? I'm not any sort of pacificist.' She pointed to the ceiling. 'My Dad flew missions trying to protect that lot.'

Bewick didn't answer for a moment, then he asked, 'Are you going to be married still?'

Sally found she had blushed and was angry with herself. 'Yes.' She looked away, flustered. 'Yes I am. It doesn't mean, though, that I'm not allowed to show interest in . . . I mean, that's not what it's all about. That's not the deal. The deal is . . .'

She stopped. Why was she defending herself? Bewick made her feel as if she were playing some sort of truth game. She resented it.

'Yes?'

She took a deep breath. 'Why did you ask me that?'

'Oh, you know . . .'

And she did know. Even though he hadn't pressed the point, he'd made her think about it. She'd been getting personal. He wanted to know where he stood, what was happening. Something was happening, she knew.

She glanced at him. He was looking down at his pint of beer. The upper-body athleticism was evident even in jacket and tie. The hands holding the pint mug looked made to fight. White scars curled around the brown knuckles. She wondered what it would be like to be on the end of Bewick's violence.

'You don't have to tell me about DNA profiling, you know,' Bewick now said. 'I know it must be very frustrating for you.'

'Please,' she said, hurt.

'OK. Where shall we start? It may be too difficult for me, you know.'

'It's difficult, but not that difficult.' She smiled. 'You're reasonably clever, after all.'

That, she realized, was the most intimate thing she'd ever said to him. Bewick's smile seemed to be one of complicity, she was relieved to see. She went on:

'Well, the first thing you have to do is to equip yourself with enough DNA. Even if you have only a minute amount in the blood or the tissue that you've found, you can make as much as you like – through PCR. I think I've told you this before, on the plane.'

'PCR?'

'Polymerase chain reaction. I won't go into it, except to say that, relatively speaking, it's quite a simple procedure.'

Bewick looked at her as if she were being kind to him, sparing his intelligence.

'It's not necessary to know,' she said.

'Sure.'

'Now, you remember I said that the Exons are the bits which code for the proteins that we're made of? And that Introns are the intervening sequences, the "junk" that we're interested in?'

'Yes.'

'Well, what you're looking for amongst the Introns, the junk, are VNTRs. That's short for Variable Number Tandem Repeats.'

Bewick looked at her, resolutely blank, and made her laugh.

'I'll explain. How many nucleotides are there?' she asked.

'Four.'

'There are. So – when two of the nucleotides sit side by side on the DNA molecule, that's a tandem. What you're looking for is a tandem repeated many times: a tandem repeat. And you want that to be sitting next to a tandem repeat which is of a very different length. Do you remember the name of any of the nucleotides?'

'Cytosine . . . Adenine.'

'Well done . . . So, you might get a cytosine/adenine tandem, in a repeat of a hundred, which is sitting next to a guanine/adenine tandem which is repeated only ten times. And so on. The point of looking for this hyper-variable region, as it's also known, is because it's sufficiently different in different people for you to be able to distinguish between each source of DNA.'

'How on earth do you isolate it?'

'Well, you don't exactly isolate it. The position on the human genome of various VNTRs is known. So you use a kind of enzyme, called a primer, that you know will bind to the particular VNTR you're interested in. You can specify primers to be made for you. So you're not "isolating" the VNTR – you're sending in something that will grab it for you.'

Bewick shook his head in disbelief. 'With this sort of knowledge we should all be immortal.'

'Well, we die for various reasons: one of them being because our genes get less efficient at replicating. If it's ever discovered how to solve that one; and it will be . . . That's going to be the real Faustian dilemma.'

They were interrupted by a burst of laughter from a group of undergraduates sitting near the door. Sally looked round and sensed Bewick following her glance. The students looked so young, so amused and alive. Sally didn't envy them at all. She was only fifteen years older, but any ethical issues to do with her science that she felt bound to think through were as nothing compared to what this next generation would have to deal with.

She turned. Bewick appeared to be looking at them with the same sympathetic seriousness. His glance met hers. 'So,' he said, 'you have your variable tandem repeats all lined up to look at. How do you look at them?'

'You label them – you make them radioactive, so they can be photographed. Then you introduce them into a gel. You pass a current across the gel, which makes the VNTRs move through it. How far they travel depends on their length – on their molecular weight. When the current is switched off, the varying lengths of each tandem repeat will be reflected in the distance it has travelled through the gel. Most importantly, they'll show up clearly enough to compare them with your other sample. You have nice little bar charts to annoy lawyers with. Bingo.'

Bewick and Sally walked along King's Parade, then down Senate House passage past the curious, ornate Gate of Honour which leads into Caius. At the bottom of the cobbled alley they turned right, past Trinity Hall, towards Trinity itself.

Bewick gave Sally a brief account of the police's post-mortem evidence: the skin under the fingernails, the smear of sperm.

'In those circumstances,' she said, 'accidental contamination isn't an issue. That's sound evidence.'

'Yes,' said Bewick, 'it'll probably convict him. I've prepared everyone for that.'

She glanced at him surprised. 'Surely it will convict him, won't it?'

'I agree, the evidence looks as good as you ever get. I'm just not sure he did it, that's all.'

'Well, as a scientist, I think you have to go with the available evidence.'

'Sure. That's what I'm doing. But part of the data as far as I'm concerned is my intuition that he didn't do it. On the other hand, the officer in charge of the case has the contrary intuition that he did, that he's a killer. I trust his intuition almost as much as my own. So you could say I have a problem.'

They found themselves in a narrow dark passageway, close overhead. They took a few steps to the end of it and there opened in front of them one of the great sights of England: Trinity Great Court under a sky sailed by white clouds; four acres of grey stone and green lawn. At its centre stood the grand fountain and in the distance, presiding over his concept, legs apart in the Holbein manner, a statue of Henry VIII.

'Yes,' said Sally, 'that'll do.'

They walked across the court.

'There's the possibility of course that you're both right: that Enwright didn't do this murder, but did do another!'

'Thanks,' said Bewick. 'Any other suggestions on a postcard please.'

'Well, there's another of life's little mysteries,' Sally said, nodding up at the statue of Henry VIII as they walked past. 'How a serial wife-killer could end up presiding over something like this.' She gestured to the court.

Near the towered gatehouse Sally paused. 'C Staircase,' she said.

'C Staircase?'

'We should stand and worship for a moment. The modern world was born on C Staircase.'

'Was it?'

'That's where Newton lived while he was a fellow of Trinity – on the top floor.'

Without knowing she had done it, she took his arm and they stood looking up at the modest building which, three hundred years before, had housed an imagination whose reverberations were still being felt throughout the planet.

They turned away to look again at the sunlit court. Sally found herself ambushed by the thought that she would never forget the moment. She withdrew her arm.

Outside the towered Tudor gateway Bewick talked of having some tea. Sally thought he meant at his house, so suggested they buy some Chelsea buns at Fitzbillies. She realized as she spoke that he hadn't meant that at all, but that his politeness would mean they went to his house anyway. It pleased her.

Sally was curious about Bewick's house. When she entered it, however, it was much less revealing than she'd hoped. Pale colours, neutral fabrics, uncluttered surfaces; it was like a hotel except for the fact that there were fewer pictures on the walls. It reflected as little as possible of the owner, it seemed. Or did it?

Bewick came in carrying a tray. He was in pain

again, she realized, as he put it down. He'd noticed her curiosity about the house just as he had about the car; even though this time she'd made a conscious effort to disguise it.

'I haven't unpacked properly yet: only some of the books.'

'How long have you been here?'

'Couple of years.'

'And before that?'

'I was renting while the divorce was sorted out.'

'Was that in Homerton too?'

'Yes it was.'

He'd forgotten to bring milk and went to fetch it. The books she could see were mostly biography, history and popularized science; some poetry, a couple of shelves of psychology, very little fiction. She heard from the kitchen the sound of glass breaking on tiles. She resisted the impulse to go and help, sensing that she'd be unwelcome. A few minutes later Bewick entered, his shirtsleeves rolled up, carrying a jug of milk.

She watched as he poured tea for her. The muscles in his forearm formed parallel ridges, as distinct as if they were carved. To distract herself, to try to think, in order to avoid what she was feeling, she asked him if he had a theory about the Kelleher case.

He looked surprised briefly. 'A theory? Not sure what you mean.'

'I mean the classic version, I suppose. Who? How?

Why? Opportunity and motive: all that sort of thing. You know?'

He made a non-committal gesture. Then he said, 'Have I told you about Giovanni Jones?'

She smiled at the name. 'No, never. Who is he?'

'He's the Chief Inspector running the Kelleher investigation. Italian mother, Welsh father. His father was a schoolboy rugby international. Local hero. Gio's mother is a proper Italiano mamma. I think I'd like to have belonged to a family with a woman like Mamma Jones running it.'

'What did you belong to?'

Bewick's voice flattened to a monotone. 'My parents were kind. They were hard working.' He paused to think. 'They were trapped by the system. They were too moral to use it.'

Sally realized he would say nothing further. 'And Giovanni Jones?'

'He's fat. He's clever. He tells outrageous lies. Claims his grandfather was an Italian nobleman; that his great-grandfather fought with Garibaldi at the defence of Rome.'

'Perhaps it's true.'

'Never thought it might be true. Perhaps. Anyway, the point of your knowing about Gio Jones is to tell you that I know him well. I respect him.

'Gio thinks he's got the killer. Mostly because of the DNA evidence which is very compelling. I argue that there are three other suspects. Gio Jones won't accept it. He says that something deep in his Celtic twilight of a brain is telling him that the lad's a killer. From an old campaigner like him, that means a lot.

'It means, as I told you, that there are two things to overcome: the DNA evidence and Gio Jones's belief in it.'

'Who are the other three suspects?'

'You really want to know?' He looked at her very directly, as if the question were about her interest in him rather than in the case.

'I really do.'

'All right then,' he said. 'Three suspects, as I said. All motivated, all involved with her. Julia's ex-husband, David Toner. He stands to get two hundred thousand from her death. He's violent. His alibi depends on the partner he's currently intimidating. Julia's gay friend, Julian Rae. She's left her house to him. Did he know that before she died? He refused to take a blood test – for HIV reasons, he claims. He also can't, or won't, account in detail for what he was doing the night she was killed. Then there's her father.'

'Her father?'

'He hated Julia. He disapproved of her. He feared and loathed her. He felt humiliated by her. He's a petty, tyrannical control freak. Psychologically he's got the perfect profile.'

'But how do you get over the DNA evidence?'

'I'm working on it.'

Sally had been watching him closely. Momentarily now she met his eyes. She didn't know what she meant to convey to him, so she looked away. 'What were you doing in Thailand?' she asked, for something to say.

Bewick shrugged, his voice bored. 'It was a project at the Bangkok Police Academy.'

'On criminology?'

'No. On how to structure their instruction courses. I was being an educationalist, in effect.'

She looked up at him again. Something didn't ring true. She remembered the preoccupied man who had been allowed to join the plane well beyond any normal flight deadlines. She remembered her initial instinct that he couldn't be a policman.

'Why did they allow you to get on the plane? So late, I mean?'

'The Embassy organized it.'

He was clearly not going to talk about it any more.

His eyes moved over her. She felt his attention like a breath on her skin.

Why were there tears prickling her eyes? Regret, she thought it was: for the fact that something was happening to her that she knew must stop, and would stop.

Or was it hope?

'I ought to be going,' she said. It sounded like an appeal.

Bewick said nothing, as if he refused to conspire in their parting. Outside the light was fading. Still she sat there. Still Bewick said nothing. She could feel the tears beginning to fill her eyes. Urgently she stood. 'The bathroom?'

'Top of the stairs.'

She could feel him watching her as she left the room.

As she turned at the top of the stairs, she paused. The door was open to the room above the street. Reflected in a good-looking cheval mirror she could see an unmade bed with a dressing-gown flung across the foot of it.

The soap in the bathroom was French and pricey, which surprised her. Was it something he'd been given? Or had he just asked for something good and paid for what he'd been offered? The thought of his choosing it himself pleased her. Her glance idled across other objects on the shelf in front of her. She checked herself. This endless curiosity about him would end in more tears if she didn't watch it.

A few minutes later she had calmed herself down. She reminded herself of her status as an engaged woman. The most sobering thought was of the wedding presents already accumulating at her mother's house.

She took some comfort from the mirror over the basin. Her deep-set eyes at least were darkly brilliant with the strain she felt. She would never be pretty, but her long strong nose gave her face distinction; her skin was perfect.

She was, she told herself, a classic candidate for pre-marital nerves. All her life she'd been wary of commitment to any substantial undertaking – even of accepting her place at Cambridge. Yet her three years at Cambridge had been the best thing that had ever happened to her. The turmoil she felt now was surely just a legitimate nervousness. It was going to be a marriage, after all, on her terms. It accommodated her work, her career. She loved James. Almost as importantly, she loved his family; his father particularly was a delightful man.

All this she repeated to herself, without daring to ask herself why she was doing so. Desperately she avoided any thought of the unfathomable individual in whose house she stood.

Feeling much stronger, she ventured down the stairs a few minutes later. As she pushed the hair back from her face she smelled the soap perfume on her hands. Her self-discipline nearly gave way again, as if dissolving in the dry fern and woodsmoke scent. She pulled herself together and continued on down.

She found Bewick standing in the still-unlit sitting-room. Outside it was nearly dark. He glanced at her; no more. 'I ordered a cab for you.'

It was if they were lovers who had argued, each wary of the other's ability to hurt.

'Thank you,' she said automatically.

Then she asked herself why. He'd driven her from the station. He saw her hesitation but said nothing.

Bewick went up to the back bedroom. From it, he had said, he could see the stretch of road where he had asked the cab to wait. Sally stared after him. What was going on? Could it possibly be that Bewick thought there was danger for her if she left in his car, from his house? That he feared he was being watched? It seemed so outlandish; but then, when she first met him, that's where he'd come from – the outlands. What had he said about the way the world was organized? By a jungle astrologer with a Kalashnikov? What had he been doing?

A car passed. On the pavement outside two women were talking about choir rehearsals. In the garden a robin was singing. Perhaps, it occurred to her, the reason for that dark withdrawn atmosphere he could generate was a streak of deep paranoia in his make-up. For a sickening second she was prepared to distrust him.

Overhead the floor creaked and she heard Bewick coming downstairs. 'Cab's here.'

Bewick showed Sally to the back door. They walked to the end of the modest garden. There was a locked door in the board fence. They went through it then turned along one of the paths which divided the triangle of back gardens.

As they reached the end of the narrow path, Sally could hear the tick-over of the cab's diesel. She felt numb and wretched. She was exhausted from the exercise of self-control. She could sense Bewick inches behind her. She stopped and he cannoned into her. She turned: she must be almost in his arms, she thought. He was a full pace back. She was astonished at the speed with which he must have moved.

Why he had, she didn't know. Had he wanted to

step back, literally, from what was going on? Had he simply wanted to spare her embarrassment? Just as she had at the airport, she stepped forward, reached up and kissed his cheek. 'Goodbye then,' she said and ran.

She was in the cab and had shut the door before Bewick appeared. He was at the cab window just as it began to pull away. The driver stopped.

She reached her hand out of the cab window. He took it and held it. They stared at each other in silence, their hands held tight. Then he reached his head forward and kissed her on the mouth.

She realized later that she had feared this moment. She didn't know what to expect. His sensitivity astonished her. He held the kiss a moment, then he was gone.

The cab pulled away. Bewick re-entered the back lane to his garden.

The man who had witnessed this parting watched Bewick until he was out of sight. The man looked nervous, shaky. He walked towards his car.

When Bewick entered his sitting-room, the light was blinking on the answering machine. He ignored it and sat in the darkened room for quarter of an hour or so, his hands palm upwards on his knees. Then he stood, drew the curtains and switched on a couple of lamps.

The message on the machine was from Gio Jones. He sounded depressed. Would Bewick ring him?

Before he did so, Bewick rang another number. He had almost given up before it was answered.

'Mr Rae?'

'Yes?'

'John Bewick. We met at Julia Kelleher's cottage . . . Your cottage, I should say.' Bewick was at his most reassuring.

'What do you want?' Rae sounded resentful.

'To talk.'

'Why?'

'I want advice. I have a theory.'

'Can't it be done on the phone?'

'Not really. Phones aren't secure.'

There was a silence before Rae grudgingly said, 'When?'

'As soon as possible. This evening?'

'All right. How soon can you be here?'

'Soon. Twenty minutes?'

'All right.'

Rae put the phone down.

Bewick rang Gio Jones at home, to be told by Eilean that he was still at City West. If Bewick spoke to him, would he tell Gio please that the dog would start putting on weight if it ate his dinner again.

'What d'you mean, start putting it on? The animal is pedigree cholesterol as it is,' said Jones. 'A long-haired salami. You sure you spoke to the right woman? Anyway, you left your address book in my car, that's why I rang. It was down the side, I only just found it.'

'Thought I had. I rang the desk – asked them to ask you.'

'They didn't. Young buggers. Soccer and sex is all they think about. Now, here's a surprise. Brace yourself. Karen's volunteered to drop it by.'

'That's good of her. Thanks.'

'She's just set off.'

'Oh, she'll miss me then.'

'This is a disappointed woman we're talking of here.'

'Is it? Tough.'

'What? What's the matter with you? Where's your manners? When visitors come to Cambridge I say: go and look at the colleges for the architecture and try to have a word with John Bewick for his world-class manners. In future I'll send them to the bus station. What's up?'

'Nothing's up. No more than usual.'

'Yes it is. Something's under your skin.'

'Got to go.'

Bewick had put down the phone. Jones felt uncomfortable: he didn't know exactly why.

He knew he didn't like the list of injuries that Toner had sustained at the hands of Bewick. The thought of having to deal with a John Bewick out of control . . . But, he reminded himself, Bewick was likely to do serious damage to somebody he thought should be damaged, whether he was in control or not. Of course it was all quite easily explained by the fact that Bewick was quite possibly looking over his shoulder half the time to see if he wasn't about to be the recipient of a soft-nosed .45.

He stood up and stretched. Outside it was fully dark now. Strings of lights moved slowly north and south in Maid's Causeway.

As he stood there he realized, to his own astonishment, that he was disappointed – on Karen's behalf. Did he care about her that much? Enough to care that the man she was in love with was going to be unavailable to her? He caught the reflection of himself in the window against the dark sky. He laughed. This is almost as insane as that stuff about loving thy neighbour, he thought.

Bewick emerged from his house into drizzle and the darkness with his bike slung over his shoulder. In a matter of seconds he was across the road, through the yard of garages and was emerging from the board-fenced alleyway which leads into Milburn Avenue. He paused there for a moment to listen for a car starting up, or moving off quickly. There wasn't one. He adjusted his bike lights and set off.

Grantchester, where Julian Rae lived, could be approached in at least two ways. The road, suburban at first, then a winding country lane for a mile or so, was the more obvious route. A second, along the cycle track across the meadows, was unlit and deserted, but it was gated: not even an off-roader could follow. Bewick opted for the cycle track.

Bewick waited for a gap in the traffic. He pulled

out and turned right. His chosen route meant turning right again in about a hundred yards.

The car hit him before he got there.

In the split second before it happened, by instinct or coincidence, Bewick accelerated. It probably saved his life. Cars were parked all along the nearside of the road. Avoidance was out.

The huge force of the car hit his back wheel at an angle. His hurt ribs sent a whip of pain around his chest. There was no possibility of control. The rearing frame of the bike catapulted him. His left leg caught a wing mirror which ripped it open. That spun him. He slid backwards across the ice rink of a wet car roof. An aerial lashed, tearing his arm. His feet crunched a windscreen. Still going too fast. Somersaulting; wide flat air. Crack. Shutdown.

Sally Vernon sat on the train, for which she had waited for half an hour. It would leave any moment now. She could then draw a line under this disastrous experiment with her feelings. One of the consequences of the day's events was that Cambridge would be forbidden territory to her for a long time to come.

She longed for familiarity, for her mother's house, for the world of restrictions, of the predictability which had maddened her when she was younger.

Rapid pips announced the train doors' closure. They slid shut. The train pulled away. Sally sat back in relief.

Her relief was short-lived. The factories, the

suburbs were passed. The train headed out into the darkness of the fens. As it did so, Sally realized to her dismay what she was going to do.

Karen Quinney made a left at the roundabout. Almost immediately she saw a couple of badly parked cars and a knot of people beginning to gather around the body on the pavement. She put on her blue light and radioed for back-up.

A man was kneeling beside Bewick when Karen arrived. There was blood from at least three wounds that she could see. It darkened the pavement by his arm. She whipped out her torch, frightened the darkness might mean that it was arterial. In the torchlight it was red. She felt a stupid relief for a brief moment; then she switched into automatic.

Bewick's eyes were half shut. He didn't recognize Karen. She radioed again, this time for an ambulance. The man who was still kneeling beside Bewick turned to her. 'He's not making sense. I think he can move everything.'

'Yeah, well don't touch him. Anybody know what happened?'

'It was deliberate,' said a tall, reserved looking woman in her sixties. Karen nodded. She went to her car and brought back a blanket. She put it over him. She then took brief statements.

The tall woman turned out to be a fellow of Homerton. 'It was quite deliberate, as far as I could tell. The car swerved in to hit him and it accelerated at the same time.' The woman was sombre-faced, shocked. She held herself very upright, and kept her eyes lowered.

'Do you know what sort of car?'

'No. That's not my sort of thing. It was a sort of dirty red. It was pretty old, I'd say. I didn't see the number plate or what the driver looked like. A number plate usually has a light, doesn't it? Well, this one didn't. It went roaring off. Whoever was driving it knew what they'd done.'

The other witness was less helpful. The car was identified as maybe a Ford Escort or a Citroen BX. The quality of a witness who knew the names but could confuse the cars, in Karen's eyes, rated somewhere below zero.

Bewick's eyes flickered as he lay in the ambulance on the spinal board with pads immobilizing his head. Karen was holding his hand, trying to stop herself feeling anything.

Bewick's eyes opened. Interrupting the ambulance man's questioning of Karen, he grunted something which he repeated as Karen leant closer to him.

'You're in an ambulance. Someone ran you out of road.'

Bewick moved his head minutely: a gesture of acknowledgement.

'Anything hurt?'

Again a gesture, which she read as 'no'.

The ambulance man muttered, 'He'll be primed up with adrenalin yet.'

'Sure.'

Bewick seemed to slip into semi-consciousness. He opened his eyes again as the ambulance slowed and switched on its siren. They were close to the hospital now. Bewick tried again to speak. Karen could see that words were forming themselves in his thoughts but that he couldn't speak them. She waited.

'It was deliberate,' he mumbled, then seemed to run out of energy.

Karen nodded. 'There were witnesses,' she said.

At the City General Hospital, Bewick was wheeled straight through to the Resuscitation Room. Karen stayed at the desk to give his details.

She asked why he was going to Resus. 'He doesn't need it.'

'We have a standard protocol,' said the receptionist.

Nearly an hour later, a doctor told Karen that there was a fracture to Bewick's skull. It would be necessary to keep him in.

'What sort of fracture?'

'Do you mean how serious?'

'Yeah, I suppose I do.'

'Serious enough to keep him in.'

'Helpful,' said Karen. 'Is he in danger is what I meant.'

'Not immediately. We're going to have a go at his wounds in a minute. He's in the corridor. Have a word with him. He can tell you what he needs for his stay with us.'

She found him where the doctor said. It was the first time she'd taken in his injuries. Blood was caked in his hair. The side of his face was puffed and most of the top skin layers had been scraped away. The ear ridges were swollen into tubes outlined with blood. She looked away.

He was soon aware of her being there. 'I can't stay here,' he said. 'When they've cleaned up my leg and my arm, you've got to get me out.'

'Might not be that easy.'

'Can you go to my place now?'

'Sure.'

'Good. It was me he was after. I can't stay here.'

She made herself look at the raw meat of his face without flinching. She would do anything for him. 'The car been following you, do you think?'

'No. He couldn't. Must have been watching one of my bolt-hole exits. Must've worked it out.'

'That's a bit sharp. Maybe it was luck?'

'Don't think so.' His energy level was dropping again.

'What about random? Some lunatic who doesn't like big guys on bikes.'

Bewick thought about this for a moment. 'It was me he was after,' Bewick managed to repeat. He took some deep breaths. 'I'll tell you what I need from my place.'

The taxi from Cambridge station was driven by a talkative middle-aged man. He aired his political prejudices and, taking Sally's silence for tacit approval, he admitted to increasingly racist and homophobic opinions.

In fact Sally wasn't taking in a word of what he said. She was tiptoeing across a pit of coals.

What if Bewick weren't there?

What would she say if he were?

Did she even know what she wanted to say? He hadn't actually identified a single feeling regarding her; he had admitted nothing . . . On the other hand, she knew.

Without this assurance, how could she have got out of the train at Ely and taken the next train back to Cambridge?

She felt a rush of elation as the taxi turned into Baccata Lane. Soon it would be resolved . . .

A young woman was walking along the pavement. Sally had time to note in the lamp-light the finely boned face, the athletic figure, before she turned cold inside.

On the doorstep of Bewick's house the woman took out a key and let herself in. She had her own key to his house. Sally told the driver to pull over.

The downstairs curtains of the house were closed, the lights were on. After a while the light came on in

Bewick's bedroom. The woman passed in front of the cheval mirror Sally had approved of. She came to the window. As she reached up, silhouetted against the light to draw the curtains, Sally saw again the elegance of her figure.

'Take me back to the station,' she said curtly to the driver. 'There's something I've forgotten.'

It had cost Karen all the cash she had on her – forty odd quid – plus some sickening, flirtatious behaviour to bribe the driver of the laundry van to take time out from his very slack schedule.

While he waited for her outside the lifts in the underground car-park, she took the wheelchair, which she had walked off with from outside the Renal Unit, up to the ward where Bewick had told her he would be.

He was sitting on the floor, leaning against the wall just inside the men's lavatory with the door ajar. He looked terrible. She had to help him into the wheelchair. She immediately headed for the lift.

He had been in a side ward so there had been nobody to object to his self-discharge, he told her, as the lift took them down to the basement. His voice was a laryngitic croak.

The laundry van had an electric tail-gate, which was the point of the exercise. The driver helped and Bewick was soon safely installed in the back of the van for the short journey to Karen's house.

'Everything's sorted. I've got your things. I've rung

Rae. I couldn't get hold of Gio Jones but I've left a message at St Margaret's for Dundas.'

'Thanks Karen. You'd better ring the hospital: tell them I've cleared off and not disappeared down the porcelain.'

Its garlands, fruit, crowns and roses still displaying their original, not very pleasing colours, the low Jacobean ceiling was thrown into deep relief by the eight trios of candles burning on silver sconces along each wall of the long, gallery-like room. At one end, a portrait of the tigress of France and founder of the college, Margaret of Poitiers, looked down on the thirty or so men who were gathered for one of the college's five-yearly reunions of contemporaries.

Alec Dundas wasn't entirely enjoying himself. He was pleasantly drunk, true, and envied no one in the room. He'd been having an excellent conversation with one of the younger dons who was much cleverer than he was, he was pleased to realize, and much more generous spirited, but . . .

He gloomily eyed the fire and the candlelight dancing on the brilliant mirrors of the sconces – a gift, he had been told, of Charles the Second to the college. The event and its setting was theatre, but . . .

Once he might have found it interesting. Now he classed such survivals with the heritage industry, that enormous barrier to sensible change which seemed determined to fix the best bits of England in aspic. Yet, he argued with himself, public life of any sort was mostly good old showbiz. From the poor tarts on the streets of King's Cross to ministers of the Crown and circuit judges, none could prosper without a dash of theatrical brio.

So this, the treat that St Margaret's could offer its alumni (aware of the necessity of constant fund-raising appeals), was surely justified and entirely civilized?

Alec Dundas thought of his father, who was much more tolerant than him, and raised his glass in salutation. His father would certainly have passed no judgement on the event. He would, however, be mightily pissed off if Alec came back from it without a decent yarn to spin. Dundas shrugged off his gloom and began listening again.

It was midnight by the time he walked through the moonlit Tudor courts to the rooms above the river which he was so pleased to have secured. Attached to the outer door was a note from the duty porter. He took it into the room to read. It involved Bewick in some way. It asked Dundas to drive halfway across Cambridge. He realized he was too drunk to do that. He went to the payphone by the porters' lodge.

'Miss Quinney? Alec Dundas.'

Karen told him what had happened to Bewick.

'It was a deliberate attack?'

'Yes. We have witnesses.'

'OK.'

Dundas wondered aloud why Bewick wanted him

involved. Karen told him that Bewick had said he wanted back-up for her.

'I can't drive I'm afraid,' Dundas told her. 'I'm well over the limit. Why don't you come here by cab. My hire car is in the college garage. You can drive us both.'

Karen glanced across at Bewick slumped in the wheelchair, his eyes closed. 'It's Alec Dundas,' she said. 'He's pissed. He wants me to drive his car. I'll have to go and get it.'

A nod from the wheelchair. In the last hour or so Bewick had developed two lurid black eyes. They flickered as he nodded, but didn't open.

Karen made arrangements with Dundas and put the phone down. She didn't want to leave Bewick. 'Sure you won't lie down?'

'Not till I'm at Beach.'

'OK.'

She went out of the room, returning a minute later carrying a Smith & Wesson revolver. She put the gun in Bewick's hand. His fingers tightened around it, then explored it like a blind man's. His eyes flickered open and he nodded again.

Karen hurried from the house towards the dead end of the cul-de-sac. She realized as she glanced around that there was only one car there which wasn't familiar to her as one of her neighbours'. It was a dark-coloured Carlton, H reg. There was no one in it.

A footpath between the houses brought Karen out

on to the ring road. The next few minutes were critical.

If this bastard knows his stuff, she thought, if he's made it to here, he'll go for it now. She walked, consciously relaxing herself, ready at any moment to run. She had planned evasive tactics and a disguised route back to the house.

She arrived at the bus stop lay-by. The late-night traffic was sparse. A minute or two later the cab she'd ordered arrived. She couldn't spot a tail. Nevertheless, she operated the cut-out by taking two cabs, so there would be no connection to be made by an enquirer between her house and St Margaret's.

Dundas was waiting for her at the main gate. He hadn't been prepared for the pair of legs which slid out of the cab, nor for the quickness of the tough-eyed young woman who had seen him noticing her legs and was informing him silently that comments were out of order. He led her to the college garage. 'Is he OK?'

'I don't know.'

'He won't stay in hospital?'

'He doesn't think he's safe there.'

Dundas nodded. He unlocked his car and opened the door for Karen, then he handed her the keys.

Bewick sat still for about twenty minutes after Karen left. Then he opened his eyes a fraction. Slowly they opened completely. He looked around the room.

Bright covers to the cushions were possibly home-made. The cushions were strewn across a grey and off-white striped sofa. A big Mediterranean unglazed pot over a metre high stood in a corner. A framed Impressionist exhibition poster, a Renoir meadow dotted with poppies, hung over the fireplace in which there were some pale logs laid very neatly over paper and kindling. On the glass-topped coffee table was a copy of *220*, the triathlon magazine, with a photo of Robin Brew on the cover. On the wall above Karen's table desk was pinned an Ordnance Survey map of Cambridge and its surroundings. The roads dominated because, as with all small-scale maps, they were not drawn to scale.

Cambridge was boxed in by the M11 to the west, the A45 to the north, and running south-west/north-east, connecting the other two roads, the A11. This triangle was the circuit Joe Enwright had driven on his superbike the night Julia Kelleher was killed.

Bewick stared at the map.

The last train deposited Sally and half a dozen others on King's Lynn station. As she walked to her car, she felt exhausted in a way unusual for her. At least, she told herself, she must now draw a line under her meetings with Bewick. At least now she could get on with her wedding . . . couldn't she?

She shivered. She realized she had been standing, key in hand, by the door of her car without moving for several minutes. She was bloody cold. She dived into the car and started the engine. She turned the heating up. She didn't drive off. She was shocked at the certainty she felt that the events of today were going to affect her whole life.

Strange, she thought, how this pain that she could see rolling towards her in towering waves left her dry-eyed.

It had always been hope that had made her cry.

Half an hour later Dundas and Karen found Bewick semi-comatose in the wheelchair. Dundas was shocked by his appearance. He had, he realized, thought of Bewick as indestructible – which was sentimentality, he now told himself.

In the car, Dundas had told Karen that he would need about a gallon of black coffee.

'I'll make some coffee,' Karen now said and left the room.

Dundas sat beside Bewick. 'She said it was deliberate.'

Bewick grunted an acknowledgement.

'Any idea who?'

Bewick managed to convey a negative,

Dundas felt impotent. He was out of his depth. He was nauseated by Bewick's wounds, the blood and oozings coagulating black and crystalline, the churned flesh. 'Any theories?'

No reply.

'Anything I can do?'

'Get me over to Beach,' Bewick croaked.

*

The electronically controlled gates opened and Karen drove in. As requested by Karen, Dundas got out and stepped into the shadow of the shrubbery to check that nothing was following. His only contribution, as it turned out. The car moved on.

At the house George and Kit were waiting. It took a few minutes to transfer Bewick from the car to the guest wing of the bungalow. He settled himself in the bed, asked for a large jug of water and for the window to be opened, and said nothing else. He was asleep. Karen put the heavy-duty painkillers down beside the jug of water. Then she folded up his clothes for him.

Kit watched Karen as she tucked the sheets and blankets around Bewick's exposed neck and shoulder. Kit noticed the care with which she did it, a tenderness which seemed at odds with the scraped-back blonde hair, the general smartness, the faultless body which was worked on to stay that way.

Karen looked up to catch Kit watching her. There was an apology in Karen's smile as if to say that she couldn't really help having got herself into this vulnerable state and should be forgiven for it.

Karen was remarkably pretty, thought Kit; but she didn't think she was John Bewick's type. Mind you, she added to herself, she'd hardly need to be, would she, with a body like that?

Dundas arrived at the house having walked up the drive. He confirmed that nothing had followed them.

He greeted George and Kit. He found himself depressed by how old they looked compared with the previous time he'd seen them.

'Who did this to him?' George asked as soon as he and Dundas were alone.

'God knows. Has Bewick hinted that he might be close to some sort of answer to this business?'

George shook his head. 'He's only told us he isn't convinced yet that Joe killed the woman.'

'If he were getting close to someone, they might have known it and tried to do something about it.'

'Yes . . . I suppose that's what I thought, really. How bad is he?'

'We won't know until he gets better – or gets worse, I guess,' Dundas said in his briskest Scottish manner, speculation fruitless.

Karen and Kit came in.

'Is John all right, just sleeping, you know?' George asked.

'He should be in some sort of trauma management really,' Karen answered.

'What would that mean?'

'Being monitored. In case he haemorrhages.'

'In his head, you mean?'

'Yes. The hospital don't like what he's doing at all.'

'Why did he discharge himself? Surely your people could have protected him, couldn't they?'

'Yes. But there's a limit. John knows that. He's weighed the risks. He thinks there's less risk this way.'

'What do you think?'

'I don't know. But I knew he wouldn't stay in hospital, so I decided to go along with it.'

'Well, we'll look after him,' said Kit.

The sky was beginning to lighten as Karen and Dundas drove away from the one-time fen island that was Beach. The flat fields were grey, barely demarcated. Then as the car dipped down on to the ditch-flanked road, walls of mist hemmed them in. The car's pace dropped to a crawl.

'Do you have a theory about who did this?' Dundas asked.

'Well, the suspect would have to be the bloke who killed Julia Kelleher.'

'No one else?'

'Not that I know of. What about you? What's your link?'

'Link?'

'To Bewick.'

'Och, John and I go back to school together. We were scholarship lads in the sixties.'

'What was that like?'

'The sixties?'

'Yeah.'

'Well, you know what they say. If you can remember the sixties you weren't there.'

She smiled.

'No, John and I were too busy being athletic and getting A levels. Luckily most of what people think was the sixties happened in the seventies, so we still got a whiff of it.'

'A whiff of a spliff?'

'Something like that.' Dundas laughed, and added in a wild Glaswegian voice, 'Virginia was never the same again.'

'What sort of athletic were you?'

'I was a runner. Bewick was a boxer and a swimmer.'

'Did you ever see him box?'

'Yes. He was quick. In everyday life he was always having to be careful about walking into things. In the ring he was slippery as an eel. Very aggressive too. That's why I asked if there might be another candidate: someone who might have got on the wrong side of him.'

'He'll have grown up a bit since he was seventeen,' Karen said. Then she remembered finding David Toner temporarily crippled by Bewick.

'Sure,' said Dundas non-committally. They drove in silence for a minute or two. Then he said, 'Few men really grow up.'

'Sure.'

Something about her manner made Dundas glance across at her. It occurred to him that she may well be in love with Bewick. For a moment he was savagely envious. Then the thought intervened of the certain difficulties of such an affair. He imagined them in his own life and was almost reconciled; not quite.

Then he imagined Bewick damaged and in danger, waiting for the tide of blood in his brain to burst its banks or recede. For the sort of journeys Bewick embarked on, the fares were ridiculously high, even if they did end with the attentions of a young woman such as this.

Alec Dundas thought about the even tenor of his own ways, cursed and was comforted.

11

Bewick woke the next afternoon. The sun was low, throwing shadows from the ornamental conifers of George and Kit's garden. They striped the curtained window of the room where Bewick lay. Voices were audible from elsewhere in the house. He took pain-killers, drank half a pint of water, then picked up his watch from the bedside table. It was nearly five. He went to the lavatory then returned to bed.

The door handle turned carefully and Kit put her head in. 'I heard the toilet,' she explained. 'All right?'

'Sure.'

'Karen's here. She couldn't get away before. Want to see her?'

Karen came in and sat on the bed. She examined him in silence for a moment. 'Everything OK?'

'Yes. I'll be staying in bed a bit longer.'

'Stitches?'

'They feel like stitches should.'

'Pain?'

'I've taken painkillers. There's something I'll need from my place, sometime . . .'

'I'll get it. Listen, you don't have double vision, nausea or anything?'

'I'm grateful Karen . . . I'm fine. Things have to settle. Then I'll be fine.'

She looked at him again, not knowing if he was robust enough to go on. She noticed how untidy his hair was, how pale he was.

'What is it?'

'Gio Jones . . . he's very concerned.' Karen was sitting straight-backed like a dancer.

Bewick smiled. It looked as if it hurt to do so. 'What about? Me or his prosecution?'

'He wanted to know if this attack could be anything to do with . . . any of your CICS work.'

'What do you think? I would've been full of goose-shot from a sawn-off if anybody'd been paid to do it, wouldn't I?'

'That's what I'd have said. Someone doesn't want you to sort out Julia Kelleher's killing, then?'

'Who knows? There are crap hit-men. Then there could be someone who wants to be taken for a crap hit-man, for an amateur. Who knows?'

'Gio Jones was thinking of some surveillance. He's thinking of re-interviewing Rae and Toner and Kelleher. He's not giving up of course on Enwright, but he's thinking in terms of an accessory, maybe.'

'No. He shouldn't give up on Enwright. He's got his evidence.'

Bewick said this amused, condescending. Karen looked at him sharply. Bewick settled himself into a sleeping position. 'Question is,' he went on, 'how it got there. As I told him before, that's the issue. You tell him to think about the M11, A45, A11 triangle.'

Jones was reading a report about a South London council estate where intense patrolling combined with widespread community initiatives had produced a marked drop in crime.

The door opened too late to prevent him flinging the report across the room as he shouted, 'Well it bloody would, wouldn't it? What did it bloody cost?'

Karen appeared. She looked at the report which had narrowly missed her and had landed fair and square in the steel waste bin. She retrieved it, read its title and said, 'Aah – This the one Hutchings gave you?'

'The only way we'll get that sort of resourcing on the Henderson is to get a good riot going. Yeah . . . not a bad idea. We could start a recycling centre for Molotov cocktails. Bring your old bottles, old rags, and any unleaded you may have nicked from a garden shed recently. Then we could get a retired revolutionary from one of the colleges to lecture them on street fighting, couldn't we? Good! Only trouble is we might get the Home Secretary round the place. Think I'd prefer an honest-to-god yob off the Henderson, after all, wouldn't you?'

'Anything but the Home Secretary,' said Karen.

'You spoke to Bewick?'

'Yeah. He looked awful.'

'I want to talk to him.'

'He's asked for nobody to go there. Seriously.'

'Why doesn't the stupid bastard stay in hospital?'

'He thinks he's at risk there. I told you.'

Jones made a disparaging noise.

'No, really. He's got a couple of smart routes from his house. If he takes one of them, it means no vehicle can follow him. The bloke who tried to kill him had second-guessed his route. Bewick reckons if he was able to do that, then someone in a hospital would be jelly tots in a corner-shop, protection or no protection.'

'Probably luck.'

'He doesn't think so.'

'Is Bewick all right?'

'You know what he's like. You can't do nothing for him unless he's planned it himself. He seemed to know what he's doing.'

'You like him, don't you?'

Karen gave Jones a steady glance. 'What does that mean, Sir?'

'Don't go all formal on me, Karen. Was only a civil observation. He's a friend of mine. I miss him, to be frank. So it was a simple question.'

Karen shook her head. 'No such thing, Sir.'

'Oh come on.'

'You don't know the shit we get. The brain-dead crap. We all get it. Every woman in the force does. Snigger, snigger, boobs, bum. Snigger . . . I've been told I'm frigid, I'm a stupid virgin, a whore, a cunt, a lesbian, you name it. So, no, it isn't a simple question,

Sir. Even you make the odd crack. So I'm not telling you what I think about John Bewick – OK?'

Jones sighed. He'd put his foot in it again. Karen's brown eyes were darkened, troubled. She'd gone beyond what was acceptable between their ranks and wasn't sure how he'd react.

'OK. I promise to try to do better in future,' Jones said, wearily. 'I promise not to tell you again that you are looking wonderful. And if I forget myself, you have permission to point out my physical graces: the fact, for example, that I have eaten sufficient focaccia this week to render my knees invisible to the owner. Fair enough?'

'Thank you, Sir.' She didn't feel like it but she gave him a smile. Despite his lamentable figure he was, after all, the most acceptable man in the building; certainly the best company.

Jones watched Karen's slim hand pull the door shut behind her and, in spite of all she'd said, he felt a stab of lust for her. It was completely involuntary and unrealistic, but he refused to feel guilty about it; refused absolutely. He had enough to feel guilty about elsewhere, thanks. Besides, he knew he actually cared about Karen. He couldn't help the caring any more than the lusting. In fact he felt more guilty about caring for her than he did about lusting after her. He wondered sometimes how much he would do for Karen, if asked. Almost anything except leave his wife and kids. In other words, not much.

Then there was Bewick. How seriously had he

taken Bewick's instinct that someone was after his neck? Not very.

Ah guilt, what an old friend . . .

He hated the fact that Bewick was in some wanky consultancy. He knew he hated that. He also asked himself if it wasn't Bewick's self-sufficiency he had always resented, his commanding independence. He remembered how the ugly part of him had said, when he heard about Bewick's accident, serve the bastard right, he deserves to get half killed. Thinking this of a friend, of a man he admired, left Jones depressed.

Could he have thought such a thing simply because the attack on Bewick had left such a gaping question in the Kelleher case? He hoped not, but he couldn't exonerate himself completely.

And now there was something else, something he knew he had missed, which nagged at him. Something which stood in a dark corner of his memory and would not step out into the light.

'You can't.'

'I have.'

'You haven't!'

'I don't mean I've told him. He's doing this bloody conference freebie in Toulouse. I mean I've made up my mind.'

'You can't do this to us.'

'Don't be a bloody fool, Mother. You know what's at stake. It's the rest of my life.'

Mrs Vernon turned away. She stood for a moment

and then walked the considerable length of her sitting-room to the French windows. She looked out at the rain drifting over her garden. 'Christ,' she said, 'you could have handled this better.'

'I know I could.'

It was the first time Sally could remember that her mother had addressed her as an equal.

'What happened?' Mrs Vernon asked. She took a long drink from the glass she was holding.

'There's nothing sudden about it, Ma.'

'I didn't say there was. What made you change your mind?'

'The way he drinks his Scotch.'

Mrs Vernon turned to her daughter. She looked at her from under half-closed eyelids; a dark, penetrating stare. It was as if she was seeing Sally for the first time, as if she were talking her language and yet not . . . yes, she knew what Sally meant. She realized she had seen it too: something excitable, greedy. Especially when you see him from the side. The blond hair beginning to recede and the smile which promised too much and . . . yes . . . the way he drank his Scotch. It was a fair description. She became aware of Sally's look of apprehension. Without thinking, Mrs Vernon stepped forward and for the first time in years gathered her daughter into her arms.

Sally was elated. I've done it, she thought, I've broken off my engagement. Actually telling James seemed like an incidental inconvenience.

Supper that evening, against all the odds, was a

happy affair. Sally was aware of loving her parents more than she had ever done. Her father said, 'If you're going to put up a black of that dimension, we'd better have champagne,' and disappeared into his cellar. Her mother defrosted a duck in orange sauce cooked by one of her Cordon-Bleu-trained friends.

'This is going to be the social nightmare of a lifetime,' Mrs Vernon said with some relish as she sucked the last of the meat from the bones on her plate.

'What put you on to him, then?' asked Mr Vernon. There was already a tribal assumption that James was the villain of the piece.

'I met someone.'

As soon as, or even perhaps before she said it, Sally realized that it was a mistake. Her mother froze. 'I thought', she said icily, 'that this was to do with James.'

Sally tried to recover the mood. 'It is. It is,' she insisted. 'Of course it is. It's just that I couldn't see it until I'd met this other person.'

Her father took a long slow sip of his favourite Jaboulet Côtes du Rhône. 'We're not going to have to go through this again, are we?'

'No. He's spoken for. There's no hope for me there. Don't worry. I'm not some feckless tart moving on to something better, Dad. This is just rejection of James. I promise.'

Everybody made an effort, but the meal never recovered its earlier hilarity.

Much later, over brandy in front of the first log fire

of the season, her father asked, 'Who is this man, anyway?'

'A policeman,' Sally laughed.

Mr Vernon looked at her for a moment and then laughed himself. 'A policeman?'

'An ex-policeman, strictly speaking. But a man who is supposed to solve crimes, yes.'

'Good God. What's he like?'

'Very large.'

They laughed again.

'He's a mystery. He's intelligent . . . you want to trust him. He's considerate . . . and very large, as I said.' What else was there? Nothing that Sally could now describe. She just remembered his presence – like a glow from a stove, a place where she felt at her ease, a place she didn't want to leave.

She shook her head and laughed again. 'I'm pissed, Dad.'

Mr Vernon watched his daughter turn away, hiding emotion.

'Do you love him?'

'Luckily, Dad, I don't know. I didn't have long enough to find out. He has this extremely attractive young blonde in tow.'

She loves him, he thought. Bad luck, old girl. He stroked her hand and said, 'What will you do now?'

'Jenny's still got her old boat in commission. She's not taking it out of the water until December. It's moored in Salvages Creek. So I thought I'd go there for a few days and mope around Scales Howe and do some reading; that sort of thing.'

Her father nodded. 'Well, we're here if . . .'

'Thanks Dad . . . There's also the small matter of telling James. I thought I'd tell his father first.'

'Whose father's that?' asked her mother, who was entering with a tray of coffee things.

'James's. I like Mr Arnott. He's always been very nice to me. I thought I'd tell him.'

'If you say so, dear.'

There was some sort of disagreement in her mother's voice. Sally let it pass, thinking it referred to some arcane protocol of what one does or doesn't do that her mother was versed in, only too well.

Jones watched Eilean shepherding their three children, Meg, Barry and Joanna, away from the breakfast table and wished he knew what Bewick's obsession with the fate of Amy Parris meant.

Moving the children proved easier for Eilean than persuading them to wear outside clothes of any description. Getting them to respond to reminders of books or homework they might have forgotten was nearly impossible. The children's blithe lack of cooperation was awesome.

What, he wondered, had been running through his own head as his pudgy schoolboy self set off for Swansea Grammar all those years ago? He couldn't remember. The hope, probably, that one of the seniors might tell him all about sex. Not that any of them knew.

Finally the last child was out of the front door.

Eilean Jones turned in the doorway and still had enough spirit left to smile. 'See you later. Give my best to John if you see him.'

Gio Jones's admiration for his wife at such moments was unbounded. After a moment she returned. 'And don't sit there brooding. Get dressed. Get shaved. Get on with it.'

'Yes Ma'am.'

'Well . . . do, then.'

Jones, who had returned from work at two that morning, grunted and grumbled some sort of reply. Eilean had done what she could. She left the house.

Standing in his vest and confronting the shaving mirror, Jones tried to suppress the resentment he felt. He still reckoned Joe Enwright was killer material.

Bewick's expansion of the evidence and the attempt on his life meant that they'd have to be looking for someone else as well now – an accomplice at the least. He knew he should be grateful to Bewick: a case against Joe Enwright alone could have gone horribly wrong. He wasn't grateful, though. This morning he resented Bewick's skill, his instinct, everything about him.

To add to life's irritations, there was that little shred of evidence he'd been trying to remember since Tuesday. What he ought to do was go through the

Kelleher database line by line until he found what he was looking for. Aaagh! The database was about the size of *War and Peace.*

Bloody Bewick.

Bewick had been making progress, according to Karen. She was going over to George and Kit's house this morning to see how he was.

Did he want Bewick better? With a tilt of his chin, Jones told himself he didn't bloody well care. That made him feel stupid.

As he ran the double blade over a stubborn patch of bristle, an image of Joe Enwright came to mind. The razor hesitated then halted. 'Something wrong, mate,' he heard himself say to the absent Bewick. He went on with the soft scraping of his face. There was something cock-eyed with the boy.

He still wished he knew what Bewick's obsession with the fate of Amy Parris meant. It was a fringe issue, wasn't it? Well, perhaps. But if Bewick was interested . . . Oh bloody hell . . .

'All right, you win,' he said aloud. He put down his razor and, half-shaved as he was, went to the phone and dialled.

'Sirius Software . . .?'

'There you are dear,' said Kit, to let Karen know that she was late. Realizing Kit and George were ready to go out, Karen apologized. She had agreed to be on duty while George and Kit went out together – for the first time since Bewick arrived.

'See you after lunch, dear.'

Bewick lay sprawled under a sheet, the blankets stripped off. The sun had been on the big windows warming up the room. Karen came in. His muscularity and the white sheet made him look like a sculptured Roman. Battered though he was, Bewick was commanding, even when supine.

He hardly moved his head as she came across the room, but she knew he was watching her. She sat on the edge of the bed. She was shaking at the thought of risking the next step.

'Hi . . .'

She said nothing. Her mouth was dry. She hoped he would say nothing. She hoped he would say something. He seemed to be waiting. Did he know what she meant to do? What in the small hours of sleepless nights she had determined to do.

She reached across, placing a hand on his chest as she leant forward. His eyes were incurious as they turned to meet hers. He did know, she thought. She kissed him. He initiated nothing, but responded to everything. She felt his immediate erection against her hip. She slipped her hand under the sheet. He was hot against her cooler hand. At her touch his eyes narrowed. He turned away with a soft, explosive sigh. Karen undressed. She was wearing only her shirt when Bewick's head turned again to look at her. She smiled as she reached up to lift it over her head.

'No,' he said.

She froze. Adrenalin pumped. She was open-mouthed for a moment. She felt sick. 'What?'

'There's no point.' He was shuddering, she could see. His breath rapid, shallow.

'I don't care if there's any fucking point,' she said. 'We can't stop now. We can't. No strings, John. We can't . . .'

She stripped the sheet off him.

'We can't, we can't,' she repeated as she straddled him. She lowered herself on to him.

They fucked for nearly an hour.

Bewick devoured her like a starving man. He told her she was the most beautiful thing he had ever seen. He told her that he didn't love her. That there was no future for them.

Then they fucked for another hour.

Afterwards, Karen lay in a warm fog, a troubled ecstasy. She was dazed, drugged with orgasm. Bewick's sensuality had been so much more intense than she expected. Although, if she was honest, she hadn't known what to expect. It had been a surprise. Through the haze of well-being lurched the memory of his voice saying, 'I don't love you.'

'You don't have to love me,' she said aloud. Bewick murmured something indecipherable. She realized she had woken him up. She heard his breathing settle again.

With painful clarity she realized she had chosen him to love because he was unreachable. The impossibility of the men she worked with, the awful six months of her early, stupid marriage had led her into a sexually reclusive state; conscientious, sexless, ambitious.

It was only the last five days, seeing Bewick injured and vulnerable, which had allowed her to think . . . what?

'There's no point . . .'

She stretched a leg. She luxuriated in her own body. Its health, its fine tone had been the only pleasure that, for years, it had given her, apart from occasional masturbation.

Now . . . she shrugged. She could go back to that if she had to. She didn't much like the sharp tart it made her into, but she was blowed if she was going to have any old self-confident oaf tramping over her life just for the sake of this, however good it was – and this must be as good as it gets. Only the best would do.

Meanwhile, never mind the disclaimers, she knew Bewick would be back for more. His pleasure had been extreme, desperate.

He'd admitted, like her, he had been living with self-control for years. She wouldn't be able to keep him, she thought. There was something complicating his life. Otherwise he wouldn't have made such a song and dance. Was he trying to get back together with his wife? There was something . . .

Be tough, she told herself . . . don't even think it. The momentary fantasy of partnership with this strange brute of a man who lay sleeping so quietly beside her was irresistible, however. Imagine . . .

Tears came. Don't even think it. She looked at him briefly. He was unknowable. Don't . . . Don't . . . She slipped gently out of bed.

'Can you tell us what Amy Parris was working on when she disappeared?'

Tessa Waring looked at the plump scruffy Welshman and felt harassed. The ambience of the outer office where she worked was cool and elegant. So was she, normally. This man was a walking disruption.

'Amy's work wasn't really my side of things,' Tessa replied.

'I see,' said Gio Jones. 'Anyone here who might be able to tell us?'

'Is it important? Only . . .'

'Very important.'

'Only Mr Hammond isn't here at the moment.'

'Oh,' said Jones, cheerful and playful. 'I'm sure Mr Hammond won't mind us knowing what Miss Parris was working on.'

'He might mind a lot,' was the severe reply, 'IT security is a nightmare.'

'I won't understand it technically.'

'Do you realize there are programmes out there specifically designed to break into other people's systems? If you have a password-protected system you can't use any word which appears in any dictionary, any names, Christian name or surname, any car registration number, any names back-to-back or spelt in reverse order. And so on.'

'I see.'

'It's more than my job's worth to point you at someone who can tell you about Amy Parris's work.'

Jones nodded. 'All right. I understand. Answer me this then – in the most general way. Was she working on something particularly sensitive?'

'As I say, everything we do is sensitive. Competitors would love to lay their hands on the way we do anything.'

'So simply by working for Sirius at all, Amy Parris would have been working on something sensitive.'

'You could say that.'

Jones nodded again. He smiled at the still tense Tessa Waring and folded his arms. He wasn't getting very far but at least he was doing his duty by Bewick. He decided on another tack. 'Did you know her? Amy? What was she like?'

Tessa visibly relaxed. She didn't mind talking on a personal level. 'Well, Amy was a bit of a boffin, you know, but very sweet. She was rather hopeless about her appearance, but she could look quite special.'

'Did she have a man?'

'I'm not sure.'

'Not sure?'

'I think she was close to confiding in me sometimes. In fact I know she was. But she never did. There was somebody, though. I think he might have been putting her under a lot of pressure. It was just a feeling I got.'

This was shorthand, Jones thought. For what? What was she not telling him? 'Pressure to do what?'

'She was good friends with Julia Kelleher, you know.'

Tessa lowered her eyes, as if this were only the admissible part of the truth.

'Yes, we know. She was in a relationship with Julia Kelleher.' Gio Jones gave 'relationship' the full South Welsh down-the-nose innuendo.

Tessa looked up sharply. 'Who told you that?'

'Julia's mother, apart from anyone else.'

'Oh . . . Well, I think it may have been to do with that.'

'This man wanted Amy to get out of her relationship with Julia?'

Tessa thought, stilled by the memory of Amy. She looked out of the window. Had it been that? She knew that she didn't want to tell too much to this man. 'I suppose . . . I'm not sure,' she murmured. She tried to remember.

Amy had been so quiet as she went about her business that to anyone who didn't work with her it might seem as if she was low in energy. It was only when you saw the fearsome number of problems she sorted in a day that you realized quite how active she was, that the quietness masked a formidable precision – she never did anything unnecessary. Tessa, who made lists, soon noticed that Amy didn't. Amy held everything in her head and effortlessly. Tessa, who prided herself on her efficiency, only briefly resisted acknowledging Amy's complete mental superiority.

From that moment of acknowledgement on, she

revised the basis of her competition with Amy. Tessa's interest in her own appearance systematically grew. She took up dance, she slimmed, she quadrupled the amount she spent on clothes, she indulged in hundred-quid haircuts. The transformation took months, but was dramatic: clients who hadn't visited the office for some time congratulated Hammond on his new secretary. It became a private joke between Tessa and Hammond.

Tessa's emergent poise and the effect it had on people gave her great pleasure. For this she had Amy to thank, without being fully conscious of it. Amy never passed comment on Tessa's change, seemed to be unaware of it, and remained the even-tempered, consistent colleague she always had been. Amy was unaltered in appearance. Her pale hair and blonde skin remained untouched by make-up; untouched, it seemed, by life.

Tessa had heard about Amy and Julia: that they were more than good friends. She thought of it as a malicious rumour. Tessa possessed a conventional streak of homophobia which she wouldn't admit to in public, even less act upon, but she did little to rethink it. The idea of two women together disgusted her and she hoped it wasn't true. With her new-found confidence, she was able to like and be friendly towards Amy and she really hoped it wasn't true. Then one day, Julia was in Tessa's office, going through some data Hammond had sent her in a memo, when Amy entered, not expecting Julia to be there.

Tessa was shocked by what she saw. Amy's face lit up as if a spotlight had been shone on it. As she laughingly asked what Julia was doing there, her easy colourless voice was transformed. It became charged with vigour, full of light and shade.

In the instant she saw her transfigured by love, Tessa was able to imagine Amy as someone's lover, which had never occurred to her before; those pale slim arms glistening with effort, electric with desire. Behind her neat desk, Tessa was astounded and illuminated for a moment, and then she began to discount what she had been privileged to witness. It made her uncomfortable to do so, but she continued to dismiss as a malicious rumour any talk of a relationship between Julia and Amy. In fact, over time, she came once more to disbelieve it herself.

Somewhere, however, she held the knowledge of what she had seen and the knowledge too that Amy knew she had seen it.

So what had happened on that afternoon she was trying to remember: what had Amy been talking about? It had been over a year ago. She had been watching Amy, who stood by the window in this very room, without a scrap of make-up as usual. How old was she? Tessa had wondered. So intelligent, so childish. She was troubled now. Tessa saw the frown deepen.

'Do you think it's fair . . .?' Amy hadn't completed the question. She went on in a different tone, impatient with herself. 'Of course it's fair!'

Amy had sighed, Tessa remembered, like a romantic heroine. Then she had taken a deep breath as if preparing to say something daringly revealing. She had checked herself again, hesitated, then looked Tessa full in the eye. 'I wonder,' she said. 'Do you know what's going on?'

Amy had looked searchingly at her. Tessa thought she had known what Amy was talking about, but wasn't going to admit it.

'Perhaps you don't,' Amy went on. 'Perhaps you don't.'

Then Muir Hammond had come into the office and Amy shut up like a clam.

Grudgingly, in simple terms, Tessa described this brief incident to Jones.

'So you knew Amy pretty well then, did you?'

'No, I didn't really. No. That's what I thought was odd. Her wanting to confide in me.'

'Perhaps she wanted to confide in you just because she didn't know you all that well.'

'Perhaps. I hadn't thought of that.'

'Not that she did confide in you.'

'No, but she wanted to.'

Now that she was calmer Tessa became irritated. The untidy Welshman offended her sense of order: it was only through order that things got done, in her book. Untidiness she equated with incompetence. And their conversation had begun to get close to something which she had no intention of talking to him about. She got rid of him . . . although she'd had to promise to arrange another meeting with Muir Hammond for the beastly little man.

Sally had explained to him, she thought, rather well. She had blamed herself, of course; blamed herself for not recognizing certain things about her own nature which she felt disqualified her from marriage at this stage of her life.

James's father, Nigel Arnott, had sat silent throughout, frowning and nodding. Now he stood. He didn't say anything until he'd finished sorting out the smouldering logs in the fireplace. Outside there was sunshine. A cold north wind was blowing leaves across the gravel sweep. The room was pleasant with the scent of wood smoke and sweet tobacco.

'Do you know what I think?' said Nigel Arnott as he turned from the fire. 'I think you're a selfish bitch.'

Sally stared. There wasn't a hint of humour in him. She couldn't believe it. It was like a personality change taking place in front of her.

'A selfish bloody bitch. Always thought you were an arrogant fucking cow and this confirms it.' His voice was lazy and savage, a short step from actual violence. Together with fear – he still had a poker in his hand – Sally experienced a triumphant sense of how right she was to be doing what she was doing. 'You'll make us the laughing stock of the county. You're a thorough-going treacherous little cunt so fuck off and don't come here again.'

Sally left the house hot with unexpressed anger,

furiously determined. James's plane was due at Stansted that afternoon. She drove straight round Norwich and headed down the A11.

There was one compensation, Jones decided, to be derived from all the pressure of re-opening the Kelleher case: he'd hardly had time even to think about Karen, never mind find the energy to lust after her. Here she was sitting beside him as he drove her to Homerton and he had barely noticed what was moving inside those black stockings.

She was unusually quiet. Bewick had asked her to go to his house and print up a copy of his file on the Julia Kelleher murder for him; so he was clearly on the mend. Why was she so quiet? Had she had a row with him?

'How was he then?'

'What?'

'Bewick; how was he?'

For one moment Karen thought Jones must know that she'd been making love to Bewick and was asking what he was like in bed.

She felt the beginning of a blush. She took a deep breath as if bored. 'He was fine. I think he's feeling quite a lot better.'

'Good. Oh! Did I get those notes to you?'

'Which ones?'

'My interview with Muir Hammond's PA, Tessa Waring. Snotty little bint.'

'Yeah, sure. I got those.'

'You'll make sure John Bewick sees them?'

''Course. What's the urgency?'

'No urgency . . . Just that I'd like him to know that I'm accommodating the inquiry to his useless ideas.'

'Sure, I'll give them to him if I see him first.'

'You're likely to, aren't you?'

'Yeah. I suppose I am.'

Slowing to some lights, Jones gave her a suspicious look. Christ, thought Karen, he's quick. You watch yourself, girl.

'Tell him I'm going to have a word with Toner as well.'

'I told him you'd brought Toner back into frame.'

'Toner's threatening to sue Bewick. I'll put him off that, I expect.'

'He really sorted Toner out, didn't he?'

'Yes.'

They were both silent for a moment. Both had heard the old rumours concerning Bewick's violence.

God, she's beautiful, Jones thought. That perfume she wears – it oughtn't to be allowed. 'What's that perfume you're wearing, Karen?'

'Cristalle.'

'It's nice. I think I'll buy Eilean some,'

They parked the car almost outside Bewick's house. Karen produced the key and they went in. As soon as they were through the door they knew something was wrong.

'He's asleep, Chief Inspector.'

Kit sounded like a mother hen.

'I'm going to have to ask you to wake him up then, Mrs Enwright – Karen says he's a lot better.'

'Well I dare say she'd know,' said Kit.

'I only want to ask him a question. Then he can sleep as long as he likes. We're at his house. It's been done over. Burglar Bill has been to tea.'

'Are you just being funny, or . . .'

'No, sorry. Not just a nervous tic. Seriously. There's been a robbery.'

'All right. I'll wake him.'

Jones waited, wondering what Kit's remark about Karen had meant.

Karen came into the sitting-room. 'I've found the floppy disk. I'll print it up at City West. It was taped to the bottom of that old food-blender, like he said. They've been through the back room he uses as a study: it's a complete jumble sale. When will the lads be here?'

'Soon. Did you switch on his computer?'

'Yeah, I tried. They nicked the hard disk.'

'This is developing into a pointless phone call.'

Kit came back on the line. 'I don't want to wake him, Chief Inspector. I'm sorry.'

'It's all right. They've got his hard disk so the question I was going to ask him is redundant.'

Karen made some coffee. She brought it through to the sitting-room. 'Do you think,' she said, 'that this is a coincidence, or–'

'Hard disks are currency. What software did he have?'

'The usual – Microsoft's latest.'

'Are there any software disks around?'

'Not that I could see.'

'Software is definitely currency, so if they've gone maybe . . .'

They shared a look, each realizing that the other didn't believe it.

'No,' said Jones. 'So matey catches Bewick on his bike and tries to kill him. Then he comes here. He nicks Bewick's hard disk to find out how much we know. Is it difficult to nick a hard disk?'

'No, Sir. How much do we know?'

'What?'

'You don't still think it was just Joe Enwright, do you?'

'No. He'll have been used, as I said before. We'll take another look at Rae, Toner and Kelleher. And there's always person or persons unknown. And we'll have to re-question the little shiteburger himself. A favourite activity – on the lines of having my teeth drilled. Excuse me.'

'Bewick told me that he rang Julian Rae about a quarter of an hour before he set off to cycle there.'

Jones turned in the doorway. 'Yes?'

'That would've given Rae time to get over to Bewick's and then wait for him.'

'Yes.'

Gio Jones left the room.

In the lavatory on the first floor of Bewick's house Jones listened idly, as he urinated, to the traffic noise drifting in through the small window.

Then he froze, his mind racing. He had remembered what had been troubling him. God!

'Jim Spilby,' he said aloud. 'Interestin' innit?' What a bloody idiot he'd been!

He hurried down the stairs. Karen was taking the coffee mugs back to the kitchen.

'I must get back,' said Jones.

'Right. I'll clear up here. Keep an eye on the team, when they get here.'

'Do that. Good. Oh, by the way,' he said smiling, 'when I told Mrs Enwright that you said Bewick was a lot better, you know what she said?'

'She fusses.'

'What she said was, "Well, she should know" – like a Sunday School mistress.'

'This is going to take hours, clearing this mess up,' said Karen and went. She was blushing.

He reckoned she was blushing. Despite the voice telling him not to, he followed her through to the kitchen, all his worst instincts aroused. He felt a sour mockery possess him. 'You do that. Get your apron on like a good little girl and tidy it up for him. Don't think you'll find it in Police Regs. but you never know.'

A moment later, it seemed, he was standing on the front doorstep having slammed the door behind him. From inside he heard, 'Well fuck you then.'

'God, I wish you would,' he murmured and headed for the car, angry with himself.

Karen stared at the slammed front door. I suppose all that carry-on means that he's guessed something about Bewick and me, she thought. Clever bastard. She realized too that it meant he cared and was jealous.

At first worried, she comforted herself with the fact that she knew Gio Jones wouldn't even hint to anyone what he suspected. Yes, she thought, he has a sort of . . . he's an honourable guy.

At Stansted, Sally broke the news to James.

'Why are you doing this?' he asked.

'I've met someone else,' she said for simplicity's sake. 'It's made me realize. I'm sorry. There's no going back James.'

He looked at her steadily, as if to judge the truth of this. 'Sod off then,' he said. He turned to the bar and ordered another drink.

She left. As she moved away, she heard a sudden movement behind her. She turned, her hand moving instinctively up to her face. She felt the jolt of the glass hitting her hand. The smoky, sharp smell of the whisky splashed her face.

Then she was running before she knew it. She didn't stop till she had reached her car. Once in, she locked all the doors.

Let's not get silly about this, she told herself.

Then she saw James running towards her. She'd been right. She started the engine. Then she realized that she had no ticket for the auto-exit. Tickets had to be bought in the airport building.

She began driving. Twelve m.p.h. was a five-minute mile. James was quite fit but nowhere near that fit. She cut the speed to ten m.p.h. Six-minute miles were tough enough. James followed her, almost within reach. She knew he would. Here was the stupid rage she'd feared and never glimpsed. Here it was, hot-faced, fists clenched, arms pumping, in her rear-view mirror.

On and on she drove, gathering a small audience as she led him round and round the car-park, speeding up when he cut the corners. Five minutes was an eternity that came and went. After seven or eight minutes his exhausted figure fell behind. She stopped the car, tempting him to come on.

From the terminal building, a couple of security guards had noticed her circuiting the car-park and were coming to investigate. She parked.

Leaving his colleague to look after her car, the other guard accompanied her to the ticket machine and back. Finally she was free to drive away. James had disappeared.

As she drove up the M11 she tried to leave it at Exit 9, the direct route to Norfolk, but couldn't bring herself to. She drove unthinkingly slowly, blind with lack of decision. Exit 11, the first of the Cambridge turn-offs, came and went. Exit 12 was the logical one to take for Homerton, but she couldn't bring herself to.

Exit 13 came up soon after. Last chance. She took it.

Jones was back at his desk. He was staring at the entry in his notebook which he'd made a week ago. He felt a coldness in his stomach at what it might imply. He had done nothing that could warrant even a raised eyebrow of criticism, but, as he'd realized at Bewick's house, he shouldn't have missed this. Now he was wondering how on earth he had.

The case had attracted a lot of notice. It would. His prisoner, naturally, was guilty as hell according to the tabloid press. Nobody is allowed to have a dying mother and to spend 25K, their entire patrimony, on a motorbike, without their reputation being shredded in the tabloids. It looked amoral, so it was blasted as immoral.

Joe Enwright was an unfeeling monster; a psychopath for our times. There were hints that killing strangers was becoming a druggy game: do your head in, do someone else's head in. This killing was portrayed as the casual product of a cancerously corrupt society: murder for sport.

Jones knew this was as stupid as you get, but he wondered now if he'd been influenced by it. He still couldn't think of Enwright as innocent.

He reminded himself again that he'd done nothing with which the pickiest superior could quarrel. He'd done everything by the book. In fact his eyes now strayed to the shelf where a copy of Police Regulations lay half-buried by magazines. Catching himself doing this amused him for a moment.

He picked up his notebook again. *'Is this the most boring reported crime of the decade?'* How wrong can you actually be? he asked himself. He should have made the connection when he first spoke to Spilby.

What he'd remembered at Bewick's house was the mention of a car in the Kelleher file. He sweated now, hot with embarrassment, as he read his jokey reporting of the theft and rediscovery of Jim Spilby's battered motor. He looked at the date: the car was stolen the day of Julia Kelleher's murder. Spilby's mates had spotted it on the Histon road the following morning. It was so glaring to him now. He reached for the phone and dialled an internal number.

'Frank? I need some help. A search on the Kelleher database. Have you got anything that'll look for reports of cars parked near the scene?'

He stood and went to the window. Outside the light was going. A string of foreign students was toiling incompetently on their identical hired bikes up Maid's Causeway. The tops of trees opposite were catching the hot colours of a sunset invisible behind him.

He asked himself again if he had unconsciously suppressed the possibility of a connection between the two cars, to protect his case – even from Bewick. He thumped down into his chair. He knew that denial, even to himself, of some such complicity wasn't on.

Suddenly he sat up and looked at his watch and

swore. Moments later he was hurrying from the building.

The house, in a smart cul-de-sac off Grange Road, was very new – only two or three years old, Jones reckoned.

He found Hammond in a pair of nearly new overalls, with his head inside the engine space of an Alvis, the folded bonnet gleaming above him, the engine pulsing smoothly. Hammond looked round at Jones and stared as if he'd never seen him before. He switched off the engine. Jones re-introduced himself and explained that his secretary . . .

Hammond nodded. He peeled off the plastic gloves he was wearing. 'Oh yes.'

Hammond took off his overalls while Jones made himself feel foolish praising the beauties of the Alvis. Hammond hung the overalls on a hanger.

'Come in. Excuse the mess. Builders.'

In the hallway two electricians were at work. Jones smiled at them. Their response was guarded. They weren't happy men. Surreptitiously they eyed Hammond as he stood inspecting what they had done. Hammond made a sour face and waved to the door of the living-room. 'Why don't you go in there?'

Jones complied. From the hallway he heard, 'You can't run it there, you really can't. Put it where I told you.'

'That'll mean moving the rad, Mr Hammond. That'll mean your plumbers, Mr Hammond.'

There was no immediate reply to this.

The sound of a few footsteps and then Hammond was talking to his office. 'Tessa. I have someone here who needs the number of the plumbers I used . . . There.'

Hammond had evidently handed the phone to one of the electricians.

'Just do it,' Hammond said and a moment later appeared in the doorway. Jones imagined with some satisfaction the faces being made behind his back. He thought he heard a stifled laugh when his thoughts were interrupted by Hammond.

'My wife.'

Jones realized he was staring at a photograph. A plump woman smiled out from it. She looked cheerful and determined. The lurid studio background, bright inappropriate blue, was what had caught Jones's eye.

'Ah yes,' Jones replied, as if she was what had taken his attention.

'Ahm, four years ago. She died then I mean. That photo is a little older.'

'Sure.'

'Summer '89. When she died.'

'Right.'

Hammond looked out of the window. He had the sort of face which Jones had seen a hundred times; ordinary, undistinctive, bland. Yet he was an exceptional man. His only oddity seemed to be his taste for greys and silvers in his clothes. As Karen had said, he looked like one of his own bits of hardware. He looked at Jones now as if confused. Jones realized that he was probably very shy.

'I can't remember why you're here, I'm afraid.'

'To try to find out as much as I can about Amy Parris.'

Hammond took a breath as if impatient, but replied calmly enough. 'I thought we'd done that. There's not much more I can tell you. She was very clever, very good. So good in fact we left her pretty much to get on with it. So . . .'

Hammond made a face. He looked as if he was trying to remember something that might be useful. Then Jones found himself on the end of a very penetrating glance. 'What's all this about then? Why Amy? What started this off?'

'The man called in by the defence.'

'Oh yes? He spoke to me.'

'Yes. Bewick. John Bewick. He was interested in her, you see . . . Well, he's had a bit of an accident, matter of fact.'

'I'm sorry to hear that.'

'Yeah, pretty serious. Well – this is speculation, you understand – we think he may have been attacked. So I'm obliged to take his theories a little more seriously.'

'Theories?'

'I have to consider the possibility that the attack on him had something to do with following a line of inquiry that threatened the murderer and his accomplice.'

'His accomplice?'

'I'm still assuming we got the killer. But he could have had an accomplice. In fact I think he did have.'

'I see. And Mr Bewick is interested in Amy Parris?'

'He does seem to be, yes. I just wondered if you remember anything out of the ordinary on the day she went missing? Mr Bewick thinks she may have been frightened of something.'

Hammond thought for some moments, staring at the carpet. Finally he shook his head. 'I'm sorry. She was very self-sufficient, you see. Very independent. She only seemed to make herself noticeable when she was needed.'

'Sounds like the perfect employee.'

'She was.' For a brief moment Hammond sounded furious with regret. 'It was such a bloody waste. An awful waste of a young life.' He was floundering now, unable to express himself, as if he'd been surprised by a journalist with a mike.

There was a silence. Jones took in the room: an uneasy mix. A pair of oriental cupboards, heavily carved, dark and gilt, which dominated the pale blue furnishings; the chrome and glass and the signed lithographs, which were vaguely familiar, probably famous.

Hammond levered himself smartly out of his chair. He walked to the window. He looked out of it for a moment, then turned. 'Well?' he said.

'Well, as I say . . . if you remember anything out of the ordinary that might have happened in the days leading up to her disappearance . . . The other thing I suppose is what I asked your secretary. Could Amy

Parris have been working on anything particularly sensitive when she disappeared? I mean something she might have found a burden in some way?'

'Everything we do is sensitive.'

'That's what your secretary said.'

'She was right. IT is a security nightmare.'

'She said that too. So you can't throw any light on Amy Parris's being on the run, Sir?'

Why had he suddenly referred to Hammond as Sir? Was it because he realized how much he disliked the man; the tetchy arrogance he had shown towards the men working in his house, his need for control.

'On the run?'

'That's what we reckon, yes. She was on the run from something.'

Hammond looked stupefied for a moment. Then he said, 'Nothing here was alienating her, I can assure you.'

A few minutes after Jones got back to his office, reflecting as he did so on the utter waste of the past hour, lanky Frank Dalmeny slid an arm around the door and waved a few sheets of paper at him. 'Print-out, Chief.'

Gio Jones took them and thanked him.

The report was fuller than he'd remembered it. On the night of the murder, a car, similar to Jim Spilby's old banger, had been seen parked just off the Old Longtoft road, about half a mile from Julia Kelleher's cottage. That was about the same distance from the lay-by on the St Neot's road, where the tinker families' occupation had dissuaded Bella from setting up her snack wagon that evening.

Jones sat down to read the report.

The car, which might or might not have been Jim Spilby's, was parked just off the road in front of a farm gate. Beyond the gate was a track through a belt of trees leading to the bleak set-aside fields behind Parbold Cottage.

In the early stages, Jones had been so occupied with finding the super bike that this car had been forgotten. Once the case had gone to the CPS, once he had only been concerned with the safeness of the evidence he'd been providing, it had remained forgotten.

He re-read the statement. The witness was reliable enough. Alan Spenser was a motor accessory salesman who had once worked in a garage. His ID of an old Ford Escort was definite.

The Old Longtoft road follows the line of a Roman road. It runs straight, dipping into the valley of Comber Brooke then rising equally straight up its further slope. Spenser's headlights had picked up the reflectors of the Escort as soon as he'd turned off the St Neot's road. He'd assumed the car was occupied by a pair of lovers, and as he drew closer . . .

Jones stopped reading. He swore at himself. Slowly his hand reached for the phone again. He looked at his notebook. He dialled. A woman answered.

'Mrs Spilby?'

'Yes?'

'Can I speak to Jim?'

'He's not here.' She sounded disapproving, as if Jim's friends should find other means of contacting Jim, rather than via her phone.

'Where might I find him then?'

'You tell me. He'll be in for his tea.'

'When will that be?'

'Tea time,' said Mrs Spilby and put down the phone.

Jones put the phone down on his immediate boss, Superintendent Hutchings, just as Inglis came into the office.

'Yes?'

'Kelleher case, Sir?'

'Yes?'

'Mary Crofton has changed her testimony about David Toner. I went over to that refuge place where Crofton is this morning. Crofton has moved in, sort of permanent like. She's helping ten-ton Sister Patience. Anyway, she told me Toner wasn't with her the night of the murder – not most of it.'

Inglis looked at Jones, who seemed transfixed, staring into space trying to think through the implications of this.

'You said you was looking for secondary lines of inquiry, Sir.' Inglis sounded apologetic. Like all the teams, he'd thought a week or so ago that the Kelleher case was oven-ready.

'Sure. No, this is good. Dead useful. You did well. Thanks lad.'

'OK, Sir.'

'Reckon you could get a statement out of her?'

'Reckon I could.'

'Great. Do that, will you?'

'OK, Sir.'

The door closed behind Inglis.

So David Toner, who was known to be violent, had no alibi for the night in question. He was £200,000 richer by the death of his wife. If there were any connection between Toner and Enwright . . . Was Enwright Toner's fall guy? Christ! He'd better sort this out.

Jones realized that what had held him back from putting Toner in the frame – apart from Enwright's DNA – was the fact that Toner was threatening to sue Bewick for assault. It didn't seem to be the action of someone who had his own violent crime to hide. Toner, though, was full of ambiguities. His strange, lurching course – early school leaver, the army, the wholefood shop, self-employed electrical engineer – suggested someone swept along by events. Meet him, however, and he exuded a peculiar confidence. Perhaps he was a natural con: a dreamer who was able to sell you his life story as that of a capable man, someone who took hard decisions and could act on them. Julia Kelleher had been fooled into marriage with him, after all. But then she was only twenty-two at the time.

★

Five minutes later his phone rang on an internal line. It was Superintendent Hutchings, again.

'Are you coming, Gio?'

Jones had promised to go straight up to Hutchings's office. He'd completely forgotten.

'Sure. Sorry. On my way.'

Superintendent Alfred Hutchings was dark haired, dark eyed, much more Italian looking than the half-Italian Jones. Hutchings was olive skinned too, with deep grey shadows around his eyes, giving him a haunted look which was quite at odds with his easy, breezy nature, whose most damaging addiction was golf – which, indirectly, was what he wanted to see Jones about.

'Had a round with Hammond today.'

'Oh yes? Don't tell me. He's feeling harassed. He's been helpful beyond the call of public duty and there's this Welsh git still asking him pointless questions and it's enough to put a chap off his swing.'

Hutchings smiled. 'He hardly mentioned it, matter of fact. But I thought I'd ask you how you're getting on.'

'We're interested in a girlfriend of the murdered woman, who worked at Sirius too . . . You play with him regularly, do you Fred?'

'Not regularly. Why?'

'Don't know. I thought he was such an arsehole, that's all.'

'Yeah, he's a bit of a dick, but he makes up a four

and plays his golf cheerfully enough. Very competitive and keeps improving. He's going to beat me soon. Lucky I'm such a good loser,' Hutchings chuckled.

'Should have heard the way he treated the fellows who were working on his house, snotty sod.'

'Suppose you have to make allowances . . .'

'Do you?'

'Genius and all that.'

'Maybe,' Jones grumbled.

'Anyway, how is it going? Last thing you told me was that the attack on John Bewick might have changed things. Still think so?'

'Yes,' Jones answered, curt, gloomy.

'May have bugger all to do with your case. I don't reckon Bewick's a man without enemies.'

'Can't discount it . . .'

Jones decided not to tell Hutchings about Jim Spilby's car. Not yet. It was going to need explaining if it turned out to have been involved. Was he going to admit to missing it first time round? Or might he be able to present it as an inspired afterthought?

'No, you can't discount it,' Hutchings agreed. 'So what're you doing about it?'

'All I'm doing at the moment is seeing if I can tie someone in with Enwright who might have had a go at John Bewick.'

'Got anyone in mind?'

Jones told him about David Toner.

Sally rang the doorbell and waited. She didn't care

what was in store for her. She just knew how important it was to be sure of how things stood. She heard movement: thank God he was in. This would soon be over.

The door opened. Karen and Sally stared at each other. Karen was wearing an apron.

'Hello.'

'Hello. I'm Dr Vernon. I'm a friend of Mr Bewick's.'

'He's not here. He was in a bit of an accident. He's fine now. He's at a friend's house. Are you all right?'

'Sure. What sort of accident?'

'A road accident, but he's fine now; really.'

Karen thought the woman was in some sort of shock. She recognized the look. It was a look she often saw.

'Come in. Come in.'

'OK. Thanks.'

Jones was on the phone. Mrs Spilby had gone to fetch Jim.

Jim arrived, dropped the phone, apologized and then sneezed. Gio Jones explained who he was.

'That car of yours, Jim . . .'

'Yes?'

'It wouldn't happen to have a piece of reflective tape on its rear bumper would it, off-side?'

'No.'

Gio Jones heard something in Jim Spilby's voice: a jokiness like he'd heard sometimes from Frank Dalmeny in the office when he was deliberately misunderstanding someone. He tried again. 'No, OK. Let's put it this way Jim: have you ever had a piece of reflective tape on your bumper?'

'Yeah.'

'You have?'

'Sure. 'Course.'

'Was it on your bumper the night it was nicked?'

'Yeah. I pulled it off.'

'When would that have been?'

'After they nicked it again.' Spilby giggled. 'I just done it. I got it in my hand.' He laughed – a long, jerky, sniffing sound.

'What? They nicked it again?'

'Yeah. Few days ago. Left it in the same place an' all.'

There was silence from Jones for a moment. Which day? He thought of what had happened to Bewick.

'Jim, you in this evening?'

Karen led the way into the kitchen. She put the kettle on.

'Are you sure you're all right, Dr Vernon? You look to me . . . I mean, have you had something go wrong?'

Sally chuckled humourlessly. She was silent and then said, 'In a manner of speaking.'

She told Karen of the frightening and ludicrous incidents at Stansted. Then she told her about the shock of James's father calling her a cunt.

'He's very traditional, with old-fashioned manners;

pipe-smoker, old tweed jackets and courtesy, you know. It was horrible.'

'You're well out of it.'

'I know, I know. That's why I think I'll be over it soon. At least my instincts were right. Half of the drive up here I've been congratulating myself.'

'I'm making tea. Want some?'

'Hot sweet tea?'

Karen laughed, 'Yeah.'

'Why not? You've been treating me as if I was someone in shock.'

'You are.'

'Am I?'

'I'll tell you something. Verbal abuse is underrated as an offensive weapon.'

'That's good. I like that.'

'So you've been assaulted twice today. I don't know what your work is, but where I work you get top-quality first-hand experience. The official name for it is canteen culture. What it means is lads together, and a load of foul-mouthed attitude. Because, one to one, the pathetic little bastards know that any woman worth her salary would wipe the lino with them. I'm a copper, by the way. What sort of doctor are you?'

'I was a medic. But it's research now. The doctor bit is the PhD bit. We get a bit of attitude in the lab, but I run my own lab now, so . . .'

'Good for you. How do you know John Bewick?' Karen asked.

Sally had been dreading this question. It left her

vulnerable, her keenest instincts liable to be exposed as so much fakery. She had always managed, through all the shyness of childhood even, to maintain some belief in herself. If she was wrong about Bewick . . . Was it possible that he was just . . .?

'We met on a plane about a fortnight ago. He wanted some advice about DNA fingerprinting, so we met again when I was next in Cambridge.'

Karen was staring at her. Why was she staring at her? Suddenly Karen looked away. The kettle had boiled. She made the tea. 'Why did you break off this engagement of yours?'

'I didn't trust him. Was I right?'

'How long haven't you trusted him?' Karen wasn't looking at her, but busying herself finding mugs and milk. She didn't appear to know the kitchen very well.

'Why do you ask?' There was an edge of suspicion in Sally's voice.

They were each suddenly facing up to the other; in the cockpit together. Yet, as women, each appreciated her rival, only too ready to appreciate the other's quality.

It was a civilized enough exchange:

'I asked,' replied Karen, 'because I'm screwing John Bewick at the moment.'

'I see.'

'But . . . it's early days. And I want to know everything about him. Including you, if you're included.'

'Do you love him?' Sally asked, looking in dread at the strong, slender arms, tanned beneath pale golden hairs which caught the light. And her mouth, tough and full, which fell now into a troubled repose, sexy even to her.

'Yes I do. I've loved him since ever,' Karen said.

'Yes . . .'

'And you?' Karen asked.

'Me?'

'Do you love him?'

'I only met him a couple of weeks ago.'

'That doesn't mean a thing.'

'In my book it does,' Sally replied.

'OK. Be grown up, if that's what you want.'

'Yes . . . Yes I do. Yes I love him,' Sally heard herself blurt out, impatient.

'Well Dr Vernon, what a monster cock-up. Tea?'

'I don't think . . .'

'Don't be bloody coy. We've got to sort this out. You say you love him. How long have you known you love him?'

'Hardly at all. I don't know if I do, even. Look, I think I'd better go. I think this thing with James has warped my judgement. I'll probably find it's some form of transference. Meeting John made me realize I couldn't go on with James, so I'm probably so grateful . . .'

Karen could see the poor cow was on the edge of tears. She was frightened by her though, very frightened.

'When did you come back to Cambridge and tell him about DNA?'

'On the fourteenth.'

The day he was attacked, Karen realized. 'And you were still engaged then, were you?'

'Yes.'

'Did John know that?' Karen asked.

'Yes. Listen, I think I'll go. I can see exactly why he's with you . . .'

Karen was given one of the most potent confidence boosters she would ever know – reflected admiration from the eyes of a rival woman.

'I'll go. It's best. I'd say give him my love but that's daft. Good luck . . .'

The phone rang. Karen answered it, quoting the number.

'Is John there?' It was Alec Dundas. 'That's Karen Quinney, is it?'

'That's right. Mr Dundas?'

'Aye. Just looking for a progress report.'

Karen obliged.

Sally watched Karen, who was half turned away, and couldn't stop herself imagining Bewick making love to her. As quietly as she could she left the house. Once outside she ran to her car and drove away. All her drive back to Norfolk, her imagination was haunted by the fairness of Karen.

Mrs Spilby had changed her dress, put on perfume and make-up for Gio Jones's visit. She was a proud woman. She had lit the log-effect fire in her lounge where she served Jones a lager in a tulip-shaped glass.

Her son shambled in wearing the pullover she had bought him for his last birthday.

'Hello, Jim.'

'Call me if you need anything,' said Mrs Spilby as she closed the door.

'Tell me about this latest business, Jim. You say someone nicked your car again?'

'Yeah.'

'Where they leave it this time?'

'Same place, just about.'

'Any damage?'

'Not a scratch.'

'You sure?'

'Plenty of scratches already. Know what I mean?'

'Where's your motor now?'

'Outside.'

'I'd like to have a glance. D'you mind?'

'Stay to dinner. Nick the vidjeo. I don't mind.'

There was a crowded history of vehicle abuse to be read in Jim's paintwork. He stood laughing silently as Jones carefully examined the nearside front of the old Escort. Jim had taken off his pullover. As requested, he started the car up and let it idle, revved and let it fall back, while the plump cop wandered up and down the road listening to it.

Well, Gio Jones thought to himself, it could be the one. Bound to sound slightly different here. He knew the effect of a different acoustic from his choirboy days. He returned to the car. 'Tell me something, Jim.

Why d'you leave your car where you do? In that lay-by, I mean? Where it got nicked?'

'The bumps.'

'The bumps?'

'Yeah. They put bumps all over the place. Wreck your suspension, them things, 'specially when you ain't got too much to start with, 'specially in the morning when nothing's warmed up. I can cut through past Mrs Shiltoe's – don't take no longer.'

Jones nodded. Made sense. He never knew suspensions were more efficient warm. Probably they weren't. 'I'm going to ask you a favour, Jim.'

'You are?'

'I reckon your motor was used in the perpetration of a crime, son. I'd like to borrow it so that forensic can have a glance. OK?'

'What'll I do for wheels?'

'We'll lend you something.'

'Will it be as good as this?'

'It'll be difficult to reproduce the patina, Jim, it may look a bit repro by comparison, but we'll do our best. Then there's your trousers.'

'My – '

'Your trousers, Jim, and your upper-body outer clothing, plus a sample of your hair for luck.'

'Me Mum washes everything.'

'An unfortunate habit I agree, but the fibres will be the same clean or dirty.'

'OK.'

'Thanks, Jim.'

Jim looked at Jones and wagged a finger. 'Told you it was interestin'.'

Karen told Alec Dundas as much as she could. She put the phone down and realized her pulse was racing: nothing to do with the phone call. It was to do with that woman.

Dr Vernon, eh? The Vernon woman wasn't any way sure of how she stood. So don't panic, Karen told herself. You handled it well.

Karen went on clearing up. But she found herself moving around the kitchen as if she had an unseen audience, as if she were on show, on trial; as if she had to prove herself more worthy of Bewick than Sally Vernon. For God's sake!

She lectured herself: she reminded herself how she knew this whole thing with Bewick had no future. Take each day as it comes. Well, fine, except this was the day she reckoned she'd met the woman Bewick was really interested in, and she didn't like it. She fucking hated it in fact. He wasn't trying to get back with his wife, was he? It was this. This Dr Sally Vernon with the beautiful skin. Not much else, mind: the else was just ordinarily OK. OK face, OK figure . . . and beautiful skin.

Stop it! she hissed to herself. You don't know.

She repeated 'You don't know' to herself like a mantra.

12

Gio Jones stood at the door of the small terraced house in Dallington. He rang the bell again and waited. Eventually he walked down the covered alley which led to the gardens at the back.

In Toner's garden stood a cobbled-together garden shed. Someone was moving inside. Jones went over to it and knocked.

The door opened. David Toner eyed him suspiciously. 'Yes?'

'Hi.' Jones stood and grinned as if the next move was up to Toner. Behind Toner he could see spreadeagled skins of squirrels nailed to the wooden wall. The shed stank of them and the woody spirituousness of turpentine.

'You're a copper, aren't you?'

'Polite of you to say so. Boss expresses his doubts on the subject a bit too often for comfort.'

'What d'you want?'

'I thought we might have a beer.'

'This isn't official then?'

'Christ no. Boss'd murder me if he knew I was here.'

'What d'you want?'

'A chat. Thought I might buy you a beer.'

Toner looked at Jones. As he did, Toner measured him for his fighting capacity as he did instinctively with all men he met. 'All right. We'll have a beer. You go and get some. I got to finish this.' Toner was glueing wooden joints and setting up cramps to hold them.

'Where'll that be?'

'Post-office,' replied Toner as if it was a stupid question.

Ten minutes later Jones had returned to Toner's with a six-pack of the requested bitter. God, he could smell the shed from here. If he hadn't been driven by an unusual combination of nervousness and guilt, Jones wouldn't have come back to the shed with its smell of animal death. But pulling in an obstructive bastard like Toner, who'd probably stand on his rights and be as uncooperative as possible, would take time and effort he couldn't afford. Get on with it, he told himself.

Toner waved Jones to a dirty armchair, decayed and gnawed, set in a bower of piled-up furniture, boxes, plastic containers and bundles of newspaper tied with orange twine.

'I won't be long,' Toner said and took a mouthful of beer.

He bent over his work with the air of a dedicated craftsman. Even Jones could see what he was doing was crap, the joints crudely cut, the wood warped. As he worked, fussily setting and re-setting the two right-angles, Toner answered Jones's idle-sounding questions.

He was a fleshy man, pale skinned. His hair was short and he wore a copper bracelet on his left wrist. His training as a professional soldier had given him a neatness of movement which could sometimes look out of place with his general bulk; prissy indeed.

He was a local, he said, born in Cambridge. Lived at various times in Cottenham, Rampton and Swaffham Bulbeck. He had joined the army straight from school and had met Julia after his discharge, seventeen years later.

Toner went very still suddenly, crouched over his badly set joints for several seconds, staring at them. Then he straightened up, ran a hand through his hair, adjusted his copper bracelet and went with his beer to sit on a stool by the open door.

'That'll do nicely,' Toner said of the woodwork.

Jones suspected that if he'd been alone, Toner would have chucked the whole messed-up job into a corner and walked off.

'How did you meet Julia?'

Toner looked at Jones as if he'd asked something outrageous. He had dark blue eyes. Hooded under a frown, as they were now, they suggested mental strength. They seemed to pull the rest of his ordinary features together, to give him an air of distinction.

'Would you rather not talk about her? I'm sorry, mate.'

'I can talk about her. Doesn't bother me. Soil

Association, wasn't it? When I was coming out of the army I signed on for a course. Environmental Awareness. I went to one of these Soil Association things.' Toner smiled. 'Tweedies and hippies! Dreamers. Still, she was there. Just a kid then.'

'You got together straight away, you and Julia?'

'Yeah, 'bout then. She wanted to get away from her mother. She was being stifled by her mother. I gave her life a focus.'

The idea of Mrs Kelleher stifling anyone struck Jones as so absurd he almost smiled. The Mrs Kelleher he'd met couldn't stifle a daddy-long-legs.

'I thought it was more her father she was getting away from.'

Toner nodded, the dark eyes alert. 'That's what people think. No, no. Her dad's OK. Dead straight. Her mother's the one. All that I'm-not-important, pay-no-attention-to-me stuff. Don't you believe it. She's ruthless, mate. No it wasn't her dad.'

The sun came out. Jones hoped it would go in again. If this stinking shed warmed up, he reckoned he'd pass out. Toner began his third beer.

'You got into all that, didn't you? Organic and stuff?'

'Yeah. I was into organic on my allotment . . . still am. We sold the surplus. It was her idea, the health food. She started going round in a van selling door to door. Soil Association types. Then the old Bedford died on her. I said instead of trying to get another van, why not put the money into a shop. That was much better.'

Jones tried to imagine Toner's allotment. If it was anything like this shed it'd look like the Congo Basin.

David Toner drained his third can. He was beginning to talk, under the influence. Jones asked in a general way about Julia's family and acquaintances. Some of Toner's charm was becoming discernible now. The dark blue eyes, when amused, were unforgettable. Jones understood how he might, long ago, have appealed to a young Julia Kelleher. He was, however, hearing only what he knew before. He eventually decided to try a direct lie. 'The lad we've got for your wife's murder, Mr Toner . . .'

'What about him?' Toner sounded deliberately breezy.

'Oh, nothing really. Something he said. I wondered how well you know him. He's a big admirer of yours.'

'Of mine. Really?'

The satisfaction was there, however disguised with indifference.

'Yeah, you really mean something to him.'

'He used to hang around Julia.'

'Well he's impressed with you.'

'Some of these young queers like real men.'

'That would be it, I suppose. Did he spend much time with Julia?'

'Yeah, some. I mean, quite a bit.'

'I wonder why? I mean, if he wasn't interested in the women. Or was he a bit ac/dc?'

'She turned queer in the end. Julia got off on women in the end. Did you know that? Did you?' Toner turned his dark, focused stare on Jones. He seemed determined that Jones should know and remember this. Was it because, in Toner's disordered mind, it excused anything that followed?

'Blimey,' said Jones, warmly Welsh and sympathetic, 'that must have been difficult for you.'

'It was after we split, mate,' Toner corrected him; then added with some self-satisfaction, 'She didn't look at another man after me.'

Jones looked at Toner to see if he showed any awareness of what he had just said – not a spark. 'Sure. Do you reckon the Enwright boy might swing both ways a bit, though? Do you?'

Toner shrugged. 'Might. Who cares?'

'Yeah. Who cares? He was very keen on you. Do you think he might have been a bit passionate about you? A bit in love?'

Toner shrugged again as if accepting what was only his due, after all. Jones looked concerned, admiring. 'Quite difficult to deal with, though, if he was pushy . . . you know. Don't know how I'd deal with that sort of thing.'

'He was all right. I can handle that. It was OK.'

Jones nodded, compassionate understanding written all over him. It was an effort to resist pushing it further. He was excited, pleased with himself, pleased with his own intuition. If they were looking beyond Joe Enwright, here was a formidable connection; with £200K at stake. If the boy had declared his feelings for Toner, then that gave Toner serious leverage. That stacked up, didn't it? The logic was good . . .

Toner got lazily to his feet and stood in the doorway, his back to Jones, staring at his messy garden.

'I think you're a bit stupid.' Toner's voice broke in on Jones's hidden excitement. 'Coming out here by yourself, without permission. No one knowing you're here. I could sort you out with my first one-two.' Toner smiled. 'You could be at the bottom of my compost heap in a couple of minutes, never mind you're obviously a heavy little bastard.'

'That a threat or a promise?'

Toner turned, slamming the door of the shed shut: sudden twilight. Jones could feel the sweat running down inside his shirt. The stench of the animal skins seemed instantly more powerful.

'What you come here for?'

Jones was shaking, trying desperately to calm himself down. He swallowed before speaking. 'Open that door and I'll tell you.'

'I want to know.'

Toner tensed. Was he about to launch himself?

'First thing you should know,' Jones lied, 'is that Detective Sergeant Inglis and Detective Constable Baynes both know I'm here. I have a meeting with them at four forty-five. I suppose they'd be knocking at your door about six. Up to you. Open the door.'

'What do you want?'

'To talk to you about the maverick bastard you had a fight with. Open the door.'

Silence; Jones's heart was thumping. This attempted authority wasn't working.

Outside in the garden there was a cawing of rooks high above.

'Yeah? So? What about him?'

Jones said nothing. He was trying to work out what Toner was up to. What benefit to Toner was there in threatening him? None that he could see. It was irrational. Was he psychotic? Jones knew that if he were, alcohol could be petrol on a smouldering fire. He had nothing on his side except his experience. Trial and mostly error had led him to believe that the only role to play here was the compassionate adult, the good parent.

'Well?'

'What I have to say could be very important to you,' Jones said gently, 'but I can't discuss it like this. All you have to do is open the door and I'll talk about it outside. There – now I've told you what I want. It's only fair that you tell me what you want. I came here to help.'

Jones also tried to suggest the entire UK law-enforcement agencies were of course available to him with a snap of his fingers, but that the last thing he wanted was to snap his fingers.

There was a long silence, then the door of the shed creaked open. Toner lumbered outside to stand on the grass. Jones followed, sucking the fresh air into him, trying to control any symptoms of the relief he felt.

'Well?'

'This bloke you had a fight with . . .'

'I'm sueing him.'

'Sure, don't blame you. Thing is, you see, it could cost you.'

'How come? I'll win.'

'But he hasn't got any insurance. He's not a copper any more. And he's shelling out through the nose to his wife and her kids. You know, usual thing. It may not be worth it.'

'He's got a house, hasn't he?'

'Has he? Never been there,' Jones lied.

'In Homerton. They don't cost sixpence.'

So Toner knew where Bewick lived.

'Sure,' said Jones. 'And then of course you'll be up against one of the best QCs in the country.'

'Eh? Get off. If he's so broke as you say, he won't be able to afford a bleeding silk, will he?'

'This is it. The bastard has posh-shite lawyers as friends. Went to school with them. I mean buddies. He'll get one of them to defend him, guaranteed. And there's another thing . . .' Gio Jones lowered his voice and leant towards Toner, who was looking thoughtful. 'There's no saying he wouldn't have another go at you. He's a violent sod. And you could bet that next time he wouldn't leave a visiting card.' Jones glanced quickly round. 'He killed a man once, that's the word on the street. Only fair you should know. I haven't said that to you.'

Toner nodded. 'I'll meditate on it,' he said. 'What's in it for you?'

'Eh?'

'Me not sueing that bastard who had a go at me – what's in it for you?'

'My job, probably. He used to be in the force. If your brief starts rubbishing the force, God knows what'll be said about me. I'd rather that didn't happen. Same time, if he has another go at you that'd be even worse, because he'd do damage, serious damage, and what'll we get accused of then? Yeah?'

'Yeah, I see. I'll meditate on it then, won't I? You meditate, do you?'

'Yeah, I've had a go,' Jones lied again.

'Who needs drugs?' said Toner, taking another gulp of beer. 'Time out of time, that's what you're looking for.'

'Sure . . . You have a think, then, eh?'

Jones drove away fast for a couple of miles then, where beeches overarched the road, he scrunched the car to a halt. He got out, flung his jacket on the back seat, and walked up and down under the trees, breathing the leafmould and listening to the birdsong for a minute or two.

He was still confused about Toner. He'd thought for a moment he'd seen what the young Julia Kelleher had been attracted to. Power, a grown-up who could handle himself, those technicolor eyes, anything to get away from her father . . . But the stupid sod was barely in control. How could she have lived with all that vanity and blindness?

Unless it was recent. Unless it was the result of trauma . . . Of massive guilt? Of some self-inflicted nightmare? Of blood on his hands? . . . Or was it just the booze?

He returned to the car, and drove back to the post-office in Dallington. He asked the woman serving where the allotments were and if she knew which belonged to Toner.

'Well you won't find him there!' she snorted.

'Won't I?'

'Parish Council are going to take his name off of it, they've had that many complaints. Hardly touched it since he had it, lazy swine! Jungle! They're going to give it to one of the youngsters.'

He drove back to City West.

As Jones opened the front door that evening his wife was just coming down the stairs with an armful of washing. Eilean stopped at the bottom of the staircase and gave Gio a weary half-smile.

'Hi. I haven't cooked. Little buggers've been a pain. One thing after another.'

'I'll go and get something.'

'Will you? That'd be so great.' She smiled at him and he knew they would make love that night.

As he headed back to his car, Jones thought about Bewick and Karen. For a moment he didn't care.

Sally rowed the small dinghy, crammed with stores and belongings, through the ruffled waters of Salvage Creek. She resisted the urge to hurry. The ebb had set in and for every stroke forwards she moved half a one backwards. It was another quarter of a mile and she might need all her energy at the end.

Her mother had asked her if it was a good idea to go off by herself like this, alone. She wouldn't be alone, she'd said: she had books. To her mother this was meaningless, merely clever. For Sally, it was the truth. There had also been a bad weather forecast. Sally said that, tucked up in Salvages Creek, she would rather relish a storm.

She was making steady progress. To her left was Scales Howe, the breeze rustling the low salty brooms and heathers on its inland shore. Behind it, the sky was dark. To her right the sun was setting behind the Scots pines on the ridge above Scalder Staithe. The saltings and the marshland between were loud with the chatter of birds.

She passed a lean low white yacht, a wooden yawl, one of eight boats moored in the creek: only two to go. She put on a spurt as she approached *Greylag* and quickly shipped the oars to slide neatly along her quarters. She reached up and caught hold of a gun-whale. Only then did she appreciate the strength of the ebb she had been rowing against. Carefully she made fast with the dinghy's painter, then began transferring the contents of the dinghy.

Twenty minutes later Sally sat in the cockpit of the old boat, a glass of wine in her hand, listening to the trills and yells of the birds, even louder now as they moved in on the inter-tidal mud. Below, in the cabin, small oil lamps glowed against the varnished bulkheads. Another time she would have been content.

Her world now was filled with hurt and longing. It was always there, mostly a grumbling ache. But sometimes, as now, there were sudden rushes of pain when her future looked as barren as the sea she could see stirring beyond the turbulent bar uncovering at the northern end of the creek.

As she sat there, a different sense of discomfort came to her. She was overtaken by the feeling that she was not alone. Slowly she turned to look at the island. There was no one there; no one at least that she could see in the fading light.

After they'd eaten the supermarket meal Jones had bought – fresh filled pasta and arrabbiata sauce, some ricotta and fruit washed down with most of a bottle of Sangiovese – they were silenced; slumped together on the sofa while they half-attended to the TV news. Eilean felt his restlessness.

'What is it?'

It was only at her prompting that Jones realized

what was nagging at him. He'd been unable to get through to Bewick since he talked to Toner. He'd tried to satisfy himself by making more than usually scrupulous notes. That afternoon he'd asked Karen to deliver them but that probably wouldn't happen until tomorrow. He realized he needed to speak to Bewick, because he was in two minds about Toner.

'Is it John Bewick?' Eilean asked. 'Try him again. Go on.'

'OK.' He kissed her and hauled himself to his feet.

Jones rang Bewick at George and Kit's. This time he was there.

'Yes?' Bewick sounded irritable.

'What's the matter with you then?'

'What d'you want?' Bewick was equally curt.

'You OK?'

'I was asleep. Been involved in a road accident. Were you told?'

This was so deadpan, Jones thought for a moment Bewick meant he'd been in another accident. 'All right, all right, just to tell you that – nothing to do with you – I've convinced myself there was someone else involved in the Kelleher murder. Party in question nicked a car to get there; probably the same car that knocked you off your bike. The path. lads are giving it the twice over.'

'We'll talk tomorrow.'

'That all you got to say, you miserable bastard? I've also been talking to David Toner. Interesting, let me tell you.'

'Have you talked to Bella Gill?'

'Bella's Snax?'

'Yes.'

'No I bleeding well haven't. Listen, you—'

'Ask Bella where she was on the night Julia Kelleher was killed,' said Bewick. 'Then we can talk about cars.'

Jones's nasal sarcasm was a credit to Welsh oratory. 'I doubt if it concerns a man of your Olympian resourcefulness, but I also persuaded the drunken, who-needs-drugs, flower-remedied, squirrel-shooting fuck-head who is sueing you, that sueing you would be a waste of time – as indeed most social relations conducted with you undoubtedly are.' He put down the phone.

Whe he returned to the living-room, Jones was humming 'Sospan Fach', the battle tune of Swansea's local rugby enemy, Llanelli. It was always a bad sign. Eilean had also heard the tone of his voice before he hung up.

'Don't let him get to you, darling.'

'Bastard,' said Jones, sitting down beside her.

The phone rang and he jumped to his feet.

'Take it easy with him,' Eilean urged. 'He needs you.'

Bewick got as close as he ever did to apologizing. 'Can we talk to Joe Enwright?'

'If you want.'

'I think it'd be worth it.'

'When?'

'Tomorrow afternoon?'

'I'll arrange it.' Jones was seething with curiosity but tried to stay cool. 'Anything in particular?'

'Just a theory I've got . . . it might sort things out a bit.'

Jones knew that that was all he'd be told. 'I wouldn't mind talking about Toner too,' he said. 'I went to see him like I said. I asked Karen to bring the notes over to you. Don't suppose you've got them yet?'

'No. What about him, apart from him being an ex-hippy, ex-army squirrel murderer?'

'I think he's a stupid evil bastard.'

'Very scientific of you.'

'And as of this morning, he's a stupid evil bastard without an alibi.'

'Is he?'

'Yeah. If Mary Crofton will go to a statement, he is.'

'Good luck then.'

'Thanks. What about you? What's your line on Toner?'

'I'll tell you after we've spoken to Enwright.'

Sally took the boat's binoculars from where they were always kept just inside the cabin. She closed the cabin doors so that her night vision wouldn't be affected. She settled herself comfortably in the cockpit and ran the binoculars along the shore-line of Scales Howe about a hundred metres away. Apart from the bobbing heads of the wading birds searching the mud, nothing moved.

For a moment she thought she heard laughter. She lowered the binoculars. It stopped. She lifted them again. She heard the laughter again, clear this time, childish and mocking. Then she heard singing.

'Speed bonny boat like a bird on the wing . . .'

Sally realized it must be that poor woman Grace Carver. She'd met Grace when she was a child, at pony-club meets and agricultural shows. Grace had been a young woman with a streak of unworldliness which marked her out, and drew the youngest children to her. Sally remembered the surprise amongst the adults – a surprise she was too young to understand – when Grace gained her place at the Slade. Nobody was surprised when she underwent a mental collapse during her final term. Yet she won a prize that term for her sculpture. Subsequently she'd had something of a career. And now . . .

Sally thought of her own pain and was ashamed. She tried to imagine the loneliness of Grace Carver. Perhaps it was worse than loneliness. Perhaps her strange island existence was peopled by creations of her own brain: unwelcome visitors, who would never leave.

Sally felt her skin creep, staring into the darkness. Then for a moment she felt a strange confidence. However distant her eventual recovery from this hopeless love might be, she knew that the thought of Grace Carver had given her a first step towards it. She waved cheerily at the place from which she'd heard the laughter. She was rewarded with a low dove-like chuckle just audible above the bubbling clatter of the mud-feeding birds.

13

When Karen arrived at Bewick's house with Gio Jones's notes on his meeting with Toner, there was no one there. She was about to post them through the front door when she remembered she still had the keys to the house.

Giving herself the excuse that she might as well complete tidying up, she went in, but after she'd been there for a minute or two, she realized she felt very uncomfortable. 'Trespassing,' she said to herself. As if she were trespassing – that was how she felt, although she had the excuse of delivering the notes. She felt so bad, in fact, that she decided to leave. She was about to put on her jacket when the doorbell rang.

Bewick stood on the doorstep. Karen was silenced by surprise for a moment. Bewick looked pale and troubled.

'Good afternoon, Sir, I was tidying up,' she said. 'What can I do for you? Or would you blush to say?'

For a moment she thought he wasn't going to smile. Then his face lit up slowly. 'Gio Jones told me you might be here. He gave you some notes for me. I wanted to see you.'

'To see me?'

'To make love to you.'

'But you don't love me. There's no point,' she said as she pulled him towards her over the doorstep, pushing the door closed behind him.

'I won't be forgiven for saying that, will I?'

'Nah, mate. The truth is unforgiveable.'

After they had made love, Karen was anxious, irritable. She looked at his slowly lifting and subsiding chest, massive but defined. He had his eyes closed, but she knew he wasn't sleeping. Her eyes traced scar lines across his skin. Some were ghosts of serious woundings.

'What is it?' he said, as if to confirm that he wasn't asleep.

'Your Dr Vernon turned up here yesterday afternoon.'

'Did she?' His eyes opened.

'She's broken off her engagement.'

Karen told him the details. She might have predicted the outcome. Bewick either couldn't or wouldn't make love for a second time.

She went to the bathroom. She stepped into the bath and ran the shower. She stood under it trying to clear her head. Why did she have to mention it? The woman had been walking out of his life, for God's sake. Why hadn't she just let her go?

At that moment she knew that Sally couldn't walk out of Bewick's life, even if she made an effort to. She knew too that she, Karen, couldn't have enjoyed a moment of Bewick's company without having told him. '*I don't love you . . . there's no point.*' She'd always known about Sally, she realized. Right from the beginning she'd known there was something . . . Or had she? Would he have loved her if Sally Vernon had never been born?

'*If I was the only girl in the world . . .*?' Would he, even then, have been looking for someone like Sally Vernon to blow in from Jupiter?

The door to the bathroom opened. Bewick was in the shower with her. He was erect; hard as wood. He lifted her on to him. From cramped and dried-up despair she opened, wet in seconds. She closed round him. He seemed to create moisture in her as he moved. He leant back against the wall. She hooked her heels behind his knees. Before, they'd moved slowly to orgasm. Now it came quickly like a rush of air. The room seemed to lighten as she came. She flung back her head and cried aloud.

The warm shower beat down on the panting bodies which slid down into the bottom of the bath, clinging and slipping, to lie folded together.

No man had been able to make her react as she had just done. Karen knew she had just experienced something she would never forget and would probably never experience again.

'You're crying.' He didn't sound surprised.

She'd tried very hard to disguise her tears. He was allowing her to indulge them. She refused to. Her voice was steady when she spoke. 'You know why.'

'Yes.'

'Say it then.'

'I didn't know she was going to be free,' he said.

'I've been thinking, "Why the fuck make it easy for him?" But I realized that it wasn't going to help me, making it difficult for you. So I'm going now.'

The shower began to run tepid. She disentangled herself from him. He made no move to stop her. She stepped out of the bath. As she began to towel herself dry, Bewick stood and turned the shower off.

'It doesn't make any difference,' he said, 'but I do love you. There was point. I wish I'd met you before.'

'You did. You didn't see me. You were too busy getting over the last version of Dr Vernon.'

'Last version?'

'You want to take a look some time at a picture of that ex-wife of yours.'

Bewick was silent. She turned and glanced at him briefly. He was sitting, wet and glistening, on the edge of the bath, his arms out on either side gripping its edge.

She ran from the room.

Only if it's the truth, she thought, as she struggled angrily into her clothes. There was no arguing with love. If Bewick and the Sally woman loved each other, and that was the truth of it, then resentment was dead childish . . .

He walked into the room to her. He held her in a hug she couldn't have fought against if she'd tried. It knocked the breath out of her. Slowly he began to release his grip. Then he walked away. In the doorway he turned. 'You've probably spoilt me for anything else.'

'You'll be all right,' she said. 'It doesn't matter in the end how well the boat sails. It's the company that counts.'

Five minutes later she was walking away down Milburn Avenue trying to quell the hurt she felt.

Jones faced Enwright across the table. Bewick was moving around as the mood took him. It was nearly dusk now; the questioning had been going on for two hours. They had been through the statements Enwright had made, moment by moment. Jones was gloomily impressed by the consistency of Enwright's evidence.

'When you left Julia's cottage that afternoon, well let's say evening, you went for a bit of a blast on the bike,' Jones said, opening the subject he knew Bewick wanted to hear about.

There was a barely perceptible nod from Enwright.

'Subject nods. You did the Triangle, didn't you? A45, A11, M11? Did you stop at all?'

The boy looked at him. 'No.'

'Where did you start from?'

Raised eyebrows by way of a shrug greeted this, as

if to say, how could it be important? Enwright said nothing.

'You blokes time yourselves, surely – mileage, time taken – so you can work out your average speed?'

Jones knew from the traffic department that there were dozens of 'circuits' like the Triangle on which bikers did their personal time trials, reaching lethal speeds. To keep ahead of the police, new circuits were constantly evolving. Some, however, like the Triangle, were always in use: on these major routes much higher speeds were possible and that's what it was all about. Jones had been told that Enwright's RC 45, tuned the way it was, could reach 150 m.p.h. in the time it took to pour a cup of tea.

'Come on, I'm not a traffic cop. There'll be no results from anything you tell me. You'd have stopped somewhere, got yourself ready, got your Casio into stopwatch mode and watched for a thin patch of traffic. Where was it? A lay-by?'

It was a shrug of admission this time.

'Which lay-by? Were the other lads there? Did it have facilities?'

There was no response.

'All right. Was it on the A11?'

There was no denial. Jones took this to be confirmation.

'It was the Cottage, wasn't it?'

The grey-blue eyes looked slowly up at him through the flopped hair. Jones knew he was on track. Having got this far, he changed the subject. 'How well did you know Amy Parris?'

'Amy?'

'Yeah, Amy.'

'She was all right.'

'I need some help here. You told Mr Bewick here that Julia loved Amy. Did Amy love her back?'

'Sure . . .' He didn't sound entirely positive. Jones noted the fact and moved on.

'Julia came to this love affair with Amy after she left her husband, David Toner.'

'Yeah.'

'According to the deposition she gave to her solicitor, Toner hit her. Do you know if that's true?'

'Yeah, I reckon.'

'You know Toner reasonably well, don't you?'

'Yeah.'

'What d'you think of him?'

'He's a shite.'

'Was he OK to you, Toner?'

'He was all right. He wanted to get me on his side.'

'Against Julia?'

'Yeah. I let him think I liked him. I wanted to know what he was thinking.'

'About Julia?'

Enwright nodded. 'Double agent,' he murmured.

'Did you and Toner go places together or anything?'

Enwright shook his head. 'No. He was a shite.'

Jones moved on. 'Let's talk about Amy. When she

took up with Julia, do you think she came from a relationship which didn't work, like Julia's didn't?'

A mumble of qualification.

'What?' Bewick spoke for the first time. His voice was hard, impatient.

'Arreckon.'

'What?'

'I reckon. There was some bloke after her.'

'After Amy?'

'Yeah.'

'After her? What? Pestered her?' Bewick was insistent.

'Norreally . . .'

'Who was still keen on her? Still wanted her? Unhappy about this thing with Julia?'

'Yeah.'

'You know who?'

'No. Julia knew him, but she never . . . we never talked 'bout it.'

Jones and Bewick exchanged a look. There was an acknowledgement between them that this was possibly true. Without saying anything, Jones indicated to Bewick that he wanted him to take over.

'Was there a snack wagon at the Cottage?'

'Yeah.'

'Bella's Snax?'

'Yeah, reckon.'

'So how long did you stop there? In the lay-by?'

A face, a shrug; Enwright didn't remember, wasn't telling.

'I'm talking about after you got back now, after you'd done your ride. That's where you ended up, isn't it?'

'Yeah . . .' Enwright frowned. He was suspicious.

'It was getting dark about then, yes?'

No reply.

Bewick was restless, impatient, glowering. He moved closer to Enwright, a walking threat. 'Come on! It was getting dark. It's a fact of nature, not a state bloody secret.'

'Yeah.'

'So what did you do?'

Enwright's face seemed to clamp shut. Bewick's speech became a low, insinuating monotone. 'I'll tell you what you did. You saw a couple of guys who you fancied go into the gents, so you followed them. Someone else followed you . . .' Jones saw that this got to Enwright. Something was beginning to make sense to the little bastard. 'The man who followed you had seen you at Julia's when you went there the first time that afternoon. When you went back to Julia's, there was no answer. Yes? But he was there. He recognized you. He followed your bike. Not easy, but he managed it. He caught up with you at the lay-by, a minute or two before you set off to do the Triangle. He waited to see if you'd come back. While he was waiting he realized what the Cottage was . . .'

Jones was watching Enwright like a hawk. Enwright was mesmerized. He was watching Bewick helplessly as if Bewick was an embodiment of a malign fate. Jones was mesmerized himself.

'By the time you'd come back from doing your burn-up round the triangle, he'd worked out what he might do – if you decided you were on for it. You were. You'd just had a billion horsepower between your legs. You were hot for it. When he saw you follow the other guys into the toilet, he went for it. After all, what had he got to lose? Julia was already dead. His life was on the line.

'It was dark in the gents – just a little light from the outside, hardly enough to see who was doing what to whom, never mind recognize anyone. So he joined in. Even gave you a bit of mild S&M and clawed your back for you. And came away with what he wanted.

'Then he went back and planted it on Julia's body. Your tissue, your semen. You were in the trap now. All it needed was for a few connections to be made, for the police to do what they always do and the trap would shut. The fact that you decided to empty your skull with jellies that night was an unlooked-for complication. But it didn't make any difference. Here you are. The charge is murder.'

Under that maddening curtain of hair, Jones could see that Enwright's eyes were still lowered. Enwright's head began to twist sideways, tucking into his shoulder. Was it possible, thought Jones, that the little bastard is going to have a good cry? He could see the tension in Enwright's body. Some huge struggle was going on inside him.

But slowly, as he watched, the sinews in the boy's neck relaxed. The head came round and lifted. The eyes half opened. Yes, thought Jones, his eyes are wet. He'd been about to cry. The gaze that met him now was trying and only just failing to be as cool and fuck-you as ever. Some satisfaction then that his voice shook as he asked, 'That means I can go then, does it?'

Enwright knew it meant he could – if not immediately, then soon. He sniffed, at last unable to disguise the catastrophic relief, blinding him with tears. Nevertheless, he wouldn't let go his defiance. His mouth opened to gulp in air. He panted, refusing to let his eyes run. 'Does it?' he blurted out again.

'No, it doesn't,' Bewick said. 'It means you start answering some questions. You start cooperating. Then you make a statement. Then DCI Jones decides if we believe you or not.'

'And what the hell do I do now?' complained Jones over a pint at The Old Muscovy. 'Apart from grovelling in front of my superiors and begging them not to retire me until after my youngest daughter's wedding?'

'Someone', replied Bewick, 'finds out who the man was that Amy Parris was involved with.'

'And then?'

'And then someone finds out what Amy Parris had on her, the thing that Julia Kelleher and the murderer were so interested in. And then someone finds out who buried her body.'

'Buried her? Someone buried her?'

'Think about it.'

Jones thought – all the way back to his office. 'Tell me,' he said finally, flinging open his office door in frustration.

'There are nine days of gale-force and storm-force winds,' Bewick replied. 'What do they uncover? Amy Parris's hand. When she was lost, the theory goes, it only needed an extra three days of similar winds to cover her completely. Completely, and sufficiently deep to stop the local dogs from sniffing her out. The dogs would have been back on the island as soon as the weather eased. The wind alone couldn't have done it.'

'Someone buried her.'

'Someone buried her.'

'Who? Why?'

Jones's brain was whirling. It was enough for God's sake to have just had his case against Enwright sliced from under his feet. He tried to calm himself down.

Jones walked to the window of his office. Outside, the low autumn sunshine was gilding the tops of trees and buildings, leaving gullies of blue shadow in between. He realized he was sweating. He sighed forcibly. He turned to Bewick. 'You don't reckon anyone killed Amy, do you?'

'No. I think now she was distracted. She got careless. She fell. Probably. Probably an accident. Why?'

'Well, if no one killed her, why would anyone want to bury her?'

'I think we should start by asking why Amy fell off the boat. Why she was distracted.'

'You say she was on the run.'

'Yes. She knew something which was dangerous to someone; had proof of it.'

'What sort of dangerous?'

'God knows. Something that could wreck a way of life. Suppose Julia thought she had it on her when she died, but didn't know what it was.'

'I get it,' said Jones. Hands in pockets he hitched his trousers up on to the top of his hips. 'Yes. When Amy goes missing, Julia goes down to Scales Howe. She finds Amy's body . . .'

'No,' Bewick interrupted.

'What do you mean, "No", you superior bastard?'

'Why should Julia find the body? There were search parties out. Professionals. The place was swarming. Why should Julia be successful?'

'I don't know. Luck? A lover's instinct?'

'Gio . . .'

'All right, all right. Who did it then?'

'If nobody found it, the body must have been buried as soon as it came ashore.'

'Who by?' Jones shouted, his frustration spilling over.

'The island's presiding spirit: sculptress and bag-lady, Grace Carver.'

Jones stared. Yes. Of course. Because it was there on her island and because that was what you did with dead bodies. He made a resigned face and shrugged. 'Sure . . .'

'Julia came down to look for Amy. We know that.

I believe she made contact with Grace Carver. She may have realized that Grace Carver had buried the body but decided to leave well alone.'

'Leaving Amy buried on the island?' Jones sounded disbelieving.

'Why not? Julia probably knew what happens at post-mortem and didn't want her lover butchered by strangers.'

'OK.'

'The killer sees Julia in the company of Grace Carver, but it doesn't mean anything to him at first. The body hasn't been found.'

'And when the body is found?'

'He realizes that Grace Carver must have done the burying. He goes to try and find her. You remember what Lund said about her? Her symptoms seem to have got worse in the last few weeks?'

'Since Amy's body was found.'

'Yes. Our man's been looking for her. I think he probably failed, as we did. But she's seen him. She suspects him. She senses something. She feels threatened. So her symptoms get worse.'

'The killer fails to find Grace, so he goes for Julia?'

'We can short-circuit this whole thing if we can talk to Grace Carver.'

Jones nodded, scowling. 'I know what this is leading up to.'

Bewick smiled. 'Pick me up from George and Kit's at eight o'clock tomorrow morning, eh?'

'I don't like the place. It's windy and it's wet.'

'Eight o'clock.'

'What about David Toner?'

'Eight o'clock.'

After Bewick left the office, Jones sat staring into space, imagining the finding of Amy's sea-battered body by Grace Carver. She would probably have performed a ritual over it of her own devising, something quite off the wall, but, thought Jones, it would have been very appropriate, probably, very right.

Despite the case against Joe Enwright being in tatters, he felt OK. He knew Bewick was on to something. He was looking forward to following it up with him. Was Amy's fate the key to the whole thing? He wished to God he'd asked Toner about Amy, whether he knew her. Jones couldn't imagine Toner being involved with Amy even on the most superficial level, but there'd been couplings more bizarre in the history of the planet.

Jones took a deep breath, walked around his office a couple of times, then dumped himself at his desk. He began looking at the notes Bewick had made following his interviews with Julia Kelleher's parents, with Percy Snaith and with Julian Rae.

Rae's cottage in Grantchester was small and charming with a carefully gardened front plot. Jones rang the bell for the second time long and loud. An upstairs window in the cottage next door opened. A balding woman thrust her head out. She peered down over a pair of reading glasses with an Elastoplast hinge.

'Yes?'

'Mr Rae?'

'He's away. What do you want?'

'Do you know where he's gone?'

'No idea.'

'I'm police.'

The woman was unimpressed by this. 'Shall I take a message? I look after the place when he's away.'

'Does he often go away without telling you where?'

'Not often. It has been known. Tell me if you need me to do anything.'

The head withdrew. The window slammed shut.

The first knock at Bewick's door was so faint he didn't hear it at all. Then the bell rang, but so briefly that it sounded as if it may have been a mistake. Bewick took his time answering the door. It was Mrs Kelleher.

'I came by taxi,' she said, as if her presence anywhere outside her own home required explanations; a reasonable assumption.

Bewick invited her in. He asked her if she wanted to take her coat off. She refused firmly, as if Bewick had suggested something improper.

They sat in the living-room.

'What can I do for you, Mrs Kelleher?'

'He's got to be stopped. I want the law on him.'

Bewick nodded as if he understood exactly what she meant.

'He didn't ask me. He must have my permission or it can't be legal, can it? Not that I'd ever give it. And he knows that. That's why he's done it behind my back. I heard him arranging it on the phone. How could he? Well, he's always hated her, and this is his revenge, I suppose.'

'What has he arranged, Mrs Kelleher?'

'To speak out. It'll be all over the papers. With family snapshots and . . . and gossip. He knows nothing about her. He can't do it, can he?'

'You mean talk to a journalist?'

'Yes.'

'Your husband?'

'Yes. He wants to blacken her name. That's what it's all about. I want him stopped; legally.'

'I'm not sure that's possible, but I'll try to find out for you.'

Mrs Kelleher had subsided. Her hand slipped inside her coat and adjusted the collar of her blouse.

Bewick went to the kitchen and phoned Dundas, whose opinion was that there was nothing Mrs Kelleher could do apart from hide all the photographs of Julia and go to a rival journalist herself.

'It won't be what she wants to hear,' said Bewick.

'It's not often a barrister's opinion comes free. What does she want? Blood?'

'Probably.'

'How are you, John? You looked awful when I last saw you.'

'I'm OK.'

'Have you solved our case, then?'

'Yes,' Bewick replied shortly.

Dundas waited for more, then, 'Well for God's sake tell me, man.'

'I'll give you a shout in a couple of days.'

Bewick told Mrs Kelleher Dundas's opinion. She hardly seemed to take it in.

'I'm sorry,' Bewick said. 'Perhaps it would be worth telling Mr Kelleher how much it hurts you, the idea of Julia's life being made public.'

'It won't be her life, that's the point . . . Anyway I can't talk to him. He frightens me. He knows how to frighten me. All he'll do is talk about the money.'

'I still think it may be worth a try, Mrs Kelleher.'

'Oh dear,' she said, suddenly assuming a bright social manner, 'look at the time. That taxi's been out there all this while. Dear dear.' Holding her coat collar to her throat, Mrs Kelleher left.

Jones was back in his office at City West and was on the phone.

'I'm sorry, we don't give personal details of our clients over the phone.'

Insistence and charm got Jones through to the head of the agency.

'That's all very well, Chief Inspector, but how do I know . . .'

'Go through directory inquiries. I'm at City West Police Station, Cambridge. Ask for me.'

There was a long, bored sigh at the other end. 'All right. What do you want to know about Mr Rae?'

'Is he working at the moment?'

'Only in the sense that he has a contract. The theatre. Rehearsals don't begin for a couple of weeks.'

'Where's that?'

'Manchester.'

'Is that usual for him?'

'What?'

'To work in the theatre out of London?'

'One works where one can get work, frankly. Though I grant you I'm quite surprised Julian was prepared to hack this one.'

'If Mr Rae was away from home, would you expect him to contact you on a regular basis?'

'Yes. He rings in a couple of times a week if he's away. He won't take a mobile. So he rings in.'

'When was he last in touch?'

Jones heard the phone being covered, muffled voices, then, 'Julian last rang in ten days ago to ask about the Manchester contract.'

'So you'd expect him to be at home.'

'Sure. Isn't he?'

'No.'

'No . . . Well, he does sometimes go to a cottage somewhere in Norfolk near the Sandringham Estate. A friend of his goes up there to shoot.'

'The name of the friend?'

'Sorry . . . Can't help with that.'

*

Home & Away Travel was in a small parade of shops with a parking lay-by beside it. Bewick could see a customer being served as he pulled up. He waited until the customer left before going in.

Bewick re-introduced himself, although Kelleher remembered him well enough, and remembered liking him.

'Mrs Kelleher came to see me,' Bewick said.

'Oh yes?'

'I understand you've made an arrangement with a newspaper.' Bewick said it to reassure, as if applauding enterprise.

'Yes I have.'

'I realize it's none of my business, Mr Kelleher, but I thought you should know how unhappy Mrs Kelleher is about it.'

Kelleher's moustache twitched as he smiled patronizingly at Bewick. 'Yes, yes. I know that. She thinks she is. But she'll appreciate it all right when I take her away on the cruise of a lifetime. They're paying handsomely.'

'Forgive me, Mr Kelleher, but I'm not sure she will. She really was distressed by the idea of further publicity.'

'Yes, yes, but you see we've had no control over the publicity so far. That's what she's thinking about. But this time it'll be our story, the way we want to tell it. We'll have control. Don't worry about her. She's stronger than people think.'

'Have you dealt with newspapers before?'

'I know my way around.'

'I don't think you should rely on the idea of exercising much control.'

'It'll be all right,' Kelleher said, determined. He wanted Bewick to go now. 'Thank you for coming,' he added, his voice cold.

'I think', Bewick said quietly, 'you should weigh up the money you've been offered and the distress you may cause your wife very carefully. I really think you should.'

In the lay-by, Bewick sat in his car staring at the bright yellow lime leaves that littered the pavement ahead. Then he started the car and drove to an address he'd noted almost as soon as he began his investigations.

Tessa Waring looked at the security screen. She recognized Bewick from his visit to Sirius HQ. She had been frightened by him even in the security of her office.

'What do you want?' she asked through the intercom.

'I want to ask you about something you told DCI Jones.'

'I'm sorry, I'm going out.'

'It won't take a minute.'

'I'm sorry. I'm late.'

Bewick heard a security lock being turned and a chain slide into the door.

Bewick returned to his car. He phoned City West to get the number of Tessa Waring's car, reparked his own and waited. After half an hour he was rewarded by the sight of Tessa Waring coming through the lit foyer of the block of flats. She walked to her car and gasped when Bewick spoke from two feet away.

'I'll really only take a couple of minutes of your time,' he said.

'No.' She was shaking.

'Miss Waring, this is a very serious matter. Julia Kelleher was murdered.'

'The police have arrested the killer.'

'The police have arrested the wrong man. Unless they find something else to charge him with, they'll be letting him go.'

She stared at him. Why did she want so much to resist him? She couldn't explain it to herself. 'All right. Two minutes.'

'Thank you.'

'Go on.'

'Wouldn't you like to get into your car? You look . . .'

'I'm warm enough,' she interrupted. 'Hurry up please.'

'You said to DCI Jones that Amy Parris asked you if you knew "what was going on?" Do you remember?'

'Yes. Of course.'

'What did she mean by that? Which way did you interpret it?'

'What?'

'Did she mean something going on within the company? Something within Sirius?'

'No.'

'You sound very confident.'

'It couldn't have been. It's a small management team. I'm part of it. I would have known something was going on, even if I didn't know what it was.'

'All right. Then it would have been, presumably, something to do with her emotional life, would it?'

'I don't know.'

'Haven't you asked yourself what she meant, Miss Waring?'

'No. Why should I? It was nothing to do with me. She made that clear.'

'Weren't you curious even? The woman was dead a few days later.'

'No. Why should I be?'

Bewick stared at her.

Tessa Waring felt hot as if she'd failed some sort of test whose rules she didn't know. She wanted to get away from this man. 'It was an accident. She was very important to us, of course. We all had to cope with it. It was chaos at work. She was one of our most important people. Very clever and a memory you could hardly credit. We were all in overdrive trying to pick up the bits. Why should I think about some chance remark? For all I know, she might have been talking about global warming.'

'It wasn't a chance remark.'

'To me it was.'

'Think of the context, Miss Waring.'

'It could've meant anything . . . I have to go.'

'All right. I'd be grateful if you could think about it, though.' Bewick was at his friendliest.

'I'll try.'

'Thank you. I'm going to Norfolk tomorrow. But I should be back some time the day after. Would you mind if I rang you then?'

'All right. I won't have anything to tell you.'

'Sure. I'd just like to check.'

'All right.'

She got into her car and drove away as if someone were after her.

Bewick and Jones drove to Norfolk. As they left Cambridge, Newmarket heaths were pale with frost. High cirrus was beginning to blur the sunshine as the predicted weather system, which was already roaring through Wales and Cornwall, moved steadily eastwards.

'Identity of third party, of the killer . . .' said Jones, who knew nothing of meteorology and was looking at the glittering slopes ahead, thinking it wasn't such a bad day after all.

'Yes?' Bewick replied.

'Know how much Julia Kelleher's cottage is valued at?'

'Tell me.'

'Hundred and forty five thousand.'

'Sounds about right.'

'How about this,' Jones said. 'Julian Rae won't take the blood test because he already knows he's HIV positive. He's also recognized early symptoms of his immune system breaking down. He's read the literature. He knows what this means.' Jones looked across at Bewick. 'Well?'

'Go on,' Bewick said.

'Suppose the friendship with Julia Kelleher had all gone wrong. Maybe she's beginning to sound like his mother. They have a row about Little Joe-sex-object-Enwright. Julia starts screaming at him. She goes too far. He hits her. Then her hatred of men comes out. The last person to hit her was her charming husband, and before that her father. She's accusing Rae of God knows what. He hits her again. And again. Somewhere in the middle of it he knows by killing her he's getting a hundred and forty five K for the treatment he's going to need.'

'What made you look at him, Gio?' Bewick asked.

'He's done a bunk,' replied Jones. 'What d'you think, then?'

Bewick drove in silence for some time. 'What about Amy? There's no connection with Amy.'

'Does there have to be? She fell overboard. She floated ashore. She was buried by a schizophrenic, who thought that's what she ought to do. Julia was killed because someone got fed up with her and needed the money. No connections. It's just as likely. More likely.'

'OK. More likely, I agree. It was more likely . . .'

'"The ordinary explanation is usually the explanation." That's one of yours.'

‘I just don’t think it applies here.’

‘Didn’t think you would . . . There you go. Worth a try. Oh! Little bit of news to make your day. Mr Kelleher, Julia’s father, has decided to sell his story to the gutter rats of Wapping. Some effing journalist rang me last night.’

‘Yeah, I heard.’

‘You heard?’

‘Mrs Kelleher told me he was going to. She wanted me to stop him. I rang Alec Dundas to show willing.’

‘Well the bastard’s done it.’

They drove in silence for a mile or two.

‘Why does there have to be a connection with Amy?’ Jones asked.

A smile spread across Bewick’s face. ‘Because I say so,’ he said.

‘All right you bugger. What about Toner?’

‘Later.’

Jones, thinking again about Toner and Amy, said nothing more until they got to Swaffham. ‘No, go on. Why does there have to be a connection with Amy?’

‘You keep quoting me. I’ll quote you. “Only bank robbers murder for money”.’

‘No, no. Get a bit subtle, will you? “Only bank robbers murder only for money.” People’ll kill for money if they want to kill anyway.’

‘OK.’

‘So why does there have to be a connection with Amy?’

Bewick shrugged. 'There has to be a connection. Amy was on the run. She's living in fear. It may be she kills herself even, at the least is careless of her safety, because someone is hounding her, she's somebody's prey. Then her lover is murdered. This isn't just a bad weekend for the girls. Can't be. Someone was after them both. Someone who was involved with one of them.'

Jones nodded. He couldn't come up with anything better.

They drove along a double-hedged lane which rose steadily to a horizon marked with Scots pines. Then they topped the rise, a moment of buffeting wind and there was the sea. On a knoll to their right stood Scalder Staithe church and below them the village huddled into the valley of Scaller Brook. Beyond gleamed the water maze of the saltings. The scoured shingles around Scales Howe were emerging from the retreating tide.

They drove into the village and stopped near the post-office.

Sally came out of the shop and there he was. Where he shouldn't be, and when he shouldn't be, for God's sake. He was the past; a citizen of the regretted past. Here he was looking at postcards outside the village shop.

She thought of walking away, of hiding in the shop, of being chilly, of being deliberately over-polite. She even thought of telling him she loved him. Instead, she did nothing.

She stared at him for several seconds. She saw him think, 'Someone needs to get past me,' and move sideways without taking his attention from the post-cards. A moment more and he looked up. Then she was caught again in the attention of those strange grey eyes which went quickly from curiosity to smiling warmth. Nervous of blabbing, still frozen, Sally smiled back but said nothing. She remembered Karen's golden athleticism and was silenced.

'Well, well, well . . .' Bewick seemed surprised too, but as if something he had foreseen were happening sooner than he expected.

'My parents live not far away,' Sally said.

'Ah, yes.'

'What are you doing here?' she asked.

She watched him think about how he might reply to this. 'I'm working on something. I think I told you.' He turned to the chubby man beside him. 'This is Detective Chief Inspector Jones . . . Giovanni Jones. This is Dr Sally Vernon.'

'Pleased to meet you.' Jones was very interested. Who was this?

'You've been mentioned, Chief Inspector – with the breath of courtesy I may say.'

'With the breath of courtesy, have I?'

'With respect even,' Sally said, and found herself amused. She liked the idea that these two men should respect each other. Then she tried to distance herself. She reminded herself that Bewick was the past she had come here to recover from. Damn this! Days by herself on a boat alone with her books, the sky and the sea seemed laughably compromised by this meeting. How, after this, would she return to her little floating nunnery? Get it over quickly and pretend it never happened: come on.

'Well,' she said. 'Nice meeting you. I'm afraid I've a tide to catch.'

'A tide?' asked Bewick.

'I've borrowed a friend's boat for a few days. I mean just holed up in the creek. I'm not going anywhere. Certainly not in what's forecast. So – nice meeting you again. How long are you here for?'

'As long as it takes.'

'Then perhaps we'll bump into each other again.'

'I expect we will. What's the boat called?'

'*Greylag*.'

She escaped. What had he meant by that? Why did he expect they would? As she hurried down to the creek where she'd left the dinghy, she found herself biting her lower lip to stop the sense of self-pity that was threatening to engulf her with tears. She had always hated her capacity to feel like this and had learnt to turn it to anger which gave her energy and was therefore productive.

As she reached the dinghy she saw the water of the creek darkened by a blast of wind which crossed it towards her, an outrider of the forecast weather.

She congratulated herself on her decision to come away from the shop when she had. Self-anger meant strength. The dinghy was in the water in seconds.

The same blast of wind spun the carousel of postcards at the post-office. Inside her shop Mrs Cahn heard the warning sign. Her customers, Bewick and Gio Jones amongst them, helped her clear the pavement.

'I wondered if we might see you again,' said the unsmiling Margaret Lund. 'I'll tell my husband.'

This time Bewick and Gio Jones were invited into Lund's sanctum: his observation room with its view over the marshes and Scales Howe.

They found Lund bent over his telescope. He gestured to Jones. 'Care to look?'

'Thank you.' Jones looked through the telescope.

'Don't move it,' Lund advised. 'It has a very narrow field of vision.'

'Right.'

'The Queen of the Howe. Grace Carver,' Lund explained to Bewick.

Jones focused on the small figure moving steadily up a ridge of dunes on the Howe, her hands in front of her as if she were knitting or telling a rosary. The bottom half of her appeared darker, more distinct. Jones thought at first that it was a trick of the lens. Then he realized that from about mid-thigh downwards, she was soaked.

'Where is she?'

'On the island.'

'She must have waded across,' said Jones.

'Not across the falls, surely?' Bewick asked Lund.

'No . . . she would have gone across the saltings somehow. She has a dinghy on a rope to get across the creek,' said Lund. 'I've tried to work out how she does it, but it's impossible. The local legend is that it's more dangerous to go across the saltings to the Howe than going across the Splash when the Falls are running.'

'Why?'

'Because anywhere before Salvages Creek you can come across quicksands. It's something to do with the mud off the saltings bleeding into the sands of the Howe. A whole family were drowned out there fifty years ago. They were stuck, not swallowed. There was an offshore wind. Nobody heard them shouting. When the tide came in, they drowned.'

Jones offered his position at the telescope to Bewick.

Sally rowed up the line of moorings against the ebb. She was nearing *Greylag* when she saw the woman. She stood at the summit of a dune, silhouetted, her arms raised, the wind rippling her clothes and hair.

Sally slowed, barely stemming the tide as her dinghy came alongside the boat. She caught hold of the gunwhale awkwardly and had to grip hard as the dinghy lost way. She looked towards the Howe again. Grace Carver had disappeared.

'She's gone,' Bewick said and straightened up from the telescope. 'And you say you've no idea how she does it?'

'No. I've watched her. I've gone down there and

tried to follow where I think she's gone. But as soon as I've gone about fifty yards I get into difficulties: waterlogged saltings, sucking mud and so on. In the old days she would have been burnt as a witch. Now she just has her life made a misery. At least nobody has locked her up, where she would surely die.'

'When do you think it'll be safe to cross to the Howe today?' Bewick asked.

'Why do you want to go this time?'

'To speak to Grace Carver.'

'The trouble is that the times you can get across are when the local dog-walkers and visitors also go across. Grace tends to disappear when they turn up.'

'In a puff of smoke?' suggested Jones.

Lund looked at him with the sort of unamused superiority which made Jones want to behave very childishly. 'As a matter of fact,' said Lund, 'that is almost a fair description. Once again, nobody knows how she does it. The landscape of the dunes seems very featureless: sand and grass. I think that she must have a faultless spatial memory, which enables her to use the landscape to hide in. At any rate, I challenge even two or three people to find her if she doesn't want to be found.'

'Does she live over there all the time?' asked Bewick.

'No, not at all.'

'Just in good weather?'

'Not really. I've once seen her over there in driving snow. Other times I've heard her mumbling away at the bottom of my garden, when it's been quite mild.'

'And she has nowhere permanent to live or work? Does she still work as a sculptor?'

'Sadly not. She was very good.'

'We've got one of her sculptures,' Jones chipped in, consciously casual, 'outside Regional HQ. A head. I gave it a glance . . . what? Yesterday.'

Bewick looked at him sharply. 'That bronze head is one of hers?'

'Sure. It's signed on the base Grace C.'

'That's certainly how she signs her work,' said Lund.

'And then there's a plaque fach, telling you what's what.'

The needle on a dial by the window leapt and a roar enveloped the room, juddering windows.

'That was a fifty m.p.h. gust,' said Lund. 'This forecast may be right, for a change.'

The roar subsided but left the three men more conscious of the wind's constant buffetings. Lund turned to Bewick. 'To answer your question – no, she doesn't have anywhere she could call home. She has a main shelter near the ruined chapel on the island.'

'She has others?'

'Yes. Vandalizing her shelter is reckoned a good laugh by the local yobbery. So she has bivouacs all over the place. She's ingenious. She told me once that she builds some very obvious shelters to draw the destructive instincts of the really stupid. The ones she actually uses are very often disguised as dumps of driftwood and other flotsam.'

'And are no doubt sculptural?'

'Quite. Yes!' Lund smiled his enthusiasm.

'Talking of which,' said Jones, hands in pockets, slumped over his stomach, smiling and looking depressed, 'is there a decent hotel round here?'

'The Royal is perfectly adequate,' replied Lund brusquely before turning back to Bewick. 'Yes, it's an interesting perspective, isn't it? Sculpture you inhabit – doing away with the architecture, which is often the excuse for sculpture in the first place.'

'Busy at this time of the year is it? The Royal?' asked Jones.

Back at the post-office call-box, they booked themselves into The Royal, which was an Edwardian hotel built at about the same time as Sandringham not many miles away. It was the hobby of the owner of a sizeable hotel group. It was barely profitable and surprisingly well appointed. Bertram Ionides, the owner, was a ruthless manager and employer, but treated The Royal like a favourite child and discouraged the publicizing of its merits.

Greylag's keel was beginning to settle into the ooze of the creek. Despite having been lowered by the tide out of the full force of the wind, in the cabin the noise of the vibrating rigging was constant now. A flag halyard was tick-tick-ticking against the mast. Sally went out on deck with a piece of light line to prevent it. Outside, the ebb had removed the surf over the bar and down the northern beach. To landward, behind a derelict sea-wall, inaudible before under the surf roar, reeds in the ditch now rustled and clattered.

Sally was angered by her feelings. She realized that she had gone over the scene outside the shop perhaps twenty times now, trying to squeeze it of meaning. She swore at herself. 'You're supposed to be a bloody scientist, woman! It's unreadable. No evidence. Forget it.'

But as her eyes swept the low horizon she knew that part of herself was hoping to catch a distant sight of the massively built man and his short, plump companion. Nothing moved however except wind-tugged heathers and wind-bent grasses.

Bewick and Jones made their way across the low central area of Scales Howe, hemmed in by dunes. They had spent over an hour, since they crossed the Splash at low water, trying to find Grace Carver. Early in their search they had heard her teasing them from quite close by; since then, silence and absence.

Now they were returning, via what they had identified as her main shelter (they thought), towards the ruined chapel. Bewick had said he was interested in the chapel and wanted to look at it but couldn't or wouldn't tell Jones why.

Jones was tired and increasingly fed up with the whole expedition. He plodded up the sand in his old wellington boots which for the first time in their lives had given him blisters. They stopped in front of Grace's shelter. Off to their right was the clothes dryer hung with flotsam Grace had rescued from the sea.

'She's been here.'

'Has she?' Jones sounded barely interested.

'She's tethered the carousel so it can't turn. Look. Very wise. It'd shake itself to bits if this wind gets any stronger.'

Bewick stood in the broken arch of the chapel's west door, staring at it. Jones sat nearby munching his way through the last of the sandwiches he'd bought at the post-office. He was conscious of the rising wind, and the fact that it was now past the time of official low water. From now on, the Splash would become increasingly difficult to return over. Bewick hadn't moved.

Jones glanced around the chapel himself. What there was to interest Bewick, he had no idea. It was a ruin, not a particularly picturesque one at that. A ruin was a ruin. He put down the plastic sandwich container and wiped his fingers.

'It's some sort of garden,' Bewick said.

Jones looked at him suspiciously. 'It's a ruin, Bewick; ecclesiastical.'

'It's a garden.'

'I don't see it.'

'Look.'

'I am looking, you bleeding Anglo-Saxon mystic; don't tell me to look. I don't see it.'

'I'm not sure I do. Somebody's taken the ivy down though.' Bewick pointed out the trails over the stone where it had been growing. There was stonecrop high on the walls, sea lavender, mares' tails . . . a salt-wind-rusted rose . . . bramble . . .

'It doesn't look to me as if it just happened,' Bewick said and continued to look.

Grace Carver glared through a camouflaging tangle of grasses at the two men. 'God, men are slow,' she whispered to herself. 'On the right trail, trying to see it and can't . . . shit beetles. Can one have powers and be as blind as this one?'

She shivered. Unseated expectations always left her with a spinning frisbee world not really in control; at the mercy of the unseen mind-wind. She feared the winds of unreason more than any violence that nature could offer. Involuntarily she looked up at a huge curve of thick grey cloud, like a ceiling lowering itself, as if intent on compressing the forces soon to vent themselves on the island. She shivered again.

What's this? What's this?

Without thought, she found herself crawling away and moving upwards. Driven, without self-examination, instinct took her to Spyglass.

To anyone without Grace Carver's experience of the island, the dune she was climbing was just another wave in a lumpy sea of sand. She knew, however, it to be the leader of the pack, the old grey wolf; the great sand mother, the biggest on the island. Snugged in behind its breaking grassy lip was the nook look-out, Spyglass.

Yes, there he was.

A tiny, solitary figure in a long coat was crossing the Splash. Even at this distance she knew who it was. She had no idea what he was doing there. She shivered again.

'She's obviously not going to speak to us.'

'No she's not,' Jones said, distracted by a curtain of rain, oil dark, slanting across a distant patch of sea.

'OK. Why don't you go back and book us dinner in that hotel?'

'Why don't I,' agreed Jones. 'What are you going to do? Oh don't tell me. You're going to go and find that woman. I'd have thought Karen was enough for any man to be kept snug by . . .'

Bewick stared at Jones. It was one of the very few times he'd seen Bewick surprised.

Jones couldn't keep the bitterness out of his voice. 'And I'd be quite obliged if you didn't do anything to upset my staff. WDI Quinney is a highly valued member of the team.'

What the hell had he said that for? He suddenly felt utterly miserable: decrepit, fat and pathetic. 'I'll go and book the meal.'

Jones marched away, trying to keep his dignity as his boots slithered and clogged in the sand. He had only gone about fifty metres when he remembered he'd left the remains of his sandwiches in the chapel. He swore at himself, not just for leaving them, but for the ingrained conscience he had about litter which he knew would make him go back.

He turned. Bewick had disappeared. Jones thought of the Gower of his childhood, of Gower's limestone cliffs facing the green swell of the Atlantic. What was this dump in comparison?

The broken medieval archway loomed above the next slope of sand. Jones's knowledge that his bad temper was all to do with Bewick and Karen didn't help him at all. He'd wanted to defend her from the pain Bewick was going to inflict. He'd wanted to be her champion. What he'd actually done was make a total arsehole of himself. All that stuff about upsetting his staff! Jones groaned aloud with embarrassment. 'Prat!'

He was startled a moment later to hear his own voice come back at him like an echo. Too late for an echo, surely? He took a couple of steps back to where he'd been standing. 'Prat!' he groaned again.

This time the echo was laughter . . . so close. No more than ten feet away.

'Miss Carver . . .?' He looked around the cwm of sand in which he stood, knowing that by the time he'd scaled any of the slopes around him, she would be gone. He understood suddenly how her subtle knowledge of the place had given her real power, not enough to protect her completely, but enough to ensure survival. The thought cheered him up greatly, without his knowing why.

The clear triangular sandwich pack had been moved. As he stepped into the arch he spotted it immediately. It had been placed where it caught the light. The wind rocked it gently and its reflective surface irridesced. Jones stared at it, as he realized he was meant to by the unseen woman. He submitted. He remained staring until his eyes swam. Was it luck or intention, what happened next?

He heard her, as if she were at his shoulder. Her voice roared, breathily at first, *sotto voce*. 'Now . . .' it said and then was taken up and lost in the noise of a huge train of wind, thundering through the broken-down walls, seeming to repeat the 'NOW' in a long howl.

Jones lifted his eyes and looked around him.

Then he saw it. It was like the moment when a chequerboard optical illusion is seen suddenly in three dimensions: as if a switch had been thrown in the brain. The entire space, he saw, breathed artifice. Curved in a doorway was a tide rime of bladderwrack and sea-bleached sticks. It was exactly believable until logic told you it was twenty feet above the highest tide the coast had ever known. A heap of tins rusted in a corner, but it was uniformly rusted as no random heap would be. As you looked, an animal lay there, watching you like an old dog on a hearth. A loose tin somewhere in the heap, carefully balanced, knocked in the wind, so that the animal had a voice.

Out of a bramble and a heap of stones where the altar had once been emerged a crown of thorns and the shadow of a crucified man.

Another thump of wind seemed to suck the air out of his body. Dazed, he looked upwards. As he did so, he heard from behind him a low growling chuckle.

Gio Jones laughed aloud when he understood. Wedged in a crack in the stone was the silhouette of a hand pointing, like an old-fashioned direction pointer. Jones's eyes followed. It pointed to a globe, whose outline was chiselled on to a big stone built into the opposite wall. The globe was recognizable by the curves of latitude and longitude, but the only country it showed was France, which almost filled the entire circle.

Did he hear her voice say it or did he see it for himself? It wasn't the pointer, it was what it was made from, the word on the ellipsoidal tin: 'ham'. Once he had said Ham the second half of the word was already in his head. Even though he was sure of what it was, it took him time to work out. It wasn't the globe exactly, but the world as the French pronounced it: 'monde'.

Jones laughed out loud. 'Hammond,' he said and looked round, his mind clambering out of a dream. There was no one there. Had there ever been anyone there?

'Hammond!' he repeated and laughed again. Hammond it was who had come to find out what

Grace knew. He had frightened her, so she had built his name into her garden; an insurance, a secret, lodged in the vault of a conundrum.

14

He had always loved guns in cases.

Shadowy behind glass, their steel silky with oil, their carved stocks sheeny with wax . . . the loveliness of the things! Sleeping beauties whose power on their awakening might change the world. Dream objects, virile fancies, artworks. He had never thought to use them. He had been waiting for them to use him.

The fever was on him. Driven beyond care, Hammond knew it was all over, that he was destroyed.

Tessa Waring had arrived early at Sirius that morning, but hadn't been able to settle to work. She'd hardly slept all night. She'd been severely shaken – that horrible bullying man had been right. Amy's question to her that afternoon, a year ago, had lain buried all this time; like Amy herself.

'*Do you know what's going on?*'

No she hadn't. That's what she'd thought at the time. But now . . .

Once, when he was a child, his Scottish Merchant Seaman father, proud of the boy's cleverness if nothing else, on one of his intermittent appearances had decided to show the boy his ship.

After the hot car ride, feeling sick, inappropriately cheered up with ice cream, the tetchy child gripped the gunwhale of the smelly launch harder and harder as it wove its way through oily water amongst gigantic vessels. He began to know a fear, a revulsion, a monstrous hatred out of all proportion. Only his profound sense of number prevented him from screaming. He dared not look up or down but stared at his thumb as the rescuing data, culled from the absent hero's old trade mags, memorized without trying, worked in his head . . . '*Fort Townshend* Passenger. Gross tonnage 3700. Length 326. Max. draught 25. Reciprocating engine 13 knots . . .' MV *Fanny Scarlett* Cargo. Wine tanker. Gross tonnage 3400. Length 334. Max. draught 23. 15 knots . . . *American Reefer* Refrigerated cargo. Gross tonnage 2300. Length 354. Max. draught 18. 12 knots . . .' This way, in here, he could master these monsters, but out there . . .

'Look Muir! This is the old girl . . . Well, take a look laddie, this is what I brought you to see . . . Come on boy! . . . Oh for God's sake!' Anger, shame, disappointment combined to make the man take a clumsy step down the launch. One hand still stretched behind him to the tiller. The other hand seized the boy's chin and forced it up. 'Look! Damn you!'

Damned indeed.

Iron cliffs swaying their huge height, black, bleeding

rust. The flare of the bow over-hanging, moving across the sky, falling, whirling, avalanching steel.

'Aaargh!' The man sat back on the thwart as if he'd been bitten, the warm vomit on his hand and sleeve. The boy made no attempt to clean his dribbled face, but, mumbling numbers, watched the contents of his stomach float away in the filthy water to be macerated in the launch's wake.

That was when the nightmare of hatred first intruded. He suspected it had been with him from then onwards, waiting its bigger moment. As at Southampton docks, echoes of its discordance had from time to time invaded the controlled place where he tried to live. Worldly success, the great palliator, the triumphant anaesthetic, had kept it at bay. Now it was everywhere. What had been occasional was now constant. No shutting of the eyes or mind could end it. The rusty walls towered, the oily water stank. Fixity and order were forgotten and he was in a place where numbers couldn't save him.

Of course there'd been something going on. Tessa remembered how Hammond's mood depended on Amy's. How his meetings with Amy, although casually spoken about, were always kept. Others, nominally much more important, were happily postponed. It had been going on under her nose – and she'd ignored it. Hadn't seen it . . . deliberately hadn't wanted to.

Then, when Amy died . . .

Tessa had arrived in the office just after Hammond had been told that Amy was missing, believed drowned. It was clear he was in shock. What hit her was the sense of his fear.

He cancelled everything for days. He'd driven straight to Norfolk.

'We've lost one of our senior staff, I'm afraid, in a tragic accident, so if you'll excuse Mr Hammond . . . Have you a space next week?' She'd trotted that out so many times. She'd managed the thing well, she knew. Telling everyone enough to elicit sympathy, without suggesting any impairment of the company's strength.

Until now, she hadn't thought much about what she hadn't been telling them: that the managing director was wandering the beaches of north Norfolk like a lost soul, looking for the corpse of the only woman he'd ever loved.

On the first night, Hammond had rung her at home from a hotel to say that he was staying over. He'd been drunk and she could tell he was on the edge of tears. Once again, it had been odd, but she'd thought he was frightened of something.

Tessa tried to settle to work, tried to eradicate Bewick from her mind.

She had begun that morning with no intention of telling him anything about Hammond's being in love with Amy. She now found the memory of Bewick standing over her like a recording angel, and wondered if she should, after all.

There was a noise outside the door. It opened.

'Oh hello, Mr Hammond . . . I wasn't expecting . . .'

He was at least an hour earlier than usual; nearly two. He looked dreadful, as if someone had drained the blood out of him. His skin looked green.

'Are you all right?'

He seemed not to hear. As he walked to the door of his office, he twice bumped into things. He was in a waking dream. His expression was fixed.

'Can I help?'

There was no reply. He wandered into his office, making a poor attempt to shut the door behind him. It occurred to Tessa that he might have had a heart attack. She followed him. 'Are you all right?'

He stood at his desk, head bowed, breathing heavily, although she could see he hadn't been exerting himself physically. Watching him, she reminded herself that he kept as fit as any man his age. She moved away from the idea of a heart attack.

'I'm perfectly all right. Wait in your office please.'

Tessa left him and returned to her desk, wondering.

Once, at the party of a smart friend, Tessa had mentioned, and proud of it too, that she was PA to Muir Hammond.

'Ah, the nerd in sheep's clothing!' someone had said. The men around him, all about Hammond's age, had laughed at this much more than it deserved. It turned out that they'd all been with him at university. There he'd been known as Supercreep. None of the women would bother with him. Then, in his last year, he was taken up by the jolly, overbearing Briony MacDonald. Under her wing he had launched his first company Dog Electronics, shortly followed by Sirius Software. The rest was marketing history.

Four years ago . . . No, thought Tessa, nearly five now . . . Briony Hammond had died, after only six weeks of illness, leaving Hammond haunted, confused. But not like this. She wondered again if he had had a heart attack.

Later, he called her in. He seemed almost recovered. Instead of telling Bewick about Amy and Hammond, Tessa transposed the proddings of conscience. She told Hammond about Bewick's questioning of her.

Hammond hardly seemed interested until Tessa mentioned Bewick's being in Norfolk, when he looked at her briefly. That was the only reaction she got from him. Ten minutes later, however, he walked out of the building without explanation. She hadn't seen him since.

People thought of him as dry and rational, sharp and peremptory. All his life, in fact, he had ridden the waves of his compulsions. It had been his strength and his secret source of power. And the secret of that secret lay in his dazzling numeracy, his easy supremacy in the golden kingdom of numbers.

He hadn't loved at all until someone had pushed open the gate into that kingdom and joined him as an equal there. Then he knew, knew love, knew what all those stupid fictions had been trying to persuade him of. Fictions which told him that he wasn't human if he didn't submit to the ache and passion, the fevers of desire whose symptoms had been a nonsense to him, had described what sounded to him like a disease, not the supreme experience of the human race.

He hadn't loved his wife and was mystified that she should resent it. He knew she could not possibly love him, who was, despite his ability to fly on gilded numerate wings, in essence grub-like, unworthy, unable, broken, damned.

Then after her death he found Amy in the world of numbers, flying on wings even stronger than his own. They danced in mental worlds no other could reach, on painted wings of beautiful numerate abstraction, untouchable.

When he confessed and declared his love, when he condescended to lay his potential millions at Amy's feet, he had no idea that Amy might have thoughts and feelings of her own. She was his. He knew. It was meant. There was no other way.

'I'm sorry,' she had said gently. 'I'm sorry.'

'Nothing ventured, nothing gained,' he had said, abasing himself as he knew he deserved.

'I'm sorry,' she had said, more gently still. He took off his glasses and wiped them, smiling foolishly.

She could not have known that he was at that

moment blind with hatred, his vision curtained with blood, that violence towards her was a hair's breadth away, that had she not walked him to the door then, that very minute, the frail curtaining membrane would have ruptured and spilled the monster which had lain within him all his life, waiting to be born.

Her refusal stunned and disorientated him. It closed him, forced him to lock himself in his grotesquely proportioned inner world. Over the coming weeks, the rage in him grew, fuelled by insane convictions about her, about himself, about how love was organized, about how life was organized; fuelled by raw infantile passion.

He began to look exhausted, ill. His clumsiness grew into a disability. He rode his compulsions still, but carelessly. They were now no longer the intuitive surges which had carried him effortlessly past his competitors, but freak obsessive waves which left him stranded.

He was tied to a rock, a raven feasting daily on his living entrails. He was sick with the disease that would finish him. He was ill with self-hatred.

Jones found himself lost again. He reckoned he only had about half an hour if he was to cross the Splash in comfort. The wind was rising uncomfortably. The thickening cloud was bringing on a premature dusk.

He walked up the slope of a dune towards a ruined hut. At least, that's what it looked like. You couldn't tell in this bloody place; probably another bloody sculpture. Grumbling, he toiled up towards it. For all his grumbling, he was elated, however. He had seen what Bewick had not – that their man was Hammond. He it was who'd solved the riddle.

There was a ripping sound. Immediately in front of him a pale wound flared in the grey weathered timber of the ruined hut. A distant thud followed at once; then echoed. With the sound of the shot and his recognizing what it was, the landscape changed. Hollows were shallower. Colours hardened. The air was brighter.

Jones had his face pressed hard against the sand. He had no idea of how he'd arrived there. Another shot. The sand kicked up in a spray. The ground quivered. Then the wooden snap of a third, closer.

He rolled. Amazing, the solid jolt of a two-foot drop. Silence for a moment. Then the hiss of the wind in the dune grasses faded in. He lay in a hollow, momentarily safe. Who was it? Hammond? He supposed it must be Hammond. Why anyone else?

Sweating, still in shock, he worked his way through some small sand hillocks to get another view of the ruined hut. Yes, there it was. It confirmed his worst fears. The shot had come from on the island – from the piece of rising ground near the chapel. He was marooned on a very small patch of desert with someone intent on killing him. He was too frightened to be frightened. He was cold with despair.

He wanted to stand up and shout, I'm not the man

you want! I'm a small, notoriously unfit Welsh coward. A flabhead who cannot possibly harm you! Another shot screamed through the top of the dune eight feet away and he knew that he was way past any version of surrender.

Think, you bastard!

So far the shooting had been nastily accurate. Hammond must have ammunition to spare, else why shoot from such a distance? Unless . . . The glimmer of hope he felt turned his bowels. With hope came fear. He prayed he wouldn't shit himself. If the man continued to shoot from a distance, it could mean he was fearful that his quarry might be armed. So if Jones could hide himself until dark, he might still have a chance. Grace Carver would be able to do it – had already done it, possibly. The man wasn't shooting at her.

Lund's words came back to him: '*She must have a faultless spatial memory.*' Well, he didn't. The place was already beginning to confuse him. For want of something to do, he moved off along a deep gully. It led to the south as far as he could tell – away from the sniper, at least. As he dragged himself through the sand, he tried to form a plan. His only hope was somehow to move towards the sniper, outflank him, and lie up in one of the pools between the lighthouse and Salvages Creek.

Jones stopped. It was a real effort to do so. The difference, he told himself, was dying anyway but later; or possible survival with the risk of dying sooner.

Risk it. You got to risk it, he needed to tell himself many times, before he laboriously turned round.

He set off on a diagonal course towards, and across the face of, the sniper.

'Hallo-o! *Greylag*!'

She felt a shiver of fear as she recognized his voice. She put her head out of the companionway. There he was on the Scales Howe shore. She heard herself inviting him aboard. She rowed across with a light line still attached to *Greylag*'s stern cleat. She had never handled the dinghy in this wind strength before.

Minutes later, they were out of the wind in the cabin. The thick overcast of cloud was already making it gloomy below. Sally lit a lamp and the gas under the kettle. The rigging roared and whistled. In the gusts the boat sailed up to her mooring buoy under spars alone, tugged and paid off. In the cabin however the flame of the brass lamp barely shuddered.

'I was told you'd broken off your engagement,' Bewick said.

'Who told you?'

'Karen Quinney. She's a Detective Inspector, she . . .'

'I know who she is,' said Sally more sharply than she meant. 'She's your girlfriend.'

'Yes. You could say that. She's left though.'

'Left you?'

'Yes.'

'Why? It's perfectly clear she's in love with you.'

Sally still failed to keep the edge out of her voice. She tried again. 'Why should she leave you?'

'Because she knew you'd broken off your engagement.'

The implications of what Bewick was saying were beginning to dawn on Sally. 'She thought,' Bewick went on, 'I ought to find out how things were with you . . . Before . . .' He gestured vaguely. His eyes were still cool.

'She said that? What an extraordinary girl. I'm very impressed.'

'She also wishes you'd never been born.'

'Does she?'

'Because she knew what your breaking off your engagement would mean to me.'

The kettle was boiling. Sally stood. There was a soft roaring in her ears beyond the sounds of the storm. For a moment she thought she might faint. Had she heard what she had heard? She turned to the kettle so Bewick wouldn't see the smile that she couldn't prevent. She started to make the tea. 'What . . . what does it mean to you?' she asked with her back to him.

'It means you might be free. Are you?'

'Yes. I'm free.'

There was silence behind her. She turned. The grey eyes were on her, watchful and calming. Bewick said nothing. He put his hand out to her, palm up. She hesitated, then put her hand in it. His closed with slow deliberation. His eyes didn't move from her face. She felt her hand touched, then explored with great delicacy. She was drawn into his arms. She was giddy with the smell of him as he kissed her.

It was a few minutes later that they heard the first shot.

By the time she had got to her feet, Bewick was already kneeling in the cockpit, the boat's binoculars to his eyes.

There was another shot. Bewick moved the glasses quickly, then steadied them. He held a hand above the lenses to keep off the rain. The boat rode forward, jerked away to leeward, pitched and yawed.

Sally stood in the companionway. 'What can you see?'

'Bugger all. Hang on . . .'

'What do you think it is?'

'Whatever it is, that's a . . . Hang on . . .

Out in dwindling light, Sally saw something move.

'Hammond!' Bewick said. 'Not exactly rifle-club kit he's using, but I think that's Hammond. Why the hell he's choosing this moment to crack up, God knows.'

Another shot. Pointless, she thought, to ask who Hammond might be.

'What's he shooting at?'

'Gio Jones. The Carver woman would have disappeared herself. Shit!'

Sally said nothing. Bewick swore at himself under his breath again. Then he relaxed. Sally stayed silent. She watched him thinking.

Bewick turned to her. 'Any flares on board?'

'I don't know.'

She found the flares in a watertight plastic canister in a locker above the pilot berth. Rain was hammering on the coachroof now, the rigging howling. The boat bucked and pitched. Bewick sorted through the flares, bracing himself against the chart table, rejecting the coloured smoke ones. Red parachute flares and white collision flares he replaced in the canister. He pondered a moment then put the smoke flares in after all.

'You're going to Scales Howe?'

Bewick didn't pause in his preparations. From the boat's rope locker he took a length of line, about ten metres. 'Gio won't get through this on his own.'

Sally watched him work the rope into a locked coil which he slung over his shoulders. She couldn't suppress the thought that Bewick might not get through it either. In that confined space he looked so powerful. Sally however had attended enough post-mortems to know what combat bullets can do to human flesh.

Above the constant roar of the gale came the cold tap of another shot.

As he slid his way down another slope, in a fog of sand blown from higher up, Jones realized he'd just seen a pair of eyes. There was no one there. He assumed he was hallucinating. This was what real fear did to you. Slowly he looked round. The rivulets of sand disturbed by the wind trickled down into the gully. Apart from these the sand was uniform. There was nowhere to hide. He was going mad.

Then he saw them again. About eight feet from the top of the dune a pair of disembodied, troubled eyes gazed at him. Then they closed and disappeared.

For a moment, Jones knew, in his dark Celtic panic, that these were the eyes of the destroying angel, the hag at the ford, the courier of death; that he should make his peace now with his remembered life, because it was not going to be his for much longer.

Welsh cynicism came to his rescue. 'Fuck off,' he said to himself. 'It's the schizo. The flotsam sculptress. She dug herself a cave.'

And, indeed, where he had seen the eyes, there was the faintest shadow in the sand, no more than a crease but enough to mask a tiny viewing slit. How she had constructed the cave, where it was entered from, how she had disguised the disturbed sand, he had no time to consider. Four feet in front of his face, a small ridge exploded in a horizontal spray and he heard the echoing knock of the weapon that had caused it.

The sky had darkened. Heavier rain now swept the island, drumming the sand, hissing, blurring the sound of the surf. Jones turned back the way he had come.

Bewick lay in the dinghy on his stomach, paddling with his hands. The saltings were deep in shadow now, and rain curtained. Nevertheless, a shot hit the water beyond him, about four feet away. At this, Bewick rolled out of the dinghy into the grey water, taking with him the waterproof cylinder of flares.

Watching from the cabin, Sally thought he had been hit. She was in the cockpit before she could think. Then she saw the blur of the flares cylinder, travelling just under the surface, steadily, towards the far side of the creek. Then it went deep enough to disappear and her fears returned. She told herself that the creek would run red if he'd been hit by battlefield ammunition – designed to tumble when it enters the body, to claw away chunks of tissue and bone. She stared. The water was unchanged.

The creek's edge was composed of a narrow beach and a miniature cliff, a vertical bank half a metre high. Well away from where her eyes were searching, Bewick now burst from the water in a crouching run and rolled under the bank. A shot greeted this. It was wide; and late. The dinghy had by now swung away, lying off the stern of *Greylag*, across the wind, held there by the flood tide.

Gio Jones heard the shots and realized they'd been fired from a different position. Hammond had come away from the chapel before they'd been fired. Which meant he must have been looking for Jones when another target had taken his attention.

Did those shots mean Bewick was on the island? They hadn't been aimed at him. They must mean the presence of someone else, musn't they? Please God.

As he crawled in the gloom just below the crest of the ridge, his head was filled with infantile thoughts . . . Please let me live . . . If I live then I promise to . . . I promise not to . . .

'Who the fuck d'you think you're talking to?' he murmured, angry with himself. The sand was sticking to his wet face and hair. The storm was screaming now. Sand, driven off the ridge by the rain, was spattering his back from head to toe. He could feel the skin being worn from his elbows and knees. There was no pain.

When the bullets next came he turned cold from his throat to his arms. He felt his bowels shift and bit his lip. 'Let's have a shred of dignity, just a morsel, for God's sake,' he hissed at himself and held on.

The shots had been in rapid succession; all in his general direction. The one that so frightened him hit the ridge so that he felt the sand under his body bulge with the impact.

Jones froze. Ahead, just visible in the gloom that was now nearly darkness, was a darker shape. He saw a head, a gun. Resigned, he closed his eyes.

It would be now; any second. Inside his head, all was calm. He said goodbye to Eilean as if she were standing beside him. He kissed the children. Their hair was shining. Karen stood in the distance somewhere. He waved at her. His arms went around his family. Come on, do it. I'm ready.

Slowly, the moan and roar of the storm came back and the lashing splatter of the rain. Jones opened his eyes. The shape hadn't moved: the head, the gun, were locked there on the horizon. He levered himself up and saw what it was he'd been looking at.

Bewick moved methodically along the shallow cover provided by the bank towards where the shots came from. As the tide raised them into the influence of the wind, the moored boats began to plunge and skew even more. The drumming of halyards was overtaken by the shriek in the rigging of the wind itself and the pounding of the surf as it crept back up the beach.

A coward dies many times before his death, Jones reminded himself. His personal best to date was two deaths in as many minutes. What he had taken for a man with a gun had been an extrusion of one of Grace Carver's driftwood sculptures. He lay sheltered inside it now. He wondered if this coffin-like space he'd clambered into might be his salvation. He lay now sheltered between two tarry railway sleepers. At last he was out of the wind. Not immune from its noise though, which growled and wailed through the structure over his head. The relief of not being outside to be shot at was huge. His eyes watered.

It took a minute to realize that he was effectively in a trap. Exposed, he was mobile and relatively safe. Sheltered, he could be identified, besieged. He knew he must get out. He didn't want to.

Another burst of fire.

Jones understood how people gave up the effort of

living, the pain of irritating bloody effort. Come on, he urged himself – now! He began to lever himself out of his hiding place.

Then the fireworks began and he was in the grandstand.

A shattering white light flowered below him near the creek. It bathed the landscape, a bowl-like auditorium of sand, for a brilliant split-second. Then it waved and flew towards the single figure who stood in it, gun in hand.

The collision flare hit the sand near the sniper, jumping and sputtering. His gun raked the beach as he dived for non-existent cover. He lay, weapon at the ready, exposed briefly in the glaring light. Then something else arced through the darkness at the edge of the light and a smoke flare landed upwind of him. Jones watched the smoke begin to billow back towards the sniper in the dying seconds of the collision flare's light. The man's face lifted: it was Hammond.

Jones was on his feet. He stood jumping and yelling behind the driftwood sculpture. He saw Hammond turn towards him as he intended, but Jones knew he would be protected. Hammond coughed in the smoke. He lifted his gun as a second collision flare, thrown spinning by Bewick, sailed high, caught the wind, and described an improbably long parabola over Hammond's head. Jones dropped to his knees as the bullets passed through the driftwood.

Then the night turned red.

In the flowing orange smoke, Hammond was on

fire. A red parachute flare had hit his shoulder. As Jones watched, he dropped his gun and flung himself down in the sand. Jones saw Bewick start out of the shadows. Bewick had a good thirty metres to cover. Jones saw immediately that he wasn't going to make it.

Almost before he hit the ground to douse the phosphorous searing into him, Hammond had begun to grope for the gun again. In horror, Jones watched as Hammond lifted it. Then time seemed to slow. Hammond's arms juddered. His mouth opened, gasping. He couldn't lift the gun high enough. Bewick was running in a ducking weave now. There was a harsh triple crack as three unaimed rounds went wide. Hammond was on his knees, screaming now as phosphorous and plastic melted into his flesh. Then he dropped forward on to his hands. Bewick's momentum carried him in a leap over Hammond's back where he crouched, still trying to bring the gun to bear. Bewick checked, swivelled and kicked out. Above the storm Jones heard the thud of Bewick's heel on Hammond's neck. Hammond collapsed. As he lurched and fell across the weapon, it juddered once more and a black stain of blood began to spread across the sand.

Bewick stood, his chest heaving, staring at the blood flowing out of Hammond. Jones saw him walk a couple of unsteady yards then sit down heavily.

Another spectator lowered the glasses from her eyes.

One by one the flares guttered in the shrieking wind and went out.

In the rocking cabin of *Greylag* a hot meal had been conjured. Gio Jones's bleeding elbows had been dressed. The paraffin heating stove roared steadily, surrounded by Bewick's clothes.

As Bewick had stripped his clothes off in the confined space, Sally had found it impossible to keep her eyes off him, especially as he was so unselfconscious about it. The power and athleticism of his body upset her. It made her think of Karen, of what she knew Karen's body must be like; of how they must be suited.

Jones had turned from the stove to see Sally contemplating Bewick's back – a landscape of scarred and bruised muscle. He had turned away before she caught his eye. He thanked God he'd decided not to provide a laughable comparison by stripping off himself.

Wrapped in blankets now, Bewick looked like a tribal chief. The meal was set out. A bottle of Château Musar was opened. They ate and drank greedily, their thoughts unable to escape the presence of the dead man who lay on the sand just across the creek.

'Who was he?' Sally asked.

'His name was Hammond, Muir Hammond,' Bewick said.

'Head of Sirius?'

'Yes.'

'My God . . .'

'Yes,' said Jones. 'You won't be able to hear the sound of the crashing stock for the sound of alarm bells ringing.'

'It was a private company,' Bewick muttered.

'Don't get pedantic with me, ex-Superintendent. There's going to be a God Almighty stink. Not to mention we arrested the wrong person for the Kelleher murder. No, you won't want to get downwind of this one.'

Gio Jones knew he was overdoing the relish. He couldn't help himself. The tension between Bewick and the woman was like violin gut.

'The press will have an orgy,' he went on. 'That horrible little ghoul Kelleher will find he's just in time to reap the full dirty purseful for his daughter's death. This will run and run. Sex, death and computers already. A heady mix. Talking of which, this wine, mmmph! Powerful. Christ look at that! Fourteen per cent. No wonder it motors. Talking of motors, remind me to get them to fingerprint the corpse ASAP, will you? The path. lads should've finished with young Spilby's much-stolen motor by close of play tomorrow . . .'

Then suddenly Jones stopped. Sally saw his hand holding his knife shaking before he put it down. Turning to him, she saw tears running down his plump cheeks. Unable to disguise them, he said, 'I think this is what you call delayed relief. I thought I was going to die out there. What am I saying? I knew I was going to die.'

For some reason Sally found this absurdly much funnier than anything else he had said and began laughing. Bewick joined in. Gio Jones, who seldom saw Bewick laugh, was ambushed into laughter himself. The small cabin rocked and resonated with it, drowning out the storm.

An hour later Bewick was in his damp clothes again and preparing the dinghy. Sally thought of reminding him that more people are lost from dinghies than from yachts, but thought it laughable to do so in the circumstances. The wind would be with Bewick and Jones for the brief, wild journey to the end of the creek.

Although one at least of the yachts had already chafed through its mooring warps and had been driven ashore, Sally insisted she could prevent that happening to *Greylag*. She couldn't prevent other boats breaking free and being driven on to her, admittedly, but *Greylag* carried a liferaft. She was much safer on board than overloading the dinghy. Bewick said he would catch the morning flood and bring the dinghy back to her.

In the cabin, the motion had quietened. The wind had swung northerly, increased and then lessened. The tide now ran in concert with the wind, the boat's movement had become rhythmic and predictable.

Sally pulled herself up into a sitting position. She had been half-lying in the bunk, listening to the roaring clatter around the mast, which still drowned out all water noises except for the bright sound of a water slop hitting the hull.

Everything had changed. Those brief minutes of pleasure and happiness she had known with him before they had heard the first shot were irrecoverable. Such things lay in a world where different laws applied. What she had seen take place out there on the sand was like a barrier slamming down and cutting her off from what she had enjoyed, a past she couldn't return to.

She had watched, avidly, as Jones had, the brief duel in the sands. She had not believed that Bewick would die. Once she had seen him in action, she had known he would win. She had known Bewick would return to her.

She was well versed in violence: the implicit violence, at least, of a cadaver gaping from sternum to groin like a ripe fruit was a familiar sight. She had participated in well over twenty PMs. Today was the first time she had witnessed the moment of a man's death.

She had also seen Bewick deliberately risk himself, subject himself to danger. She knew that in the past she could have been cynical about this. When she saw Bewick in action, however, she saw something that thrilled and repelled. Irony wasn't open to her.

She tried reminding herself that Bewick hadn't sought the risk. It wasn't some sort of self-challenge. He had been facing an imposed threat unprepared. It was a level of spirit and courage which she had never seen before, but then . . .

It had ended in death.

She had seen in Bewick a man prepared to kill. She hadn't sensed anything like this about him when she first met him; nothing. Would she, she now asked herself, have been surprised if someone had told her what he was capable of? Duty, sacrifice . . . They were so rare, so perverse, so powerful. Is that what she had seen taking place on Scales Howe?

She didn't know, and until she did . . . She realized that she was actually frightened of him. The image that came to her was not the duel with Hammond, but the moment in the cabin when she had first seen his extraordinary body with its bruising and its scars, like the sculpture of a warrior ideal damaged by time and carelessness. She was able to ask herself whether sexual fear was involved. That wasn't it. If only it were.

She tried to recapture the sense she had once had of his presence being a drug to her; the sense of warmth she felt in his company which was literally an alteration of her body's chemistry. It was gone. It was the past. She couldn't even remember it properly.

Sally was on her feet. She clambered from handhold to handhold in the rocking hull and began to tidy away the debris of her brief stay on board.

Gio Jones gave a doctored version of what had happened on Scales Howe to his opposite number in the Norfolk CID and promised the availability of Bewick to make a statement.

A team, including the police surgeon, was beginning to gather in the lounge of The Royal, waiting for the tide to drop and the weather to moderate. As soon as he could, Jones excused himself. He was exhausted. Catching sight of himself in a mirror on the way to the lift, he wasn't surprised they let him go so promptly. He looked a wreck, a joke. The dressing-gown made him look sinister. His hair, thick with salt and sand, stood up like a vaudeville madman's.

'Great,' he murmured. He longed for the approval Eilean somehow managed whenever he needed it.

15

Grace Carver had worked now for two hours, burying the entrance. She knew that in this wind the surface dampness would have dried out by dawn and the dune would resume its camouflaging uniformity.

She tried to rid herself of the mind set which was personalizing the grains of sand as she moved them, giving them souls and motives – some helpful, some enemies, dark with hatred, who hindered her in any way they could. It became worse. She was shifting the entire population of the world with her hands. She was a benign deity burying the last refuge of the gods from the malice of the dark beasts who roamed the underworld, never dying, never entirely alive, always ravenous. Raven, ravenous, ravening, raving . . . She hadn't taken her pills.

With this thought, the sand reverted to being something describable by a geologist.

'I suppose you'll be joining that Sally Vernon on her boat, will you?'

'No.'

'Why the hell not? Woman's mad about you.'

Bewick shook his head. 'This'll get to her. It'll have to be sorted out.'

'What will?'

'What happened. I killed Hammond.'

'He'd have killed you, for fuck's sake.'

'Doesn't matter. It makes a difference. She can't ignore it.'

After washing down the pills with some milk that was only just right, Grace wandered over to the washing carousel: a tree whose strange fruit swivelled and tinkled in the wind. Hidden in the middle, near the stem, hung a small plastic pouch on a piece of red cord. Grace removed it. She climbed to the top of the nearest dune.

Over the leaden sea and below a sombre sky, streaks of yellow marked the horizon. Above, briefly, a shooting star.

'Lustrous gashes,' murmured Grace. 'Crystal tresses.'

Everything was stowed in its rightful place. Sally had packed away her bedding. She had even refilled the lamps. Her two bags stood packed on the cabin floor. All she had to do now was wait for Bewick to turn up with the dinghy.

Above the chart table was a check-list of things to be done when leaving the boat. She looked through it. The only item left was switching off the gas.

In the cockpit, the wind was no more than a strong breeze. She delved into the gas locker and shut down the cylinder. As she straightened up she heard the squeak of oars. Like a character in a play whose arrival has been heavily anticipated, but delayed to the acute moment, Bewick's broad back emerged through the half light. He was in a wooden dinghy and was towing *Greylag*'s tender.

He came alongside with no sense of occasion – as if he was fulfilling some ordinary arrangement. 'Your tender as promised. I borrowed one of the dinghies on the beach.'

It was as if he had never touched her, as if the events of last night had obliterated the past. Sally stared. What did he mean?

As if he understood, Bewick said, 'Should we have time, perhaps, to think about this, about things?'

'Do you need time to think about things?' she asked.

'No. No I don't. I meant you. I thought you might.'

It was exactly what she wanted, but she didn't enjoy his anticipation of it at all. She resented it furiously, even as she felt relieved. 'I think that might be a good idea. Shall I ring you . . .?' she asked, 'When . . .?' She searched his face. There wasn't a flicker of acknowledgement that he'd been right.

'Yes, you ring me,' he said mildly.

She watched him keeping station with his oars, moving in time to the dinghy's motion, compensating, easing.

'Ring any time,' Bewick added. 'Day or night. I like being woken up. I have bad dreams.'

Bewick transferred the line from the inflatable to *Greylag*, then rowed away.

Sally watched him, hardly believing her own silence.

Outside the post-office, where they had stopped to buy some strong mints for Gio Jones, they were accosted by Grace Carver.

She thrust the plastic pouch into Bewick's hands. 'This is what all the fuss was about, I think you'll find,' she said in her county-smart voice, as if she were pointing out the obvious. Then she suddenly turned and ran.

Bewick opened the pouch, which was re-sealable and waterproof. He slid out the computer disc. Then he returned it to the pouch and handed it to Gio Jones.

Jones nodded off at Swaffham, but woke again as Bewick slowed behind the queue of cars waiting to turn into RAF Lakenheath. He yawned and stretched. He remembered he was on his way home and rejoiced.

'Halleluiah!' Jones said with brio.

Sunlight flickered through the trees lining the road. He stared at the dispiriting buildings of the airbase. He yawned again and thought of going back to sleep.

'Did I tell you,' Bewick said, 'I've come round to your way of thinking about Joe Enwright? I reckon he's a killer too.'

'What!' Jones screamed. 'What the bleedin', soddin', fuckin' hell're you on about?'

Bewick smiled. 'What happened to the car?'

'Car? What car? What are you on about?'

'Calm down, Gio. I mean Enwright's father's car – after it crashed.'

Jones calmed down. 'It was a wreck, scrap. It would've gone for scrap,' he replied.

'Got a record of who took it?'

'Probably. But I know who would have done anyway. Amos would have picked that one up. You know, Monty Amos, Muldoon's half-brother.'

'Monty? That makes sense. You sure?'

'No one else would've dared, not on Monty's patch.'

'True. These things change, though.'

They drove to Amos's Breakdown at New Eastwick Fen, where seven acres of wrecked cars and vans lay spread out under a creamy grey sky.

A short pot-holed track led off the Cottenham road. As they closed the doors of the car, a decaying caravan nearby exploded with the barking of Alsatians. One of them was at the filthy window, throat stretched. Another Alsatian immediately responded. It was in the small grim house beyond. Here, all the curtains were drawn, piled up on the window-sill, thick with dirt.

'I almost prefer Disneyland,' said Jones.

Bewick didn't reply but wandered over to the house.

Jones could see rain falling out of the clouds, miles away, somewhere over Rampton, he reckoned.

The dogs didn't give up. Bewick knocked at the

door of the cement-rendered house and the barking became a frenzy. No one came.

In a shed beyond, before the dump itself, Jones could see the crazy rocket fins of a sixties American car. Beyond that was a crane, its crab jaws hovering over a sea of wrecked vehicles, in places piled five high. He watched it pick up a car and move it.

'Arternoon, Mr Bewick.'

They turned.

Monty Amos gleamed, like the car in the shed. From his hair to his 24-carat earrings to his snakeskin waistcoat to his tooled cowboy boots, there was a gloss to him. Jones had forgotten that the man was such a style lunatic.

'Afternoon,' said Bewick.

Jones took in Amos's brown eyes, permanently bloodshot, that offered no greeting.

'Hello Monty.'

'Giovanni Jones as well. Must be serious. What's the agenda?'

'A car you pulled out of the river by the Twenty-pence Inn about a year ago. Still got it?'

'What you payin'?'

They haggled briefly, then walked over to the crane.

'Andy!' yelled Amos at the crane. 'C'm 'ere!'

The crane stopped. Andy jumped down, looking nervous.

'These gentlemen here're reckonin' to pay money for a sight of that Mazda we pulled out of the Old West River.'

'Yeah?'

Amos turned to Bewick and Jones. 'The papers said police frogmen got the bloke out. Loadershite. It was Pete from up the road with his wet suit. We lent him a rim to weigh him down.' He turned back to Andy. 'Still got it, have we?'

'Mazda?'

'That's what I said.'

Andy fiddled with his eyebrow stud. 'Yeah, reckon.'

'Find it, then.'

The three men followed Andy into a small town of stacked wrecks with main streets, side streets, cul-de-sacs, and in the middle of it all, a small piazza. This was where Andy took his breaks. There was a smartly striped deckchair sitting in the mud and a folding picnic table placed to catch the sun at lunchtime. All around stood walls of crushed and rusted steel.

Andy led them through his domain into a final street where wrecks were stored whose future was uncertain. Amongst them was the Mazda.

'Check it out,' Amos ordered and invited Bewick and Jones to a beer back at the van. The van in question was an American caravan with sliding patio doors composed of small leaded panes. Amos took three Budweisers from a cold box. He gave a bottle opener to Jones and then took the cap off his own bottle with his teeth.

Jones asked him about his half-brother, Muldoon, the trucker.

'Going straight,' said Amos. 'What am I saying? Going? Gone! Gone straight.'

'Pull the other,' said Jones.

'Straight up.'

'Straight up my arse.'

'No thanks.' Amos laughed. The gold in his mouth caught the light. A plump teenager in jodhpurs knocked at the window. Amos waved her away.

Twenty minutes later Andy came in. 'Yeah,' he said. 'Somebody fucked with the servo on the brakes.'

'Could it have happened by itself?'

'No chance.'

'So . . .' said Jones as they walked back to the car.

'Mrs Enwright good as told me he'd done it. She told me he'd serviced the car, that he wouldn't go with his father to Ely that night. Claimed he knew his father would be drinking.'

'His father did drink. That's why we didn't look at the car too closely. But look here, why would Mrs Enwright grass on her own son?'

'Perhaps she doesn't like him, just like we don't.'

Jones had taken over the driving. He glanced out at the black fields, the low blur of mist, the silver line of a water-filled ditch, the big emptiness of the fens. For the first time he felt some compassion for Joe Enwright. He compared the boy's life with his own and briefly he felt abundantly happy.

'I know he's not expert at admitting sexual

relationships,' Bewick said, 'but you might get the psychiatrist to have another go at him. Find out what went on with his father: then you can let the charming child go with a reasonably clear conscience.'

'There'd be no case against him, that's for sure. Not with one of your posh lawyer friends biting chunks out of young Andy from the dump. Where do you want me to drop you, by the way – I'm going home to my wife.'

'Homerton, if you've got the time.'

'Sure. Tell me, what gave you this idea about Joe Enwright?'

'Sally Vernon.'

'Yeah?'

'I told her about the case and what you thought about it. She said perhaps we were both right: he didn't kill Julia but did kill someone else. I laughed at the time . . .'

A farmhouse passed, huddled into its barns and trees, surrounded by the dark spread of peaty fields. Jones glanced across at Bewick. 'You going to see her again?' he asked.

'I told you. It's up to her. I doubt it.'

'Yeah?'

'I'm not reckoning to see her again. She broke off her engagement because he was a violent bastard. She's not going to bother with another.'

'That's what you are, is it?'

'Not to women. But it's something I do. You know it is.'

Jones knew it was.

Sally drove to her parents' house. She had phoned to say she was coming. Her father, unusually, came out to greet her. More unusually still, he gave her a hug. His sweater smelt of woodsmoke and the Eau Sauvage that she or her mother gave him every birthday. As they walked to the house together, he gave her a shy smile of sympathy and said, 'All right?'

Sally nodded. Her father seemed at a loss for a moment, then added, 'Your mother's playing bridge at that bloody awful Cartwright woman's. Want some tea?'

In the tidy kitchen her father set about making tea. He watched Sally surreptitiously as he did so.

'He was there, Dad,' she heard herself say before she began crying. Her father stood frozen, the tea caddy in one hand and a spoon in the other, helpless.

'Sorry,' she said. 'Won't be a moment.' She ran to the lavatory. She washed her face, cried again and washed her face again.

When she emerged into the familiar hallway with its grey flagstones and fading wallpaper, she didn't feel any better, worse if anything, but was no longer tearful.

Her father was in the sitting-room by a smouldering log fire.

'I've been thinking about you honey,' he said as if

wanting to open the subject of Sally's tears. Then he retreated. 'Lot of wind last night.'

Sally watched him sadly, wondering if she would ever be able to reach across the divide. 'Yes, it wasn't too brilliant.'

'That why you came back?'

'No. I told you. He was there.'

'James?'

'No. Not James.'

'Ah . . . This policeman fellow of yours, you mean?'

'He isn't "mine", Dad.'

'Sure. 'Course.'

'But, yes. Him.'

Vernon began pouring the tea. His eyes lowered, profoundly uncomfortable. 'Want to tell me about it?'

Sally felt her eyes prickle with tears again at this effort of her father's. She told him what had happened the night before.

'This man, Bewick, sounds . . . well . . . I mean his going to help . . . it wasn't just in the heat of the moment. Sounds suspiciously like bravery to me. What do you think?'

'I've been thinking that he was probably a bit of a violence merchant who enjoyed risking his own skin.'

Vernon looked at her with a smile. 'That describes a lot of men,' he said.

'Does it? Does it describe you?'

'Not really.'

'Quite.'

'I'm no model. Surely, what matters is what they

do with it? If this Bewick chap is that type, then he seems to know how to use it.'

'That may be what matters in the abstract, but I don't like it. And anyway, why do they have to do anything with it? Why can't they just deny it? Or confine it to rugger?'

Vernon shrugged. 'When you talk about his risking his own skin, by the way,' he said, 'it depends what you mean. Intelligent people who risk their lives, I mean who consciously know they're doing it, are very, very thin on the ground. I never did.'

'In the war, you mean?'

'Well it wasn't playing bridge with the Cartwright woman,' Vernon said crossly.

Sally knew by the quality of his irritation that he was, in his embarrassed way, giving her permission to ask about it. What she wanted to ask was, had he ever killed anybody? Sally's father was gentle towards his wife and daughter, fair in his business dealings, astute enough to have earned them a comfortable life. If he . . . She couldn't ask it, not directly. 'If it hadn't all been in machines, Dad, if you'd been a soldier not a pilot . . . you'd still have done it?'

'They had to be stopped,' he said ruminatively, as if he had to remember what it had all been about. 'That was a conviction I held. I'd thought about it a bit. Your uncle Patrick was in an eight which was rowing in Germany just before the war: the Goering Cup at Bad Essen. I went over with him for a sort of holiday. It was very ugly what was going on. We knew then that they'd have to be stopped. Even without the anti-Semitism you could see it was all wrong.'

'Were you frightened? When it started, I mean?'

Brisk footsteps outside announced Mrs Vernon's return. Sally knew the moment had passed, probably for ever. She went to her father and kissed him on the cheek.

'He sounds all right to me, this chap,' he said.

'Maybe . . . I don't know, Dad.'

'We're never not at war, you know,' Vernon said. 'In one way or another. It's just a question of numbers, of how many are committed.'

'Sure.'

Mrs Vernon came in. 'What a nice surprise,' she said, as if to her it was no surprise at all.

Sally lay with the curtains open, watching the moon creep across a dark cloudless sky. The wind in the ash tree near her parents' house waved a web of black branches. The tail of the storm moaned quietly through the ill-fitting frame or, in squalls, coughed in the chimney. With the wind noise came the memory, keeping her from sleep again.

She was back again in *Greylag*'s cabin, possessed. It had been the possibility of love, hadn't it, which had turned that small space into paradise?

Yes, it must have been that.

And was that no longer possible?

John Bewick had been infuriatingly right. She needed to understand – not why she had left James, but why she had come so close to marrying him. Until she knew that, she could not move on.

Was that all John Bewick had done, after all? Shown her that she couldn't continue with James? Perhaps so. It was enough, even if it was all. She knew it was more, but couldn't describe what that was.

So here she was again; like the young Ph.D. she had been at twenty-five, unattached, yielding to the tides of her work, living for it. What was that word? To describe a dedicated life? Conventual. That was it. She was pleased to have defined herself, felt braver for doing so, even if it were to accept some sort of nun-like status. Conventual.

Watching the moon's journey she fell asleep.

Mrs Kay looked up from her desk, her glance searching. 'Are you recovered?'

Bewick appeared stupefied for a moment.

'We heard that you'd had an awful accident. We have a friend who works in A&E who reckoned you were lucky to be alive.'

'Yes thanks. Bit of bruising now. Nasty at the time.'

Mrs Kay didn't look as if she really believed him. She had a gleam in her eye. 'Mr Halliday won't be in today.'

'No?'

'He met with an accident, as it were, in Glasgow. You all seem to be at it. I've had to renew all his credit cards. He was mugged. I don't think it's too serious, but he's working from home until the facial bruising settles down.'

On Bewick's fax machine when he returned home was a note from Gio Jones. It briefly outlined the financial condition of Sirius Software; debts of over fourteen million and rising. There were also some notes of an interview Jones had had with Tessa Waring, where she'd got around to discussing the relationship between Hammond and Amy Parris.

The computer disk Grace Carver had given them described complex movements of money (source unknown) through a series of unknown accounts. These money movements were not yet understood, although Frank Dalmeny was working on it.

In the car-park of City West, Gio Jones was supervising the return to its owner of Jim Spilby's car. Jim had turned up for some reason in a jacket and tie and looked even more uncomfortable than usual. When he first met Spilby, Jones thought his stepping from foot to foot was because he'd been cold. He now realized it was a habit, as if Spilby was terrified of being nailed to the floor.

'So I can take it away, can I?' Spilby asked, although he'd already been handed the keys by Jones.

'You can, Jim.'

Spilby seemed reluctant to go. Had he been expecting some sort of ceremony, Jones wondered, a citation on vellum?

'Jim, I'd just like to say how appreciative we all are, me and everyone at the station, for the loan of your motor. It was a privilege. The material removed from it will undoubtedly be the keystone in the case we are building against our prime suspect; deceased. Drive carefully and good luck.'

Spilby was smiling. Jones clapped him on the shoulder and he got into his car.

Jones turned. Karen was a few feet away, smiling at what she'd seen. She was about to speak when Spilby started the engine. With a coughing roar and a plume of black smoke, he drove off.

Karen handed Jones an envelope. 'This came. Sent by Mrs Kelleher. She found it, she says, in one of Julia's books.'

'Yeah?'

'A letter from Amy Parris. Christ, it could've saved some bother.'

Gio Jones sat at his desk reading the letter.

My darling,

It's three in the morning and I know a fax will wake you up so this comes by hand when I set off (soon). Something has happened which is worse if possible than that disgusting proposal he made me – and the more I think about *that* the worse it seems. It was like a man offering a child unlimited sweeties if . . . And then his creepy self-prostration when I said 'no'. Yukk. Well, he won't give up, and it's getting more and more manic. I know how grim I've been. Forgive me, darling. It's him that's doing it. I'm depressed and you're depressed. I feel infected by him as if some virus had come into the world which transmits madness.

Anyway, this evening at work I found something hidden (not very carefully) in my files. I don't like the way I found it. I'm sure he put it there deliberately, knowing (hoping) I'd find it. What it amounts to is fraud, a scheme for moving accounts around which is far too clever for its own good and is actually highly illegal. I think, as a matter of fact, it would work for a number of months because it's so complex. I suppose he thinks that during that time he'll come up with the glorious invention that will come to the rescue of the company and then go back and unpick the fraud.

I brought the file home on disk and worked on it all night till now. I think he must have tagged the file somehow to show it had been opened (and copied perhaps) because someone came and rang my doorbell at about nine and I'm sure it was him.

This got to me more than I can say. I wandered round in one of my manias feeling violated. I can't face him. Fear and disgust. The thing under the stone that is blind and vulnerable and packed with poison. No. No. No.

I'm heading off for a few days – let the wild wind see what it can do. Apart from anything else, I've got to decide whether or not to go to the police. And then – do I confront him? Do I resign? (Would you be able to keep me in the manner to which etc?) Common sense needed. I'll phone. At least in all this vile muddle one thing is clear to me—

I love you, Amy.

Gio Jones blew out a long slow lungful of air. 'Bloody hell . . .'

'No wonder her flat was done over a few days after she went AWOL. All the computer kit was taken, wasn't it?'

'That's right, that's right . . .'

Karen could see he wasn't listening. She noticed for the first time that Jones looked almost presentable. He was wearing a tie she hadn't seen before, quite nice. His suit, too, looked unusually uncrumpled.

'On the run . . .' Jones said. 'He had a dream.'

'Eh?'

'Our man Bewick. Clever sod dreamt that letter, you know. That's what he said. Had a dream where Amy Parris was on the run. Bloody hell.'

'How is he?' Karen asked, cool.

'Don't ask me, woman. You should know.'

'I should?'

'God, we've known each other long enough . . .'

'I haven't seen him since you both went to Norfolk, Sir. So I'm asking how he is.'

'You haven't seen him?'

'No. I thought he'd stay on there for a few days.'

'Oh, why?'

'That's where she lives isn't it? Dr Sally Vernon?'

'Ah yes. See what you mean. That's all over.'

Karen stared for a moment. 'What is?'

'John Bewick reckons this Sally woman won't want another violent bastard in her life,' said Gio Jones. 'I don't see it. Do you see it? Woman's mad about him.'

'She's got her own life. She runs her own lab and all. Perhaps . . .'

'Sure. She'll come round to it though, violent or not, wouldn't you think?'

'Course I'd think. But I'm prejudiced. So is he a violent bastard?'

'Not towards women. Never has been.'

'No. Not towards women,' Karen said slowly, as if testing the truth of it as she spoke. No, he wasn't – she was sure of it. A small flame of hope was flickering, quickening her blood. 'So,' she said, 'you think she'll come around to him, do you?'

Gio Jones shook his head.

'Who can tell? God knows. I could see she fancied him rotten, that's all. I don't know. Women are impossible to predict, best of times, and when they're genius level, forget it.'

He watched Karen carefully, knowing he had given her an opinion she wanted. Nothing registered on her cool honey-coloured face. She nodded. 'Sally Vernon is clever, I could see that. Yeah, that might . . .'

She didn't complete the thought. Like Gio Jones, her instinct told her that Sally Vernon hadn't really disengaged herself from Bewick's life; perhaps never would. Nevertheless she foresaw the possibility of extreme pleasure for herself now, of joy even . . . She didn't care if it was doomed. She was an addict. She relaxed, her expression softened, her eyes brightened.

Jones frowned and then launched himself at the door. 'Got to go,' he grumbled. 'Can't sit here watching you finish up the cream. I gotta luncheon appointment.'

He walked out.

She watched him go, dazed with what he had told her. The light in Gio Jones's grotty little office brightened; in every channel of her body she felt a warmth.

In Oncology, the Ward Sister walked along the shining corridor past one of the old private rooms, now a side ward, then she checked and returned. Something had caught her attention.

All that morning she had passed the tableau in the small room where the boy sat with his mother, her right hand in his, his left arm across the pillows in a gesture suggestive of protection, although it was perhaps simply more comfortable that way. She had noticed the two of them because their positions seemed not to have changed for hours. Now the boy had taken his arm down from the pillows. He was slumped forward as if passed out. She glanced up automatically, although she knew the light over the door wasn't flashing: nobody had asked for help.

She went in.

Joe Enwright was holding his mother's hand in both of his. His back was bowed in a way that suggested utter defeat. His face was turned to his left shoulder, his flopped hair obscuring it.

On examination, Mrs Enwright proved to be dead, as the Ward Sister suspected she might be – she had been living semi-conscious on a cloud of morphine for days. What surprised her was the body's temperature: she must have been dead an hour or more.

The Ward Sister put a hand on the boy's shoulder. 'Do you want to stay here?'

The boy released his dead mother's hand. Then he seemed to uncoil as he stood up. He was a good-looking boy. His face was wet from tears. 'No,' he said. 'That's it . . .'

He made no attempt to wipe his face, nor did he look back at the bed, but walked straight out. She expected to find him waiting for her outside the main ward, but she never saw him again.

The Strawberry Fair restaurant by the river was the smartest in Cambridge. Bewick and Dundas sat in the palm-decorated conservatory and watched the college eights on the river while they waited for Jones.

Dundas listened to Bewick's clear account of the past week's events. It was more measured but quite as competent as his own summaries. Dundas was full of admiration. He didn't risk himself in the front line – Bewick did, and bore the scars.

'What will you do now?' Dundas asked.

'Ah,' Bewick said smiling. 'I've been looking at my contract from CICS. It allows me time off until the end of this week, unless I've been incapacitated in some way that requires medical supervision, in which case that period is added.' Bewick patted his jacket pocket. 'A chit from matron. I've got a fortnight plus.'

'Any plans?'

Bewick shrugged. 'I might go to Paris . . .'

Bewick nodded at the river to change the subject. They watched the rowing. A women's eight went by.

'Beautiful,' Dundas said.

'Less of that,' said Jones, out of breath as he arrived. He slid the Amy Parris letter under Bewick's nose. 'There you are. If that doesn't make you smug, nothing will. This is nice, Mr Dundas. Choice. And all paid for by a barrister! Beats Bella's Snax on a wet Tuesday.' He settled himself in his chair. 'When do you think those lasses will be rowing back?'

As they sat over coffee, the subject of Amy Parris's letter came up again. Any evidence which turned up this late would at least help Jones's explanation of how it was they'd made the wrong arrest.

Bewick and Jones decided to walk over the footbridge to Chesterton to see if Mrs Kelleher had any more critical material tucked away in her bottom drawer. They thanked Dundas for the meal and sauntered over the concrete footbridge across the river. A few remaining brown and golden leaves clung to the planes and maples lining the bank as it curved away to the locks at Jesus Green.

Ten minutes later they were in Chesterton outside Number Four Erasmus Close. The small grey Rover was parked outside as usual.

Both men came to a halt. The front door was ajar. In a normal household that would hardly cause comment. Here it might mean anything. Bewick and Jones looked at each other.

Jones moved to the door. 'Mrs Kelleher?'

'She's in the kitchen. Look.'

Bewick nodded to the garage at the side of the house. Reflected in the garage window they could see Mrs Kelleher's head and shoulders. She was concentrating on something on the table, reading probably.

Relieved, Jones rang the bell. It sounded loud and clear.

'She's ignoring it,' Bewick said. He brushed past Jones and walked quickly into the house.

'Gio . . .' From inside the house, Bewick's voice was low and ominously controlled.

Jones went in.

Bewick was standing in the living-room with its sentimental trinkets. There was blood everywhere: on the floor, the walls, even on the ceiling. It had squirted, heart pumped, splattering and smearing most objects in the room. Brian Kelleher lay across a chair. There was a gross wound in his neck, its lips purple. His clothes, blood sodden, were drying to the texture of board. Kelleher's face was streaked with the rust of his own blood. His neat dark moustache was now ginger, strangely flamboyant. His eyes were open as if staring in disbelief at the slaughterhouse chaos of his own death.

Jones went to him. He was cold and stiff.

They found Mrs Kelleher seated at the kitchen table. It was the first time either of them had seen her looking calm. She was reading *Hello!*

The room was immaculate. At the other end of the table was a kitchen knife with a ten-inch blade. It lay on a folded drying-up cloth.

'I couldn't let him do it. He must have known that. In fact I told him.'

'Do what?' Jones asked.

'He wouldn't let me talk about it. He wouldn't, even though I tried. I really tried. Next thing I knew the man was here and Brian was telling him wicked things. About Julia. Wicked, filthy lies. About my Julia. He couldn't leave her in peace, even now.'

'Where's the man now, Mrs Kelleher?'

Was that shadow across her face shame, or what?

'He's with Brian.'

They found the journalist behind the door of the

living-room, hidden by the sofa. His mouth was sagged open revealing the gap between his front teeth. One of his hands lay by his head, as if his last gesture had not been to defend his vital organs but the little wart on his forehead.

His throat was cut, gaping; lurid in the shadow.

READ MORE IN PENGUIN